GLENS OF THE DEAD

Where
Fearsome Legends
Are Born.

MATT HAY

Glens of the Dead

©2019 Matt Hay

First Edition

All rights reserved

Edited by Christina Hargis Smith

Cover art by Jeffrey Kosh Graphics

Published by Optimus Maximus Publishing, LLC

ISBN- 10: 1-944732-46-2

ISBN- 13: 978-1-944732-46-2

To Matt Hay, Senior

Thank you for everything, Dad.

"Here's tae us. Wha's like us? Damn few, and they're a'deid."

A traditional Scottish toast

GLENS

OF THE

DEAD

A Novel by

MATT HAY

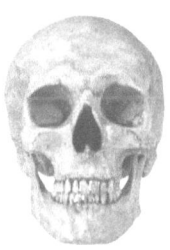

Optimus Maximus Publishing, LLC

Brick, New Jersey

PR⊕L⊕GUE

⊠

Lanark, Scotland 1301AD

Mist descended over the moss-covered shallow glen. Shadowy figures dotted the landscape, forms obscured whilst trudging forward, torches dimly lit the way ahead as their damp robes dragged along the ground. A teenage girl stood alone; golden hair dripping in the dampness of the light drizzle which enveloped her, nerves jingling as butterflies flitted in her stomach in anticipation of what she was about to do.

Taking a deep breath and gulping down the excess spittle forming in her mouth, Maggie hesitantly stripped, removing one garment at a time, neatly folding them in a pile on the grass. Finally naked, her long arms wrapped over small breasts while she bounced lightly on the balls of her feet in effort to conserve body heat in the chilly night air.

Doubts continued to plague Maggie's mind. Worry invaded, thoughts swirling about what was transpiring tonight. Did she have the stomach or willpower to go through with it? Since joining the Satanists, there were many acts that she was uncomfortable with, most involving blood and nudity, but over time the nefarious ceremonies were easier as she became more involved with the local community. She was first introduced to them by Moira, a friend who also lived in Lanark. However, unlike

Moira, fascination of Satan and the preaching zealots in the town enthralled Maggie, despite the initial debauchery. Never before had she been exposed to a ceremony with the Grand Disciple and being part of a ritual with such a high standing figure caused the nerves currently making her body shake.

Gingerly, Maggie made her way over to a small group of lassies who were also bare, goosebumps highlighting their pale, milky skin. A low murmur radiated from all directions, voices were praying, or…summoning? Maggie was not sure as the words were unfamiliar. This was the first large gathering which she had attended, although she went to many of the sermons at various secret locations in the town, often run by a lesser zealot. The others looked more experienced with their bodies peppered in scars, many shaped like bite marks. Some looked old, but there was a number of fresh gashes which had only just healed over. A few ladies wore masks. One looked like a goat, another a cow, or maybe a bull, and the third was possibly a horse. It was tough to make out in the torchlight. The priest in town at the last meeting forewarned about the debauchery and pain caused to one another, but this was natural and celebrated by the Great Lord. Maggie was told that a special place would be reserved in Hell for those who followed their Master's wishes. Many of the Satanists bore a pentagram, the symbol etched into the top of their left thigh. Continual participation in the gatherings meant her standing could be elevated, which would eventually result in the carving of the unholy mark, or so she was told. Whether this was true, Maggie did not know.

Shaking, from the chill and uncertainty, Maggie hummed along to the chorus which was accompanied by what sounded like a gong but it was muffled by the chanting. As she moved, picking up the odd word or two, before reaching a small hill where the larger group was gathered. Sat atop was a middle-aged man surrounded by more figures, naked and clapping a rhythmic beat which Maggie mimicked as she drew closer. Wearing a dark black robe of silk which skimmed his ankles, and deep sleeves that hid his hands, Maggie assumed he was the Grand Disciple as he was similar to the description given by the dark priests in Lanark. Either side of him sat a large golden idol of a man, who Maggie assumed was Satan, with horns protruding from his head and a snake-like tail wrapped around him, similar to the ones seen in the small grottos in town. Between thirty and forty young girls assembled around the base of the mound, each bare as the day they exited the womb, on their knees bowing to the Satanic figure. Maggie mingled with the crowd, her hand suddenly grasped by a pretty brunette whose body was covered in carved symbols, most of which she had never seen before. Smiling, the woman tried to put Maggie at ease, kindness showing in her emerald eyes.

"Is this your first ceremony?"

"Aye," replied Maggie. "Does it hurt much?"

"There is more pleasure than pain; you have nothing to worry about. The Dark Lord will look after you this eve."

"Thank you," Maggie spluttered. "Do you mind if I ask a question?"

"What do you want to ken? Make haste, the Grand Disciple will be starting soon."

"You have a lot of markings on your body. Most I dinna recognise. Will I get these?"

"In time, fair maiden, if you serve the Dark Lord as I have, then you will be rewarded with his mark. Each symbol depicts what I have done to serve my Master over the years. Now hush, lass, he is about to begin."

The chanting intensified before the Grand Disciple raised his hands in the air, dancing around in a circle. The singing gradually quietened until it was just one, the voice of the Grand Disciple.

"Nascentes morimur."

"Nascentes morimur," the naked ladies responded solemnly.

Without warning, the Grand Disciple dropped his robe, revealing a scrawny, white figure, flesh covered in engraved symbols. Maggie quickly turned her head at the initial sighting, not keen on staring at an old man's penis.

"Fool!" hissed the auburn-haired lass. "Watch the ceremony!"

Forcing herself to look, all Maggie could see was the small member now standing at attention. Each time she tried to concentrate on the chants, that little cock kept staring at her, almost hypnotically. There was nothing erotic at all about it, she just found it interesting that someone with such a miniscule penis could command so many nude girls.

Suddenly, the strange ritual ended as the Grand Disciple's hands dropped to his side. A ring of fire ferociously erupted, entrapping everyone within. The blazing heat intensified as the flames grew and danced about. Maggie was afraid that her tender skin would burn and blister. A reassuring squeeze of the hand relaxed her slightly. Calmer, she gazed once more upon the Grand Disciple.

"Tonight, we stand united, linked in a circle as one in our worship of Satan. The Dark Lord will reward each of us with a sacred place in Hell, with your every need and desire met. The Day of Reckoning will be upon us soon and we can either hide away from the Christians or we can stand tall and rule this land in the name of Satan and all who follow him."

"*Rule the land!*" chanted the crowd. "*Rule the land!*"

"Soon, my followers, we will be able to put our plan in motion, people will be cowering in fear of us all. Soon, the Dark Lord will return and Satan will walk again!"

"*The Dark Lord returneth! The Dark Lord returneth!*"

"We must continue to destroy the followers of Christ. The enemies of the Dark Lord are trying to root us out and undo all the hard work we have undertaken in his name. Many have died standing up to these despicable god worshippers. Let us now celebrate their sacrifice to our cause."

"*Hail the dead! Hail the dead!*"

"As strong as we are, we must become stronger, as united as we are, we must become one. To create, one must destroy, to love, one must feel pain."

"*We want pain! We want pain!*"

Suddenly, the flames dropped and the fire almost extinguished in time with the Grand Disciple's hands thrusting downwards. Gasps filled the air from the captivated audience. Striding forward, with surprising strength the Grand Disciple grabbed two linked arms and wrenched them free. Snatching a large ornamental knife from the ground, he admired the intricate carvings on the hilt, inset with rubies, the blade made from the finest silver. The Grand Disciple traced the weapon along his palm before swiftly slicing a small gash in his inner wrist. Blood swelled into a thick globule then slowly trickled from his withered skin. Several discoloured drops spattered to the grass between his feet.

Pink tongue extended, a buxom blonde came forth and lapped the deep crimson liquid from the wound while he caressed a full breast, tugging hard on her nipple. Suddenly lashing out, he slapped globe, a forceful crack sounding as flesh hit flesh, causing a sharp cry of agony to escape the maiden's lips. This routine was repeated with a fiery red-haired girl who wept tears of joy as each painful blow struck.

Stepping back, the Grand Disciple raised a gnarled hand, coated with dark blood flowing from his wound. "My blood is *his* blood, when you drink it; *your* blood becomes *his* blood. Let us all feast on each other's blood, becoming one with one another. Satan is our Master and he will possess each and every one of us."

"*Satan is our Master*!"

One young lady after another took turns using the knife to cut one other, allowing the person next to them to lap up their life fluid. The ritual continued with each girl experiencing both pleasure and hurt around the circle. The pressure intensified as more pain was administered with every new participant. Moans filled the air as they were sent into a frenzy, fulfilling desires with the flesh and body of their sister Satanist.

Maggie's knees quivered as the girl beside her was engulfed deeply in the experience. Maggie trembled in anticipation knowing she was soon to receive her initial offering of Satan. Heat from the flames coupled with the encompassing excitement intensified her insides, she felt on the edge of bursting.

Suddenly, chaos ensued just as Maggie was about to get her first taste of Satan's blood. Snarls and screams exploded in the distance as the entire gathering turned nasty. Head straining to try and see what was going on the other side of the large circle, Maggie could scarcely make out naked women fleeing across the field in all directions. Blood slick maidens were chased by others. Gurgled moans resounded from the pursuers. The skinny priest was in his element, screeching in delight at the carnage unfolding before him.

"It is here! The Dark Lord has shown us the future. The Day of Reckoning has finally arrived, let us enjoy it, feast on each other, my lovelies. Tonight, we are reborn, ready to conquer the world!"

Despite the chaos, Maggie focussed attention back on the lass who was receiving her mark. Feeling scared, frightened that participating in the ritual may have been a mistake. There was no going back now, though. Those waiting, gripped tightly by the next link in the chain, had no way to escape the inevitable. The fingers on Maggie's right wrist loosened, indicating it was now her time to be sliced. Knees weakened as the busty lass turned to her with the knife clenched in one hand.

"It is time," she murmured, staring deep into Maggie's eyes. "Satan is our Master and we shall taste his dominance and gorge in his essence. His spirit is a part of each one of us and what we do now shall only strengthen our bond to him. Through the combination of pain and pleasure shall we grow. The darkness can only bring light, the agony can only bring ecstasy, a new age is about to dawn upon us, let us taste the start of that."

With skill and precision like a clan warrior, the blade pierced through the delicate skin of her wrist, a vein burst open, ready for Maggie's consumption. Dropping the weapon to the ground, she grabbed the back of Maggie's neck, pulling her into the inviting wound. The ferocity forced Maggie to her knees as she lapped up the fresh blood. The taste was not as expected, there seemed to be a foul flavour which made her gag slightly. Maggie felt her hair being tugged by the roots. As she jerked back, the teeth of the other girl bit into her lips with the acid taint of blood from the wound leaving a bitter aftertaste.

Suddenly, it was over and a grin spread over the face of the woman, a sadistic smirk that frightened Maggie a little. "You have tasted the soul of our Master. Now it is time for you to pass this on. You are one of us now, destined to-"

The formal speech was interrupted by a piercing scream as teeth sank into the woman's neck from behind. Chunks of flesh were torn free before she collapsed to the ground, screaming as the attacker jumped atop her and unbelievably, began feasting.

Maggie shrieked at this abhorrent act. The revulsion of seeing a woman eaten was too much and she did what anyone would do in the same situation. She ran, as fast as her legs could go. Maggie stumbled in the pitch-black darkness during her escape from the unfolding horror. Cries of the dying sliced through the night, following Maggie as she fled.

Daring to look behind, Maggie could see the pulsating orgy was now a feeding frenzy. The Grand Disciple revelled in the middle, dancing in glee at the debauchery and mayhem. Thankful that they were all now in the distance, Maggie's pace slowed to a stumble as she felt an acute pain in her belly. She wondered if it was from moving too quickly after what was ingested.

A short time later, Maggie was sprawled on the ground, guts heaving, spewing out the filth from the ceremony. Overwhelming pain ensued and Maggie lost control as violent tremors took over and her body thrashed about the glen. A sharp, bright light flashed, followed by an all-consuming darkness as Maggie died, alone on the moor.

Her dead body rose, now withered and smeared with blood, vomit, and dirt. The head rolled to the side as unresponsive hands struggled to gain purchase on the thick grass. Each attempt to stand caused the body to crash back to the ground. Finally, as if a force was driving it, Maggie's corpse was able to stay upright. A low, animalistic growl gurgled forth from the back of the throat as it turned and limped away, looking for flesh to devour, roaming the night as one of the living dead.

CHAPTER ONE

THE STAGGER INN TAVERN

Two brothers, both tall and well-built, settled down at a roughly hewn ash table located to the left of the door after buying two tankards of ale from the burly bartender.

The noise of the room reverberated against thick stone walls, making the place seem busier than it actually was. Lanterns ablaze, flickering light illuminated the way for patrons who relieved themselves in a barrel, which sat by the village drunks who were passed out on a bench at the far corner of the establishment. It was not somewhere anyone wanted to go near due to the stench of stale urine. Most customers tended to go outside to the woods for a piss, rather than pick their way through the vomit and faeces left by the rougher element of the village. Heat radiated from a massive stone fireplace, where flames licked the side of a dark, iron cooking pot. The scent of freshly stewed beef tickled the hairs at the end of their nostrils. A large brown rodent, dirt covering its coat, scurried past. A fat white cat was in close pursuit, panting with the long, bloodied tail of its last victim protruding from the side of its mouth.

Donald, a red-haired lad of sixteen years, took a generous sip from his wooden cup as the dark ale sloshed around. He slowly surveyed the tavern, looking for anyone he recognised. Several booths were occupied by travelling strangers. Patrons varied from muscular, armoured warriors to garishly clothed peddlers. No matter who they were, people engaged in sociable chatter which was only interrupted when one of the serving wenches replenished the tankard. The two curvy, young ladies worked the customers with joviality and flirtation, encouraging the clientele to buy more alcohol. Both girls were dressed in ankle length, full skirted, brown dresses. Perky breasts overflowed with not-so-subtle bends at the waist. Shoving their assets into the eager faces of men was a sure-fire way to get more sales. Free drinks and tips were popular rewards for their hard work, but more often than not, a pinch of the bottom and a lustful stare was the only compensation received.

Donald stared at the massive heads of boar and deer mounted on the walls. The hunting prize of some local laird, one who had displayed the poor creature after his dogs had done most of the work. It annoyed Donald to see them used as decoration, but as they had hung there for years, he was not keen on disrupting the status quo of the much frequented Stagger Inn Tavern. The drinking establishment was often used as a stop-off for a weary traveller on their way to Edinburgh or Lanark. His brother, Malcolm, who sat beside him, loved to listen to the stories of life in the big town and the exotic places visited like Perth and Inverness. Travelling on the open road was appealing to Malcolm. He often wanted to just pack a bag and set off to find adventure and make a fortune, but the responsibility to look after his mother and Donald, whilst da was off fighting for the clan, was too great. Donald often saw the yearning for adventure in Malcolm's eyes whenever a traveller entered the alehouse. He usually sat for ages chatting away to them, whilst Donald remained bored, feigning interest at the same tedious stories told in different ways.

A slight movement to the right disturbed Donald's thoughts as his brother was making hand gestures towards a group of adolescent girls sitting a few tables away. A pretty, immaculately dressed brunette with lengthy, curling locks was furiously signalling back, her face reddening as the exchange went on.

Exasperated, Donald said, "For fuck sake, Malcolm, go over and talk to her, I really dinna mind. Yer ignoring me anyway."

The silence from Malcolm was deafening as he turned and gave a look, which could have felled a charging bull at a hundred paces.

"I get the message, I will shut up then," stated Donald, defensively, before returning to visually scouting the room whilst lazily rolling a finger through the froth of his ale.

Unfortunately, there was no-one that he socialised with in the tavern. The usual drunks and old folk from the village were in attendance, and apart from the girl's table, he did not know, or care about, a soul. The only person Donald showed interest in was Mhairi, Morag's sister, but she rarely visited the pub. It was a shame. Donald spent a lot of time chatting and playing with Mhairi when they were younger. Malcolm's overprotectiveness of him since the accident had all but isolated Donald from his former friends. If, like today, he was alone, most stayed away, knowing Malcolm would take them aside the next day and have a serious word. Instead, he went back to fantasising about fighting on the battlefield. Visions of slashing at an incoming enemy cavalryman took over as he fell further into his reverie.

With a shake of the head at Donald's daydreaming, knowing his brother could be lost in thought for a while, Malcolm took the opportunity to slip away. Easing into the seat beside Morag, the previous time spent flirting across the tavern ensured he was engaged in chat with the lovely teenager the moment his rear hit the chair.

"Morag," said Malcolm softly while gently holding her delicate, white hand and stroking its silken skin, "your eyes sparkle like the stars at night, just as the moon catches them in its silver glow. My heart flutters each time that your eyes blink. In fact, it has just skipped a beat now."

Squeezing his large, rugged fingers, Morag gently replied, "Oh, Malcolm, your kind words make my face blush. I am not worthy of such praise."

"But you are, my dear," said Malcolm, lovingly. "Every day I bathe in the golden pool of your aura."

As the conversation continued, Malcolm noticed the other women were intently listening in, staring with lips slightly parted in awe. Blushing at the unexpected interest, he motioned Morag to move to a free table located to the right of Donald.

Whilst they were shifting across, Malcolm glanced over at his brother, hoping that he had popped out of the trance. However, the glazed look in Donald's eyes told another story. Malcolm was worried. Fifteen minutes passed before any movement was spotted from his sibling. Donald did this sort of thing often. Normally it subsided quickly, but the episodes could go as long as a couple of hours before he finally snapped out if it. The frequency of the incidents varied. They started a few years ago when Malcolm and Donald were playing by the river, one of the local lads made a makeshift swing from a stolen length of rope. All the boys used it, either swaying from side to side, being prodded with a stick to see if they would twirl or fall off, or building momentum to jump off into the river. The furthest across usually got first pick of the apples off the tree in Old Angus's field. That day it was just Malcolm and Donald. Donald's confidence was sky high due to winning the leap for the last four days. Wanting to prove to Malcolm that he was the best in the village, he climbed the tree and ran across the branch before leaping off and trying to grab the swing, looking for a huge boost. However, disaster struck when he missed the end of the rope and fell, hitting his head on a huge rock by the side of the river. Donald was knocked out, blood pouring from the scalp wound.

Malcolm panicked, carrying him to the local healer in the village. It took a few weeks, and a lot of herbs for Donald to get back to a semblance of his former self. By that time their mother and father were very protective of Donald and smothered him. Donald was not allowed to go anywhere without one of the parents and the once carefree lad slowly, but surely became a recluse. The daydreaming started soon thereafter. It was infrequent at first, but they got worse when their father left to fight in the Douglas Clan Army a couple of years ago. Malcolm and his mother tried everything to bring him round. From awful herbal concoctions to repeated slaps across the face, nothing seemed to work They were frustrated to be so helpless. It was something they lived with and Malcolm spent more time looking after Donald and keeping him entertained than with his friends or with Morag, which at times put a strain on their relationship.

The sturdy tavern door swung open, the ferocity nearly taking it off the hinges as three brawny blokes entered. They were dressed in full Douglas colours, a blue coat with a white tunic stained rusty with blood. Behind them strode a smaller chap who sported a pair of black and white checked trousers. Scars marring their faces and limbs were obvious signs that they had been in many battles. A crude, filthy bandage was wrapped loosely over a weeping wound on the thigh of the warrior to the right. The shorter man looked less intimidating than the others as they strode purposefully into the room, sitting down at an empty booth.

"Wench!" bellowed the soldier with the mop of messy black hair. "We have just travelled from Kirklinton and I dinna ken about the others, but I am dying of thirst. I need four tankards of your finest ale and there is an extra wee tip for you if you bring them here quickly."

"Ease off on the wee lassie, Big Davie," ordered the smaller lad. "The poor thing looks terrified of you. You can last a few more minutes without ale."

"Ach, come on, Jamie, you are taking all the fun out of this. I was going to give her a wee something anyway," Big Davie retorted.

"Do what you like, you fool," joked Jamie, nodding towards the barman. "Dinna blame me when Big Angus bashes your head in. He gets quite protective of his lassies."

Malcolm glanced over at the huge server who had a massive smile on his face. Shaking his head, the bartender signalled to the small blonde wench who was clearing empty tankards from one of the tables. "Jenny! Go and get the man some ale. Dinna take any of his nonsense though. Big Davie Douglas is not as hard as the legends say. Watch his hands, they tend to wander."

Malcolm had fond memories of drinking sessions with Big Davie. They had spent many an evening staggering home after consuming too much whisky. Davie could drink most people under the table, which meant that some nights Malcolm needed the gentle giant to keep him from sleeping in a bush.

A light tap on the shoulder was a reminder that Morag was there, looking slightly annoyed that his attention had strayed. Malcolm and Morag were courting for the last six months and he grew very fond of the tenacious teenager. Although comfortable with one another, both agreed that things would move slowly. Frustratingly for Malcolm, they never went beyond hand holding and kissing. Malcolm wanted to see what lay beneath her dress but respect and love for Morag mean that he did not want to force anything that she was not ready for.

"Malcolm Douglas," said Morag in a firm quiet tone, "I think that my handsome man would prefer to spend time with his friends than me. If that is the case, then I shall have to consider retiring for an early night."

"I am sorry, Morag. I havena seen Big Davie or Jamie for a couple of years. It would be good to catch up with them, but you are right, it is rude of me to ignore you, and I apologise for that."

"Oh, Malcolm, I dinna mind you talking to them, I would prefer not to be ignored though. Please call them over, I am sure you have loads to talk about."

"Morag, you are an angel." Malcolm planted a kiss on her cheek before calling over to the other table, "Big Davie! Get your fat arse over here and bring that cheeky wee runt with you!"

"Malky, is that you? Hold on, me and Jamie are coming."

The giant clansman sauntered over, tankard in hand, swigging the ale, the froth sticking to his bushy black beard. The cuts on his arm were now more visible and from what Malcolm could see, they looked to be at least a week old and healing nicely. Flinging his bulk onto the chair next to Malcolm, Big Davie dropped a monstrous hand onto Malcolm's shoulder, giving it a hefty clap before gently lifting Morag's and delicately placing his lips upon it.

"Madam," Big Davie gushed, "it is a joy and a pleasure to make your acquaintance. Please excuse my ruffian friend Malcolm, he can be quite uncouth at times."

"Uncouth? That is rich, coming from you!" Malcolm said, playfully punching Davie in the arm. "This is my lass Morag." Malcolm turned to Morag, with a mischievous glint in his eye. "Morag, you already ken David Douglas, bastard son of Brian Douglas, also kennt as Big Davie. He spent much of his childhood here in Forth until his uncle could not stand the sight of him anymore and sold him to some traveller. He is noble born but there is not a noble bone in his body. He would rather spend time brawling in a tavern than attending court in a dress." The fake introduction brought a snigger from the young lass.

"Oy," retorted Big Davie with pretend indignation. "Less of that. It was my da that sold me to the traveller, my uncle wanted to sell me to a priest. And I will have you ken that I look quite fetching in a dress."

15

Malcolm snorted at that comment and extended his hand out to Big Davie before giving it a warm shake. "Big Davie, mate," he said with passion, "it has been far too long. How are you doing? Have you heard any news of my father?"

"Malky, you wee goat, you ken that I am not one for telling stories, I much prefer to drink and I ken that your lovely wee lass does not want to hear me talk all night."

"Actually, David, I would love to hear your story," answered Morag politely.

"Nonsense!" barked the big clansman. "Wee Jamie has all the facts. I tend to forget stuff. Da reckons that my brain gets addled due to all that whisky." He paused, thinking for a moment. "Or was that ale? Ach, it is probably both. Anyway, I need another drink and you need to listen to Jamie." Bellowing, as only Big Davie could, "Jamie, you wee prick! Get your arse over here, our Malky wants to ken about his da and can you get one of those wenches to bring me over another ale? Mine seems to have strangely disappeared somewhere. Must be witchcraft."

The jovial conversation continued until the small, dark-haired man sat beside Davie. Though slighter in stature than his companion, Jamie had a strong aura, it was as if, inadvertently, his presence alone commanded the room. "Big Davie, sorry about the delay. I was chatting to a charming young lady who was most eager to get you a tankard of ale. I may have suggested that you had a wee thing for blondes. I hope you dinna mind," Jamie said with a not so subtle wink.

"Ha ha! At least I ken where I will be sleeping tonight. Your cousin Malky here has been waiting for you. He wants to ken about his da."

Shaking Malcolm's hand, Jamie said, "Sorry, Malcolm. The other lads are trying their hand with the local girls and I have been laughing at how skilfully the lassies manage to fend them off."

"That is fine, I am used to Big Davie disappearing on me. The last time we were here, he left with a group of lassies. I found him lying in a bush on the way home, naked with a smile on his face."

"Aye, that sounds like Big Davie. He has not changed much over the last couple of years. Your da cursed his name every time he pulled him out of the bed of a young maiden."

"Jamie, it has been too long since we last saw each other. If I remember correctly, you were showing off your wee baby to ma and da, a bonnie wee thing she is."

"Aye, that is right. The last I saw her; she was just chasing the ducks with a stick. She took a few pecks but it is a lesson well learned. I miss my daughter. She will be a big girl by now. I hope to see her before we go back to join your da in Cumbria."

"Speaking of da, have you heard anything about him?"

"Dinna worry, Uncle Cammy was alive the last time that I saw him. Although the English may not be. Between him and Ian, the Southerners have not stood much of a chance." Jamie turned to Morag, "Your da fights like a madman, Morag. I have not seen anyone, apart from William Wallace himself, fight with more bravery. You should be proud."

"Thank you, Jamie," responded Morag, softly. "I am proud. I just wish that he was back home with his family. I miss him terribly."

"I understand that, but I have seen him in action and not one enemy got near him. He is a fearsome warrior. The last I saw, they had just finished sacking Kirklinton and were heading south to see if they could make some inroads into Cumbria. Hopefully, their march will stop future English invasion for years to come."

"I agree, Jamie. I pray for a time when we can live at peace in our land without the threat of war. I just wish that everyone would just get along and stop this needless killing."

Wiping froth from his beard, Big Davie's belch nearly ruffled their hair with its force, before interjecting with a more sombre tone, "That is the downside of war, lass. Too many good people die in the name of some trumped up noble hoping to make a name for himself. War is a nasty business and I often wish I could just walk away and live a normal life. Unfortunately, duty and my da say otherwise."

"Your da is a fine man," said Jamie before taking a gulp of ale. "It was your da who spotted the potential in me and spoke to William Wallace and Cammy about making me flag bearer. I have learned so much from them in the last couple of years and the laird makes sure my family is well looked after. I am nothing but grateful to your father."

"My father is an arse. If he spent as much time with his family as he does with his precious clan, then perhaps I would have grown up to be a decent man. Instead, I am an uncouth, battle hardened brute who drinks too much. What woman would want this mess?"

Malcolm almost fell out of his seat from laughing so hard. "You big oaf. I ken a few who find you attractive. All I hear about is how brave and muscular Big Davie is. You would not believe the amount of times I hear women fawn over you. You have the pick of the country."

"You almost sound jealous, my friend. You with an attractive young lass on your arm as well. One whose sister has a fine pair of legs."

A loud crash from the other end of the lounge interrupted their conversation. Malcolm tried to get a better look but there was a crowd of bodies obstructing the view. A cry of pain pierced the air, followed by strange moans and the ripping of flesh like a wildcat feeding on the carcass of a rabbit.

"That does not sound great," said Jamie, worried. "Angus willna be happy if that is one of his barmaids being abused. Look, he is going over to see what the disturbance is and bust some heads if necessary."

Malcolm watched as Angus strode purposely towards the commotion. Just as the bartender reached them, one of the thrashing men turned and sank yellow stained teeth into Angus' neck. Breaking through the skin, the terrible wound spurted. Malcolm sat in shock as a red chunk flapped from the attacker's mouth. Blood sprayed everywhere as Angus fell to the ground clutching his ruined throat. Malcolm could not take his eyes off the unfolding horror. A tight knot of fear sat in the pit of his belly as the aggressive man turned and they locked eyes.

CHAPTER TWO

CHAOS

The atmosphere intensified as the general noise level changed from chatter and light-hearted humour, to terror and confusion as gargled screams and loud moans dominated the tavern. Fear and anguish was evident amongst the group as they shot each other looks in silence whilst listening to the horrific sounds erupting from the other end of the room. Malcolm thought he could see the injured clansman who had arrived with Jamie thrust his head onto one of the barmaids and take a huge chunk out of her bosom. Rubbing his eyes in disbelief, Malcolm stared back at the troubling scene, but both the attacker and victim had fallen to the floor and out of visual range. The strange looking fellow, who had taken a bite out of Angus, started to move towards the group and was about halfway across the room and closing in on them.

"There are more coming in behind him," remarked Jamie as he started to rise. "Our weapons are outside, we may have to do this the old-fashioned way."

"What about Donald?" Morag asked.

Malcolm looked worried, before replying. "If he doesna snap out of it soon, we will have to shift him ourselves. Unfortunately, due to him being a big bastard, only me or Big

Davie can carry him. If that happens, the others will need to block our escape. We need to get out of here."

"Our horses and swords are in the stable. It would be a good place to retreat to," Jamie said.

"Heads up!" called Big Davie. "Incoming!"

The sturdy chap rose and grabbed a tankard to wield as the shambling man came towards him. Big Davie could see pieces of tissue hanging from various areas of his body. Unbelievably the man was covered in bite marks with blood pouring out of gaping wounds. Davie balked, there was plenty of disgusting sights seen on the battlefield, but he never saw anything like this. Gastric juices, mingled with digested food, excreted from a gash in the stomach. The smell alone was horrific. The greater shock was that none of the injuries seemed to slow him down. With a burst of speed and an animalistic growl, the fellow reached out, attempting to grab and sink teeth into Davie's arm. Dodging neatly, Big Davie quickly brought the oversized mug crashing down on the back of the attacker's neck, the sheer aggression caused the man to collapse to the ground, skull cracking as it bounced on the hard stone.

Malcolm was certain that the force of the blow was enough to knock him out for a while and was astonished to see a hand attempt to rise and take a lunge at Big Davie's feet. Luckily for Big Davie, his massive leather boots prevented any damage and a swift kick to the head knocked it out of range. The body sprawled face down a few feet away.

"What the fuck was that?" shouted Jamie aghast. "I have seen Big Davie hit someone with less strength and knock them out for a good few minutes!"

"Fuck kens. But whatever it is, it never stayed down. I am starting to feel a wee bit uneasy. We should dispatch them quickly and get out of here," Big Davie replied.

Another two figures came into view, one was a tall blond chap with a bloody, half-eaten stump where his ear should have been. The other was a short, rotund, ginger-haired lad with a mangled eye dangling out of the socket. Malcolm watched in awe as both limped towards the group with teeth bared, aggressive snarls filling the air.

"I dinna ken what this is, but they are definitely not normal, and they are obviously dangerous. I will go back for Donald, if you guys can hold them off. I will meet you at the stables," remarked Malcolm.

As Malcolm moved towards Donald's table, Jamie and Big Davie stood side by side, ready for the shambling patrons. Big Davie still had the tankard in hand, poised to strike, whilst Jamie kept watch, holding the nearest chair in hand, ready like a stalking wildcat, tensely waiting for the incoming attack.

Malcolm took a look behind, trying to gauge how long he had to get Donald out of the tavern. His brother was still sat in the comatose trance. These strange episodes enveloped him each time the daydreams started. This was an all too familiar state for Donald. When they first started, Malcolm often took advantage and painted Donald's nose red or shaved off his eyebrows with a knife. Donald never flinched once, despite the attempts to bring him back to reality. Mother got angry when Big Davie helped out, trying things like hanging Donald upside down from a tree. She never really liked his friend. Now this problem meant that Donald was reliant on Malcolm to get him out of the delicate situation.

Morag froze in shock behind the men, hesitant of what to do next. As tough and resolute a person she was, it was her caring and gentle nature which left Malcolm unsure of how she would react if attacked.

"Morag! Over here. I need you to open the door and clear any obstructions whilst I carry Donald. I canna do this on my own, I need your help."

Morag turned to look at Donald before quickly walking over to him. Malcolm was amazed by the elegance of her stride as she glided by, her flowing skirt not impeding a single step. Smiling, Morag lightly touched him on the arm before surveying the obstacles on route to the exit. Several chairs and benches protruded outward and Morag moved swiftly to push them back under the tables, kicking any strewn mugs which landed on the floor during the chaos out of the way. Eventually, she reached the tavern door and stood watch on the unfolding situation.

Meanwhile, Big Davie, sick of waiting for the shambling patrons, strode to meet his foes, cautious as they snarled at the sight of him. Scarlet tinged drool dripped from the salivating mouth of the first man as he approached the giant lowlander. Bright eyes were blazing red against the background of ashen, grey skin. The rapid transformation left it resembling a beast more than a man and the feral actions matched this observation. Shrieking, the creature thrashed out at Big Davie, teeth bared, trying to bite into his huge hairy arm. Ever the warrior, Big Davie, belaying his immense size, nimbly dodged the attack. Gigantic fist raised, he slammed down on its head, forcing it to fall to the stone floor. The ferocious blow split the scalp to the bone, further crushing it open, causing fluid and brains to ooze. The corpse twitched a couple of times before lying still, dead in a pool of its own filth.

The second monster was now in range and Big Davie, not yet tiring a bit from the exertion, took no chances. Kicking out with a massive boot, the would-be attacker flew across the room, crashing to a halt onto a table six feet away. Big Davie stood in shock as the thing rose, unsteadily getting back to its feet, preparing for another charge. Big Davie wiped his brow and watched as another three crazed patrons staggered into view, each with the same murderous, hungered look. The middle figure was Angus the barman, who was almost unrecognisable as his skin was now as pale as the moon passing behind a cloud. Pristine white shirt and black trousers were in rags with scratches and bite marks evident on his muscular body. Davie maintained position, ready for the incoming onslaught, hoping to buy enough time for the others to escape.

Jamie looked at the second monster carefully, searching for any potential weakness as it limped towards him. Davie's boot had caved in part of its face, scraped away flesh, exposed bone protruded from the cheek. The power of the kick had crushed the side of the head, a long sliver of bone pierced the eye, ripping it from the socket. The orb now sat proudly upon the point of the shard, like a prize, mucous spilling out of the pulverized sinus in a gelatinous green muck on the side of the displaced nose. Jamie balked slightly at the sight of the ghastly deformity, but had to be on his toes as the being seemed to ignore the injury and powered on with the goal of maiming him.

A sudden burst of speed caught Jamie off guard as an arm reached out to grab him. Quickly recovering from the surprise, like lightning, Jamie dodged to the left and flicked a punch, dislocating the attacker's limb. The hairy hand fell limp to the side, hanging useless whilst swaying at the movement of the persistent predator.

The monster almost caught Jamie by surprise for the second time in a few seconds as it paid no attention to the pain and swung the other fist towards Jamie's head. Jamie ducked and agilely, grabbed its fingers, and dropped to the ground to try and twist his enemy to the floor and prevent any potential injury. Jamie was horrified as the figure flopped on top of him, falling awkwardly to the unforgiving surface below, the weight of the burly beast trapping the unfortunate soldier. Jamie could feel the hot, putrid stench of its breath as he stared into the vacant, bloodshot eyes of the ashen man. Thrusting forward, the foul fiend attempted to bite down. Straining, Jamie wrapped his hands around the neck of the aggressor with a mighty effort and squeezed with everything he had left. The pushback from its biceps was constant as Jamie struggled to contain the pressure bearing down.

Sweat poured from the slight man as he weakened with each passing second. Hissing from the vile fiend continued, with its mouth opening to reveal dull, brown teeth. Strips of flesh stuck between the discoloured ivories as a pungent smell escaped. Jamie choked back a gulp to prevent the ale sitting at the top of his stomach from ejecting and spraying everywhere. Worry etched across Jamie's face as his life flashed before him. The horrors he endured whilst fighting on the battlefield paled in comparison to what was happening now. A vision of his beautiful, red-headed, wife Fiona, and Elaine, his gorgeous, brown haired daughter, gave Jamie hope and reminder of something to fight for. Blood coursed through veins as he felt a boost, giving extra strength which Jamie used to push at the creature. Despite the additional help, all he could do was hold it back from pressing its advantage any further. Jamie well aware that it would not be long until he was depleted and done for.

Eyes briefly closed; Jamie prayed for forgiveness for his sins. Accepting fate, Jamie asked God to look after his family and keep them safe from all the conflict and illness in the world. Weakening each second with the monster bearing down on him, Jamie asked the Lord to keep his friends safe and let them escape the terror. Finally, his remaining stamina dissipated, and arms gave way as the body of the undead crashed atop him. Prepared for ravenous bite to rip flesh from his skin, Jamie tensed, anticipating the onslaught and his eventual demise.

Nothing happened.

Surprised, Jamie slowly eased one eye open, peeking out, not knowing what to expect, hoping that that by some miracle that he was still alive and everything had disappeared. Slowly adjusting to the light, Jamie could barely make out his attacker lying to his left with a large spike embedded in its brain, blood leaking down the side of the wound, the other half of the body sprawled on top, trapping him. Exhaling the breath he was holding, relief washed over Jamie, cleansing his earlier acceptance of death. With full vision restored, Jamie looked up to see Malcolm's hand attached to the other end of the iron weapon.

"Malky! I dinna believe I have ever been so glad to see your ugly mug. I thought I was a goner there."

"You nearly were. That thing was close to having you. I need to remove it from you, then we should get out of here. Morag and Donald are unprotected and Big Davie looks like he has company."

"I am grateful, cousin, I truly am, but I have to ken where you got that spike?"

"It was Morag who found it. It is the poker for the fireplace. She passed it to me when I dropped Donald at the door. Now, move it!"

Malcolm carefully removed the iron rod from the head of the corpse and wiped it on the ragged shirt of the man before pulling the dead weight off Jamie. Extending an arm, he pulled up his friend, hurrying towards the exit before the situation worsened.

"Big Davie, move your fat arse now! We are leaving," Malcolm called out as they reached the door.

Still worried about the extended length of Donald's daydream, Malcolm hefted his brother, slung him over the shoulder, and exited the tavern as Big Davie ran for his life, hotly pursued by a large group of the snarling men.

"Move!" shouted Big Davie. "There are loads of them behind me. We need to get to the stables. Run for your fucking lives!"

CHAPTER THREE

REVENGE

The sun had set not long before, and the full moon shone brightly in the sky to light the way along the narrow dirt road which led to the village of Forth. Visibility was good along the rough terrain as an armed group of clansmen continued the tough march from Peebles. Their yellow tunics were soaked with sweat as the twenty-mile walk had taken its toll.

A red headed chap with pale skin and freckles was at the head of the formation, flanked by two larger blokes. Stopping suddenly, he turned to study those behind, checking for signs of exhaustion and fatigue. Several soldiers were bent over, trying to regain their breath as the punishing walk, alongside the searing heat, pushed them to the limit.

"For fuck sake! You stupid bastards are out of shape. I have seen pigs last longer than you fuckers. Take five minutes and rest. We have got a few miles to go. I want those fucking villagers dealt with tonight."

"Yes, Hamish. Sorry, Hamish," chorused the reply from the tired voices of the group as they stared collectively with venom towards their hated leader, Hamish Balliol.

Hamish had a reputation for pushing the men too hard, which caused a lot of resentment. This, coupled with being the son of the head of the clan in Peebles, meant that he was not the most popular person in town. Hamish did not care about that, focusing more on the orders from his father to raid Forth and other strongholds of Clan Douglas. Hamish took particular pleasure in carrying out the instructions due to a longstanding hatred of Malcolm Douglas and Big Davie. Hamish used to take regular beatings from them and each time went home bruised and battered, vowing to exact vengeance. Many evenings were spent training and practicing with various weaponry, and tonight was when he could put the skills he had honed to good use.

Hamish was keen to be in Forth as soon as possible and was dismayed to see most of the soldiers taking long drinks of water out of their flasks. It was frustrating to be delayed yet again by another break. One was looking worse for wear. Brian Balliol, a shepherd from the other side of the border who resided in a small village in Northumberland. Brian fought in a few battles against Wallace and the Clans allied to him. He sported a large wound on his arm which was crudely bandaged and appeared to be infected; green puss seeping from the injury.

"Brian," said Hamish, concerned, "your arm looks sore. Are you able to continue?"

"Aye, it looks worse than it is, gies a couple of minutes and I will be alright," replied Brian, unconvincingly.

"You can have a few minutes, but if you start to falter, you will be left behind. I canna afford to carry anyone. It is already dark and I want to launch our attack soon."

"I will be fine, Hamish, I am just as capable as anyone else."

"You better be, Brian, or I will kill you myself."

Hamish never saw the look of hatred that Brian gave as he turned and walked to the front of the line. Continuing to chat and appraise the group, Hamish checked the condition of each of his team on the way to the head of the column. Stopping beside his two personal guards, Sandy and Tam, Hamish took a long drink from a waterskin before checking that his broadsword and spear were both in good working order.

Suitably refreshed, Hamish turned to the rest of the small army, numbering at around forty men. Puffed out with self-importance, he barked, "Clan Balliol, rest time is over! Get moving, we march for Forth and the beginning of the destruction of the Douglas Clan."

Cheers sounded from the troops as they formed into pairs before marching behind Hamish towards the village of Forth. Hamish rubbed his hands with glee at the thought of Malcolm Douglas finally getting his comeuppance.

They walked for another couple of miles with Hamish distracted, plotting the demise of Malcolm, Jamie, and Big Davie. All the time, anger and hatred grew within his festering mind. Hamish imagined the many different ways of killing the hated enemy, smirking with the thought of slowly slicing off each body part. Hamish was barely aware of the concerned looks from Sandy and Tam as his muttered curses and vows reached their ears.

Hamish continued along the stone road, oblivious to the discontented chatter. Time dragged as the rest of the group made pace with Hamish who had slowed down in his reverie. One of the men grunted and moaned behind. As his maniacal rantings continued, Hamish paid no attention. The low curses upped a notch with both Sandy and Tam able to hear every word.

An agonising scream of pain emanated from the back of the squad, finally rousing Hamish to his senses. Turning, he scowled at the rabble, scouring about for the person that created the disturbance, his rage building at the lack of stamina shown by whoever it was that halted the march.

"What the fuck is going on?" Hamish yelled.

"It is Brian," came back the reply from near the back of the column. "I think he is dead. Hold on, I will check his breathing."

"Hurry up! If he is dead, we will leave him for the rats to eat his carcass. I have not got time for this."

Hamish squinted as he watched the young fellow at the back bend over and feel the side of Brian's neck, checking for a pulse. The lad turned around, still pressing down, shaking his head at Hamish.

Shocked, Hamish watched as the previously deceased Brian, rose and sank yellowed teeth into the boy's buttock, wrenching into flesh and severing a chunk of muscle out of the soldier's arse. A pained roar resonated as blood spurted from the injury, a pool forming in the dirt. Spitting the flesh out, Brian fell to the ground and greedily drank the liquid, like it was the finest wine in his father's cellars. Brian moved with vigour, pouncing from the light refreshment to quickly tear into the lad's throat, further soaking his already stained shirt.

Hamish gasped with horror as the boy took a last breath and passed into the afterlife.

"What are you all fucking staring at?" screamed Hamish. "You are supposed to be warriors. Kill him!"

The stunned expressions on the faces of his subordinates changed to a look of determination, ready to strike at their fallen comrade who had now finished feasting on the fresh corpse of his first victim. Behind Brian's reanimated body, the mutilated form of the cannibalised youth began to rise. Flesh hung in loose strips from his form, and, as if the corpse lay exposed in the hot sun for weeks, festering into a putrefying mess, a foul, moss-coloured slime oozing from the torso. The gut wrenching, rancid ichor immediately attracted a swarm of flies, ready to fill their miniscule bellies.

The advancing troops stopped in shock at the emergence of the second abomination, hesitating, unsure of the next move. Swords hung in the scabbard, men aghast at the sight of the advancing foe. Fear had frozen the once hardened warriors as nightmares manifested before them. They stood awaiting fate to deal its cruel final blow.

"Snap out of it!" yelled Hamish to his panicked comrades. "Defend yourselves, kill those things."

The soldiers were brought back to reality after Hamish's orders rung in their ears. Weapons raised, the men desperately tried to garner some advantage by frantically stabbing into the chest of the advancing beasts. Unfortunately, it was to no avail as each strike never felled the intended target. The Clansmen thought the job was done, but this assumption proved fatal as the figures shambled forward, skewering the blade through them until the grip of the handle was lost and the monsters tore into the flesh of their surprised victims.

Hamish continued to watch in disgust as two more of his men were set upon and savaged. Nothing like this had ever happened before. Hamish was at a loss at what to do next as he stood in amazement as a few more were mutilated. At this rate, not many of the force would remain to invade Forth and take revenge on the Douglas brothers. A decision had to be made soon or there would be no-one left to invade the village. Retreat was the best option but Hamish's stubborn pride stood in the way of the withdrawal.

Anger coursed through the blood vessels as muscles tensed and an already sweating face turned red with rage at the sight of his team falling like trees during a thunderstorm.

"Fucking hell, you bunch of idiots!" Hamish screamed at the remainder of his raiding party. "Dinna just stand there, kill them. I want them all dead!"

Calm overtook Hamish as the squad moved as a single unit towards the ever-increasing shambling fiends. Sandy and Tam attempted to join the fray but were yanked back by their leader.

"Look," he growled at them, "there is a good chance that we'll lose this battle. If we do, then we will need to make a run for it. When I shout run, we move as fast as we can towards the village and find a cottage to take refuge in and regroup. You are my protection, I pray that it does not come to this, but it looks like God is against us."

The two guards nodded in response and held back, taking position a few yards in front of their leader. The seasoned veterans had fought in many skirmishes against the clan's enemies and had built up quite a reputation as two of the most feared warriors in Clan Balliol. When Hamish's father ordered them to serve as Hamish's personal guard, in private they complained, but publicly they were loyal to the Balliols and followed the orders given. After several raids with Hamish as commander, they had come to respect their overbearing leader.

Hamish watched with concern as the battle raged on. With the resurrected creatures numbering at four, each blow dealt by Hamish's force was ineffective as the creatures ignored the pain. Despite the blood flowing from numerous wounds, the monsters surged past the thrusting swords of the next wave of troops, launching themselves, ripping through woollen shirts as their teeth tore through the skin before feeding. Roars of agony followed as the defenceless victims were slammed to the ground with the weight of the dead atop them. A battle for survival ensued, one that the rest of the army had no chance of winning.

Hamish was paralysed with fear as his fallen comrades weakened with each passing minute. Vital fluid pooled around as the creatures delivered their final blows, feeding on the robustness of the unconscious men. Once finished, the abominations turned and snarled at the remainder of the incumbents, hungry, looking for more nourishment, seemingly unsatiated despite full bellies. Hamish could now see their grey, withered faces and vacant, scarlet eyes. Already, over half of his force was gone with the rest about to be engaged by the fiends. Hamish knew that all was lost; it was best to make a retreat and live to fight once more.

Tapping his bodyguards on the shoulder, Hamish nodded to them and motioned towards the road that led into the outskirts of Forth Village. Looking forlornly at the remains of the ravaged soldiers, Hamish lamented on the revenge that was cruelly snatched away from him. Malcolm Douglas would have to wait another day. The payback for the torment suffered at the school, ran by the monks in Peebles, would come, just not the way he had planned it.

The trio fled from the slaughter, looking to make as much distance between themselves and the carnage as possible. The initial light jog upped to a quicker pace with cries of hatred heard as the abandoned troops realised that Hamish had left them to a gruesome fate.

Hamish risked a look back as tortured screams pierced the night. Seeing the last of his former brethren fall as the figures turned to outlines with each passing second, Hamish broke into a sprint, urging the others on, an attempt to put as much distance between them and the devastation. It was going to be a long night for Hamish, but it was better than being dead or one of those things.

CHAPTER FOUR

THE STABLES

Frantically, Donald rebounded back to reality from the vivid dreams. Disturbed by the scenes that frequented his unconscious psyche, Donald felt overwhelmingly disoriented, struggling to gain bearing while scanning the darkness as the moon hid behind the snowy white clouds blanketing the night sky.

Becoming more aware of the surroundings with every passing moment, finding himself slumped over, Donald thumped in a rhythmic motion against something firm. With the realisation he was moving in a method outside of his control, it was difficult to ascertain exactly where he was going due to the enveloping shadows.

Donald was annoyed with himself. Too often he zoned out due to boredom, his imagination was usually more exciting than sitting in the tavern listening to a lovesick Malcolm gush over Morag or the local lads fantasise about which lassie they wanted to court. It was always the same, the boys salivated about the size of the lady's breasts, each description more outrageous than the one before, with one unfortunate girl having her tits compared to a pair of pumpkins. There was a lot of boasting about who had the best place to take a maiden back to for sex. Gus preferred to use his da's barn whilst Jock was a wee bit more morose and preferred a graveyard. According to Jock, the cool wind hitting your bottom, combined with the smell of death was one of the most erotic experiences. This usually went on for a while until the topic degenerated into penis comparison, each description becoming more outlandish than the next, with one daft lad claiming that his penis was the bigger than a fence post. This had brought a chuckle from everyone. Donald was more interested in an imaginary world of battling with the English and the evil Balliols, his legendary prowess with the sword unmatched by anyone in his head.

Malcolm worried about him, although was never direct about it. Donald was not stupid and could tell from the hints, and the secret whispering with mother, that his elder brother wanted to help but did not know how to go about it. Donald hated this and worked on trying to improve things, but the increased tediousness of his life, mainly due to the long hours out in the countryside, had left him wanting adventure. The unlimited possibilities within his mind proved to be more appealing than sitting and watching sheep graze in the meadow all day.

Donald could now hear what sounded like heavy breathing under him and suspecting that he was being carried, Donald tapped lightly on what he thought was a shoulder.

"Donald? Are you back?"

Donald wasn't expecting the voice of his sibling, he feared Malcolm was kidnapped by the Balliols or worse, the dreaded English and their evil soldiers.

"Malcolm, where are we? And why are you carrying me?"

Malcolm slowed to a stop and called out to the others to wait whilst he lowered Donald to the ground. Steadying his feet, Donald glanced around and saw his cousin Jamie, Big Davie, and Morag walking ahead.

"What is going on? The last thing that I remember is that we were in the tavern. What happened?" Donald asked worriedly.

"Ach, it is nothing that we canna handle. The folks in the tavern just turned a wee bit crazy and started biting people. There are few of them behind that are chasing us down. I suggest that we make haste or we could be in some trouble. Move your arse to the stables, laddie. We can regroup there," replied Big Davie.

Donald stood there, even more confused than before, and watched as Big Davie and Jamie turned and jogged off ahead, with Morag not far behind. A gentle tap on the shoulder soon had Donald moving as well.

"Come on, brother, I dinna want our cousins to get too far ahead of us."

It took a few seconds for the Douglas brothers to catch up with the rest of the group. Strange thumping echoed, filling the night while the occasional scream pierced in the distance. All of this was making Donald feel uneasy, shaking with fear of whatever was out there, nerves jangling at the visions that his mind was creating.

"How long until we get there?" Malcolm called out to his cousins ahead. "I am starting to get a little freaked out here."

"Ach, Malky," laughed Big Davie, "you have nothing to worry about. I will give you a wee cuddle once we get there. Will that make you feel better?"

"Away and shite, you big lump," retorted Malcolm, shaking his head. "I will boot your arse when I catch up with you."

The nervous banter continued, helping to soothe frenzied thoughts as the party neared the massive wooden building where the horses were temporarily housed whilst their owners had a drink at the tavern. In most villages, the stables would be close by, but in Forth, citizens like to socialise in peace and it could get very noisy as the animals took time to settle down for the night.

Soon, the group neared their destination and Donald could see that Morag was struggling slightly with the unplanned run. Morag was bent over trying to catch her breath as they slowed to a walk on the approach to the stable entrance.

Donald placed a hand gently on her shoulder. "Are you struggling, Morag?"

"I am fine, thank you," Morag replied in a soft, almost musical tone. "I am just not used to running. I think spending all that time sitting down sewing has left me a bit sluggish compared to you lads."

"If you are struggling, let us ken," said Malcolm, overhearing the conversation. "I suspect that this is not the last time that we will be on the move, I dinna want you to fall behind."

"Dinna worry about me, Malcolm Douglas, I am more than capable of looking after myself."

"If you two are finished with your romancing, we need to get the horses and get out of here," Big Davie said with a chuckle.

Donald shook his head and watched Malcolm throw Big Davie a mock scowl. Donald knew that his brother was just trying to wind up the big clansman and take the heat out of a tense situation. Big

Davie returned the favour with a wink and a blown kiss, which Malcolm snatched out of the air, clutching it to his chest.

"Will you pair stop acting the fool?" interjected Jamie. "Those things will catch up to us soon and I dinna fancy another battle with them if I can avoid it. Morag, can you stand watch please whilst the rest of us go inside and get the horses and weapons?"

"I will stay with her. I am not wanting her to be on her own if she is caught by surprise," Malcolm stated.

"Your decision, cousin, I dinna have time to argue with you. If you get in any sort of trouble, just shout."

"Will do, just keep an eye on my brother, dinna let him do anything daft."

Donald followed Jamie and Big Davie through the doors into the stables, giving Malcolm a playful punch as he passed. Donald was sick of Malcolm's babying. Years of training with the sword had proved he was a capable fighter, yet Malcolm always had someone keep an eye on him, whether it was at school in Peebles or out playing in the fields with their cousins. With Malcolm or a friend normally watching, there were times that Donald felt trapped by the constant attention, which was part of the reason he was keen to leave home and start off on his own adventure.

Upon entering the structure, the stench of horseshit was pungent. The pit of Donald's stomach started to ripple with the overwhelming smell, which was unusual as Donald normally spent part of the day mucking out the barn. The way ahead was dim, with only the light of burning torches preventing the place from being in total darkness

"For fuck sake!" exclaimed Big Davie as he turned to talk to Donald. "Is that your brew? Check your tunic for stains, you disgusting bastard."

"No," replied Donald laughing, "mine is much worse than that. I think your nose is too close to your own arse."

In a low voice, Jamie instructed, "Will you two shut up, I am trying to listen to that noise."

Silence ensued as the group could hear a scraping of metal against stone and a low groaning sound, like the cry of an animal in pain. Donald's skin exploded in goosebumps as his already strained nerves were frayed even further.

"Where are the stable hands? Should they not be here to tend the horses?" asked Donald.

"Aye," replied Jamie. "They should, but there is no sign of them."

Donald surveyed the small, dusty passage ahead before continuing. It was what you would expect it to look like with various items like stirrups and horseshoes hanging on the wall. Normally, the doors to where the horses were housed would be half open, but they were all closed. Very unusual. Donald hated the feel of straw beneath his boots but understood that it was needed to keep the place clean.

Jamie took the lead position as they moved slowly along the corridor, with Donald sandwiched in the middle, and Big Davie bringing up the rear. Donald watched the smaller man carefully as he scouted around, looking and listening with expert skills, wary of any possible threats, always ready for any danger that may unexpectedly appear. Donald admired his cousin; the years of war had taken its toll on Jamie, but that experience was invaluable now as he took time to ensure it was safe before they continued.

Jamie stopped beside the big doorway on the left, a weather-beaten surface with splints of timber hanging off due to lack of proper maintenance. Edging it open, Jamie tried to peek through the gap to ascertain if any danger lay within, but soon jumped back, startled, as a small swarm of flies buzzed through the crack and immediately flew around, trying to nip at exposed faces and limbs. Frantically swatting, they tried to beat the pesky insects away to avoid being bitten. It took a few seconds for them to disperse, leaving a sour taste in Donald's mouth.

"That can mean one of two things," said Jamie arms flailing at the remaining beasts. "There is either a huge pile of excrement on the floor or a dead body and I dinna smell any shite."

"Out of the way," Big Davie demanded as he pushed Jamie to the side. "I am tired of doing this carefully. It is time to do things the Davie way." Big Davie flashed a huge grin before raising a boot, flashing his massive calves, and kicking the door with such force that it slammed off the wall and settled back into the position that it was originally in.

Turning around, his face scarlet with embarrassment, Big Davie smiled sheepishly at Donald whilst shrugging his shoulders. "I may have to use a little less force."

35

"Aye, I think everyone now kens we are here." Donald laughed.

Turning forward with a sigh, Big Davie gave the door a gentle push and stood there in shock at what was happening before him. "Fuck me!" Big Davie exclaimed. "You have got to see this."

Donald moved up beside Big Davie, jaw dropping at the scene. Two men were kneeling in front of a dead horse, gorging on flesh they ripped out with bare hands. Donald's stomach started to churn as blood flowed down the flank of the stallion, forming a dark puddle, the thickness seeping into the cracks of the floor.

"That is disgusting, I think I want to vomit," Jamie uttered.

"Look," Big Davie said, scanning around the room, trying not to look at the horrific sight before him, "I see no weapons. I suggest that we close the door while they are distracted and move onto the next stable. Bolt it shut, so that those things dinna get out."

"We have one problem with that idea, I think you broke it," said Jamie as he struggled to get the door closed.

It took a few moments to manage to get it back into place, unable to lock it due to the mechanism, mangled after it struck the stone wall. Conscious of time, Big Davie took the lead as the trio continued to the next cubicle, hoping to find their weapons and mounts intact. Donald noticed Jamie continually scouting and looking around as they rapidly proceeded along the hallway. This time there was no careful checking to see if there was any movement behind the door, Big Davie quickly opened it, standing ready for what may appear. Donald could feel the tension, the previous banter finished after the disturbing scene they just witnessed. Donald shuddered as he thought about the poor horse being ripped to shreds. *What had happened to the men? Why were they feasting on that poor creature?*

This time, however, things could not have been more different. Before them stood a large brown mare, front legs in the air, aggressively neighing. Scarlet eyes, discoloured by the yellow tinge around the iris, stared vacantly at them as Donald balked at the remains of a heart, severed by the oversized teeth of the huge beast flapping at the side of her bloody mouth.

"What the fuck is that? That creature has turned savage. I have never seen anything like it before!" Donald yelled.

"We have," replied Jamie, "the same thing happened to the people in the tavern whilst you were out of it. There is no use standing around here gaping, we need to get out of here, fast."

Confused at what was going on, Donald turned tail and headed back up the corridor with Jamie and Big Davie trailing not far behind, the heavy breathing of the larger man could be heard in the background.

"Where to now?" asked Big Davie, a couple of feet to his rear. "I dinna think we are going to get any weapons here."

"I dinna ken. I reckon that we should head away from the centre of the village as these things seem to be breeding and there could be lots of them there," Jamie replied.

"We will get the others and figure it out then," said Big Davie.

CLIP CLOP DRAG, CLIP CLOP DRAG.

The sound echoed in the corridor around them, a slow and deliberate noise that continually repeated as they walked.

Donald paused slightly to catch his breath and chanced a glance over his shoulder, two large horses trotted slowly behind the one just found in the stable. Its hooves pulled in the straw, shambling eerily towards the group. The horses looked more like ghosts than the animals they arrived on.

"Run!" shouted Donald. "There are three of the fuckers now."

Sprinting for safety, Donald tried to make up the short yardage to escape but was soon interrupted by a pained yell from behind. Turning, he saw Jamie sprawled on the floor as Big Dave barged past him, the slavering beasts closing in on his prone cousin.

"Go, lad! Run as fast as you can!" yelled Jamie, realising that he was not able to get back up in time. "Go find your brother, I am beyond help now!"

"*No!*" Big Davie screamed, aware that his comrade was in trouble. "No man shall be abandoned! I am coming for you."

Donald could only watch, frozen in fear, as Big Davie barrelled past, towards his distressed friend. The threat looming ever larger, Jamie tried to stand up.

CLIP CLOP! CLIP CLOP!

"Neigh! Groan!" wailed the monstrous mares, a yard from Jamie as Big Davie launched in front of him, huge fists slamming into the teeth of the feral fiends, knocking each one to the side, giving Jamie just enough time to get off the floor and run towards Donald.

37

"Run! We dinna have much time!" bellowed Big Davie as the creatures recovered.

A few seconds later, Donald reached the door and threw it open to reveal dark skies ahead. Stepping through, he surveyed the surroundings, desperately looking for his brother, but there was no sign of Malcolm or Morag as a stony silence told of the sense of dread.

CHAPTER FIVE

SHADOWS

Morag sighed. Tired from the excursion and late evening outside the stables. She strained her grainy eyes, attempting to see if she could make out any movement in the dark field around them. Owls hooted, warning their prey of imminent death, taking attention from the shadows that danced at the corner of her vision. A wee tingle shivered along her body as she thought of the terror that they had experienced so far that night, similar to the shock of accidentally seeing your father naked for the first time. Morag suspected more was to come and hoped that her nerves would hold in the coming hours ahead.

Malcolm was beside her, standing guard, looking every bit the handsome man that she had grown to love. Muscular arms rippled in the deep glow of the moonlight as he surveyed the landscape for any possible threats. The poker used in the tavern earlier was gripped tightly in a large, hairy fist. Morag watched as Malcolm softly tapped it. He was so brave in the tavern. If it was not for him, they would all have died and who else would have carried Donald and at great personal risk? This was a different side of Malcolm she saw, one that was caring and not the awkward, unsure man she grew to love.

Unexpectedly, she felt the gentle squeeze of Malcolm's hand caressing her silky skin with a dainty touch unusual for a fighting man. Morag did not remember slipping it in there and the tenderness caused her to pull back, withdrawing from the moment, flushing a deep crimson in embarrassment.

"Sorry," Morag stuttered as she tried to recover the situation, "I have no idea what came over me."

"It is fine, lass, I like it when you hold my hand."

"I enjoy holding it, Malcolm, but we need to concentrate here, what if something happens?"

"Nothing will happen If I just stand here and caress your fingers, Morag. Your ma willna suddenly appear around the corner and catch us. Even if she does, so what? I love you and I dinna care what she or anyone else thinks. We were holding hands in the tavern, what is so different about that to doing it out here?"

"Ma does not visit taverns," retorted Morag defiantly. "Neither does my brother, so they would not have seen us."

"It is none of their business," said Malcolm, his voice raised slightly. "I love you, Morag Douglas and I am not afraid to let my feelings show."

"What we do in public and in private are two different things," Morag snapped, "we are supposed to be looking out for threats, not discussing our love. I am scared, what if those creatures from the pub find us and attack us? I am too young to die."

"They willna catch up with us. We shut the door behind us when we left."

"Do you not think they can open doors? Angus could open the tavern door with ease."

"Aye, but whatever that thing was, it wisna Angus."

"It had Angus's hands, legs, and brain. If Angus could open a door, then those things should be able to."

"You might be right, lass. I dinna ken though."

Satisfied that the argument was in her favour, Morag turned to face the landscape, happy that all was once again right with the ever-complicated relationship that they had. Malcolm was a caring man who Morag loved with all her heart, but every once in a while, he did need reminded of who was in charge. Morag looked up at the looming night sky, trying to make out if anything was in the distance. The fight had distracted both of them and it did look like there were shadows dancing in the field ahead, probably jigging away to the sound of the bagpipes playing at a Ceilidh. Convinced her imagination was running wild, Morag said nothing to Malcolm as she did not want to disturb his concentration again, fearful that if she did, a real threat might appear.

A few more minutes passed, and Morag could swear she heard faint moaning. Worried that they were in danger. Morag lightly tapped Malcolm on the shoulder.

"Do you hear that?" she whispered with concern.

"Hear what, lass?"

"That noise, it sounds like someone is hurt or one of those creatures in the tavern."

Morag watched as Malcolm strained to try and catch the faint groaning in the wind, tilting awkwardly as his back arched for a better listening position.

"I canna hear a thing, Morag," said Malcolm doubtfully. "Are you sure it was not just the wind?"

"I am positive, it came from around the side of the stable. I think someone is injured. What if it is ma out looking for me? I would hate myself if she hurt herself out there when I am here with you. We should take a look."

"If you are sure there is something there, we will investigate. We need to be quick about it though, the others will be out soon and we are supposed to be standing guard."

"Thank you, Malcolm, it is probably nothing but I want to make sure."

Malcolm took the lead as the couple gingerly made their way around the side of the building, treading carefully, trying not to trip over any loose rocks or rogue tufts of heather sticking out of the side of the walls. It did not take long to sidle around, but the further they moved, the louder the sound got.

"I can hear it now," declared Malcolm in shock. "Whoever it is, they are definitely in trouble, we had better hurry. Stay behind me, Morag, I dinna want to lose you."

The journey continued to the far side of the stables and as they reached the corner, a low guttural sound, like a faint roar, emanated. Yelping, Morag almost tripped Malcolm as the pace quickened. Jangling nerves spurred already shaky legs onward, continually nagging away, saying there was nothing to worry about and it was just her imagination, but Malcolm had heard it too, so it must be real, whatever it was.

"Malcolm," she stammered, "I am scared, what was that?"

"It was nothing, lass. Probably just a wild animal like a feral cat or dog. Nothing to concern ourselves with," Malcolm replied, trying to sound assured.

Although the words were calming, Morag knew that there was a lack of conviction in his voice. The usual confidence was not there, causing him to shake slightly, but that could be the chilly air. She felt the uncertainty when she accidentally pushed against him, almost causing them both to fall.

"Will you be careful!" Malcolm hissed. "You are going to get us both killed out here. Stay close but watch where you are walking."

Morag felt sheepish at the lecture, ashamed at being berated by her beloved. It was tough to see by the meagre light from the shadowy sky; she could not tell what the shapes were in the distance. She decided it was probably a good idea not to know. Not wanting to face another tongue-lashing, Morag dropped back slightly to give Malcolm more space to manoeuvre.

Horrified, she watched as an arm flailed out at Malcolm, almost putting a dent in the side of his face. Fortunately, instincts kicked in and the blow crashed into the wooden beam that supported the stable as Malcolm dodged deftly to the right. Another limb struck at him but this time it was met by the large metallic spike that Malcolm was holding. This was soon followed by a swinging punch which sent the dark figure sprawling on the ground.

Morag marvelled at the quickness of Malcolm's reactions and knew that years of practice honed his skills, ready for this moment. Morag felt useless as her only training was with a short bow da had constructed. Often, hours were spent firing small sticks of wood that lay by one of the oak trees that stood in the forest to the west of the village. Morag endured many days collecting the "arrows" for her temporary weapon and quite a lot of time was taken to retrieve the ammo expended. With no sword hand, the lack of fighting skill meant that Morag was reliant on Malcolm for protection. It was worrying that she was so vulnerable, not able to defend herself if Malcolm was to fall. This and the dark foreboding night sky did not help ease the fear.

The clanging sound of metal falling on the stone path below brought Morag back to her senses as she saw the poker Malcolm used to fight with lying on the ground behind him. More of the creatures were ahead and Malcolm was struggling to hold them at arm's length with his bare hands. Morag could see Malcolm's tenacity in fending off the attackers but knew that it would not be long until he was on his knees, injured, or perhaps worse. If that happened, she was an easy target and this was frightening. Crouching down, Morag picked up the fallen spike and almost without thought, she rushed behind him. Four of the men were now squaring up to Malcolm, with more approaching. He managed to hold off three but the last one was proving elusive. Morag could see bared teeth as the monster lunged towards Malcolm's unprotected shoulder. Instinctively, Morag's arm shot up as she skewered the incoming cranium before it made contact with Malcolm, the impact shuddering through an unsteady arm. Her palms soaked from the exertion of the first kill, it was tough to get a grip on the rod as it protruded from its forehead. Quickly wiping the sweat upon her dress, Morag finally managed to get another hold of the poker, wrenching it back and forth until it popped out the skull and plopped to the ground. The wrought spur clanged to the stone as her arms flopped with exertion. She watched with relief, coupled with sadness, as the man slumped to the ground, gore and brain splattering from his lifeless body. Momentarily frozen in shock, flabbergasted that she had just taken the life of a fellow Scot, tears flowed down Morag's cheeks.

"Thank you," said Malcolm, turning quickly to look at her after shoving over the other three attackers. "I was a goner there. We need to get out of here before that lot get back up and there are more of them coming."

"I will lead, you follow. Here take this," replied Morag, passing him the poker, "you have more of a need for it than I do." Turning, Morag started the journey back, through the unforgiving darkness, praying that Malcolm was able to hold off the pursuing creatures.

CHAPTER SIX

SHELTER

◘

Panting, the red-haired Borderman leaned against a sturdy timber fence at the edge of the village, trying to desperately catch his breath after fleeing from the cannibalistic soldiers a couple of miles back. Beside him stood two rugged warriors, each armed with hefty long swords, sweat pouring off their brows. They were used to enforced marches or short-range battles, but not extended tiring runs trying to escape a blood thirsty enemy.

"For fuck sake," said the frustrated flame headed chap, "a few weeks out of battle and you two are running like a pair of old maids. I thought da trained you better than this."

"Sorry, Hamish, I think we may have overindulged recently. Too many feasts and not enough fights," replied the taller, raven-haired man.

"Typical. You are supposed to be elite soldiers, instead I get a pair of spoiled nobles complaining that their feet are too sore. Look, we are almost in the village, we need to find some shelter and get cleaned up a bit before planning our next move. I dinna ken about you pair, but I could do with a good piece of ham and flagon of ale to wash it down, instead of standing here like a bunch of old women," Hamish snapped back.

"That sounds bloody brilliant," replied the smaller blond, licking his dry lips in anticipation. "Where is the nearest tavern?"

"Sandy, you are an idiot. Are you wanting to lose your balls as well as both your legs? We would be more welcome in a monastery than the local alehouse. No, we need to find somewhere less public, an unoccupied cottage for example."

"But that is stealing," replied the other chap. "My da told me that stealing was wrong. He said that thieving was for cowards and Englishmen."

"Tam, your da was wrong," Hamish declared. "The English are our friends and one does not steal from our enemies; one takes back what is rightfully ours. You are either with me or you can go back snivelling to your family, what is it going to be?"

"There is no need to be like that, I swore a blood oath to you and our clan. I dinna intend to break it," Tam complained.

Hamish sneered. "Make sure that you remember that. We are in the middle of enemy territory and exposed, we need to rely on each other or we will end up jailed or even worse, hanged, and I dinna fancy swinging from a noose."

"You have got a point," replied Tam. "We need to find some shelter for the night. Where do you suggest?"

"I have not been here for a couple of years. If my memory serves me right, there are a couple of cottages that are isolated from the village out in the fields over yonder." Hamish pointed to the darkened area behind the wall to their right.

"What if there are more of those things there?" asked Sandy, concerned after their recent encounter. "We had to run for our lives earlier."

"We will just have to be better prepared," Hamish retorted, annoyed at the apparent unwillingness to fight by the two so-called warriors. "Get your swords ready, you pair of cowards, we are not losing another fight to those creatures, whatever they are."

"What *do* you think they are, sir?" asked Tam.

"Who kens? We dinna have time to stand around here and discuss it. We need to move."

It took a few minutes for the trio to traverse the rough rocky path at the edge of the village. Hamish yelped a few times, stubbing a toe off the edge of a stone hidden by the deep expanse of the shadowy eve. Pain throbbed through the front of the unprotected boot and shot up into the base of his leg in no time.

"Fuck! Fuck! Bastard son of a Douglas whore! Fuck!" Hamish cursed as he hopped furiously in agony. It was a few seconds before it subsided and he continued through on the path.

Despite the injury, they finally reached the boundary. A few years ago, sheep and cows wandered from their pastures and roamed through Forth, causing no end of bother. The locals became angry after various theft of pies left out to cool in the shade, with drunken ewes lapping up spillage from casks of ale tipped over in the hubbub, or the rams who chased the children into burns. All this chaos forced them to build the boundary. Hamish remembered the stories from the times that he spent in the hamlet, the camaraderie and the bond that connected the locals sickened him. The memories fuelled his foul mood caused by the events of the night so far.

Before long, they climbed over the four-foot-high structure and dropped down into the pasture below, Hamish grinned as he could hear Sandy cursing after stepping into a steaming pile of dung dropped by one of the cattle. The glee soon turned to frustration as Hamish felt his foot squelch into a soft, moist mound that ponged similar to a bucket after one of the servants had shat in it.

"Aaahhhh! How much shite can come out of a bloody cow? I hate farmers and their fields filled with useless animals that spend all day eating and shitting. I would much rather be sat by the fire in a nice tavern, supping on ale with a buxom wench on my lap. Instead, I am stepping on cattle dirt in a field with you pair of idiots. What a godawful night this is turning out to be."

The remainder of the trek through the field was done in relative silence with the peace only being disturbed by an occasional "eewww" or an odd curse escaping from the drying lips of one of the trio. Eventually, they reached the end where a sturdy oak gate led onto the next pasture lay. Frustrated that this was taking longer than he had hoped, Hamish kicked out at the wooden exit, using more force than intended, smashing through the barrier. More pain surged through his already aching limb as splinters scraped along the bottom of his shin.

"Ow! You wee bastard!" Hamish screamed, falling to the ground. "Fucking farmers should look after their property better."

"Are you hurt, sir?" asked Tam, concerned that his leader may have broken his leg. "That looked sore."

"I am fine, it is just a flesh wound, now help me up so that we can get out of this hellhole."

Hamish glowered at the clansman as Tam pulled him to his feet. Discomfort etched across scarlet cheeks. Dripping sweat mixed with blood and shite that had stuck to his face from the arduous trek through the meadow, Hamish's body complained about the day's journey. All he could now think about was finding shelter and the possibility of a good bath.

Hooting owls and howling wolves in the distance ensured a much quicker trot through the next pasture. The three men were covered in all sorts of mud and filth. Hair, matted with cow dung and grass, hung down foreheads into their eyes. Taking a few minutes to brush off what they could, the weary travellers continued down the narrow stone way towards the faint candlelight that lit a small thatched building in the distance. Hamish surmised that it was a cottage as grey smoke could be seen puffing from the straw roof, forming small clouds that Hamish mistook for flying sheep in the distance. Conscious of the myth that counting them would put you to sleep, Hamish shook off his grogginess and drudged along the trail towards what he expected to be the night's lodgings. A tantalizing scent of beef tempted taste buds as he visualized the stew being cooked in the pot inside. A loud rumble escaped his empty stomach and Hamish realised that they had not eaten since midday at Cosy Inn in Linton. Reminder of the hot lamb broth and fresh bread dripping with butter soon moistened once dry lips, spurring the party onwards to their destination.

Sounds of barking dogs slowed the pace slightly as they approached the farmhouse. Tam was particularly nervous around the animals. Clouds overhead finally cleared, allowing the moon to take centre stage and shine bright. Twinkling stars helped to guide the weary travellers to the front of the home. Hamish motioned for the others to draw their weapons whilst he stood at the massive oak door and rapped loudly on the ram's head shaped wrought iron knocker. Hamish was impressed with the craftsmanship of the skull and was soon thinking of ways to remove it from its occupancy.

Hamish's devious musings were interrupted as the sturdy barrier dramatically swung open. Before him stood a chubby, dark-haired woman who looked to be aged in her early forties. A hard life had put grey streaks through a tidy mane that was formed into a bun to keep it out of the eyes. Dressed in a lengthy white robe, the lady carried a small, brass holder with a dripping candle, which she used to illuminate the faces of the three strangers intruding on her night.

"How can I help you, fellows?" The lady smiled as she surveyed the guests standing in her yard. Pleasantness soon faded as upon Sandy's chest, she spotted the clan badge of the Balliols, the sworn enemy of the Douglas clan.

Noticing the change in attitude, Hamish placed a foot against the exit, preventing the closure of the door. The woman ran back into the house screaming at the top of her lungs. With a quick flick of the wrist, he motioned the others to chase after. Hamish watched as a couple of big sheepdogs barrelled towards the Bordermen. A small whimper emanated from Tam at the sight of the crazed canines, but the mutts were soon cut down with ease by Sandy and Hamish as they drove swords through the bellies of the beasts before continuing after the fleeing female.

"For fuck sake, Tam, you need to overcome this irrational fear. Dogs are not something to worry about."

"Sorry, sir, I am just not keen on them. I was bitten by one as a child and I am a bit nervous whenever they are close."

"Just follow us. Sandy will keep you safe, despite being smaller than you, you coward."

Carefully pulling the door shut and turning the key, Hamish could hear the continual panicked yelping of the lady of the house. Turning attention ahead, Hamish's jaw dropped as the fallen canines unbelievably scrambled upright. Heads lolling to the side with tails drooping, the reanimated hounds dragged padded paws, slowly staggering after their killers. With vicious growls and slobbering maws, the murderous intent was clear.

"Oh fuck." Tam was visibly shaking now.

Not believing what he was witnessing, Hamish thought back to his clansmen who also seemingly rose from the dead and devoured the fighting force he brought to Forth. Once again unsheathing his sword, determined not to lose Sandy and Tam, Hamish stalked behind the hairier black and white canine and swung full force to decapitate man's best friend. Body collapsing, blood gushed from the severed neck. Never ending it seemed, the artery sprayed over the stone floor, running in rivulets across the surface before settling beside the coat rack that housed the jerkins of the farm's occupants. Surmising that there were others that lived here based on a pair of leather jerkins that hung on the furthest hook, Hamish knew he needed to dispatch the remaining animal and concentrate on securing the place before its departed owners returned.

Turning to face the other hound, whose attention was firmly focused on him, Hamish noticed the lifeless expression within the glazed, bloodshot eyes of his enemy. It was almost as if it had no control of its own form. Trying to control his initial shock, Hamish dodged to the side as the beast suddenly burst into life and leapt towards his throat. Thankful for the years of training which honed his instincts, Hamish responded with a swift swipe through the back of the mongrel, slicing it in two. Hamish panted heavily from the fight. Watching carefully, he noticed the bodies were now still and both halves of the corpse lay a couple of feet apart. Not confident of death, Hamish gave the other dog a swift kick to see if there was any reaction.

Satisfied there was no response, Hamish concentrated on the screams coming from upstairs. Rapidly moving past fallen chairs, he climbed the steps two at a time before arriving at the back room where he found the woman lying on bed, stripped of all her clothes. Her hands were tightly bound to the bedposts. Sandy was midway through removing his tunic, ready to rape the unfortunate farmwife.

"Get your clothes back on," demanded Hamish, annoyed at the lack of control from his men. "There will be plenty of time for that later. We need to check that there is no-one else here and get some food in our bellies first."

Hamish turned to look at the woman. A farmer's wife for sure, breasts sagging due to advancing years. Her arms and thighs were still quite shapely and firm from life on the farm, although she was a little old for his liking. Crying continued as Hamish could sense the fear pulse through her quivering body.

"Oh, do stop that," Hamish demanded harshly. "No-one is going to hurt you... yet. You are giving me a sore head. If you dinna stop that incessant crying then I may have to change my mind and let my horny friend loose upon you."

The woman soon ceased the desperate sobbing, cheeks now flushed red with tear stains. Trembling uncontrollably, fear and anticipation of the horrors that had lay before her flowed deep into her bones.

"That is much better," said Hamish in an almost mocking tone. "Now, dear, what is your name?"

"My, my, my," stammered the woman, the terror overpowering her voice.

"Come on now," Hamish said, trying to make himself sound kind and gentle but failing, "you can tell me your name. My name is Hamish Balliol. You have my name, now, what are you called?"

"My name is Jean, Jean Douglas."

"Oh good! *The* Jean Douglas, mother of Malcolm and Donald, surely not. Are you she?" Hamish clasped his hands in evident glee.

"Yes," whispered Jean in a resigned tone, "they are my sons."

"This is my lucky night. Do you happen to ken where your sons are?"

"No, they never told me where they were going."

"*Liar!*" Hamish's hand swooped down and imprinted on Jean's cheek, the force of the punch flailing her head to the side.

Wooziness overcame Jean for a moment before she defiantly straightened herself and glared. "Go to hell, you bastard!" Blood rolled down her chin, spittle and fragments of a broken tooth sprayed upon Hamish's cheek.

"You will tell me, bitch!" More blows rained down on the poor, defenceless mother, each strike with more power than the next, but nothing came from Jean's mouth.

"If you willna tell me, I will beat it out of you." Hamish positioned himself atop the thrashing prisoner.

"For fuck sake, will you two idiots hold her still?"

Sandy and Tam each held a leg as screams of hatred turned to cries of pain whilst Jean endured the torture handed out to her from the vengeful Borderman as the explosion of violence continued for a few minutes before finally, mercifully, she was knocked unconscious.

CHAPTER SEVEN

FINDING MALCOLM

The eerie, moonlit sky highlighted the large field that lay before them. The gentle clip-clop of horse hooves came from behind, each step taken getting a little louder than the last. Worry etched over Donald's face. Squinting his deep brown eyes, Donald tried to locate Malcolm and Morag. Figures could just be made out in the distance, feet dragging slowly, slumped as they walked. None looked like Malcolm.

"Malcolm! Morag!" Donald yelled with hands cupped together to try and further the range of his shouting. "Where are you?"

This repeated a few times before Donald felt the unexpected weight of a hand rest upon his shoulder. Concern for Malcolm's safety heightened. Donald was now convinced that something terrible had befallen his elder brother. The sound of shoes hitting the stone floor was getting louder and Donald knew that it would not be long before the rabid mares were upon them.

"Donald," said Jamie, fingers still resting on Donald's collar, "if we dinna leave now, then we could be horse food and I dinna fancy being stomped to death, do you?"

"No, let us head to the back of the stables, I reckon we have a better chance of finding them there than out in the open."

Walking gingerly to the right, Donald led the other men around to the end of the wall, continually calling out for his missing sibling. It was unusual for Malcolm to leave him like this, normally they were inseparable as Malcolm was so protective. Sometimes it was smothering, but Donald did not mind knowing that Malcolm would do anything for him, especially with their father fighting down south against the English. Donald surmised that the couple must have found a secluded place to canoodle in. Suspecting that Morag was getting impatient with Malcolm's gentlemanly ways and was keen to get him alone to have more intimate relations, Donald was surprised they had picked now to be frolicking in a field.

Groans drifted from the other end of the meadow, momentarily freezing Donald to the spot. His mind teased, telling him that a large beast wasn't far behind. In reality, the only heavy breathing, huge animal was Big Davie as he puffed and panted, struggling to keep up with the nimbler lad.

The edge of the building loomed near and the lack of response from Malcolm hastened their pace. Various scenarios popped into Donald's head about where he might be. Visions of strange men ripping his throat flashed into an already fragile psyche. Wary of the dreams coming, Donald slapped a cheek to keep from slipping any further from reality.

A hand clapped upon his shoulder jolted Donald back to full awareness.

"Laddie," said Big Davie softly, "try and hold it together. You are no use to us or Malcolm if you zone out. Stay with us, we'll find the big eejit."

"I'm fine, Davie, I will be alright. You are right, Malcolm and Morag must be the priority here, we need to find them."

"Aye, you just keep that thought in your head. Me and Jamie will see you through this, we may not be much but we willna see you hurt. Dinna forget that."

"Davie, I do appreciate you looking out for me but I am old enough to look after myself. I can fight, you ken. Malcolm has been training me with the sword. I'm no Balliol."

Big Davie laughed. "I've seen that brother of yours trying to use a sword. He uses it like a woman trying to stab a needle in cloth, no bloody skill."

Donald chuckled and rounded the corner. Big Davie was good at putting people at ease and that was what he needed tonight. It was a long time since he had seen the large clansman, it used to be two or three times a week that Davie would come around for dinner. Donald enjoyed the mock fights and pranks that Davie pulled on Malcolm.

The visits often perked Donald up, but the nights passed too quickly and an evening of fun and banter was over before he knew it. It was good to see him again, despite the current situation.

The groaning grew louder. This time it seemed to surround them rather than come from a distance. Deep, guttural sounds were followed by a sharp scream. Donald came to an abrupt halt and was greeted by a sudden, painful thump as Big Davie bumped into him. Force from the clumsy blow almost sent the smaller man sprawling, but hours of balance training with Malcolm kept Donald upright, preventing what could have been a dangerous fall.

"For fucks sake, Donald!" Big Davie started to complain before being rudely interrupted by Donald.

"Shhhh! Listen, can you hear that?"

It took several seconds for the loud sounds to morph into a quieter, more human grunt.

"I dinna hear anything but those bloody animals, there sure are a lot of wolves out there tonight," Big Davie exclaimed.

"Are you deaf or something? Even I can hear that. Have all those blows to the head affected your hearing?" Jamie declared from behind.

"Och away, there is nothing there, you two are having me on."

A loud shout pierced the night, coming from the other side of the barn. A sudden realization hit Donald as his face paled in response to the noise. "We went the wrong way! That was Malcolm, I swear it was him and they are at the other side of the stables. We have got to go back and help!"

"We canna go back," said Jamie. "Those fucking horses are back there. We need to keep going forward. God only kens what is out there. Whatever it is, I dinna bloody like it."

"Neither do I. You are correct about taking our time. As much as I hate doing it, it is the right thing to do," Donald stated glumly.

Despite words spoken calling for the party to move at a more measured pace, Donald was striding faster towards the far edge of the shed, concentrating purely on where the shouts were coming from. He could sense that Malcolm and Morag were in danger. Hastening progress towards them, he wanted to get there before anguish took over.

"Slow down, lad," puffed Big Davie, struggling to inhale in the humid conditions.

Donald could hear him panting heavily behind and slowed down accordingly. "Are you okay?" Donald asked, concerned for the struggling man.

"Aye, I will be fine, just slow it down a bit. I think all that alcohol is making me sluggish."

Nearing the edge of the building, their speed eased to a walk. Big Davie's heavy breathing still evident, the group continued to be enveloped by the grating, croaking noises. From the forest to the west, just at the edge of Donald's vision, wolves howled intermittently, adding to the worry and dangers of this haunting night. Donald tried to shove the fear to the back of his mind and keep focus on his missing brother.

"Malcolm!" Donald yelled once more. "We are coming."

A faint shout came from ahead. Donald was hopeful that it was Malcolm, but was unsure. It very well may be old Peter who lived on the other side of the village and could often be heard shouting at the cows when they mooed too loudly for his liking. Or, just as easily, it was Donald's imagination. With the excessive daydreaming lately, he couldn't be sure either way.

"Did you hear that? Did you hear Malcolm shouting this time?" Donald asked anxiously.

"Aye," replied Jamie, "I heard it. Just keep going, we will catch up to him."

This seemed to settle Donald as he turned the corner to face the shorter distance to the back end of the stables. Still, nothing was there. Yet, the moaning increased in pitch and he could now hear a strange scraping sound like shuffling feet.

Worried that Malcolm was in peril, Donald's pace quickened, his hand reached out and lightly trailed the dark outline of the stable. Donald thought that he saw shadows moving at the edge of his vision, but each time he turned to look, nothing was there. Feeling that something bad was about to happen, a sense of dread filled him. Determined to shake it off, Donald took a deep breath, steadied his resolve, and kept pushing on towards where Malcolm and Morag were.

"Laddie," called Big Davie from behind, "do you want me to take the lead?"

54

"Thank you, but no," Donald replied confidently. "I am faster than you are and I have much better hearing. Your offer is appreciated but I can do this."

"That is fine, laddie," puffed Big Davie. "Just be careful. I have your back."

"It is not my back that I am worried about," Donald replied as they continued the arduous trek around the massive stable. A rough, stony ground formed the basics of a path, a track so beaten by weather that parts of it had started to crumble away, leaving the trio exposed to a potential fall. Donald's nerves twanged. Although he had walked along this route many times before, it was different doing it in the dark and with fear pushing you along. One false step could send him tumbling to the ground which would likely result in Big Davie following suit and landing atop. That was something that he did not relish.

It was less than a minute before they reached the next corner, Donald continued to call out for Malcolm as they walked. Big Davie's heavy breathing had subsided a little. The chaotic noises were close to fever pitch as they rounded the building to see a group of about five or six people ahead, all advancing towards two shapes at the far end. The taller one was brandishing some sort of weapon which seemed to be holding them off.

"Malcolm!" shouted Donald in the excitement of seeing his sibling. "Is that you?"

"Donald," called a faint voice in the distance, "be careful, those men are rabid and attacking us, we need help but-"

The reply was cut off as the figure of his brother lashed out at a shadow that had appeared before him. The shape slumped to the ground after Malcolm shoved a pole through the back and killed him. Donald watched as Malcolm fended off more before the fallen chap rose from the ground and continued his attack.

"Come on, we have to help him, he canna last much longer!"

"Donald," replied Jamie, with a hint of caution in his voice, "we have no weapons, we are of no use to him. The best thing that we can all do is make a run for it and head for the road."

"We have got to help them!" Donald screamed in frustration. "They are going to get killed."

"Donald Douglas," Big Davie commanded with authority, "you will start to run towards the road and we will follow you. We can do nothing against that." He turned to roar at the fighting clansman, "Malky! There are too many of them! Head for the road at the other side of the grass. We will meet you there!"

Frustrated and angry, Donald turned to glare at Big Davie before heading away from the fracas with the others in tow.

CHAPTER EIGHT

THE PRIEST

The inviting smell of beef and assorted vegetables greeted the awaiting palate of the middle-aged priest. Dressed in a flowing, white night gown, he stood eagerly over the large cookpot that sat over the fire in the church kitchen. Oak logs crackled in the heat of the flames which danced like roses swaying in the wind.

It was an exhausting day for Father Patrick Murphy, whose legs ached after spending much of the afternoon removing the ever-growing weeds from the graves in the cemetery. They were left untended for a few weeks due to his journey north to pass on the word of God to the MacDuff Clan, who lost their preacher from illness. Patrick had agreed to go there to help out, and a young priest in training took the sermons in the large church located in the centre of the village. Upon his return, it was a few days to get his affairs back in order. Once done, he created some free time in the gardens of the old graveyard. Tidying the fallen leaves and trimming the shrubs and heather that had overgrown at the side of the stones was back breaking yet soothing work for the priest.

Bending over the boiling pot, the mouth-watering scent wafted out, the aroma enticing the hungry priest. Father Patrick took an old ladle and scooped out a hearty portion of stewed meat. Bringing it to his mouth, he checked the tenderness of dinner. The soup's heat burned his lips slightly, causing a curse to escape as the boiling food was tipped it back into the cookpot.

"That was stupid, Patrick," he muttered, before wandering over to pick up a large, wooden plate from the table. "You knew it was hot, you silly old man. So why did you think that it was clever to taste it?"

Head shaking in disbelief at his foolishness, Patrick returned to the steaming cauldron and scooped out three overflowing spoonfuls of stew, tipping each onto his platter, watching as the thick, gravy ran to the edge. Carefully carrying it back to the table, Patrick settled onto the bench before tearing a soft wedge of freshly made bread gifted to him by the local baker. Filling a goblet with deep red wine, he gulped down a huge amount before tucking into dinner, brown liquid spilling down his chin.

Twenty minutes and a swipe of the mouth with a cloth later, thoughts about the recent trip up north plagued the forefront of Father Patrick's mind. The highlanders did things differently, they spent more time out in the fields tending their flocks. A lot of advances from bored wives, stuck in their cottages or shacks with their children to look after, any spare time was spent darning socks or knitting woollen jumpers in preparation for the colder winter nights. The pious nature of the Catholic religion stopped him from taking up the offers of these lonely ladies. There could have quite easily been a few romps with the numerous frustrated women. One in particular had taken his fancy. A flame-haired lass with skin as white as the clouds, by the name of Eilidh. Her voluptuous hips, complemented with a revealing, low-cut dress, and an inviting, teasing smile, had tempted him on many a night. However, during those times of temptation, Patrick had sought solace in his books, the word of the Lord guided him from taking the attraction any further. Sighing, his thoughts wandered regularly to her striking emerald green eyes. Patrick smiled at the memory of her soft, silken touch upon the top of his hand.

Abruptly, he was brought back to his senses with an incessant loud banging. Constant thumping against the thick oak door where the congregation made their way into the church's main hall to listen to a sermon echoed through the priest's quarters. Patrick was not expecting visitors at this time of night. Normally after a meal, he would retire to the chair beside the sheepskin rug by the fireplace to enjoy the warmth and crackle of the flames while reading one of the books picked up from a travelling peddler or local scribe on his journey. Many an evening was spent with a quill and parchment recording his travels from memory and musing over the many towns and villages he had visited.

Rising from his seat, Father Patrick carefully moved to the other end of the church. The persistent banging continued; the throbbing beat pulsed through him. That, coupled with the wine consumed, had introduced a small thrum to the side of his head. Pain grew with each rap.

"All right!" he bellowed. "I am coming! Will you cease that infernal noise! My head is pounding!"

Shuffling quickly to entranceway, Patrick located the log used to block intruders from coming in unannounced. Normally God's house was open to all, but Patrick did not like to be disturbed whilst he slept. Many years of experience told him rest was essential in order to cope with the day ahead, along with a nice bowl of chopped fruit for breakfast.

Patrick felt force being exerted against the outside of the door, and despite the extra pressure, was still able to remove the crude barrier, nearly falling onto his backside as a small group of people rushed into the church, slamming the door behind them.

Stunned, Patrick watched as a pair of large chaps leant against the sturdy structure, loud groans and shallower thuds reined against the oak, whilst the intruders strained to prevent anyone else from entering.

"Dinna just stand there, Father," barked a smaller man at him, "get that wood back in place. We need the door blocked before they break through!"

"Before who force their way in?" Patrick asked, slowly recovering his senses.

"Never mind that just now. Bar that bloody door, they canna hold them off for much longer."

"Sorry," mumbled Patrick as he hoisted the log atop the supports before standing back to see it bend slightly, but not breaking.

Taking a few moments to adjust to the dim light at this end of the church, Patrick recognised the four males and female who unexpectedly burst into the room. The Douglas brothers, Malcolm and Donald, who were normally inseparable, had lost their boyish joviality. Patrick could see stress masking their faces. Even more concerning was grime splattered over them. Malcolm had what looked like blood caked on his arms and torso. Patrick noticed, gripped in a fist, a fireplace poker similarly covered in the crimson liquid and gore. Shocked, Patrick wondered what the young man endured to be in such a state? Why had his typical juvenile humour disappeared? Looking at the next pair, he recognised the Douglas' cousin Jamie who was not seen since he moved out a few years ago with his heavily pregnant wife. Patrick was surprised to see him in the village. Local gossip said that Jamie was in Lanark preparing to march south to join the clan's forces. Beside him was Malcolm's childhood friend, David Douglas, someone who Father Patrick knew had spent many a night in Forth, usually with a good drink in him. David was a part of the Douglas Clan army that normally fought with the united forces of Scotland. The legend of Big Davie was often told throughout the land and Patrick had heard many tales of his strength and character. Only a couple of weeks ago, he was privy to the stories of Big Davie being discussed over an ale in the Highlands. The locals exaggerating more each time the yarn was spun.

The last, but by no means least, was the only girl in the group. Patrick knew Morag Douglas as a shy but very clever young lassie. Although she was normally seen in public on the arm of Malcolm, Patrick had spent many an evening at their house in the village and often conversed about the word of God with Morag and her family. Patrick was surprised to see the normally immaculate girl in the same state as Malcolm. Whatever had happened, the usual banter and camaraderie had vanished and been replaced with a hardness and purpose that was usually etched on the faces of soldiers preparing to combat the enemy.

"Father, sorry to intrude, but we are being pursued by a foe, the likes of whom we have never experienced before," began Jamie, hurriedly. "We are going to barricade ourselves in the best that we can, but my fear is that this could be in vain. Is there another exit here? And what can we use to block the entrance?"

"Jamie, there is no need to apologise to me, son. There are the wooden pulpits that you can use. They are very heavy and it will take two very strong men to move them. There is a way out to the garden at the back, but it is enclosed by a wall, built to keep foxes and other wildlife from munching on my vegetables."

"Davie, Malky," Jamie called, "get those big benches piled up against the door now. Morag and Donald, can you look about the place for anything we can use to defend ourselves? Father, please can you show me your garden?"

Patrick watched as the group burst into action. Davie and Malcolm struggled with the cumbersome pew as they tried to drag it along the floor. The other pair busily searched about the main hall. Patrick signalled to Jamie and they walked together towards the rear of the building.

"Jamie, you are most welcome here at any time, but I am very worried about what is going on. What is it that you are running from? Are we being invaded?"

"I dinna ken how to explain it," replied Jamie whilst hurrying along beside him. "It all started a couple of hours ago in the tavern. Normal men have been turning into rabid monsters, killing and maiming other people who themselves then have turned into these things. I have also seen it happen to the horses in the stables. Each of these creatures has a gaping wound or some sort of major injury. It is like they have died and their soul has not taken the final journey up to Heaven, so they have returned to the lands to haunt the living."

"Heathens!" hissed Patrick with a worried look on his face. "This sounds like the Devil has found a way to touch the sinners and unbelievers which has resulted in these Heathens who walk the earth instead of taking their natural passage to Hell. I am afraid that this could be the start of the end of mankind. The good book prophesises the return of the Anti-Christ. I just hope that this is not the lead up to his coming. If it is, we could be doomed."

"It is an interesting theory, Father," Jamie replied as they approached the small stairway which went outside. "One that I think we should discuss at another time. Let us be on our guard for now as we dinna ken what awaits us."

Patrick took the lead as they made way through the small door and into the inky night beyond. It was quite a big garden, deceptively so, despite the wall surrounding it. Patrick spent many an evening cultivating the variety of vegetables which grew throughout the warmer months and fall. It meant he was able to feed other villagers who struggled crop-wise over the harsher weather. Fortunately, this was something that rarely happened as the locals normally helped each other out during the tough winters. There was a real community spirit around Forth that Patrick admired. Things were different tonight though he now noticed. Usual sounds of animals in the woodland beyond had gone; no wolves howling, or owls hooting before striking down their prey. An eerie silence abounded. An overwhelming uneasiness quickly engulfed Patrick as he led the younger lad around the garden.

"If you feel out to the left, you will get an idea of how high the wall is. I am sorry, Jamie, I should have thought and brought a candle for us to see better."

"Ach, it is done now." Jamie reached out to try and feel the stone barrier. "It is not that high, is it?"

"I am afraid not. I had a lot of problems, when I was out visiting parishioners, from the local wildlife taking a fancy to my crop. I felt that the erection of the wall was a better idea than killing all those animals."

A pained scream erupted, followed by what sounded like the shriek of a wounded animal thrashing about after being attacked by a wolf. The priest's skin exploded in gooseflesh from head to toe.

"It sounds like those things may be close by. I think it might be an idea to go back inside and work out what our next move is," Jamie stated with worry.

"We should not be disturbed; the wall will keep them out."

"I would prefer not to take any chances. I have faced too much danger tonight. I could do with a quieter night."

"From what you are saying, that seems unlikely to happen."

It did not take long for both men to hurry back inside the church. Jamie turned and slammed the bolt across before returning to the pastor.

"What are you doing? I never keep that locked. What if we need to get out in a hurry?" asked Father Patrick.

"I am more concerned at those things getting in here."

"You should have faith, young Mister Douglas. They are Heathens, God would not let creatures of the dark one into His building. We are quite safe here."

"I do have faith, Father," answered Jamie, indignantly. "I have seen too much death tonight to take unnecessary chances. Now let us see what the rest have done, I have a feeling that we may have a long night ahead of us."

CHAPTER NINE

TRAPPED

✪

Sweat poured from Malcolm's brow as he hauled large benches across the cold, stone floor. Big Davie grumbled in complaint as they struggled to pull them up the small steps before the entranceway. Three other pews were piled up as a barrier to the threat outside and they were already starting to strain from the pressure thrust upon them by the growing horde. Gut-wrenching sounds echoed through the high beamed ceiling of the hall. Malcolm froze mid lift as memories of the blood-thirsty horrors came flooding back. Torn flesh flapping from between yellow teeth stained with the blood of the ravaged tavern victim was burned into Malcolm's mind.

Malcolm almost fell as he felt an over-enthusiastic push from Big Davie in an attempt to get the cumbersome seat up the stairs. Cursing, he glared over at the grinning fool, muttering under his breath whilst trying to regain some balance. "You clumsy oaf! That nearly took my head off. Calm down, we still have another couple of these to shift."

"Aww, poor wee Malky. Do you want me to kiss it better? Can you not cope with some hard work?" Big Davie mocked.

"Och, will you not give it a rest. There are monsters outside and you want to kiss me in church, what would God say about that?"

"Fuck, I forgot that we were in a fucking church, I am going to Hell for blasphemy. What a fucking idiot!"

"You had better watch your tongue in front of the Father." Malcolm laughed. "He will condemn your soul and you will spend eternity shovelling shit for the Devil."

"Ach, I think all that killing and sex has already marked me as one of Satan's minions. A few swear words willna make much difference."

"Sssshhhh," hissed Malcolm in response, looking off in the distance. "He might hear you and you ken how sensitive he gets about that, especially in here. "

"Shit, my damn mouth keeps running away with all these curse words. I am just fucking out of control, what a cunt I am."

Malcolm roared with laughter at the oafishness of the larger man. The light relief broke the tension built over the last few hours. It was good to see his friend happy again, even if it was at the expense of his religion. The hilarity soon faded as the banging intensified and Malcolm could see a look of worry creep onto Big Davie's face.

"Malky, I am not sure how long this barrier will hold. We could have company sooner rather than later and we have no weapons to speak of."

"I have this poker." Malcolm pointed to the metallic spike resting against the side of the wall. "I hope Donald and Morag are able to find more."

"*Donald*!" Big Davie's thunderous voice vibrated through the hall, candle flames dancing to the beat of the gruffness of his tone. "Your big wimp of a brother needs a cuddle. Get your scrawny little ar…feet over here!"

Malcolm collapsed to the ground guffawing at the inadvertent slip. Big Davie stood over him looking miffed at being the butt of his humour.

"Malcolm Douglas, that was not funny. I am trying not to fucking… fuck, I did it again! Stop fucking laughing, it is not bloody funny. Fuck, I am going to the big bad fire. Shit, I hope the fucking priest is not listening. Fuck. That is enough Malky, you are such a dick. I am going to tickle you for that. Bastard."

Rolling, Malcolm tried to dodge the incoming attack as Big Davie landed on top of him, oversized fingers moving rapidly up and down Malcolm's sides and underarm pits. Unexpectedly, the merriment soon turned to pain as the attempt at a tickle failed badly as Big Davie, not knowing his own strength, rubbed vigorously at Malcolm, turning his side red with excess pressure.

"Ow, get off, you big eejit," yelped Malcolm, writhing to escape Big Davie's grasp. "That is fucking sore, you bastard."

"I guess that I am not the only one going to Hell for swearing in a church!" Big Davie giggled as he rolled off Malcolm. "Satan will be paying you a visit in the morning."

"Fuck off, you cunt," retorted Malcolm holding his tender side. "As usual, you take things too far. Total arsehole."

"Brother," Donald said as he came into view, "if Father Patrick catches you swearing in church, he will tan your hide."

Malcolm glared at Donald as his unfortunate arrival played to Big Davie's amusement, the clansmen squealed with laughter, flailing about the place uncontrollably.

"What is wrong with him?" asked Donald, watching as Big Davie started pounded the floor with a fist, whilst clutching his chest, struggling to breath as the giggles had taken over.

"Och, it is just Big Davie being Big Davie. Ignore him, he will eventually go away," replied Malcolm, smirking at the sight of his friend on his knees on the ground. Malcolm was wary that his brother wouldn't understand the mocking that went on between the pair as a look of seriousness and tired aggravation was wearing on Donald's face. "Are you alright?" Malcolm was worried that the night was going to be too much for Donald, he kept an eye on him recently due to the frequency of the daydream attacks he suffered from. With all that was going on, Malcolm feared that another incident could leave Donald exposed and vulnerable to one of those monsters.

"Aye, I am fine. It has just been a long night. I could do with my bed."

"Hang in there, brother," said Malcolm, wincing as Donald's fierce embrace enveloped him, almost knocking the wind out of his lungs. "It will all be alright; we will be back home soon."

"Can anyone join in?" Big Davie asked as he barrelled in, hugging both the brothers, almost squeezing the life out of them. "I can feel the brotherly love."

"Get off, you fool," chortled Malcolm. "You will squeeze us both to an early grave."

Malcolm watched as Donald stood shaking his head and chuckling at Big Davie's antics. Part of Donald's problem was that he got overstressed too easily, which is why Malcolm was particularly concerned tonight. Malcolm could feel the tension lift as a result of Big Davie's jovial nature. It was a relief to know that his brother could be distracted by the silliness and almost childish behaviour from the loveable rogue. With all that was going on, drifting off into another fantasy could become very dangerous for Donald. Malcolm hoped that the tension and distraction would help prevent it.

"Donald," Big Davie began quizzically, his relaxed mood now more serious and pensive, "did you manage to find any weapons during your search? I am worried that if they break through, we have nothing but Malky's wee stick to defend ourselves with."

"Oi! I have killed a few of those creatures with my poker whilst you stood there with your mouth open admiring my superior strength. Maybe if you watched what was happening, then you might do better, rather than trip over your own two feet."

"Will you give it a rest!" Big Davie laughed, turning around to look at his friend, knowing that he was trying to wind him up. "I am trying to get some useful information here; all you can do is mock me, and in a church of all places. What sort of person have you become, Malcolm Douglas? What would your ma say?"

"She would clip his earhole and paddle his arse for disrespecting the church," replied Morag, stepping into view. "Much as I suspect that your uncle would do to you, David Douglas."

"Miss, yes Miss," teased Big Davie looking sheepishly at Morag. "Sorry, Miss, I willna do it again."

"Liar," whispered Malcolm, mischievously, as Big Davie guffawed at the comment.

"Malcolm Douglas!" scolded Morag. "If you have something to say, then say it. It is rude to whisper. Come on, spit it out."

"Sorry, Miss," replied Malcolm hanging his head, trying not to burst into a fit of giggles. "I was merely suggesting that Big Davie may not be telling the whole truth, mainly due to the fact that he talks through his arse half the time."

"Malcolm!" Morag chortled. "That would explain the smell earlier in the tavern."

More laughter came from the group as Big Davie mock-punched Malcolm in fake indignation. Malcolm responded by over-dramatically falling to the floor clutching his arm as if stabbed.

Donald smirked. "Idiot. Do you think ma would let me disown you?"

"Right," said Big Davie, suddenly turning from the clown to the voice of authority. "Donald, I need to ken if you have found anything?"

Trying to regain his composure, Donald replied, "Well, we had a good forage about the place and apart from religious trinkets, all we could find were some gardening tools, an axe that has dulled over time, and the knife that Father uses to cut his meat. It is not much, but better than what we have."

"That is great, we might have a better chance against these creatures than we did before."

"Heathens," Father Patrick interrupted as he hurried towards them with Jamie not far behind. His red face was sheen with perspiration due to the heat and walk. "I have discussed this with young Jamie here. My theory is that people die, then not long after they come back to life. I believe that once they die, their souls go off to Heaven, they are rejected by God due to their lack of belief and as a punishment, they are left to wander the Earth as a lost soul, making them Heathens."

"That is an interesting theory, Father," replied Malcolm respectfully. "How do you suggest that we send them to Hell, where their souls obviously belong?"

"That is simple, young Malcolm," said Patrick, sounding patronizing without meaning to. "The only way to release the soul is to remove their heads. From what Jamie has been telling me, these things seem to have some thought. Well, they canna use it if we decapitate them."

"Are you sure about this, Father?" asked Jamie, not looking convinced at what Patrick had just told them. "It seems to be a bit extreme."

"Of course. I am the word of God, what I say comes from Him. Now enough of all this talk, you all must be hungry, come and get some stew.

Malcolm followed the others as they made way over to the oak table nestled by the fire, bellies rumbling after all the recent hard work and running. The smell of beef boiling in the metallic pot tantalized taste buds. A small trickle of saliva escaped his lower lip. It took a few minutes for Patrick to fill the bowls and the group were soon tucking into the food laid before them.

"Mmmmm," Donald mumbled, greedily shovelling the meat into his mouth, gravy dripping onto an already blood-stained top. Donald ripped a piece of bread from the loaf perched in the middle of the table, before dipping into the dish and wolfing it down. Malcolm smiled at his sibling's ferocity whilst greedily gulping his own portion, the tender piece melting as it touched his tongue. Meanwhile, the wailing and thumping continued. The group looked around nervously as they ate.

"I wish they would stop that noise," said Morag, worriedly as another forkful of stew was stuffed into her mouth. "I am scared that they will get in here."

"We are quite safe. The doors are made of solid oak and there is no way anyone is getting in here, not with the extra barrier that the lads created," Father Patrick replied.

"What about the back way? It is a good door, but if there is enough pressure pushing against it, it will surely buckle," Jamie said.

"I am not worried about that entrance. The wall will stop them coming in, we are quite safe here for the time being. Perhaps a good night's sleep may be the best thing for us all?"

"We really should try to get home tonight. Ma will be worried and I am sure that Morag's mother will be the same," Donald said.

"I think you may be safer here this evening." Patrick had a worried look on his face. "I dinna think that it is a good idea to be out wandering in the dark with the Heathens baying for our blood. Anyway, we have loads of space and I can get my lute out and we could have a good sing song to try and lift our spirits."

"Perhaps you are right. Although I think that singing may be going a bit too far," Donald said reluctantly.

"Nonsense! There is nothing like a good tune to boost spirits. If you chaps finish up your supper, I will fetch the lute from my room."

Once the plates were cleared away, the warmth and lure of the crackling logs on the fire was too much for the group. Settling down beside the flames dancing away like villagers at Harvest Festival, the atmosphere was more relaxed, although the unease of the situation had them all on tenterhooks.

"Do you think he will actually play the lute?" asked Donald, his brow furrowed as he hastily looking round the room, unable to stop his left leg jiggling up and down. "Those things are out there; they could burst in at any time and he is going to strum away as if nothing has happened. Do you not think that this is a little strange?"

"Look, the Father is good enough to give us some shelter and a meal, the least we can do is listen to him whilst he tries to entertain us. If they manage to break through, we will be ready for them, for now let us relax and have a little bit of fun whilst we can," Jamie said.

"It still feels wrong." Donald was still not convinced by his cousin's argument.

"Donald," Malcolm interjected, "would you rather be outside being chased by those things or sat here by the fire? I would rather have shelter for the night than risk certain death by stumbling about in the dark being harried by those monsters."

"That is what I like to see." Big Davie laughed. "Brotherly love. Are we going for a group hug again?"

"Get away, you buffoon!" exclaimed Donald, chuckling away. "I just think that it is not right what we are about to do, that is all."

"Objection noted," replied Jamie, all serious. "Now, keep it to yourself and try not to offend our host."

"Och, Jamie, I would not say a word to him, I am just a little unsettled by it all."

An uncomfortable silence ensued for the next few minutes, each lost in their own thoughts, disturbed only by the banging, scraping, and wailing from outside. The vibration caused by the ruckus pulsed through the church, causing the candle flames to dance in time with the beat. The air had cooled a little, which did not help ease the rising tension.

Malcolm felt Morag snuggle into him. Her warmth and gentle touch brought a comforting smile to his face. Softly, he eased an arm around her shoulder, pulling her in carefully to feel the love in his embrace.

"That is nice," murmured Morag contently as she rubbed her hair along the front of his wide chest, purring with each casual motion.

Malcolm responded by rested his head atop of hers, breathing in the scent of her auburn locks brushing against his nose. Malcolm watched contently at the others who were lying stretched out, enjoying the warmth of the fire.

Exhaustion from the night's exertions hit the group hard. Donald leaned against one of the large pillars that supported the building, his long legs crossed. The tiredness had finally caught up with him. Donald's eyes struggled to stay open, the sound of a gentle snore escaped his lips as he dozed off to a light slumber. Jamie and Big Davie were sat, a little bit further away, looking through the array of weapons that Donald and Morag had retrieved earlier.

A contented sigh escaped Malcolm's mouth, enjoying the calm whilst it lasted. Malcolm was a bit concerned that Patrick was gone for some time. *Surely it did not take that long to find a lute*? Just as Malcolm decided to disturb Morag and get up and see where the priest had disappeared to, Patrick came striding into the room carrying a long, rounded wooden instrument with numerous strings stretched out along the length of it.

Walking towards a stool that was sat at the side of the fireplace, Patrick perched onto the seat and began to strum it and started singing. It was a tune that they all knew. Invigorated by the soothing music, the group started to join in. Soon, the worries of the night started to dissipate and everyone was in a jovial mood, all apart from Donald who had woken up by now and fidgeted nervously, continually looking around.

Malcolm felt Morag starting to sway, brushing gently along his torso as the music seeped through her body. Malcolm moaned as her legs rubbed up and down the inside of his thigh. Malcolm's slumbering member reacted instantly, hardening as her movements became rhythmic. The sensual pleasure and excitement building evermore as her hand gently caressing his inner thigh. Malcolm knew that this was wrong, to be aroused in a church must surely be a sin, but there was not one care showing. The enjoyment was almost complete, the mood, lighting, and music added to the moment. Lustful thoughts of Morag naked invaded his mind.

Out of the corner of an eye, Malcolm noticed Donald rise suddenly to his feet and sidle steadily to the right, his neck craned, stretching as if trying to look at something. Of what, Malcolm was not sure. Whispering apologies and cursing as his brief lapse of sensual pleasure was halted, Malcolm gently moved Morag off and wandered over to where Donald had positioned himself.

"Are you alright, Donald?" asked Malcolm, concerned that Donald could enter into one of his dream states again. "You seem preoccupied. What is wrong?"

"Look," replied Donald, pointing off into the distance, to the far end of the hall close to the exit, "Do you see that, over there?"

Malcolm followed where the finger was extended, the weak candlelight making objects difficult to see. There may have been a shadow moving about, but Malcolm was sure that his eyes were deceiving him. "I dinna see a thing. Are you sure it is not your imagination?" Malcolm noticed the worry in Donald's face turn to frustration, almost anger at the lack of faith his brother had shown. Before he could think of how to calm the situation, Donald interjected.

"Really? You dinna believe what I am telling you? I can see the shadow of someone over there. I think one of those things has gotten in here. You have two choices, you trust in what I have said and we go investigate, or you ignore me and sit down. If I am right, then it is on your conscience if I get injured or killed. Do you want explain to ma how you got me hurt, Malcolm?"

"I never doubted what you told me, Donald," snapped Malcolm. "I never saw anything with my eyes, it does not mean that that you are wrong. We will go and take a look to make sure."

The pair crept carefully towards the darkened area near the back entrance to the church, trying to keep as quiet as possible so as not to disturb whatever may be there, or their friends who were still sat enjoying the tuneful music. As they walked, all the time the groans outside getting louder, a cool breeze could be felt the closer that they got to the exit.

"They are in the building," whispered Donald, starting to panic. "The bloody door is open. We are all going to die!"

"Will you be quiet," hissed Malcolm. "Stop panicking, the wind is probably coming from the gap at the bottom. You are overreacting."

"You are probably right, but what if it is those creatures? What do we do?"

"We will take a look and if something is wrong, we will go running back to the others and get out of here as quickly as possible. Head to our house, I think."

"What if the others dinna want to come? What if we get separated?"

"Will you pull it together? Nothing is in here, we willna have to run, and the rest are perfectly safe. Now get a grip."

Creak!

Malcolm groaned inwardly, it sounded as if the hinges of the old door were opening. Sensing the danger, Malcolm knew that the hellions had found their way in, and a sinking feeling told him that they may be trapped.

CHAPTER TEN

THE ROAD TO CARNWATH

"For fuck sake, Sandy, hurry up."

Frustration can often lead to mistakes which is a lesson Hamish never learned in all eighteen years of his life, one laden with luxury and filled with servants seeing to his every whim. People were too scared to impose any discipline or order due to fear of his father. Hamish played on insecurities and often manipulated them to suit his own purpose, which is what he was trying to do with Sandy and Tam.

Although they were still in the Douglas cottage, Hamish was keen to leave as soon as possible, wary that Malcolm and Donald could be back at any time. If the brothers found him still in the house after what they did, Hamish did not fancy his chances against them, especially in an enraged state. Hamish needed proper provisions and a blanket before departing, which meant that Sandy and Tam were tasked to search the cottage.

Revenge on the Douglas brothers was at the forefront of his mind, but no action could be taken without more men. Having Sandy and Tam was great, both were seasoned warriors who had fought many a foe in battle. Despite the numerous scratches, bruises, and injuries, they were undefeated. Hamish admired their prowess and loyalty, but also knew if strict discipline was not maintained, then no respect would be given by the pair. This was needed in order to convince Uncle James, who lived in Carnwath, to provide him with some more men to continue the campaign. Hamish could go home, back to Peebles to get the soldiers that were required to properly raid this and other Douglas owned villages. However, the thought of returning with just Sandy and Tam was not an option as his da would never forgive him for failure and the likelihood of future command would be laughed out of the room. There was every possibility of a serious beating being handed out if the humiliation was ever discovered back home. No, there was a job to do and no matter how limited his resources were, Hamish needed to find a way to achieve it.

"Sorry, sir," Sandy hastily replied, "I am just packing up the food so that we can carry it easily. I willna be much longer."

"Have you seen Tam at all? I have not heard from him in a while and we need to be leaving now."

"He was scouring the outbuilding, looking for weapons and a new pair of boots, he said that his pair had split during the cross-country walk earlier."

"Thanks, I will meet you outside the kitchen door when you are done. I am just going to get him, he is probably asleep somewhere, you ken how tired he gets when it is dark."

Moving swiftly through the cottage and into the fresh night air, a slight breeze caught Hamish upon entering the courtyard. Moonlight highlighted the rough, natural path made by constant treading of leather boots over the years. Careful not to trip on any rock or branch errantly laying on the ground, Hamish made his way to the barn where he expected to find Tam. Taking in deep breaths, savouring the fresh country air, Hamish paused to enjoy the beautiful, inky sky. Its blackness highlighted by the full, silver moon, engulfed by glistening stars blinking like a cascade of fireflies playing in the valleys. Mesmerised by the shimmering show, Hamish stood watching, at peace, taking some time to snap out of his reverie.

"For fuck sake, Hamish, get a grip. We dinna have time for this shit," Hamish scolded himself.

Taking his own words to heart, Hamish quickened the pace to reduce the time to reach the oversized shed, at time stumbling on unseen obstacles along the way.

"Tam!" he yelled as he reached the entrance. "Are you in there?"

"Hamish!" replied a muffled voice from inside. "What are you doing out here? I thought you were still in the cottage?"

"I was, but I came out looking for you. You are taking ages, what is keeping you?"

"Sorry, sir. I am just coming out, give me a couple of minutes."

"Hurry up, you idiot. I want to be out of here soon. What are you doing? Pleasuring yourself?"

A stony silence greeted Hamish for a little bit before a strangled reply came, "No, I was not. I just found some weapons and was, erm, examining them."

Hamish laughed, that was one of the most pathetic excuses ever heard. He suspected what happened in the bedroom turned Tam on and the soldier was relieving the frustration. Still, it sounded like he was finished and they needed to be leaving soon.

"Right," Hamish replied with sarcasm, "when you are done, can you bring your weapon and whatever you find in there with you. I will meet you outside the kitchen door."

"I will be there soon, I willna be long" said a sheepish Tam.

Hamish returned to the kitchen and was pleased to see Sandy standing there with a medium sized brown sack lying on the grass.

"That didna take long. What have you got in there?"

"I managed to raid the cupboards," Sandy exclaimed with a look of pride on his face. "I have some bread, ham, eggs, chicken, and some wine that I found hidden in the pantry. I think old Ma Douglas liked a wee tipple when her lads went to bed. They are all wrapped up in a few blankets that I found lying in there. Did you find Tam?"

"Aye, I found him. The dirty wee bastard was playing with himself whilst we are doing all the hard work. He said that he found some weapons, but I am dubious about that."

"Ssshhh," hissed Sandy, trying his best to hold back a laugh. "Here he comes now."

Hamish turned to see the other bodyguard limping towards them, a couple of rusty old swords and a hunter's axe clutched in his grasp, struggling to manoeuvre along the rough path. Toiling with the load, Tam stubbed his toe a couple of times, comically jumping up and down whilst trying to keep the weapons from dropping to the mud below. Tam's lack of co-ordination was legendary in the Balliol army and he was often ridiculed for falling over or stumbling. Most folk had blamed the drink but Hamish knew that it a result of the number of blows to the head Tam had received from many battles. His da often tried to talk him into retirement, but Tam was insistent on fighting on for the good of the clan and promised to never let the Balliols down. Rather than use his problems as an excuse, it made Tam more determined to slay enemies and be the most elite fighter in their army. Despite this persistence, Hamish worried that one more hit would cause permanent damage. This is why the soldier was put on Hamish's personal guard duty with Sandy, rather than be a part of the main force.

"Why are you standing there gaping?" demanded Hamish, looking at Sandy in frustration. "Go and help before he skewers himself. The way he is going, he willna have a cock left to play with."

Sandy helped Tam, then the group spent little time in getting the supplies organised before starting off down the road, out of the village, and on their way to Carnwath.

A sense of relief washed over Hamish at finally being out of that house and away from a potential attack from the Douglas brothers. Hamish felt safer on the move than stuck in one place, although knowing they would need to rest at some point, he wanted to get as much distance between them and Forth as possible. Shelter was essential and a long sleep needed before they collapsed from exhaustion.

Deep into the night the trio travelled. Strange noises joined the usual night sounds, enveloping the soldiers with unease. Wolf howls became more urgent, followed by growling, snarling, and eventually a strangled gurgle, before it all quietened. Hamish noted a lack of owl hooting, which was worrisome, as usually the cacophony of the predator bird hunting prey was prevalent. Oddly, the constant bleating of sheep from the surrounding fields was an unusual event. Typically, the flock slept at night. Hamish wondered what was disturbing them, but was not feeling adventurous enough to investigate. At this time of year, one would expect to find swarms of midges, nipping away at skin, bringing out large bites that would itch for hours afterwards. The continual scratching often left Hamish's arms and legs red raw and there was nothing which could abate it apart from sitting in a cool bath; even that did not fully help. As he walked, none of the incessant insects disturbed him, in fact, there were no bugs of any kind flying in the air. Pausing to ponder this, Hamish wondered what had driven them away. Whatever it was, it could not be any worse than Scotland's most evil creature.

"So, Hamish," Sandy interrupted about half way along the track, "what is the plan?"

Well, that brought an awkward quandary. It was certainly tempting for Hamish to reveal the cunning schemes that had just been formulated but letting the soldiers in was risky. *What if they think I am mad?* There was too much at stake to trust to that pair. Although it was tempting to get it all out in the open.

"Erm," replied Hamish, still trying to decide how much of the truth to tell, "I want to make as much time as we can tonight before finding shelter, then in the morning we head to Carnwath to visit my Uncle James. I plan to meet with him and then work out our next steps from there."

"Do you think we will find somewhere to sleep?" asked Tam after a big yawn. "I dinna ken about you, but all this walking is tiring me out."

"Aye, if memory serves me correctly, there are a few old huts that the shepherds sleep in when they are out at night tending their flocks. It is not ideal but it will be better than nothing."

Reaching the road junction, the chatter faded as they came close to where most of the group was lost earlier that evening. Feeling wary to be back on the same route, Hamish knew it was necessary if they were to survive the night. With extra caution, the soldiers journeyed onward towards Carnwath, only stopping briefly to examine the remains of the kit hastily dropped in battle.

"Such a waste, all that life gone, we lost almost all the men tonight," declared Tam, slowly shaking his head.

Looking forlornly at the dried pools of blood splattered around, Hamish replied, "Aye, and if I had not been alert, you pair would have also been in trouble."

"Sorry, sir," Tam said, feeling slightly embarrassed. "We are grateful for you intervening, but I ken we would have survived. Those things may have taken out the rest of the men but we would have won."

Hamish stared at the man with awe and slight derision, amazed that the seasoned warrior believed himself capable of killing all those men. Hamish saw what happened, knowing how quickly the soldiers had turned into monsters. It was frightening, and though the fight in

Tam was admirable, Hamish knew the trio would have been slaughtered in mere minutes had they not fled.

Suddenly, the air exploded. A snarling beast emerged from the shadows, teeth bared, hackles raised, with claws fully extended, it aimed for Tam's throat. Chunks of decaying flesh flapped between the toes of what looked to be a wolf. Gore streaked all over its matted fur.

Shock prevented Hamish from reacting, but luckily for Tam, his clumsiness helped, and in trying to run away, he tripped over a branch and flew onto the ground, avoiding the claws of the incoming lupine.

Drawing his sword, Hamish moved in front of his grounded friend, wary as the animal turned to face them. Crimson eyes glowed in the night sky, sharp canines bared as it started to pace, sizing him up, ready to begin the next attack. Hamish knew they would have a better chance if all three were on their feet. Despite having the weapon, there was no guarantee it was sharp enough to pierce the tough hide of the beast. The creature's head rolled slightly to the side it dragged a hind leg as it looked for an opening to strike. Hamish kept eye contact with it, hoping to buy Tam enough time to rise and defend himself. Sandy was beside Tam, trying to help the man up.

Hearing movement, Hamish softly spoke whilst keeping his concentration on the predator. "Are you on your feet yet?"

"Not yet, sir," replied Sandy. "Tam looks a bit groggy, but once his head clears, he will be fine."

"For fucks fake, can you pair of cretins not do anything right? This bloody wolf is looking hungry and I think it wants a big lump of a Balliol for breakfast. I am not sure how long I can hold it off for."

"Sorry, sir," Sandy mumbled, panting and grunting. "I will be as quick as I can."

"You idiots are lucky that I am here or Tam would be dead."

Hamish's attention once again focused on his foe as it pawed the ground, snarling a challenge to fight. Suspecting that this was the prelude to initiating combat, Hamish started swinging an arm, moving slowly forward, trying to reduce the distance between them in the hope that he would not get knocked over when it finally chose to make its move.

"Come on then, you bastard!" Hamish sneered as he tossed the sword hilt from hand to hand "Do your worst, I am ready for you!"

Feeling as if the animal read his mind, Hamish cringed as it leapt high, aiming for the throat. Jaws open, the beast was ready to lock onto Hamish's Adam's apple, but the man was ready and dodged, stepping deftly to the side while driving the sword up. Slashing into the stomach of the monstrosity. Unfortunately, the blunt blade left only a lengthy scratch, barely seeping blood instead of gutting the underbelly.

Frustration caused him to sharply turn around, almost losing balance due to the speed of the motion. Pounding the weapon against the stony surface below, a metallic ringing vibrated as a look of defiance showed the wolf he meant business. Hamish Balliol, a man who would not be defeated by an inferior beast.

"Is that the best that you can do?" taunted Hamish. "You are weak, a pathetic creature who lives in the woods because it is scared of men. You dinna frighten me, I am superior, I am better than you, I will be the one who ends you. Fear me, wolf, for I am a Balliol! I was born to fight, I was made to destroy, I will be the last thing that you see before you descend to the lower depths of Hell. I will win, it has been decided!"

With that, Hamish moved with lightning speed towards the wolf. At the last moment, jumping in the air just as the creature also began to leap, he drove the weapon down, between the ribs, lacerating internal organs. Landing steadily as the monstrosity fell, Hamish looked at the still body, blood flowing out onto the ground around it. "Run! Move, before the rest of the pack show up. We dinna have long," Hamish exclaimed.

"What about the sack of food?" asked Sandy, finally getting to his feet and helping Tam up.

"Leave it! I would rather starve than become wolf food, now move!"

The trio scrambled once again back on the road, initially running, but the darkness and their ever-tiring bodies slowed the pace to a light jog. After about three miles they eased into a steady walk as exhaustion and thirst made legs feel heavy and complaints started to rain in from Tam and Sandy.

"Will you two quit your whining?" Hamish snapped after a few minutes of hearing their gripes. "I am tired too."

"But, Hamish, we really need to stop, just for a wee breather, I just need to get some air, the heat is killing us," complained Tam.

"Look, since you two are acting like babies, I will stop once we get around the bend ahead, I dinna want to be caught by surprise again."

Although it was difficult to see, a corner did indeed appear in front of them, almost hidden by overgrown blackberry bushes heavy with ripe, juicy fruit.

"Thank you, sir. My feet are bloody killing me. We need to find a burn to soak them in," Sandy said.

"Do we now? Do we also need to find a barrel of wine to drink, a nice rump of beef to eat, and a luxury cushioned coach to travel in? Who do you think you are? The Pope?" Hamish asked incredulously.

"Well you keep saying that you are the most important person in Scotland," answered Sandy defiantly. "We should be travelling in style instead of walking through mud, blood, and shit. I am fucking sick of it. I am tired, hungry, and need a good fuck. Does it look like I am going to satisfy any of my needs? No, not one. Is it any wonder that I am pissed off?"

"Erm," said Hamish, trying to contain the laughter which was close to exploding inside, "you could eat the fucking berries on the bush over there."

"What berries?" inquired Sandy, failing to notice the tasty treat hanging off the foliage at the side of the road. "Are you taking the piss?"

Chuckling, Hamish reached over to the hedge and pulled the biggest, sweetest fruit that he could find and waved it in front of Sandy's nose, smacking his lips to tease his fellow clansman. Sandy tried to snatch it out of Hamish's hand but each time he got close, Hamish pulled it away, dancing, before finally dropping it into his mouth and devouring the food.

"Fuck me!" exclaimed Hamish, reaching out to try and grab more. "That is the most divine fruit that I have had to eat in a while, you should try some, Sandy, that is if you can find any."

"Bastard," Sandy muttered, reaching over to pick off as many of the berries as possible before greedily stuffing them into his cheeks like a starved beaver.

"Calm down, Sandy," said Hamish, bemused at Sandy's vigour. Purple juice stained his cheek as each handful found their way past eager lips. "Leave some for us."

Sandy looked sheepish, face turning the colour of a raspberry ready to be picked as he tried to sneak the remainder of the gains behind his back to stop Hamish from seeing how much there were.

"There is no point in trying to hide it," chortled Hamish, "I can see how much you have. Dinna blame me if you are sick after gorging on all that shit. You are worse than a child."

Suddenly, a cry came from behind as Tam uttered a warning, a surprised exclamation, like one normally heard when someone, or *something,* had jumped out in front of you.

"You pair are nervy tonight." Hamish was frustrated that yet again their rest time was interrupted by the ravings of a so-called seasoned veteran. "This had better be good."

"I would draw your weapon," replied Tam warily. "That wolf that you killed is back and is not looking happy."

Hamish turned as the large, grey creature limped towards them. Wounds still seeped blood, hind legs dragging, its foreboding eyes staring through him, like the devil was possessing it

"That is no wolf!"

CHAPTER ELEVEN

ESCAPE

The door banging repeatedly against the frame sent a panic through Malcolm as the cool breeze whistled quietly around. Shadowy figures lurked just yards away. The rancid smell of rotten flesh wafted up the sinuses making them gag in the putrid air. Candles peppering the walls near the entranceway flickered for a moment before extinguishing, plunging the place into darkness. The only light left came from the fire behind, illuminating the brother's shapes, making them stand out as obvious targets to the intruders.

"Donald," Malcolm whispered, "we need to warn the others. We have to move now."

Nodding, Donald turned and walked as quickly as his legs could carry him with Malcolm hot on the trail, the grunting noises fading the further they moved away from the shadows. Tuneful sounds of the lute playing priest and the joyful voices of his friends eventually drowned out the incoming foes. Malcolm hurriedly approached the group, sat in the main hall, annoyed he had to interrupt their joviality, sad to have to shift them so quickly.

"Intruders!" shouted Donald as he approached the others. "Grab your weapons, those monsters have breached through at the rear of the building."

The music stopped abruptly as Father Patrick stood in shock, staring at the young clansman. The shock paralyzing, it took a few seconds to regain his senses. Looking incredulously at Donald, he finally spoke, "That is not possible, the door is very secure and there is no way that those Heathens could have gotten over the wall."

"Come on, Father, I was out there with you, there was no guarantee that the border was going to hold them and the doorway was not fully secure. It would not have taken much to break that lock," Jamie argued.

"Right, lads, grab what you can and head for the woods, we need to get out of here," Big Davie called out in haste.

"I am with Big Davie, there is little light here and I, for one, dinna want to be trapped in here with those creatures trying to kill us. I say we head for the woods and then to our place, there should be less trouble out where we live," Malcolm said, following not far behind Donald.

"Don't just stand there, let us pair up and fight our way out. Father, you are with me. Big Davie, can you team up with Donald? And Morag, I am sorry, lass, I am afraid that I will have to leave you with Malky. Arm up lads, we dinna have much time," Jamie commanded.

The partnerships seemed fair to Malcolm, there was no-one that he would rather have fighting at his brother's side than Big Davie. Davie had seen numerous battles against both the Balliols and the English and his legend grew with each story. Rumours stated that he stood over seven feet tall, some had the giant killing a thousand Englishmen on his own. Unbelievably, there were even tales of him entering the pits of Hell and defeating Satan himself. Malcolm laughed and loved each story heard about his childhood friend, but he knew the truth which was far from the lies told. Big Davie was a big, kind-hearted fool who only fought when he needed to, standing toe to toe with the enemy and battling with more bravery and intelligence than anyone he knew. Big Davie would kill for his country and clan, but was as peaceful as a dove when with friends, unless someone or something threatened them, as what was happening tonight. Malcolm saw the determined look on his face. The man was focused on surviving, escaping, and keeping Donald alive. For this, Malcolm was grateful and able to concentrate on protecting Morag.

Spinning on his heels, Malcolm watched as the poker was swiftly grabbed and rolled about Morag's hands before a wry smile confirmed the decision to use it as a weapon.

"Good choice," muttered Malcolm, placing a calming hand on her shoulder before snatching up the large kitchen knife for himself. Carefully caressing his thick fingers along the dull metallic blade feeling the sharpness, Malcolm allowed it to nick the fingertip slightly, drawing a droplet of blood which fell lightly to the floor.

"Malcolm, be careful, I'm not wanting you to get injured before we even try to get out of here. Let me have a look at that," said a concerned Morag.

"It is fine." Malcolm put the tip to his mouth and gently sucking the crimson liquid in. "It is but a scratch. You just concentrate on staying close to me. Do exactly what I say. When I say run, grab a hold of my hand and go as fast as you can. It is time to move. I willna let anything happen to you."

"And I willna let any harm come to you, Malcolm Douglas," Morag mumbled.

"Sorry, what was that?"

"Nothing, it was just wind."

"I understand. The others are moving, we need to go now, my sweet. Dinna stray from my side."

With the oversized blade in his right hand and Morag to the left, Malcolm steadily made his way towards the rear exit, eyes struggling to adjust to the fading light. The cacophony of thumping wood vibrated throughout the passageway and snarls crowded the route. Shadows haunted his vision and it soon got to the point that Malcolm was unsure whether they were real or not. Several times Malcolm lashed out with the weapon only to find fresh air as dancing figures continued to fool his senses. Frustrated, a growl escaped his lips. Exasperation overflowed at having to flee and confront this terror. A gentle, calming squeeze from Morag was enough for him to retain concentration. Turning quickly, he flashed her a smile of gratitude. This momentary distraction meant that Malcolm almost missed the arm flailing towards his head. Blocking, he pushed it to the side and stabbed towards the torso of the rabid man. The blade's edge penetrated the tattered, grubby white shirt, piercing skin, causing an eruption of blood from the wounded belly.

Aghast, Malcolm was shocked to see that this did not affect the monster. The gash haemorrhaged, yet the creature continued on, its other fist slamming towards his head. Ducking, Malcolm grabbed the creature and yanked it by the hair towards him, thrusting the weapon through the eye socket and into the brain. Removing the knife, a gelatinous goo seeped out as the monstrosity slumped to the ground, lying as still as a graveyard during a calm night.

"Did you see that, Malcolm?" Morag asked, shaking with fear, slipping her quivering hand back into his. "It only died when you stabbed it in the head. It is just like before; I dinna think you can kill it any other way."

"Hush, lass, you will bring more of these things upon us. Now stay close, there is more out there," Malcolm hissed, trying not to face her, attempting to keep focus on what lay ahead.

Although the room was almost totally inky black. Malcolm could feel the slight waft of a cool breeze ahead so he continued in that direction, hoping that the way out was not far away. The bizarre bellowing groans intensified and on more than one occasion, Malcolm though he heard the clash of battle, although could not be sure. Morag squeezed his hand even tighter now. Jangling nerves shuddering through her. Fear intensified but only served to harden his resolve as Malcolm vowed to get her out of this mess.

A scream busted through Malcolm's train of thought as Morag wrenched her hand from his. Panic set in and Malcolm spun around. Not knowing what to expect, he narrowly avoided a wide-open maw trying to sink itself into his shoulder. Swiftly bringing the knife aloft, he was about to stab the vile beast when a fireplace poker flashed by and into the head of the Heathen.

Yet again, Morag was forced to kill to save his life. Weapon hanging limp on her side, she stood in shock. Tears streamed down her soft cheeks, skin reddening with each salty drop. The metallic pole clanged gently to the ground as Morag lost her grip. Seeing the pain and anguish that was haunting her soul, Malcolm stepped in and wrapped his arms around Morag. Pulling her in, hugging tightly for a few seconds, wishing that the embrace could last forever and keep her protected and away from the terrors of this awful night. Sniffing, he held back his own flood of grief and felt Morag sob into his green linen shirt, steadily becoming more sodden as the crying intensified.

"Dinna let me go. I canna do this anymore," Morag pleaded as she continued to bury her head into the comfort of his firm shoulder.

"I have to, love," Malcolm replied as he parted the embrace, regretting doing so almost immediately. "There are a lot more of them out there. We need to get out of here. I promise that I will hug you again, my sweet lass, but we must not stay still. We must go."

Her eyes once more met his, the deep emerald orbs boring deep into his aching heart, her passion emblazoned within that look, a gaze that he struggled to break away from.

"I understand. Lead us, Malcolm Douglas, take us out of here and deliver me safely to your abode," Morag whispered softly.

Determination flooded her features. A new fortitude overtook her, making Malcolm smile. Pride washed over him. Even with all that she had endured, Morag still had fight within, a will to go on and battle, in spite of the dangers they were sure to encounter. Malcolm admired that, loved the fact that she could pull herself together and be so strong when it was all going downhill around them.

Facing forward, with the knife in one hand and Morag in the other, Malcolm strode ahead purposely towards the exit. His resolve was forged with iron, enhancing the need to get out of this hellhole and keep Morag from witnessing any more horrific killing. The shadows had lessened but the relentless hammering on the front door continued. Malcolm was unsure if it was from the very faint breeze or more trouble awaiting them. They were not hanging around to find out.

"Morag, I am going to move at speed to where I think the exit is. Dinna let go of me for any reason. If you are in danger of any kind, scream."

Shortly, they had reached the door without any further incident; surprising considering all the chaos going on. With relief, he sighed as the touch of the metallic handle was the start of the escape from the horror inside.

Feeling the squeeze on his hand, Malcolm yanked open the wooden barrier, weapon ready for anything ahead. His panicked mind projecting a snarling, grey-faced man with crimson eyes and blood-soaked clothes was going to attack on sight, tear a chunk out of his neck, and leave him for dead whilst he feasted on Morag. It was easy for the imagination to run wild when scared. Malcolm's fingers were now trembling, barely able to hold onto the weapon, trying not to shake too much and let Morag know of his fear.

The cool wind hit his face like a wet kipper slapping against the cheek of an unsuspecting fisherman. The fresh air was a welcome change from the staleness inside the church, the smell of rotting carcass mixed with burning wax had made his eyes water. It was good to get back outside. Malcolm was surprised that no Heathens were in the immediate vicinity. The unmistakable pained gargling nearby indicated that more lurked in the area. A clammy sense of death permeated. They would have to hasten or be prepared to fight for their lives.

"I think we can make it to the woods if we run," said Malcolm, turning slightly to Morag, trying to adjust to the faded light behind her.

"That may not be an option." In a panic, Morag lifted the iron poker, pulled back, then thrust the rusting rod towards the darkness beyond. The motion repeated as Malcolm could see blood adorn the weapon, each time she drew it back. "I am occupied at the moment, give me a second and then we will make a break for it."

Worried that Morag may be in trouble, but also concerned about what lurked in the shadows around, Malcolm decided to pay more attention to what was going on at the rear, knowing that Morag could get overwhelmed at any second. Suspecting their chances of escape could be slim, he hoped this decision did not doom them both. Malcolm knew that there could be no guilt in saving his beloved, he must act quickly or become one of the Heathens.

Eyes finally adjusting to the darkness outside, Malcolm readied the knife and positioned himself beside Morag, ready for the next move. More monsters closed in, meaning they needed to shift rapidly to survive. Quickly, he pulled her back, ready to face the oncoming hungered beasts.

"What did you do that for?" whispered Morag, sounding annoyed at him taking her place.

"I am not losing you tonight," he replied determinedly, dodging an incoming fist swinging towards his neck. "You dinna get rid of me that easily. Now keep watch behind me, we may have to make a break for it. I am not sure how long I can hold them off for."

"You can do it, Malcolm. Nothing can stop you," Morag said, trying to sound encouraging but failing due to the fear in her voice.

"Thanks, lass." Malcolm caught the wrist of the latest attacker before pulling it towards him and thrusting the blade through the temple, the momentum carrying through to the brain, causing the Heathen to fall lifeless to the ground.

A scream from behind almost had him spinning around, scared that Morag could be in severe danger before Malcolm heard her voice, soft yet firm, speak in a low tone.

"Big Davie, you gave me a fright, you big oaf!"

Malcolm could feel unmistakable laughter of his friend pulse through. Relief washed over with the knowledge that Morag was safer, she had even more protection, albeit by the largest fool in Scotland. Malcolm was confident that they were in a better position now with the help of the jovial jock. Pushing out with his huge leather boot, crafted by a cobbler in Carnwath, which da had specially made for his name day, Malcolm wondered what happened to da as his foot connected with another beast that had taken the place of its fallen comrade. The force of the blow sent it sailing a few feet in the air, a dull thud resounded as it landed out of sight. Malcolm hoped that father was safe in England, praying that none of the Heathens were present in Cumbria where they were raiding.

"Davie, you large lummox," called Malcolm with a sense of relief, "am I glad that you are here. Is Donald safe?"

"I am fine. Big Davie has been powering through those things, I swear that they were starting to run away from him. You seemed to be struggling though, I think we need to head for the woods. If you get an opening, shout run and we will go with you," replied the familiar voice of his younger sibling.

"Have you seen any sign of Jamie and Father Patrick?" asked Malcolm as a set of gnashing teeth narrowly missed his arm. Sidestepping, he brought an elbow down on top of the cranium, sending it to the unforgiving surface below. A follow up stomp on its head with the sole of his boot dispatched the attacker swiftly.

"Nope, the last I heard was the priest launching himself at the enemy shouting 'Heathens' with Jamie not far behind, trying to keep them off of his back."

"Hopefully, they dinna get themselves killed. That priest is certainly a strange one," Malcolm declared in annoyance.

Another grey thing, clothes soaked in blood seeping from numerous wounds covering its body, launched towards Malcolm. The knife flashed as he jumped in the air to avoid the incoming assailant, twisting in mid-flight before thrusting down on the base of the neck during the descent, the ferocity separating long flowing blond hair from its shoulders.

With nothing else nearby, Malcolm took the opportunity and went for the clear path ahead.

"*Run!*" he shouted, turning and sprinting towards the trees in the distance. "Aim for the forest and yell if you are in trouble. We can do this, together we willna fall!"

Spinning, Malcolm could see the others pacing about as his eyes slowly focussed back to the moonlit garden. The outline of the woodland became clear and he was now running flat out, blade still gripped tightly in his palm, ready for anything that came out of the dark.

Before long, the short yardage to the wall was crossed and they were over the barrier and into the trees beyond, stretching their legs, heading in the direction of the Douglas brother's cottage. The horrific groaning and growling sounds faded from the carnage left in their wake.

CHAPTER TWELVE

DELAYS

🜨

It was an arduous trek through the woods. Normal forest sounds of owls hooting in the trees and scampering rabbits were replaced by bloodthirsty shrieks of the rabid Heathens. The initial sprint slowed down to a light jog with the group wanting to get as far away as possible whilst keeping something in reserve for any unexpected surprise. They had avoided many hazards along the path, but an outstretched, thick tree root had gone unnoticed, sending Malcolm sprawling ahead of Donald as he fell headfirst onto the leafy surface below.

Morag rushed over upon hearing the commotion, concerned that Malcolm had hurt himself during the fall. Malcolm lay writhing, knee bent, holding his ankle in an attempt to relieve the swelling on the limb.

Donald prayed it was only a sprain and not something more serious. "Are you alright?" Regretting the question as soon as it escaped his lips, knowing it was stupid to ask, but only trying to show concern for his brother's wellbeing.

"Do I look fine?" Malcolm snapped, the agony evident on his mud streaked face. "I think I went over my ankle during the fall, it is bloody sore."

"No need to snap my head off," Donald replied, looking annoyed at his brother. This was typical of Malcolm, strong and commanding one minute, but the instant he had an injury, even a burst nose, he turned into a bubbling mess. Both of the women in his life always fell for Malcolm's act, which was laughable, but he forgave him because Malcolm was normally supportive during one of the unplanned daydreams.

Donald backed away as Morag examined Malcolm's injury, grimacing in response to his cries of pain each time she rotated the joint.

"I think you have twisted it," said Morag, still prodding and poking at it. "Can you try to walk on it?"

"It hurts a lot, I will try, but I am not sure if I can."

With the support of Morag, Malcolm gingerly stood up, heavily favouring the injury. Face contorting as he tried to put weight on the damaged leg, a small grunt of anguish escaped each time that pressure was put on it.

"It is no good. You need to go on without me, I will just slow you down." Malcolm sighed in frustration.

"Nonsense, I will help you along, if you hold onto me and hop, it is not that far to our home, a couple of miles at most," Donald replied, refusing to give up.

"What if those things catch up to us?" Malcolm asked with concern, not wanting to be a burden to the rest of the group.

Donald laughed. "Then the Legend of Big Davie will have another tale added to it. The last I heard, he was seven-foot-tall and killed a five hundred strong English Army with his bare hands."

"Really?" exclaimed Big Davie blushing. "I keep hearing the stories but I try not to pay attention to them. It is all getting very silly, I take out a few English on my own and the next thing I ken, I have more fables than the great William Wallace."

"Just be ready," replied Malcolm, face straining with the pain, "we may need those famed fists again before the sun rises."

"Haha. I have the axe that I borrowed from the church. I will be fine; my holy hand weapon shall protect us all from the Heathens." Exaggerating, Big Davie swung it a few times, pretending to lop off a couple of heads before spinning and, with a flourish, the axe rested on his shoulder before he knelt in front of Malcolm, sporting a huge grin.

"Get up, you fool," snickered Malcolm. "If all those people knew the real Big Davie, your legend would be a whole different story."

"All seven feet are here to serve, my lord. May I get you an ale, or perhaps one would like a bowl of stew?"

"Ach, away. If that is the patter you use on the wee lassies that you chat up, it is no wonder you end up alone most nights."

"The Legend of Big Davie says otherwise. The ladies ask me why I am called Big Davie and I invite them back to my house for them to find out."

"Big Davie!" Morag exclaimed in shock. "That is disgusting, have you no honour or respect?"

"No, ma'am. No decency nor morals either," Big Davie replied, trying to keep a straight face.

"As much as we all like to listen to the big man make a fool of himself," Donald interjected, "we need to get a move on. If we stay here for too long, those creatures will soon catch up with us and Malcolm is in no condition to fight."

Deferring to the younger lad's words of wisdom, the group prepared to leave. Donald moved over to help his brother and Big Davie took the lead, brandishing his newly acquired axe. A pace or two behind, the fireside poker in hand, Morag surveyed around looking for danger. Donald and his encumbrance slipped in-between them, with Malcolm hopping more than walking. His leg seemed to be bothering him a lot. Shouldering the extra weight, Donald was determined to get Malcolm quickly back home to rest.

Ahead, Big Davie was looking like the man mentioned in the rumours that circulated the towns and villages in Lanarkshire, muscles rippling in the shimmer of moonlight, eyes roving, watching out for potential conflict. At the rear, Donald saw a complete contrast to the burly clansman. Morag could not have looked more nervous. Her already pale complexion had whitened further as the combination of fear and the cool night air had her visibly shaking. The metal rod clattered a couple of times on the rocks, causing Donald to wince. Morag looked dizzy, almost to the point where she could have fallen.

"What have you been drinking, lass?" asked Donald, trying to get Morag to relax. "You look like you have been sampling some of Malky's home brew."

"I had a mead at the tavern, a lot less than Big Davie," Morag replied, still looking nervous.

"The rumour is that Big Davie drank a whole keg of ale and could still kill fifty Englishmen single-handed the next day," said Donald with a wry smile on his face.

"Och, that is out of date," Malcolm continued, catching on to his brother's mischief. "The latest is that Big Davie drank two kegs of ale, a keg of mead, had sex with ten women and killed two hundred people all in one night."

"You went too far there, Malky." Big Davie laughed, his face becoming a deep crimson. "Any more of that and I will damage your other leg."

The mood lightened as the banter continued during the remainder of the trek through the woods. Morag had become less nervy and Malcolm was starting to put some slight pressure on his ankle, which settled his mind a little.

Once they exited into open land, the moon highlighted the road and fields around. There was nothing ahead which was concerning as sheep normally grazed out here at this time of night. Donald wondered what happened to them. Had all the commotion and strange goings on frightened them away? Donald knew the group were close to home, so he hurried along the stone path, trying to push the rest of the party along which did not help Malcolm who still struggled with his injury.

With the slow pace it took about another hour to reach home. The Douglas cottage stood out like a beacon in the dark sky, unexpectedly looming ominous as they approached. Flanking the door, two large shadows stood, ready and waiting. Neither were bigger than Malcolm or Big Davie, but silhouetted against the farm building, they certainly looked dangerous. As the group neared, they started to relax as the features of Jamie and Father Patrick came into view.

"What kept you?" called Jamie, looking rather bored and tired. "We have been waiting here for ages. Has Davie been playing with the sheep again?"

"Fuck off," replied Big Davie, his usual joviality gone as the rigors of the evening started to affect him. "Poor Donald has had to carry Malky home. The lazy shite couldna be bothered walking."

"Piss off, you big fool." Malcolm laughed, hobbling in behind his enormous friend. "I twisted my ankle in the woods and it took us a bit longer than expected to get here. What are you two doing outside? Has mother not let you in?"

"I suspect that she is in her bed sleeping. The door is locked, and we didna want to disturb her, so we decided to wait on you lot," Jamie explained.

"Hmmm," thought Malcolm aloud, "that is most unusual. Mother normally keeps the place unlocked. She does this in the hope that father will get home early from the campaign across the border. I have not kenned her to lock it since he went away. Have you tried the kitchen entrance around the back?"

"Erm," answered Jamie, looking rather sheepish, "we never thought of that."

"Donald, do you want to go with Jamie round the back and check if the door is open whilst I rest here for a bit? My leg is killing me and I need a sit down."

Staying alert, Donald and Jamie carefully made way to the other side of the house. That it was blanketed in darkness worried him. Normally there were a couple of lanterns lit so that their father would be able to see if he returned home early. This, coupled with an eerie silence, put Donald on edge as the dogs would usually bark at the first sound of any visitors. Sometimes they were so loud mother put them out to the field for a bit of peace and quiet.

As they turned the corner to the rear of the building, Donald noticed that the door was wide open and a strange odour, smelling almost like rotten meat, was wafting out from inside. Concerned, Donald motioned to Jamie to go back to the others, not wanting to face whatever may be inside on their own. For obvious reasons, he felt safer with Big Davie beside him.

CHAPTER THIRTEEN

HOME SWEET HOME

The entrance to the kitchen loomed ahead as Morag approached with the rest of the group. Teeth were heard chattering behind her, both Father Patrick and Donald not used to being out in the middle of the night, along with the rhythmic tapping of Malcolm's stick, which he picked up at the side of the cottage. Jamie took the lead, which surprised Morag. She thought Big Davie would be first into the home, his massive bulk surely a deterrent for any foe. The wiry smaller soldier was quick to organise the group before they entered the building. Morag noticed he'd done also before in both the tavern and church. Jamie seemed to be the natural leader of the group.

Malcolm was still struggling, using herself and Donald for assistance. She would be glad when they could get inside and Malcolm could rest the injured leg. Morag was worried there would be lasting damage to the ankle if he continued to put pressure on it and she did not want to spend the rest of her life looking after a lame farmer. Big Davie stood just behind Jamie, the mountain of a man's presence settled her and put everyone more at ease. Morag was not sure if it was the light-hearted nature of the loveable rogue or his sometimes over-exaggerated reputation, but whatever it was, she was happy to have him with them.

Father Patrick brought up the rear, nervously glancing around. Morag remembered having many a dinner with the priest, who often went to their house for an evening meal, a chat, and a sermon. Morag liked listening to his stories and, although they were mainly religious in nature, it was better than watching her brothers fighting. In particular, when her mother was ill, Father Patrick was there every night, cooking, cleaning, and looking after them all whilst her da was away fighting. As a family, they never really spent a lot of time with other villagers, but Father Patrick always made them feel part of the community.

"Morag, Donald," called Father Patrick, worriedly, "I will help Malcolm in. You look as if you are struggling."

Close to exhaustion but resolved to see his sibling settled in, Donald replied, "It is fine, Father. I can manage."

"Nonsense, young man. You must be keen to see your mother and get freshened up. I insist." With that, Father Patrick went over and took Malcolm's arm, helping him hobble towards the kitchen door.

"Thank you, Father," said Morag, relieved, "I appreciate it."

Donald and Davie both tripped and fell, making a ruckus and to her surprise, only Jamie remained on his feet, avoiding the hazards left lying on the kitchen floor. Morag could just make out both Donald and Big Davie struggling back to their feet. Supressing a yawn, Jamie helped the pair up as Donald fetched a candle from the old chest in the corner and lit it before they burst into the hall.

From the other end of the corridor, not seeing any movement, Jamie called out, "Aunt Jean! Are you there?"

"Hush," demanded Malcolm, hobbling over. "Ma might be in bed. We dinna want to wake her."

Shaking her head, Morag responded, "I think it may be a bit late for that."

"Sorry, I forgot how late it was. I will go up and check to see if she is awake," Jamie replied, head hanging in shame.

Malcolm looked a bit pensive. "Take Morag with you, she kens the place well."

"Malky!" Big Davie called from the other end of the room. "Get yer arse over here. I have found your dogs."

Morag and Malcolm rushed over, with Father Patrick providing support, to find Donald on his knees, head buried between them, sobbing away. Jamie and Big Davie were standing beside him, obstructing the view. Looking at the options, Morag decided she was more likely to see what happened by going around the group than barging past the large lump.

Morag sidled through to find a position that would give her a better look. What lay ahead not only shocked, but turned her stomach. Spread on the floor were two huge, black and white pelts of the dogs that often greeted her when she visited the farm. A few feet away, in a pool of blood, were the severed heads of the hounds. Morag reckoned they lay for a couple of hours due to the mass of flies swarming around the corpses. She felt a churning inside, forcing her to look away from the horrific deaths and focus back on the teary-eyed men that surrounded it.

"Fucking bastards!" snarled Malcolm, just behind her. "When I find the men that did this, I will cut off their balls."

Morag's face paled. "That is awful."

She approached Donald and tenderly lifted his head up, embracing him as the grief poured out upon her now sodden clothes. His crying lasted several minutes before Donald looked up, bleary eyes stared blankly behind her, teardrops continuing to pepper his face.

"Who would do something like that?" Donald sobbed. "They were innocent dogs, loving animals. They couldna harm a fly. This is not right."

"Whoever it is, I will find and kill them. This is not acceptable," Big Davie vowed, his face scarlet with both anger and sorrow.

"We need to find ma," Malcolm said through gritted teeth.

Taking charge, Jamie said, "I am on it. Morag and I will go upstairs. Davie, check the rest of the house. Malcolm, you and Donald stay here. I will find Auntie Jean."

Taking a moment to give Malcolm a sympathetic hug, Morag followed Jamie up the narrow staircase. With one last glance behind, she could see and feel grief and anger from the Douglas brothers. Father Patrick tried to offer comfort to them both, beside the mess below. Both siblings hung heads in prayer as Father Patrick held their hands, knuckles white from the strain. Unable to contain her anger, Morag struck the wall with the poker, a loud clanging vibrated through the room, drawing looks from both Jamie and Malcolm before she quickly ascended the stairs.

Upon reaching the top, Jamie insisted on taking the lead, and informed that at each room, he would check if it was empty before letting Morag in. Morag cursing oaths under her breath, annoyed at once again being treated fragile maiden.

There were two doors on either side of the short corridor, each closed, giving no clue if anything was amiss within.

"The door on the left is the brother's room, the other is where Jean and Cameron sleep," Morag whispered in Jamie's ear.

"I will try my aunt's bedroom first. Watch my back please."

Warily standing guard, Morag extended the weapon like a wildcat, coiled, ready to strike. There were no noises in the other room, the front door was locked, and Big Davie was downstairs still searching, the unmistakable thump of his boots like the beat of a war drum at Bel Tine.

Jamie popped back around after examining the room. His face had turned ashen white, looking like he might vomit.

Heart pounding, her mind replayed a vision of Jean lain out on the floor, covered in blood, similar to the dogs. Shaking it off, Morag placed a steadying hand on his shoulder and asked if he was okay.

"Sorry, lass, I am just a little taken back by what I have seen in there. It is not a pretty sight."

"What is in there? What has rattled you so?"

"It is best that you dinna ken. Malcolm would not want you to see that."

"I dinna care what you think, I am a big girl and can look after myself," Morag replied, anger and frustration evident in her voice.

Forcefully, she barged past Jamie to see what was going on, before standing pale-faced in shock at the sight. A naked body thrashed away on the bed whilst shackled to the frame, covered in gashes and gore, with flesh a gaunt, grey, sickly colour. The sheets were soaked bright crimson with blood pooling under her body, but lying there so long that it was starting to crust over. Full breasts sagging with age, once rosy nipples now charcoal, almost pure black, withered and wrinkled like the rest of the skin on her torso. The full mound of pubic hair, before a bright, pearl white, was now matted with a deep ruby streak caused by the gaping open wounds all over her skin. The woman was in obvious distress but looked like one of the monsters chasing them all night. Holding back revulsion, Morag stepped closer to take a better look to see if she knew the woman.

Though the facial features were swollen and discoloured, suspecting that it was Malcolm's mother Jean and trying to avoid looking into her vacant eyes, Morag still recognised the matron of the Douglas family. The woman who nurtured Malcolm and Donald was now nothing but a naked, living corpse. Breath caught in her throat, Morag finally inhaled when Jamie startled her from behind.

"Step back, lass, there is nothing that you can do for her. She is one of them now."

"There must be something that we can do! That is Malcolm's ma."

"I ken, but the only hope for her now is to put her out of her misery. I will go down and get Big Davie's axe so that I can do the needful."

"Wait," demanded Morag, trying to think of something that would delay the inevitable before noticing something on the wall above the bed, "do you see that?"

"See what? All I see is a poor woman that has been beaten, stripped, and turned into one of those monsters. Her suffering needs to end, Morag, it is not right."

"No, you dinna understand," said Morag frantically pointing at the artwork, "look above her, are you blind?"

The scripture was faint, seeming to be written in blood. A dark grisly message that shook them both.

MALCOLM DOUGLAS, YOU ARE NEXT. I WILL BE WAITING FOR YOU IN CARNWATH. HB

"What the fuck? That is fucking creepy."

"Aye. Look, I have seen enough of this, I think we should let Malcolm ken about this, let him decide what happens to his mother. The message is for him, whoever has done this clearly hates Malcolm," Morag said.

"I think you are right. It may be best if it comes from you though, you seem to have a calming influence on him."

"I will do, but I want Big Davie blocking the stairs, it is not a good idea for either Malcolm or Donald to see this."

"I agree," said Jamie, relieved that he did not have to tell Malcolm about this. "I also think we should secure the place and spend the night here. Everyone is exhausted and heads will be much clearer in the morning."

"Come on then, I dinna want to spend one more moment in there," stated Morag, moving out of the room, back into the corridor.

CHAPTER FOURTEEN

CARNWATH

A deep rumble vibrated almost loud enough to throw him across the room. Stirring, thinking it was thunder, he pulled the blanket back over his face, trying to block out the disturbance. Another clap sounded, this time eyes slowly opened, the blurriness meant that it took a few seconds to focus the dark background around into some semblance of a picture. Gradually, sight returned while carefully rolling his neck around, trying to remove the stiffness from lying in an uncomfortable position. A large figure dozed, slumped in the corner, dwarfing the rough cloth rug that he lay under, chest heaving up and down in time to the grating noise destroying his eardrums. Grumbling, he walked over, trying to keep the makeshift cover from falling, and booted the chap swiftly in the side. A wry grin crept over his face at the thought of the pain inflicted and the silence which ensued after the kick.

The peace lasted for just a couple of minutes before the drumming torture continued, deep snores awakening him fully this time, grogginess soon turned to rage at being woken with such force. Channelling the anger again, he strode over to the originator of the deathly throb and stuck a long, hairy foot into the back of the offender's head. This time, cries of pain and furious mutterings were heard as the still heap started to stir. Sniggering, the aggressor stood ready, waiting for the outcry that was sure to come.

"What the fuck did you do that for?" came a bass voice that echoed through the small area that they were resting in. "I was dreaming about a sexy redhead with huge breasts and my head kept...."

"That is enough of that," interrupted the red headed man who delivered the hit, "you were snoring like a bear, Tam. I would not be surprised if everyone in Peebles was awake with your damn ruckus."

"Sorry, Hamish. All that walking last night left me exhausted. My wife tells me that I can be loud when I am tired."

"You were lucky that I was just as exhausted. We have been asleep for long enough anyway; we have to get to Carnwath this morning."

"I ken, I am still in shock after seeing that wolf," Tam replied, sighing and trying to hide back under the small piece of cloth.

"That was no wolf! It looked the same as one of those creatures that our troops turned into. That is why I removed the creature's head. You are fortunate I did. It was going to kill you."

"It was not," replied Tam, unsure, "I had it just where I wanted it."

"You were lying on the ground. It was ready to tear your throat out," Hamish mocked.

"I was using the ground to my advantage. I was going to kill it."

Hamish stood and just looked incredulously at Tam, knowing the truth, shocked his bodyguard was unwilling to suffer disgrace. Sandy was too far away behind them, and as useless as Tam could be at times, he was still a damn good fighter and loyal. Hamish did not want to lose such a good ally.

"Aye, alright then," Hamish said, still not believing him. "You had better get Sandy up, I want to leave soon."

Hamish stretched his limbs as the clear blue sky provided little protection from the morning sun shining brightly into his eyes. Shielding them with grubby hands, he explored the area to get an idea of any potential pitfalls. The heather filled slope was damp with morning dew, the deep purple flowers shimmered in the green meadow around them. The stone wall blocking the field from the main road stood out in the distance at the bottom of the small hill they were strolling down. With little effort, they were through the gate, tied off by Sandy the night before, and back on the road to Carnwarth, the blazing sun beating at their back.

Sweat flooded from Hamish's forehead as the sweltering heat and lack of food had left him feeling tired and eager to find shelter. They were on the move for roughly a couple of hours and their feet ached like dozens of bees inflicting a vicious sting.

"I hate to say this, but I miss home," complained Tam, trying to keep pace with Hamish who was quicker than a horse being whipped by its rider.

Sandy looked incredulously at him. "Not me. I enjoy spending time with the lads and having a drink, but apart from that, life in Peebles is boring. I enjoy being out in the field, the smell of fresh air and you dinna ken where the next sleep is. All I have back in Peebles is a shitty small house and some furniture I beat a noble up for."

"Do you not miss your family? I miss my wife and children. I miss seeing the kids playing near the river and my wife's freshly baked bread."

"At least you have a wife. I have a crotchety old mother who does nothing but moan at me, especially when I dinna attend church on the Sabbath. No, the sooner we are back with the rest of the soldiers, the better."

"Sandy, I honestly think this might be it for me. I am getting too old for this shit. I have more than served the Balliol Clan. It might be time for me to retire."

"Tam, you are an old fool. There is no better fighter than you. I reckon you could best Big Davie with one hand tied behind your back. Look, Hamish needs us both. We need to be extra vigilant or it may be the last air we ever breathe."

The village outskirts rose into view as a shadowy outline in the distance. The sight spurred a renewed sense of urgency in their step. A place to rest and some breakfast was the top of the agenda, and if Carnwath was relatively free from the bloodthirsty creatures, then a quick visit to Uncle James house should provide some temporary respite.

Unusually, no-one was on the streets or even in the farms on the approach. None of the domestic animals were out in the fields either. There was no sign of any cows or sheep, the meadows as barren as Hamish's stomach. Even on the road they travelled on, there was no traffic or any disturbance. Normally, coaches or horsemen would have passed by, but there was not even the sound of the wooden wheels trundling on the stone.

"That is weird, where are all the people?" Hamish asked, taking care to keep to the middle of the road.

"You are right," replied Tam, squinting as the glare rebounded off the hilt of Sandy's sword. "Normally this place is hectic. Every time I have been here, the town is bustling with women chattering to each other outside those houses, trying to sell off their poorly made bracelets or tempt some handsome noble in for some fun, if you ken what I mean. I would have been tempted but the wife was with me."

Shaking his head, Hamish could only laugh. "That is funny, I dinna remember this street as a place for whores."

"To be fair, you led a sheltered life. Your da tried to keep you away from the seedier elements of towns and villages. You never got to see the beggars on the streets or the orphans relying on kind hearted women to pass on some bread, or if they were lucky, a bowl of soup. You spent your time in noble houses and in the affluent districts. The reality is that this street was where the prostitutes sold their wares. It used to be called the Cattle Market, which was ironic as you could not milk any of those cows."

Laughing, they rounded the final bend. Looming forth like a sentry, an immense cross stood erect in the three-way junction at the town centre. The road to the left would take them home to Peebles, the one on the right would go through the heart of Carnwath and then a few miles later into Lanark itself. Due to the number of travellers between the two towns, this was normally a busy time of day but again there was no-one in view.

The normal hustle and bustle, accompanied by the shouts of the market traders trying to attract customers, was not to be heard. The smell of butchered meat and fresh vegetables was also absent. If not for the putrid stench and sound of creatures feasting on what Hamish assumed was flesh in the distance, then you would think that Carnwath was desolate. Trepidation blanketed Hamish as the surrounding stillness was indicative of trouble. His hand slithered to the thick hilt of the sword, ready. Uncle James stayed not far away, fortunately, it was only about half a mile down a side street on the way through the town, which eased Hamish's already chafed nerves.

Drawing his blade, Hamish instructed, "Keep your weapons handy, I dinna like this one bit. I have a bad feeling about this."

"Aye, it is very creepy out here. It reminds me of a battlefield littered with corpses. Where the fuck is everyone?" Sandy replied with his great sword in hand.

"I have no idea. Be on alert, they must be somewhere, and I dinna want to get ambushed. I plan to stay alive today."

"As do I," stated Tam with conviction.

They turned at the junction and continued along Lanark Road, keeping a steady pace while passing a long row of two storey buildings, each constructed differently than the next. The absence of kids playing in the streets and the smell of freshly baked pie was missing. It unnerved Hamish, who remained vigilant, expecting an attack at any minute. After a short investigation, avoiding the roads where the odd monster was either banging on a door or nibbling on a victim, they found the entrance to the side street where Uncle James stayed, or so Hamish remembered. It was down another road, one that was blocked off at the end by a stone wall that served as a barrier to the bens beyond. James's abode was a few houses down on the left, two away from the end.

"This is too quiet," said Hamish to the others, whilst standing in front of the door, "I hope he is home."

"He better be, I am bloody starving," Tam said, rubbing his stomach.

"Och, you are always hungry," Sandy laughed, "it would take less to feed an army than to fill your belly."

"I am not that bad. I just get a little peckish at times."

"You got banned from the laird's house for eating all the pheasant," mocked Hamish, knocking the sturdy wooden door. "Uncle James, are you there?"

"No!" shouted a voice from within. "There is nobody here!"

"Em, you are there, I can hear you. Who are you? What are you doing in my uncle's house?"

"Who are you? I am not just going to let anyone in here. What if you are one of those monsters?"

"I am Hamish Balliol and this is my Uncle James place!" Hamish yelled, starting to get agitated. "Now, tell me who you are or I will be forced to take action."

"All right, son, stop shouting, you will draw unwanted attention. Your uncle is not here. Now please go away."

"Look, whoever you are, you obviously have not understood my last question, so let me put it more plainly to you. Who *are* you? Open the door or I will kick it in."

"It is not important who I am," said the voice, mysteriously, "it is important to you where James Balliol is though, is it not?"

The guttural sounds were getting louder. Movement could be heard nearby. Hamish knew that they did not have long before a group of the creatures were upon them, from where, he was not sure, but he did not fancy hanging around to find out.

Turing to Sandy and Tam, Hamish whispered, "We have two choices here, we continue to talk to this fool or break in there. We are going to get some uninvited guests soon and I would rather not be out on the streets to meet them. Are you ready to fight?" Hamish smiled as both men nodded in agreement, turning back to the door, he yelled, "If you ken where my uncle is, tell us now and I will leave you alone. If not, then I have to use force. Do you understand this?"

Murmurs could be heard from behind the wooden barrier. Hamish could not make out what they were saying but it was taking forever and he was getting anxious. The rabid screeching intensified, his impatience growing as the tension thickened. With time running out, Hamish signalled to the soldiers before aiming a kick at the entrance. Recalling the words of his father, '*Aim for the side of the door, opposite the lock. That is the weakest point and a good strike both high and low would get into most places.*' Hamish executed this manoeuvre and was met with success as it cracked under the increased force and swung open, slamming against the wall. At the other end of the corridor stood a frightened looking man, quivering whilst holding a short sword. Hamish did not recognize him. The stubble faced chap was a good few inches shorter than Hamish and sported cropped, blond hair, grubby from not having washed it in a few days.

"Sir! We have company, a few of these monsters have just turned into the alleyway, it willna be long until they are upon us!" Tam exclaimed from the rear.

"If you pair keep them busy, I will sort out this mess and you can come in once I am done."

"It would be great if you could hurry, I dinna like our chances here."

106

Annoyed, Hamish strode in towards the scared chap in the hall, deftly blocking the man's half-hearted swing of the weapon, before striking him squarely in the chest, causing both the fellow and blade to fly a few feet back. Casually, Hamish placed a boot upon the hand splayed on the floor, the bones cracked a little. An excruciating scream pierced his ears as more pressure exerted on the fragile digits.

"Now," Hamish calmly stated, "where is my uncle?"

"I din..din..dinna ken…" stammered the man, a small puddle of urine forming around him.

"Wrong answer." Hamish forced down harder. The broken crunch of each finger serenading painful cries before the intruder fell unconscious.

Kicking his side a couple of times to make sure he was fully out, Hamish quickly checked the rest of the rooms above, hoping to find his missing uncle. James was nowhere to be seen. Hamish could hear skirmishes outside and quickly checked the ground floor for another exit. It did not take him long to find it hidden in the kitchen. Opening the door, he looked out, trying to determine if there were any threats. Fortunately, there was no-one in the alleyway and any obstacles were soon removed, clearing the route there to make the escape easier.

Hamish could still hear the sound of metal cutting into bone and the thump of body parts hitting the ground, which concerned him. Returning to the house, hefting the unconscious body on his shoulder, Hamish shouted at the others to follow as he trudged into the alley.

Sandy and Tam were soon nipping at his heels, the undead not far behind but losing ground. Conscious that they had to find a secure location to rest in and plan their next move, Hamish proceeded to check the door handles of each house they came upon, hoping to find one open. Just as a few of the monsters came into sight, blood and detritus dripping from broken teeth, the third attempt was successful. Hastily throwing open the door into a narrow hallway, shadows formed as a result of the sunlight streaming inside. Beckoning the others in, Hamish passed the stunned man over to Tam before slamming the door shut and bolting it.

"Sandy, we need something to block this door. If we dinna barricade it, then I think that we will have some trouble!" Hamish yelled with worry.

Hearing voices chattering away in the distance, Hamish motioned for Sandy to investigate. They were not alone and he was keen to keep any intruders out.

CHAPTER FIFTEEN

HEATHENS

Bleary-eyed, Malcolm awoke from a disturbed slumber, vivid dreams haunted the little rest that he managed to achieve overnight. Visions of his mother lying on the bed, blaming him for leaving her in the house alone whilst they went out to the tavern. The image of his dastardly foe Hamish Balliol standing over and killing her left Malcolm shaken, nerves jangling. All this time Morag had stayed, cradling him back to sleep when he woke sobbing, unable to get the nightmares out of his head.

Malcolm turned Morag over gently, her slight figure lay to the left, ears pricked at the noise of the bed creaking. Returning the favour, Malcolm stroked the flowing, auburn hair lovingly, trying to settle her down again. Thinking back on the evening's happenings, Malcolm found his cheeks wetting, thoughts of his monstrous parent entering his mind. Wiping back the tears with the sleeve of his cream nightshirt, a smile finally appeared, grateful that Morag was there when he went up to look at the writhing figure last night. It was heart-breaking for both and they spent a lot of time hugging and comforting each other, but they got through the worst of it.

The pain was still evident in his ankle and that did not help matters either. Morag strapped it heavily before they went to bed, which left him again feeling nothing but gratitude for the care shown by his betrothed. They decided rest was needed before facing whatever jeopardy lay ahead in the morning. Morag wanted to go out and check on her family in town. The group agreed it was too dangerous to go out in the dark, so she was left frustrated and anxious.

Malcolm needed to travel into Carnwath to hunt down Hamish but the decision was made that they should see if Morag's family were alive first before seeking out revenge. Morag's elder brother Rabbie was the only fighter left to defend them from the threat. Her da, Ian, was away fighting with the clan against the English in Cumbria with Cammy, his father. Both men were out battling the Earl of Lancaster's army, who travelled north to support their Cumbrian neighbours, trying to send the Scots back home. The Earl of Richmond was no friend to the Scots, the combined Army had enough foes to deal with without the possibility of the undead to add to their woes.

The thumping of gigantic footsteps thundered below as Malcolm suspected Big Davie was wandering about downstairs, probably looking for food. Malcolm gave a wee, wry grin to himself, certain that the Legend of Big Davie never mentioned how much food was eaten in a day. Malcolm was grateful to have the loveable rogue with them. He did not think that they could have survived out there without the presence and prowess of the hulking man. At times, when things had looked at their most bleak, Davie's confidence and humour buoyed their spirits. Big Davie took one of the two watches last night with Father Patrick, just in case Hamish or the dead had decided to pay them a visit. Although it was likely not needed, Malcolm was sure that Hamish was well on his way to Carnwath by now.

Jamie was a godsend last night. Malcolm was barely in any state to deal with himself, never mind Donald. Jamie had cradled, hugged, and talked to Donald, helping deal with the pain and grief. Donald never went into her bedroom, which was just as well as Malcolm thought that this would make things worse. Jamie had remained with Donald in his room, making sure that there was someone for him to talk to which helped to ease some of the pressure building. Malcolm dealt with the situation better than expected and did not snap at Jamie when he suggested removing his ma's head. Malcolm saw she was restrained and thought that leaving her tied up and secluded was a better idea, just in case there was a way of reversing the infection or whatever had happened to her. It was similar to the men in the pub and during the fighting, Malcolm noticed the seeping puss coming from their wounds, a possible clue to what caused the people to turn into monsters.

Morag was restless now and Malcolm smiled as she threw an arm over him, snuggling in before trapping him with an exploratory thigh. Contentedly sighing, Malcolm stared at her shapely limb as it gently stroked his calf. Knowing that they needed to be on the road soon, Malcolm bent forward and touched his lips tenderly, caressingly, just above the brow of her forehead, the skin smooth, like a fine lace that had just been woven by the most skilled dressmaker.

Long lashes fluttering fully open, Morag stretched like a barn cat after a filling meal. Sunshine glistened through the small window, hitting her blue eyes just right, making them appear like bright stars in the daylight. Malcolm stared into them for a few minutes before finally breaking contact and wishing her a good morning.

Morag yawned back at him. "Malcolm Douglas, it is such a comforting feeling waking up beside you. How is the foot?"

"It is still a wee bit sore, my love, but much better after the rest."

"Give me a couple of minutes to fully wake up and I will have another look at it, see if it is any better than last night."

Rising slowly, Morag carefully disentangled from his toned limbs. Malcolm watched lustfully as she stood up, a white gown borrowed from his mother, flowed whilst gliding to the end of the bed. The outline of her body teased through the fabric, his member becoming erect of the sight of the voluptuousness. The arousal soon turned to pain as Morag gripped his heel and carefully rotated it in both directions after unwrapping the strapping that was applied before bedtime.

"Are you feeling any pain when I do that?"

"A little, but not as much as yesterday. How does it look?"

"The swelling is down, there seems to be some bruising. If you dinna put too much stress on it, you should be fine."

"I use a staff to help me keep balance when walking the hills to tend the sheep, I could use that to support me on the journey."

"Good idea, my love, I will walk with you on the way back into the village. I hope my family are all right."

"I am sure they are," said Malcolm, not convinced this is where they should be going. "I just feel that we should go after Hamish before he causes any more trouble, I dinna like that man one bit and when I ken he is in the heart of Douglas territory, it makes me very uneasy."

"We will go after him, but you did promise that we would check on my kin before you hunt him down. I need to ken that they are still alive."

"I intend to honour my word, my sweet, but I dinna want to spend too long before going on the road. Hamish canna be allowed to get away with this."

"Well," retorted Morag with an impatience in her voice, "let us not waste any more precious time. We should stir the others and set off for the village."

It took them longer than anticipated to get dressed with Malcolm continuing to be the gentleman, turning his back as Morag changed, although his mind was imagining the naked body behind him. Blushing, he tried to keep his concentration back on the task at hand and the plan for the day. It was a short distance to Morag's abode, then assuming everything was good, they would set off for Carnwath in the afternoon and arrive just before the sun sets. Big Davie's uncle stayed in Carnwath, so he knew that they could settle down for the evening there before initiating the search for Hamish the following day.

When they eventually entered the kitchen, the rest of the group were sat round the table tucking into fresh bread and soup, trying to build up some strength for the day ahead. Malcolm could see the scarlet streaks on Donald's cheeks caused by endless tears overnight. Malcolm felt his own face, certain that it was also a bit tender due to grief.

Approaching his young sibling, Malcolm gently touched Donald on the shoulder, breaking him from rapt attention on Big Davie. Jolted from his reverie, Donald turned, eyes welling when catching sight of his big brother. Unable to hold back, Malcolm engulfed Donald in strong arms and held him in a much-needed embrace.

The moment of tenderness seemed to last for hours but it was only a few minutes as none of the others dared to disturb the time shared by the two. Eventually, Malcolm let go and put his hand on Donald's head in a reassuring manner.

"The hurt will last for a while. For me, the pain will always be there and mother will never be forgotten."

"She is not dead yet, we could still find a way to bring her back," Donald said with ferocity.

A frostiness overtook his tone. "It is unlikely. I am grieving now so that I dinna have this continually on my mind. I suggest that you do the same. We may find a cure or a way of bringing her back, but I dinna hold out hope. We must go on, Donald, and make sure that Hamish canna do this again. First though, we must fulfil a promise that I made to Morag and return to the village to check on her family. It will be a long, tiring day, so grab whatever weapons you can find and fill your water skins, we have a lot to do."

Malcolm could hear Father Patrick mutter "Heathen" when he spoke about his ma, but he was not ready to deal with the priest yet. He just hoped that Donald hadn't heard. The group needed to be united, Malcolm could do without them at each other's throats. Thinking about it, he would have a word with Patrick before it got too much out of hand. Jamie explained Patrick's theory last night in the church, it seemed unconceivable his mother was a Heathen. Malcolm knew that he could not rule anything out and did not think that Donald would share the same opinion or patience as him, which meant getting Patrick to stop being so vocal about his theory. It would have to wait until they were on the road to Carnwath, Malcolm had too much on his mind and was not keen to initiate the discussion straight away.

Everyone quickly packed up their belongings and hit the road again. Malcolm was feeling a bit better because he found his long sword, hidden in the clothes trunk in his room, and let Morag continue to carry the poker she wielded earlier. Morag fetched his old shepherd's staff and this made walking easier as they strolled along the path back to the village. Morag was by his side and did as much for him as she could. Malcolm was grateful for the love she showed. In so many ways, she made life a lot easier with a strength and resilience he never knew she possessed.

Jamie stayed with Donald, still keeping an eye on him as they led the rest along the route. Malcolm could see Jamie occasionally put his hand on Donald's shoulder and the chatter became quite intense. Malcolm was glad Jamie had the chance to talk to Donald as he went through something similar a few years ago when his da was killed fighting the Balliols. Malcolm knew Jamie held no love for that clan and he would be the first to join them when they finally left to hunt down Hamish.

Big Davie and Patrick were at the rear of the party. Big Davie continually kept watch with his big axe over one shoulder, whistling away as they walked. Patrick was more tired and pensive, it looked like he was lost in thought, trying to reason what had happened over the last day.

The continual sunshine was not normal at this time of year. Often the weather was intermittent with some days being wet and others being windy. This heatwave lasted a couple of weeks so far and with the time spent out tending sheep, Malcolm must have sweated out a small river. The hills behind provided as stunning backdrop for the stone path that snaked through the green fields, which were unusually sparse of farm animals at this time of day, no sign of the usual grazing or bleating by the sheep.

Before noon arrived, the group passed through a small gap in the wall to enter the outskirts of Forth. There were no people about which was not normal before lunch time. Typically, women would be standing about chatting or the odd trader passing through. The place was as still as a graveyard. The smell of rotten flesh and the scraping of fingers against doors nearby creeped Malcolm out a little as the fear of being eaten alive by one of those creatures played on his mind.

"Draw your weapons," Jamie called out. "There is trouble nearby, we need to be ready to defend ourselves. Malcolm, how is the foot? Are you able to fight?"

"My ankle is still sore but I am ready if we are attacked. You dinna have to worry about me. Let us just find Morag's house and get on with it."

"Aye, if you are sure. I wouldna like to lose you, cousin, you are a good fighter and smell better than Big Davie," Jamie said with concern.

"I resemble that remark," Big Davie retorted with a smile. "It has taken many years of sleeping in hedges or barns with farmer's daughters to accumulate this unique pong."

"I am sure that the girls just love the aroma of cow dung in the morning," joked Malcolm, trying to use humour to mask his fear as they continued along the street.

"They spend half their day in fields with cows and sheep. It is an improvement on a bull dropping a huge shit on your foot."

The uneasy merriment continued as they progressed along the road, playful punches and giggles helped relaxed the party which lightened everyone's mood after the emotional turmoil they went through recently. After a few minutes, they rounded a sharp bend which preceded the row where Morag lived. The chatter and antics soon dissipated as they approached, everyone drew their weapon, ready for any potential conflict.

Hope, followed by dread, crept through Malcolm's mind as a large congregation surrounded Morag's front door. Desperate pounding and clawing fingers sought to gain purchase within. Gnashing teeth and monstrous bellows of hunger joined the cacophony.

"Do you think my ma is up there?" whispered Morag to Malcolm, trying not to draw any attention their way.

"I am not sure, there is definitely someone up there though. The only way we will find out is by clearing the mob away."

"Weapons ready," commanded Jamie, "And-"

Before Jamie could finish his sentence, Father Patrick charged into the horde. The mace he picked up from the church swung in a round arc, spikes glinting with each rotation as it passed over his head. He rushed across to the first Heathen, with the force of the attack caving the skull in, blood and brain fluid leaking out of the collapsing corpse.

Face beat red and spittle flying, Patrick screamed, anger and passion vibrating through his speech, "Heathen scum! The Lord shall smite you down by my hand. Fear me as I have been chosen by God to banish you to Hell!"

"Oh fuck! We had better go and help him out," Big Davie yelled. The clansman sprinted forward, giant axe gripped in both hands, with the rest of the group following not far behind, ready to take care of the Heathens. By the time that Big Davie had sunk his huge blade into the first victim, Patrick had already crushed four as he aggressively hunted for more to kill.

It took Malcolm a few seconds to join the melee as his ankle could not bear the weight of a sprint. Throwing the staff behind, he faced familiar crimson eyes boring deep into his soul. Deftly sidestepping, which caused a sharp pain to shoot up his injured leg, Malcolm brought the long sword up through the base of the Heathen's neck, cleaving it neatly off where it landed several feet away on the stone path. Malcolm grimaced as the remains of his victim slumped in a bloodied heap. Trying to keep balance, Malcolm steadied himself, ready for the next infected to make their move. The others had thinned out the numbers to a few, which were dispatched quickly. The raging priest was largely responsible for the swift culling of the Heathens. Soon the doorway was clear with nothing but filthy detritus was left before them.

"Ma!" yelled Morag, at the top of her voice, frantically. "Are you there?"

"Keep it down, lass," Jamie admonished. "You will bring more of them on us. We should only fight when we need to. Let us not invite trouble."

"Sorry, I just want to ken if my family is safe."

"I understand, lass, I would just like to keep things as calm as possible."

They were interrupted by raised voices behind. Malcolm turned to see Donald with his hands at Father Patrick's throat.

"You bastard! My mother is not a Heathen and none of the villagers that we just killed are either. They were my friends!"

Patrick's face was starting to turn a deep purple before Big Davie was able to prise Donald's fingers from his scarlet streaked neck. Gasping for breath, Patrick stared in shock at the ferocity of the younger Douglas lad. Malcolm almost felt sorry for the priest, though did partially blame himself for the attack as he never took the time to have the talk with Patrick.

Anger blazed in Donald's eyes as he struggled to break free of the legend's grip. Malcolm watched as his brother started to sag, knowing that he could not escape Big Davie's strength.

"Calm the fuck down! We dinna attack anyone for their beliefs, especially not Father Patrick who has been there for our family during times of hardship. A man who has taken great effort to integrate himself into our community and be a friend to all of us. A man who has fed the needy with his own food and went without so children in the village were fed during the harshest of winters. This is not behaviour that I would expect from you, Donald," Malcolm declared.

"But...He called our ma..." Donald stopped, interrupted by the shouting coming from above.

"Morag," came the voice of a woman, hanging out the window from the next storey, "is that you?"

The group turned around to stare at the dark-haired lady making the noise.

"Yes, ma," replied Morag, with tears streaming down her cheek. "Is everyone safe?"

CHAPTER SIXTEEN

LUNCH

Heart pounding, Morag jumped for joy at the sight of her mother Sheena. A sigh of relief washed over like a huge wave exploding from the sea, and now all she wanted to do was hug and tell her that how much she was missed and loved.

"Ma, can you let us up? We have dealt with the monsters that were trapping you here."

"Oh, Morag, we could get out at any time, the back door was clear. I will send your sister down to let you in, dear."

Moments later the door to start rattling. A metallic clang rang out as the barricade was removed from the inside. Unfortunately, at the same time, sounds of gnashing teeth echoed as a large group of the infected came around the corner. Morag estimated between fifteen and twenty of the shambling, grey villagers, all seemingly focused on the small group of weary travellers who were still mulling on the porch.

"Morag, take your sister and get inside quickly. Barricade that door. We will be up soon," Malcolm shouted.

"Malcolm, you are hurt, you need to come up with us. You are in no condition to fight."

"Just go, I will do what I have to do but I willna put you at risk. Please move!" Malcolm screamed in frustration.

Stomping her foot in anger at being excluded from the action, Morag moved inside the doorway and helped Mhairi block the door with the huge wooden plank that rested on the supports at either side.

"I can look after myself," Morag snapped in frustration as she climbed the short staircase to the top. "Stop babying me, Malcolm Douglas!"

Feeling Mhairi's hand on her shoulder, Morag shrugged it off and smiled at her little sibling, bright red hair shining as the girl entered the light in the hallway, a mass of carrot freckles enhanced her impish beauty, highlighted by her deep green eyes and toothy smile. The pained love for her family, stowed away during all the chaos, soon returned at the sight of her sister. Not expecting to see them alive, and although there was always hope, in private Morag mourned her family since the Heathens struck last night. Now, dreams were reality and the thought of seeing her mother again swelled her heart with joy.

Morag barged past Mhairi and shot through the entranceway looking for ma. Seeing her turn around at the window, she launched at the woman who had raised her. Squeezing tightly, Morag held on in the deepest embrace as she sank into the loving bosom.

"I thought you were dead!" Morag shrieked. "I am so happy to see you."

"Morag, sweetie, I kennt you were alive, I told Mhairi that you would be all right. I am so glad to see you, honey," replied her mother, joy evident in her voice.

"Me too, I am thankful that Malcolm looked after you," Mhairi cried from behind Morag.

"Him, take care of me? It was more like me making sure that he did not die. I carried him, fought beside him, defended him, and nursed him," Morag declared indignantly.

"Leave her be, lass," said Sheena. "She didna ken what you have faced. In fact, you dinna ken what we have endured. It has been an awful time."

"Before we get into stories, where is Rabbie? I have not seen him at all since I arrived."

"Rabbie is on the road to Moderwell. He left a couple of hours ago. He heard a story that you and Malcolm were off west to try and get help. One of the lads in the village told him that you had went along the Kilmarnock Road, Rabbie grabbed his stuff and went off after you. He was worried about you."

"Oh no! That is awful, we have to go after them. Shit, Malcolm is outside fighting with the others just now. I have to see how they are doing."

"Wash your tongue out, young lady! You willna curse in front of me or your sister!" Sheena exclaimed in shock.

"Sorry, Mother. It is hanging about Big Davie; he is a bad influence."

Mhairi stood aghast, hands on hips. "He has always been lovely to me. Big Davie is as kind and generous a man in the whole of Scotland."

"He always seemed to get himself into trouble though," Morag retorted, "Malcolm used to tell me about all the times he was caught thieving. He was a rascal before he left the village."

"He was always polite and generous when he was with me. He would not hurt a fly unless provoked. Malcolm, as per usual, is wrong."

"What does that mean?" demanded Morag. "Malcolm is never wrong about people, especially Big Davie who he kens for years."

Mhairi smirked. "Really! What about when he vouched for Paul last year? The very same Paul who made off with half the chickens in the village and sold them all at the market in Carnwath."

"You canna blame him for that. Paul was his second cousin. How was he to ken that Paul was a rogue?"

"That is not the only time your oh so perfect Malcolm was wrong," began Mhairi before their mother interjected.

"Will you two stop bickering and watch the fight? Honestly, I swear you never argued this much when you were bairns. Whatever happened to the quiet pair of lassies who used to sit and knit or read a book?"

Taking their mother's advice onboard, Morag soon found Mhairi standing beside her as they watched the rest of the group fighting. Father Douglas was in fine fettle, mace swinging like a pendulum as it felled Heathen after Heathen with each vicious strike. Big Davie appeared larger than he actually was while thrusting the axe through the air with such ferocity it easily beheaded quite a number of infected. Any that got too close met the force of Big Davie's boot, which launched it a few feet before landing on the rough surface where another of the group delivered the killing blow to the head.

"Oh gosh! He is very handsome and strong. Davie is very impressive with that huge axe of his. He is doing much better than your Malcolm," Mhairi gushed.

"My Malcolm is hurt; he is fighting on one leg and still able to kill the attacking creatures. I am very proud of him."

"Heathens!" shouted Father Patrick as he bashed in the skull of a dark-haired man. "We are fighting Heathens, Morag!"

"I am going to fucking kill him," Donald declared from below, fending off the lunging arm of a withering old lady. "*Stop* calling them Heathens or I will turn you into one of them!"

"For fuck sake, will you pair stop it? It was your bickering that brought them upon us. Concentrate on killing the infected, not each other. This is not the time!" Jamie shouted in frustration while thrusting the sword clean through the neck of a Heathen, blood coated blade emerging out the other side.

"Sorry, Jamie," they answered in unison as both men fought with passion and skill, culling through the numbers of the aggressive beasts.

"They are not the fearsome fighting team that I expected. In fact, apart from Big Davie, they are all a bit disjointed," Mhairi said, almost disappointed.

"They have their issues, but I would trust each and every one of them with my life, especially Malcolm."

"Big Davie!" shouted Mhairi from the window as a Heathen lunged towards him. "Behind you."

"Thanks, Mhairi!" called Big Davie, spinning to catch the incumbent with the clenched fist of his off-hand, knocking it off its feet."

"Just concentrate, I dinna want to see you hurt," replied Mhairi, blushing as she watched Big Davie punch another Heathen with his bare fist, the power pushing it back a few yards before it could recover. Noticing a foe closing in on Jamie's left flank. Morag shouted the same warning.

Looking up, Jamie shrugged his shoulders at the two sisters and turned back to the action, narrowly avoiding getting bitten by the incoming monstrosity. Stepping to the side, Jamie impaled his gore coated blade through the eye socket of the infected. Blood spurted as it sank to the ground. Rivulets ran through the hard-packed dirt, joining together in an ever-growing pool.

The rest of the threat was soon over as the lads worked together, fighting side by side in pairs with Donald and Big Davie on one flank, Jamie and Malcolm on the other, with Father Patrick and his flailing mace taking care of the threat in the centre.

"That was amazing!" shouted down Mhairi. "You were all so brave."

"Thank you," said Big Davie with a huge grin on his face. "Can you let us up now? I am starving after that battle. I think I have worked up an appetite."

"Mother has said that she will prepare some food. I will let you in, she is very keen to meet you."

It took a few minutes for the warriors to get inside and congregate around the large table in the kitchen. Bread, ham, and cheese was served along with milk and water. The drinks were greedily gulped down to alleviate deep thirst from the battle. Food was hastily shovelled in to feed the hunger.

"My, you have a big appetite," Mhairi gushed to Big Davie, thick eyelashes fluttering seductively. "I reckon that it is not the only big thing that you have."

"Mhairi!" gasped Morag in shock at the forwardness of her sister. "Mother will hear you and you will get in trouble again."

"Och, I am just having a wee bit of fun with Big Davie, it has been too long since we last met," replied Mhairi defensively.

"He can be a bit overwhelming at times," stated Morag, trying to hide her surprise, before turning to Big Davie, "stop listening in, you big vain fool. If your head gets any bigger, we willna be able to get you out of my house."

Big Davie laughed, which Mhairi giggled at, eyelashes batting in his direction. The food was soon demolished, and the hilarity turned to more serious matters.

"Malcolm, we need to go and find Rabbie. Ma said that he went to Moderwell to look for us. I would feel awful if anything was to happen to him," Morag said with firm determination.

"What about Hamish and Carnwath? You said that once we had checked on your ma that we could go on the road and hunt him down before he kills many more people. That man is a danger and must be stopped!"

"Is your revenge more important than finding my brother? It is our fault that he is out there. If we had headed here instead of your cottage, then perhaps he would not have left!" Anger seethed in her voice, her worry for Rabbie and annoyance at Malcolm combined to toy with her already tumultuous emotions.

"Is there any reason that is stopping us from doing both?" Jamie queried, his voice of reason helped prevent further argument at the table.

"What do you mean?" asked Morag, still shaking,

"Three of us could go to Carnwath to go after Hamish and the other three could head to Moderwell and find out what happened to Rabbie. We could meet up in Lanark in a couple of days."

"That sounds like a good idea, what about Ma and Mhairi?"

"They seem to be safe enough here. If they are in any danger, they could always head out to Malcolm's cottage where there is less chance of trouble."

"I quite like this plan. How would we split the group? I want to go after Hamish and Morag wants to go after her brother," Malcolm asked.

"I hate it," replied Mhairi, "I would quite like to go with Morag and Davie. That huge hunk of a man needs better company than my grumpy sister."

Flashing a scowl at her sister, Morag retorted, "That would leave ma on her own. She needs someone with her. Sorry, sis, you need to stay here."

"That is not fair," said Mhairi, stomping her foot. "You get all the fun."

Jamie continued, ignoring the interruption from Mhairi, "I think Morag needs Big Davie for protection and Donald would do well to learn from our legend on the way. You dinna ken, they could create tales about the legend of Donald Douglas!"

"That would leave you and Patrick with me, that makes sense. I think keeping Donald and Patrick separated is a good idea. The quicker we get going the better, I am eager to get on the road after that rogue," Malcolm said.

"I agree," replied Morag, "I want to get after Rabbie before evening."

"I want to come with you. I want to learn from Big Davie too," Mhairi announced, still trying to weasel her way into the group.

"You would be better safe here with mother. I would rather that she was not alone."

"It is decided," said Jamie, starting to rise, "let us thank our lovely hostess for the delicious food and take our leave."

At this point, Sheena entered the room. "Och, no need to thank me. It is good to see friendly faces, and you did me a favour by getting rid of some of that pesky vermin. It was the least I could do. In fact, before you leave, why do you not all go and get changed into fresh clothes. The clothes you have on are all grimy. Malcolm and Donald, you are both about the same size as our Rabbie, you could borrow some of his clothes. Jamie, you are similar build to my husband. I am sure he would not mind you taking some of his clothes. I am afraid I dinna have anything large enough for David, but I can give him more stew whilst he waits. You could all get dressed in my room. It is not very big, so you will have to go one at a time."

"Thank you, Sheena," said Malcolm, gratefully, "That is very kind."

"No need for thanks. Morag will take you up, she can put on a fresh dress whilst she is up there."

It took about quarter of an hour for them all to put new outfits on. The lads all wore shirts and trousers, keeping it simple and convenient. Morag wore a long brown tunic with a thick pair of white stockings underneath.

"That is much better, you all look so much better now."

Malcolm replied as they headed for the exit. "Thank you once again Sheena. Now, we really must take our leave."

CHAPTER SEVENTEEN

SECRETS

"I thtill think we should thtay in the kitchen," a high-pitched voice, which Hamish assumed was male, but could not be sure, was heard from the far end of the building.

A second man piped up, this time the deepness of the tone was unmistakable. "For the moment, that is prudent, but if those monsters should visit, we should be prepared to find shelter elsewhere. Your brother would not be pleased with me if I let you die."

"There is no danger of that, the creatures are harmless. We are in no danger."

"Are you serious. I have seen these beasts converge on people in the streets and rip them to shreds. I do not fancy being devoured like that."

Hamish could not hear much more as the conversation soon faded to whispers. Whoever was there obviously did not want to be heard. Hamish quickly checked the man he was carrying, thankfully he seemed to be still unconscious. Sandy and Tam were busy trying to keep the strange creatures from coming through the door. Sandy was using his strength and weight to keep them at bay whilst Tam was hauling chairs and other furniture, gradually building a barricade to prevent intrusion. Hamish propped the prisoner against the wall and traversed cautiously to the kitchen located to the rear to investigate who was making the noise. It did not take long to get there. Sat at the long, rectangular table were two middle-aged men. One was balding with a bushy brown beard whilst the other was clean shaven with neat blond hair swept to the side. Hamish immediately recognised his missing uncle, James Balliol, the senior clan member in Carnwath.

"Hamish, old chap! Am I surprised to see you, what are you doing here?"

"What am I doing here? Where the fuck is here? And why are you not at home?" Hamish asked in shock.

"Now that is an interesting tale. First, let me introduce you to my good friend and our new ally, Andrew Baird."

Hamish extended a hand towards the balding man whilst James continued, "Andy, this is my nephew, Hamish Balliol, from Peebles. I have no idea why he is here, but his presence may be to our advantage."

Andrew Baird eased out of his seat and stood tall, although just a couple of inches shorter than Hamish, and extended a well-manicured hand.

"It is an abtholute pleathure to meet you," gushed Andrew, unable to hide his speech impediment. "You are a long way from home. May I athk what hath taken you tho far out of your way?"

"Clan business. I am on a mission from our glorious leader in Peebles, one that I canna discuss with outsiders," Hamish answered gruffly.

"Oh, come on," James declared with a huge grin on his face, "Andrew has just helped me finish writing a treaty between our two great clans, making us allies against the rebels in the area, the Wallace sympathisers. You can say anything in front of him."

"An alliance?" queried Hamish, his voice starting to shake. "That is wonderful news, father will be pleased."

"He will be once it is signed. Your arrival has been most fortunate, it means that you can escort us to Lanark to get the clan heads there to sign it before returning the treaty to Peebles."

"I have a personal matter to take care of first before we leave," Hamish stated cryptically. "Plus, we have to find a way out of here, there are loads of those things at the door. Sandy and Tam are doing their best to keep them out, but that barricade willna last long."

"May one athk what your busineth ith?" interjected Andrew, his lisp now very prominent as he spoke. "We cannot thtay here too long, we must be on our way with haste."

126

"No, one may *not* ask. One may keep their fucking mouth shut and be grateful that one will have three armed guards to escort them to bloody Lanark."

"Hamish! You will not speak like that to my friend. Andrew is a very important member of the Baird clan, you must treat him with the respect that he deserves," James harshly admonished.

"Thorry," replied Hamish mockingly, "it ith wrong of me to dithrespect you. I am thure that you are a decent chap. Pleathe accept my humble apologieth."

"Hamish!" James warned with a growl. "Any more of this insolence and your father will hear about it."

"You are motht gracious," replied Andrew, not picking up on Hamish's teasing, "I am tho honoured to have thuch a skilled fighter to protect uth."

Hamish tried his best to hide a snigger, taking a few seconds to regain composure, ensuring not to face further wrath from his uncle. Andrew was a strange chap who looked like a typical aristocrat. He was well dressed with unnaturally pale hands, probably never having done any honest labour in his life. Hamish hated the upper class with a passion. It was the laziness that annoyed him the most, sitting on their fat bottoms whilst servants slaved away doing all the dirty work. The bullying angered as well, Hamish had beheaded a few lords for their treatment of maids and the beating given to pageboys, it caused ruckus with his father, but the point was made and the nobles in the area tended to tread more carefully when he was nearby.

"Please excuse me," said Hamish almost too politely, "I have to check on my soldiers and there is a young man who I found in your house, Uncle James. I am most keen to find out what he was doing there."

"You are excused. Please try not to use the more extreme measures of persuasion. You are a guest here and I would not want to offend our host."

Bowing, Hamish exited the room. Muttering about hating snobs, he went to the hall to check on the others. The intruder was still lying slumped against the wall as Sandy and Tam continued to reinforce the blockade. Thumping of bone against wood echoed. Hamish was shocked at how loud is was, surprised that they could not hear it in the kitchen. The banging was accompanied by a whining and that odd, grating sound of gnashing teeth which made Hamish uncontrollably shiver.

"Those bastards give me the creeps," Hamish said without prompting, which caused Sandy to jump slightly.

"Aye, me too," replied Tam, trying to drag a large cabinet through, "I just wish that they would go and annoy someone else."

Glum, Hamish said, "That is not going to happen. Look, we have to leave soon. My uncle is through there with a high-ranking member of Clan Baird. They have an important treaty that they need to get to Lanark but before they do, I want to leave a wee message for Malcolm who I hope is following us."

"What message is that, sir?" queried Tam, confused as he pushed the furniture against the door.

"I met a chap in Berwick a few years ago, he was from Norway. A big blond-haired fucker called Lars. He had a huge golden beard and stank of fish, the rank bastard. He told me about a ritual that the Vikings once used kill their enemies, send them to somewhere called Valhalla. I have no idea what that meant but the ritual sounded painful. I think our uncooperative friend in the hall may experience this soon."

"What about the monsters at the door? How are we going to get through them?" Sandy asked.

"We are not. Once my uncle and his daft friend are done, we will make our exit through the rear and out into the street. We need to head towards the town square and then try and avoid those bastards on the road to Lanark."

"I am starving, sir," said Tam, rubbing his belly. "Does your uncle have any food?"

"I never asked him. If he doesna, we can always run a quick raid on one of the other houses on the way out of town. My stomach is starting to rumble too and I fancy some wine."

"A flagon of wine would do nicely at this moment," interjected Sandy, "I am gasping for a drink."

"Concentrate on keeping us safe in here. I am hoping that we can leave soon. Keep an eye on that wee shite against the wall. If he moves, let me ken. I am going to see if our host will provide us with refreshments."

Striding back into the kitchen, Hamish could see the two noblemen sat at the sturdy table, still chatting to each other as if nothing was going on outside, ignoring the chaotic sounds from the creatures trying to get in. For a few seconds, red mist descended, anger briefly turned his face red, ready to explode at the pair who did not seem to notice what was going on. Subconsciously, Hamish began to tap his foot irritably on the stony floor, the noise echoing against the thinly constructed walls of the building.

"Oh, do stop that," grumbled James without looking up, "you are really annoying me. Go and find something useful to do."

Hamish snapped, patience starting to wear thin, "We dinna have time for this, it willna take long for those creatures to breach the barrier that Sandy and Tam are erecting. We need to be out of here and on the road to Lanark. If you pair could finish up, I will take care of the intruder when we are back in the centre of Carnwath. I have a message to leave for someone who has been giving me trouble for years."

"Pray tell, nephew, who has annoyed you so much that in even the gravest and most dangerous of times, you need to leave something for them?"

"Yeth," chimed in Andrew, trying to support his friend, "who hath pithed you off tho much that we have to risk our liveth?"

"That is personal and not something I wish to share just now," Hamish stated cryptically. Although the feud with Malcolm was well known to those close to him, it was not something that he wanted anyone outside of their inner circle to know. It was bad enough the raid on the village was bungled without father finding out about the obsession for making Malcolm and Big Davie's lives hell. There was already too much suffering at the hands of the Douglas Clan, Hamish saw no point adding to it by bringing his da's wrath upon him.

"I understand," mocked Andrew, "we are jutht about ready to go. I would appreciate it if you could take care of your problemth quickly pleathe."

"Thank you, Andrew," said James, standing up and dusting himself down. "Now, let us not delay my young nephew any longer."

"I thuppose you are right. Call your men, Hamish, we should make our exit."

CHAPTER EIGHTEEN

LEAVESTAKING

It took a few minutes to drag the mutilated bodies away from the front of Sheena's house. Sweat flowed as they worked tirelessly in the warmth of the midday sun. The stench was unbearable as heat bloated the flesh, gases giving off fumes that made one turn green. Black clouds of flies gathered around the corpses, greedily sucking up the spilled blood.

Malcolm's stomach churned as he dragged each carcass away from the battle scene. The pain in his ankle had subsided after a prolonged rest during dinner. The additional strapping Morag added helped give better support, making it easier to put pressure upon it. Sharp jolts still shot through his leg each time that he missed a step, but the improvement had put a huge smile onto Malcolm's face.

It was nice to spend some time with Sheena; he had grown fond of her over the last few years. Although she had on occasion given him the cold shoulder, today nothing but warmth and care shone through. He suspected the gratefulness her daughter's return was the main cause of the change of heart. Malcolm could see fear and worry etch over her features as Morag told her that she was going off to find Rabbie. Sheena's kind face had turned from sorrow to disappointment upon learning that Malcolm would not be going with her daughter. It was something that Malcolm wished he could change after seeing the distress in both Morag and Sheena, but he had to stop Hamish Balliol before the man caused more hurt and death to the ones he loved.

The mood was slightly subdued as they trudged along the path that led out of the village, the blazing sun beat on perspiring scalps, slowing the already sluggish pace. Although he could tell that Morag was annoyed, she still walked beside him, helping to support the weight and keep his ankle from hurting too much. Donald was in the lead, talking to Jamie, who made it his mission to impart as much knowledge onto the young man before they split. Big Davie was just in front, chatting to the cheery priest, trying to keep the mood of the group light-hearted and away from the earlier tension that had developed between Donald and Patrick.

Malcolm's mind wandered to the image of his mother lying tied to the bed in her room. The infection, or something equally sinister raging inside, turned her into one of those beasts. Beautiful hair matted in blood with clumps fallen out, skin now a gaunt, wrinkled mess. The monster within thrashing about in the prison made for her by his enemy Hamish. A tear slithered down his cheek. Moving his head to hide it from Morag, Malcolm quickly wiped it with his sleeve, hoping that more would not follow. The squeeze of his hand indicated differently as she turned and smiled at him. Nodding back, he tried to keep his mind away from ghastly things, but it was proving difficult. Malcolm wanted to remain steadfast, keeping grief in check until he found somewhere private to let it all out.

Stay strong, Malcolm thought, willing himself, knowing that he needed to keep going and focused on getting to Carnwath to find and punish Hamish for his indiscretions. Aching to go with Morag to find her brother, Malcolm knew responsibility was to his mother and clan, a loyalty that he took very seriously, sometimes too much so.

The pit of Malcolm's stomach folded. The closer that they got to the main road, he knew he would not only be leaving Morag but his brother too, and the thought of not being there to protect them was frightening. Malcolm knew that they would have the best protection in Scotland with Big Davie by their side, despite that, guilt consumed about having to leave them to go on his revenge mission and remove the Balliol threat to his family. Feeling the squeeze of Morag's hand again, Malcolm focused, trying to put the impending separation to the back of his mind, instead taking in the stunning scenery beyond. Swooping meadows flowed into the glens, surrounded by a sheet of white daisies waving in the beautiful summer's breeze. Malcolm was lucky to have such amazing natural land around him. Years spent tending sheep and looking after the farm helped him appreciate it. He was further fortunate to build up a muscular frame due to all the heavy lifting of animals and tools required in farming. He was grateful to his parents for the privilege of growing up in the clean air of the countryside rather than the dirty hustle and bustle of a major town like Lanark.

It took another ten minutes to reach the main road that went past the village. The winding stone surface flowed naturally through Carnwath; it was rumoured to have been built in Roman times. Wear and tear recently showed on the route and ongoing repairs were often done by eager residents, which Malcolm could see in the distance. However, all that was left of them was half eaten corpses, strewn about the road, flies swarming to and fro looking for food. The intensity of recent events felt like they happened last week and not less than a day ago.

Stopping at the junction, Malcolm reluctantly removed his fingers from Morag's soft grip and the group tearfully said their goodbyes. Hugs passed between everyone with advice and best wishes given.

"Once you find Rabbie, head onto Lanark, wait for us at the Douglas clan house in the centre of town. If you get there first, tell our chief about what has happened in the village and the attack on ma by the Balliols. They canna be allowed to invade into our lands without consequence. Good luck on the journey, and, Morag, I hope that you find Rabbie."

"Thank you, Malcolm. I shall miss you for this short time that we are apart, but I ken we will meet in Lanark soon. Each minute that I am away from you will be too long in my heart." Leaning forward, lips pursed, she placed them gently on the side of Malcolm's cheek, her hand once more slipping into his and squeezing hard, a strength which showed Malcolm how much that she cared about him. "I will miss you," Morag finally said, tearing herself away from the comforting grip of his embrace, the warmth and love flowing between them before they parted company.

Malcolm watched Morag walk off, each movement of her hips mesmerising. His eyes followed in time with the sway of her curved bottom until she faded off into the distance, a memory now of his time with her until they met again in Lanark. He was tempted to run after her so that she would not leave him alone with nothing but his fond memories to occupy the rest of his journey.

"Are you going to spend all day standing there like a lovesick puppy?" asked Jamie, anxious to get moving. "You are starting to drool."

Snapping out of the elongated trance, Malcolm turned around to face his comrades to see the smile on Jamie's face. Patrick impatiently tapped his feet, looking nervously around, grasping a wooden cross, expecting an imminent attack. Both seemed anxious to be on the road again which made Malcolm feel guilty about delaying the departure.

"Come on then," Malcolm said reluctantly, "I want to get to Carnwath before dark. I dinna fancy facing those things again in the middle of the night."

Turning, the trio readied weapons and started trudging along the uneven road towards their destination and on the trail of Hamish Balliol.

The going was slow but the pace steady. Fortunately, they did not encounter anything along the route from Forth towards Carnwath. Corpses being greedily devoured by swarms of flies lay at points along the way. The stench was overwhelming, unbearable for the group really. Using their shirts to cover mouths in hope to prevent gagging was failing.

Malcolm's thoughts were almost singly taken up with regret, guilt ridden by abandoning Morag and being separated from her. Both Jamie and Patrick had tried to strike up conversations with him, but one-word answers and unintelligible grunts soon put them off and they walked a few yards ahead chatting to each other along the way.

"I keep hearing you mention the term Heathens," began Jamie, "pray tell, why do you believe they are so?"

"Can you not see the mark of the devil on them? It is clearly his work afoot."

"I must have missed that. From what I have seen, people get infected and die. Then, they come back to life as these monsters. I say come back to life but I have yet to see any life in those horrible creatures," Jamie replied.

"There is no life in them. Their soul is not pure. The devil has it."

Lowering his voice, Jamie said, "A bit of advice here, Father, I understand and ken where you are coming from, but I would not be so vocal about it near Malcolm. He has been through a lot with his ma and he needs support, not conflict. I ken you are a good man, Father, but I dinna want to see my cousin hurt."

"You are right, Jamie. Malcolm needs care and the Lord to guide him through this trying time, now more than ever. We all need the Lord to help us get to Lanark in one piece. I have a feeling it is not going to be an easy journey."

Conversation about religion continued between the pair as they walked into the village. Father Patrick and Jamie spent quite a bit of time arguing about what happened, Jamie believing that the creatures were as a result of some sort of infection gone wrong, whereas Father Patrick was insistent the monsters were demons sent to roam the land in the form of humans as a punishment for their Heathen ways. They were both interesting theories and Malcolm listened to each argument with intrigue.

Houses became more frequent on the road in as they traversed down the slight incline towards a sharp bend which Malcolm knew was the last corner before entering the centre of Carnwath. Malcolm used to love coming here as a child on the back of the cart with his da and Big Davie before they continued onto Peebles. They always stopped for a chat and some raspberries picked from a bush on the other end of town, although often, there was no filling Big Davie and a further visit to a local farmer was needed to satisfy the man's appetite. Malcolm smiled inwardly at the ribbing given to his friend for the amount of food he ate.

Davie spent most of his time in the village, living with his Uncle Peter after running away from his father Brian, who was a noble that stayed in Lanark. Big Davie hated the lifestyle of the rich and despised Lanark and its residents with a vengeance. After about the twentieth time escaping to his uncle's house, it was decided that Big Davie should live permanently in Carnwath. Davie integrated with the locals, heading out early most mornings to explore the village and countryside. Big Davie was at his happiest, playing in the burn or climbing trees looking to see if there were any eggs in the bird nests. The locals normally caught him and many a time Big Davie was scolded by one of the farmers and hauled back to his uncle on the back of a cart.

It was not long after Donald's accident when the two really became firm friends. With all the attention and fuss over Donald, Malcolm had to escape and soon found Big Davie, bored trying to see if he could hit a tree with a stone from the other side of the burn. Malcolm joined in with the game and they egged each other on, the rocks getting bigger until Big Davie missed and almost killed a poor rabbit wandering past. They quickly crossed over to check on it, but the sight of the pair frightened the creature into scarpering down a hole. It was from there that their comradery grew and Big Davie became a part of the family. Malcolm was gutted when Big Davie's da summoned him to battle at the same time as his father, more furious about having to look after Donald alone when they left.

Rounding the corner, they almost crashed into two men who were running away from a group of infected several yards behind. One man was short, yet stocky, with light brown hair, wearing a woollen shirt and leather trousers. Rugged features indicated that he was in his early thirties. The other was bald, taller than the first by six inches. Similarly dressed, though with a scar adorning the right cheek, he was roughly the same age as his partner.

Weapons brandished, the trio stood ready to meet the eight or nine Heathens that were in pursuit. Seeing that they had done so, the pair being chased turned and stood their ground, willing to fight now that the odds were even. The lead attacker was dragging a foot, blood dripping from its lips, signs of a recent feeding. Unfortunately, that last meal did not look as if it was enough, the beasts appeared to be in a constant state of hunger, even after a recent feed. With a final spurt, the Heathen lunged towards Jamie, teeth bared, arm stretched, ready to rip the flesh out of him. Jamie ducked under and stepped inside before slashing along the throat of the Heathen, blood cascaded like a waterfall. This proved fruitless as an attempted bite narrowly missed Jamie's wrist as he dodged back from ferocious fangs.

"This one is feisty," commented Jamie commented while avoiding the other hand as it tried to grab a hold of his wrist, "I wonder what has riled him up?"

"He has probably not had sex in a while." Malcolm laughed, coolly decapitating the Heathen, flicking droplets of blood from his sword. "I ken how that feels."

"There is nothing wrong with celibacy. It teaches discipline and respect. Big Davie would benefit from it," Patrick interjected while bashing through the skull of the creature that he was facing. Brain bits exploded through the hole the mace made.

Malcolm nearly tripped over with laughter as he narrowly avoided an infected trying to take a lump out of his leg. Steadying, he kicked it squarely in the nose then stomped on its head once it slumped to the ground. "Could you imagine Big Davie being celibate? You would have more chance of stopping the pope being Catholic than preventing the legend from fucking wenches."

"Hold on, you ken *the* Big Davie? The scourge of England himself?" the smaller stranger said in astonishment as he scurried out the way of an attack before cleaving at a Heathen with his axe.

"We all do. My name is Malcolm of the Clan Douglas. I come from the village of Forth."

"Pleased to meet you," said the wee chap, surveying the cluster of dead bodies strewn before them. "My name is Steven of the Clan Galbraith, my friends call me Wee Stevie."

"The pleasure is mine. What do your enemies call you?"

"Sir," Wee Stevie stated stone faced.

"Well, Wee Stevie, I will try and not call you sir then, friend. The priest is called Patrick and the other chap is my cousin Jamie."

"This giant of a man that I seem to be lumbered with is named John, he is from the Clan Wilson. We only met yesterday. We were both passing through town when people started turning into these strange monsters and we ended up fighting and running for our lives. We found somewhere to hole up overnight, but something has stirred up these beasts today and we were harried from our lodgings and have been trying to avoid these creatures since."

"Heathens," declared Father Patrick, "they are called Heathens. People who are not Catholic and have been rejected by Heaven and forced to roam the earth as punishment for their sins."

Malcolm watched bemused as Wee Stevie stood there and gave Patrick a look of disbelief. Admittedly, he was not sure either if the priest was correct or not. What Patrick said made a lot of sense, but if Malcolm was to believe, this would mean that his own ma was a Heathen and he refused to think that she was not anything but a good Catholic woman who had done her best for her husband and children. His theory was certainly something to explore further, it may be that he was onto something, but Malcolm was not sure what. Perhaps the Head of the church in Lanark would be able to put some clarity on it.

Weariness invading his voice, Jamie said, "I dinna ken about everyone else, but I could do with a rest and something to eat. Is there anywhere that you ken of that is safe and has some food and possibly ale?"

"We could try the local inn," John replied pensively. "My concern though is that there could be a few of these *things* inside."

"That sounds like a plan, I am sure that we can handle anything that we find."

"Right, if you could show us where it is, we will follow. I could do with resting my ankle for a bit," Malcolm stated with a sense of relief.

Keeping weapons drawn, the group followed their new friends into the village, alert in case of any rogue infected appeared, nerves still tingling after the previous encounters.

CHAPTER NINETEEN

DREAMS

The road to the north of the village was not as well travelled as the southern route. Villagers tended to go to Carnwath or Lanark rather than venture into Lothian or Falkirk. This was mainly due to keeping things within the clan. Although friendly with many other clans, they found most of the goods were purchased from Douglas members or neighbouring families within Lanarkshire such as the Wallaces.

It was with a heavy heart that Morag trudged along, each step harder at leaving the others behind. With everything that had happened, she felt closer than ever to Malcolm. The thought of bulging muscles, the cute way his eyebrows raised when disapproving of her actions kept Morag moving. As each moment passed, her pace slowed to match the sense of loss that was felt at the start of the journey. It was necessary though; the guilt was almost overwhelming, knowing that Rabbie had sacrificed everything to look for them. It hurt so badly, it was her fault and there was nothing to be done but look for him.

"Lass, I am worried about you," Big Davie said, interrupting her thoughts. "We have been walking for a couple of miles and you have not said a thing the whole way. The meadows are blooming with flowers, the bushes are bursting with berries, and you have not commented on any of it. You look like a lovesick wolf cub. If it was night time, I would not be surprised to see you howling at the moon."

"You are a fool, Big Davie!" Morag laughed, striding along faster now. "A loveable rogue but a fool, nonetheless. I am just lamenting over losing Malcolm, we have grown so much closer recently, I find myself missing him."

"I am sure that he is feeling just the same, but you have to remember that this was your decision and the slower that you walk, then the longer it will take for you to be reunited."

"Those are wise words, my friend. Will I tell the tales of Big Davie the Sage to add to the legend? The man who has more intelligence than the King of Scotland!"

"Will I ever be rid of these ridiculous tales? Everywhere that I go, some local who has never met me, who doesna ken who I am, tells over exaggerated stories of my so-called exploits. Most of them are made up. I am afraid that I canna live up to the myth that I have become. I am scared that if I do eventually meet the woman of my dreams, she will believe the lies that has been told about me and I will end up a lonely old man with no children to pass on my legacy to."

"You will find someone. Your true love will look past the fables and want to ken the real you. They willna care about what some peasant in Linlithgow is saying, they will only be interested in who you are, not who the public portrays you to be. You are an amazing man, David Douglas, you just need to find a way to cope with this silly legend or it is going to ruin your life."

"I guess you are right. Now look what you have done. Your moping has made me depressed. I think I need to run about in a field throwing flowers in the air declaring my love for some tavern wench."

"Can you not be serious for one minute?" Morag giggled, throwing a friendly punch in the side of his bicep.

The banter continued for a couple of miles, each quip improving her mood as they made better time along the route. The junction at the Calder Road came up and they bore left on the road towards Moderwell, continually watching for even the slightest sign that Rabbie had passed by. All the time they were talking, Donald spoke to himself, unnoticed by either Morag or Big Davie as they were too engrossed in their own conversation. It was only when Donald started spouting oaths and slowed down that Morag paid attention. By that time, it was too late as he slipped into a trance, standing frozen to the spot.

"Donald?" asked Morag, starting to panic. "Are you okay? Donald?" Morag's face went pale as no response came from his lips, which seemed to be uttering something unintelligible. Hurrying over, she shook Donald vigorously, trying to snap him out of the apparent catatonia. It was to no avail. Donald just stood there, remaining rigid, not responding to attempts to get his attention.

"He has descended into one of those daydreams that he goes into," Big Davie said concerned. "Malcolm told me about this. He can go for hours and nothing can bring him back to reality. I just wish that we had paid more attention to him. Try slapping him, hard."

A loud crack boomed as Morag struck Donald with as much force as she could muster, the noise reverberated around which made her fear that it would attract some of the infected milling about nearby. The blow was so mighty that he toppled over, falling sideways towards the stony ground. It was only the quick thinking of Big Davie that saved Donald from splitting his skull open on the unforgiving surface by diving and catching hold of him to cushion the impact.

"I am so sorry," whispered Morag, cheeks turning pale in shock at what had just transpired. "I never meant to do that to him."

"Remind me to never annoy you," said Big Davie as he settled Donald down on the ground. "If that doesna bring him out of his trance then nothing will. I fear the only thing that has happened is that he now has a scarlet face. Probably embarrassment at being knocked to the ground by a woman."

"Enough of that," warned Morag, chuckling along with the burly clansman's infectious humour, "or I will knock you to the floor next. That would soon ruin your reputation as a living legend."

"Does Malcolm ken how feisty you are? Because if he doesna, then he is in for a shock."

Morag laughed and threw a fallen acorn at him. "Wheesht, you leave Malcolm out of this, you big fool. This is between you and me, now get your fists up and prepare for a beating!"

"I relent to your superior skills, I yield to thee, fair maiden," Big Davie mocked, bowing to her.

Morag shook her head at the antics of the giant man, knowing that Big Davie making light of the situation was his way to try and ease the tension, make things seem less problematic than they actually were. She knew that this time the fun was short lived, as Donald's unexpected dreaming was going to cause them major issues, inevitably slowing them down.

"So, what are we going to do about him then? We canna leave him here," Morag asked, her mirth now back under control.

"Ideally, I would like to find a cart and pull him along in that, but I ken we willna find one out here. I guess that I must carry him to Moderwell with you being my eyes, ears, and protector. Are you able to protect The Legend or will I have to fight any foes whilst carrying your beloved's brother?"

"I can hold my own," replied Morag, brandishing the fireside poker menacingly, "I have gotten quite used to using this by now."

Big Davie chuckled, backing off. "All right, you will have my eye out with that. I will hoist Donald over my shoulder, and we will walk the rest of the way, hopefully he will wake up before too long."

"We will rest regularly, I willna have you collapsing with exhaustion, Big Davie. Even a living legend needs respite, I willna allow you to falter. I willna let you risk your life due to being too tired to fight. If I could share the burden, then I would, but Donald is too heavy for me. Unfortunately, I must rely on you, but we will get through this together. I am sorry to burden you with this."

"Ach, it is what it is. We must do what we have to in order to survive. It is not that long before we get to Moderwell, if we are lucky, we will arrive before dark. Luckily, it is summer and the evenings are long. Right, enough chatter, let us be on our way."

Standing over the slumped body of Donald, Big Davie hoisted him over his right shoulder, struggling with an axe in the other hand, before trudging along the stony road. The route was surrounded by heavily laden blackberry and raspberry bushes. Morag happily picked the best of the fruit and fed Big Davie as they walked. Davie stopped every once in a while, to move Donald onto the other side.

"You are unusually quiet," said Morag, trying to break the tension built up around them. "Are you alright?"

"I have not got time to talk, I have this big lump on my shoulder. I think Malcolm should stop Donald from getting second helpings at night, he has gotten a lot heavier over the last couple of years." Big Davie puffed.

"Do you need to rest? Your pace has slowed over the last few furlongs and you look tired," Morag asked, trying to stifle a chuckle whilst being serious.

"I will be fine," replied Big Davie, trying to hide the fact that he was struggling. "I could go on for miles yet. In fact, I may break into a jog at any time."

"Sometimes, I dinna ken if you are being silly or not," Morag scolded, her brow furrowing with concern at the well-being of her friend. "I would rather that we rested for a wee bit than you collapsing to the ground with exhaustion. I dinna fancy trying to carry you, Davie, I think I would break my back."

"I think we should stop soon then," Big Davie agreed, his face reddening even further due to the heat and exertion. "Malcolm will kill me if I dinna bring you back in one piece."

"I will scout ahead for somewhere shaded then. Once you are settled, I will find us some more fruit and refill our water pouches."

"Thank you. I honestly am very grateful for everything that you are doing for me. It is such a relief to have such a caring woman helping me out. Malcolm is a very lucky man."

"Och, wheesht," said Morag, her cheeks turning as red as the berries on the bush, "I am not doing anything that you would not do for me."

"No, you have gone beyond what any normal person would do, that makes you amazing in my eyes."

Morag turned and moved onward, carefully treading along the road, checking for an opening that may lead to a clearing or a small sheltered area just off the track, one that provided enough shade that would allow them to cool down and replenish their energy. The apples on a nearby tree looked tasty and she grabbed a few as she passed, picking up the loose fruit on the ground and only picking off low branches. She did not want to stay long, the area was too exposed, and a surprise attack would have them trapped.

This was so hard, Morag had to stay strong for the lads but the tiredness was setting in; there was nothing more tempting than wanting to laze about in the comfort of her own bed. The dense green foliage went on for a while, often intertwining with other shrubs growing beside, making passage through almost impossible, but the berry laden branches were high quality. Just as she was about to give up, Morag finally spotted a small well-trodden path that led into the heart of the shrubs. In the middle was a clearing that was shaded by a tall, overhanging oak, acorns still in full bloom on the branches. Relief washed over as she walked into the shaded area, looking forward to a few minutes rest.

Satisfied, Morag turned around and hurried to the main road, knowing that Big Davie was still struggling with the dreaming Donald. She soon caught up with the Lowlander who was almost on his knees with the exertion needed to haul Donald along. Face red, relief washed over him at the first sight of her.

"Please tell me that you have found somewhere," pleaded Big Davie dragging his feet along the path. "This is killing me, there are times that I wish we could have just left Donald to fend for himself."

"I ken you, Big Davie," replied Morag firmly, "you would not have abandoned him, nor me for that matter. Despite all the nonsense uttered about you, you still remain a good, kind-hearted, and humble man. I found a clearing about half a mile ahead. It is perfect to take a break at and it is shaded from the sun, so ideal for us to get some strength back and have some fruit."

Smiling, Big Davie nodded approval and the good news seemed to spur him on as each step taken was with a renewed vigour with the goal of some respite from the burden. Morag took the opportunity to replenish their supplies and opened up a small canvas sack that she carried, picking as much fruit as she could along the way.

It was about quarter of an hour later that the pair finally reached their resting place, Morag used an apple to spur Davie on, the big lump powering through exhaustion to get to their destination. Big Davie carefully removed Donald from atop his shoulder and propped him gently against the tree before flopping down on the ground next to it, letting out a long sigh of relief which was followed by a loud rumble as his stomach betrayed how hungry he was.

"Sit up," Morag demanded as she noticed Big Davie, lying spread-eagled, "you sound hungry, you will get a sore stomach if you eat whilst lying down. Have some of the fruit I have picked. It will help with the hunger."

Both Morag and Big Davie tucked into the selection of wild berries and apples. It was not long before the sack was emptied and both were lying on the grass, bellies full, letting the exhaustion seep away, as first Morag, then Big Davie, dozed off and fell into a light slumber.

CHAPTER TWENTY

THE CARRIAGE

✪

"For fuck sake, how exciting was that? I thought we were goners at one point!" Sandy exclaimed as the group ran out of the village and onto the road to Lanark.

Hamish chortled, thinking of the narrow escape that they had in the centre of Carnwath as the creatures closed in whilst they beavered, trying to make sure that Malcolm got the latest message. It was close at one point, they only just managed to get away without being pursued. It was luck more than anything, with Andrew finding a side street to bypass the gathering horde. Hamish hoped that the flood of the creatures in the main square would be enough to slow Malcolm down, giving enough time to sort out the business, and put his plans into motion in Lanark.

He knew that going there was risky, the Balliols were not popular, often treated with derision or challenged to fights by over-rowdy clansmen. This all came about due to their alliance with the English and the betrayal by the clan chiefs. Father had explained the reasons. It was not a lack of patriotism, far from it. Before all this happened, Hamish loved Scotland, the country he was born and grew up in. Unfortunately, he experienced first-hand the backstabbing Scottish nobles. Often the Balliols were put down and even made fun of by some of the more influential clans, which led to the separation from the alliance. The Balliols went on to lead the English insurgents, which before William Wallace came on the scene, had put John

Balliol on the throne of Scotland for a short time. That came to an abrupt end when Wallace led his rebellion and drove out a lot of their support, chasing them back over the border. He knew the Lowlands were vulnerable at the moment due to their campaign in Cumbria and Lancashire. The Balliols made the decision to strike at them before they returned and tried to drive them out of Scotland.

"I was more surprised than anything when that wee arse told us that he was part of the Douglas Clan," declared Hamish with hatred, "I was already going to gut him, I think Malcolm will be quite surprised with what I have actually done to him."

"You took an unnecethary risk," said Andrew, bent over with his hands on his hips, trying to get his breath back. "We could have been eaten or worse, killed by those monsterth."

"We were in no danger." Hamish laughed, clearly enjoying the discomfort of the plump nobleman. "The blood ensured that the monsters were not going to be interested in us and we got out of there before they got too close. In any case, there is nothing like a good afternoon run to get the heart racing. You should try it more; it would help with that fat belly that you are carrying."

"That ith an inthult, Hamish Balliol," blustered Andrew, taking offence to the flippancy shown by Hamish, "I am offended and demand an apology. You hath slighted my honour."

"I have merely stated the truth. You are tubby, pampered, and a very spoiled man. If you took more care of your money and spent less time frittering it on wine and whores, then maybe I would have a bit more respect for you. If it wasn't for Uncle James here, I would remove your cock and force you to eat it to save the prostitutes from having to suffer for much longer," Hamish replied, enjoying Andrew's anger building up.

"Thith is an outrage," spluttered Andrew, his cheeks turning a deep violet, "I will not stand for thith any longer. James, you need to do thomething about your uncouth nephew. He ith a disgrace!"

James interjected, seeing that this would not end well for his friend and the treaty between their clans. "Right. Calm it down, Hamish. Andrew is our friend and ally. You must show him the respect that he deserves. We need him and his clan in order for us to thrive against the English haters out there."

"Sorry, Uncle James, I just get frustrated when I see nobles hide behind their fortunes and it is soldiers like Sandy and Tam that fight their wars for them. I would like to see them with swords, doing what Sandy and Tam do. It would open their eyes to what we go through to keep them in their big houses. No offense, Andrew, I am sure that you are not like that."

"It ith fine," said Andrew, his composure starting to return. "I do understand your frustration. I do thit in my houthe and do a lot of work to enthure that there ith ath little fighting as possible but there are those in power who do not share my philosophieth and are alwayth looking to go to war."

"It is those idiots that I mean, Andrew. There are times that I just want to punch them in the throat. Anyway, this is not getting us anywhere, we need to be moving again," Hamish replied, warming slightly to the portly fellow.

"If it helpth any, I want to thee a united Scotland," said Andrew suddenly. "I want to thee thith hatred and divisiveness stop. I also want to thee us ceathe the hostilitieth with England. I guess I am an optimist but it would be nice not to have to worry about being attacked in your own houthe."

The statement from Andrew left Hamish stunned, he had always believed that nobles were abhorrent, loathsome creatures who just wanted to live off the depravity of the poor whilst they got richer. It surprised him to see one that held similar beliefs. Andrew was the first gentleman outside of the clan who had these views, even some of the elders were not as forward thinking. Maybe he should give him another chance, possibly find out more and see if the rest of the Bairds had similar thinking.

This revelation distracted Hamish and he found the others had readied themselves and started off, leaving him several yards behind. It did not take long to catch up and soon they left Carnwath and the surrounding hills as they walked along the road towards Lanark.

The route between Carnwath and Lanark was short, but well-used as the village served as place where visitors to Edinburgh, Linlithgow, Peebles, or even Berwick would pass through. The hamlet prospered with local markets bustling with shoppers. Taverns benefited from the plentiful coin spent by the weary travellers, grateful for a flagon of ale, some fresh fruit, or a hearty bowl of stew to give them strength and warmth during the rough Scottish winters.

After a couple of miles, they spotted the first wagon. The large carriage, covered in deep emerald cloth, was stopped. Its horse nowhere to be seen. Tooth marks on the straps told Hamish that the occupants would not be back and there was no further sign of them on the road ahead.

"Right, guys, prepare yourself," Hamish ordered, looking every bit the commander that his father had trusted him to be. "Sandy, you cover the rear, I dinna want any unpleasant surprises from behind. Tam, you are with me at the front. Keep your eyes peeled for any movement from the cart ahead and especially from the fields around us. I dinna want to be caught in some clever bastard's trap."

"What about us? What do you want Andrew and I to do?" asked James, deferring to the younger man.

"I want you to stay in the middle between us. You two are not armed and dinna have the fighting skills or experience that we have. It is safer for all if you stay between and let us protect you. The best way to help is to holler if you see something that we dinna spot. I have a bad feeling about this and I dinna want to be caught unawares."

Hamish and Tam strode warily towards the seemingly abandoned carriage, but not a sound could be heard and nothing stirred inside. Hamish felt very nervous; a niggling feeling told him that there was something nasty waiting.

Quickly searching around the wagon, nothing jumped out and everything looked to be in place. There did not seem to be anything untoward but Hamish could not get rid of that nagging itch, he was sure that he had missed an obvious sign but was unable to put a finger on what it was. Approaching the door to the abandoned cart, Hamish made some hand signals to Tam who just shrugged back at him.

"What? Why are you flapping your hands about?"

"Did you not learn anything from all those years in battle?" Hamish hissed with exasperation. "I was signalling that I will open the entrance and you stand ready to strike at anything that might attack us."

"Oh. That makes sense, I was wondering what all that was about."

"Just stand ready! If I die because of your actions, I am going to beat the fuck out of you! Do you understand that?" Hamish snapped in frustration.

"Yes, Hamish, sorry." Tam looked very confused at this statement but never said anything else as he knew that he would face further wrath from Hamish.

"Whoever you are, I ken you are inside. If you come out peacefully, I promise that no harm will come to you. If you continue to hide, we will come in and I will gut you from head to toe and end your pathetic existence. You have until the count of three."

There was no response from the potential occupant. Determination was set on Hamish's face, he was not going to be made a fool of. "ONE!"

The first number boomed out louder than he intended. It disturbed the unusually still afternoon which soon garnered disapproving looks from Andrew and James who stood a couple of hundred yards away. The carriage still held a deathly silence from within.

"TWO!"

The next was slightly quieter but it had the same effect. Tam shuddered at the chilling threat from his leader. Still, the wagon remained quiet.

"THREE!"

The wheels vibrated slightly; a faint squeak could be heard from the rusting spokes as there appeared to be movement within. Anger ignited at the audacity of being ignored, an irked Hamish decided that actions were needed. Walking up to the door, he booted it as hard as possible, watching as the barrier disintegrated with the force of the kick. Splinters sprayed everywhere, nearly piercing his skin. Hamish peered around the corner. The pungent smell of death invaded the nasal passages and he balked at the overwhelming stench that filled his lungs. Hacking to escape the taste, Hamish narrowly avoided throwing up his meagre lunch. Looking to his right, the source of the disgusting odour was rotting away. A blood-soaked body lay covered in a swarm of flies nipping around the decaying flesh. The constant buzzing starting to grate in his mind as he began to swat away the annoying insects. The sanguine fluid had both dried up, forming a sticky mess, and in other places, crusted on the flaking skin of the decaying corpse.

The elongated exhale of a hiss forced Hamish to spin around, his eyes searching for the source of the disturbance, ready to strike at whatever lay within. Nothing caught his immediate attention, causing him to relax slightly, thinking that it might be something under the carriage, possibly a snake or another animal that had wandered unknowingly looking for food or shelter. A sharp movement from a beneath a small sack tucked under the cushioned seat caused Hamish to flinch before squinting as he adjusted to the poor light. A flash of grey fur peeked out from underneath the cloth bringing a sigh of relief. It looked like a fox or possibly a squirrel foraging for food and not a potential flesh-eating threat.

Lightly stabbing the outside of the pouch with his sword, Hamish prodded and poked until another loud hiss came from inside and a large dark paw with razor sharp talons swiped out, trying to bat the metallic blade away. A cry of pain squealed from the creature and the limb was soon withdrawn, a large cut bleeding from the contact with the sharp weapon.

Not disheartened, Hamish eased his weapon in again, this time tapping it against the creaky, wooden floor of the carriage, hoping to move the animal towards the exit and away from him. Hamish was not happy to see it hurting. For all his hatred of his fellow man, he loved animals and often spent time out on his father's farm or in the stables grooming horses or milking the cows. It was for that reason that a smile crept across his face as a flash of fur sped past and through the space that he had created earlier, out into the rich countryside beyond. Although Hamish only caught a passing glance, his knowledge of wildlife told him that it was a wildcat which could often be found in the moors. Although fierce, they do not normally seek confrontation unless threatened. Hamish was glad it chose to run instead of standing and fighting.

Sad to have disturbed the feline's home, Hamish rummaged about underneath, finding a small bowl, promptly filling it with water from the skin on his belt and leaving it for the creature if it returned. There used to be a pussy that petered about the yard when he was a lad. They had developed a friendship over the years, Hamish had often smuggled out food or milk to keep his pet fed. He had fond memories of Murphy, who had passed away peacefully of old age a few years ago. It was amazing how similar Murphy was to this scared, wee creature.

Hamish smiled before exiting, keen to get back on the road and not delay their journey any further.

CHAPTER TWENTY-ONE

CARNBLOODBATH

Standing outside the entrance of Miller's Inn was Malcolm and the rest of the group as they prepared to enter the tavern. There was no sign of the Heathens at this end of the village as they all seem to have congregated further along the street.

Jamie stood to the left, his wiry frame caressing a short sword which he held ready for whatever might appear within. Malcolm held huge respect for Jamie due to the number of battles that he had fought in against the English. Although Jamie was the flagbearer, he did participate in the majority of fights with his weapon dispatching more than a few enemies. A lot of people mistook his small build for being an easy kill but his close combat skill soon had them rethinking their strategy, if they lived long enough to do so. Jamie's position in the clan meant that he spent a lot of time with Malcolm's father and William Wallace, the most feared warrior in Scotland, enabling him to pick up a lot of tactical knowledge which he had used to help them survive since these creatures started appearing.

Patrick stood to the right of Jamie, his simple brown tunic disguising the strength of the man underneath. A man whom Malcolm had grown to respect due to his passion and prowess in recent fights against those creatures. During sermons to the Forth congregation, which were told with the craft of a storyteller, he often left thinking about the words of wisdom emanating from the scholastic priest. Patrick worried him with the recent theory about the infected. His ma was a kind woman, she never done anything wrong in her life. A faithful wife, a loving mother, and a good Christian who went to church on a regular basis. Malcolm knew that she was not a bad person so could not understand why she would not pass peacefully to her eternal resting place.

On the other side stood the new members of their group. Wee Stevie. What the chap lacked in height, he made up for in personality. The dark humour and sarcasm had made him likeable and fun to be around. It was not often that you found someone who took the worst of life's circumstances and joked about it. Beside him stood the drier and sullener John Wilson. Older than Wee Stevie, John was an impressive looking man, his silver hair shone in the sun, highlighting his handsome features.

He knew they were out in the open too long and ran the risk of the infected picking up their scent and hunting them down. "Right," declared Malcolm, his sword raised ready for action, "open the door, Wee Stevie, we are going in."

"Are you sure? Would you not rather stay out here and offer yourself as food? I have some bread in my bag, give them a nice flagon of ale and they can have you for their dinner," asked Wee Stevie with a hint of mischief in his voice.

Malcolm laughed. "Aye, very good. Maybe we could offer John as dessert. On second thought, he doesna have enough meat on him for the infected to get a good meal. I do believe that the bloody door is patiently waiting for you to open it."

Holding the metal handle, Wee Steve tugged hard. A long hallway unfolded ahead with no sign of life within. There were a couple of rooms on either side with an exit at the far end. The silence and lack of blood indicated nothing was disturbed recently.

"We are clear inside," said Malcolm, "I am going in. Jamie, you come in behind me with Wee Stevie and John. Patrick, if you could guard the entrance whilst we check for any surprises. If any of the infected come close, shout up to us. Hopefully no one is in here and we can get some food."

"Will do," Patrick replied, keeping his eyes peeled up and down the street, continually scanning around. "The Lord will protect us from the evil that walks the village. We will be fine because we walk in the light."

Malcolm waited until everyone followed then approached the entrance to the first room immediately on the left. He grabbed the handle and carefully opened the door, revealing the kitchen area beyond. There was no sign of any life which made him exhale a huge sigh of relief. Motioning for Jamie to check for anything that they could salvage, Malcolm waited as he searched through the pantry within, pulling out some carrots, turnips, and other vegetables that had not spoiled, which he thrust into a sack and placed it at the exit, behind Patrick, before moving inside.

Entering the next area, the putrid smell of death immediately hit Malcolm's nostrils, almost overwhelming him as the bile sitting in the pit of his stomach began to rise, his eyes blurring with the sting of the salty tears.

"God please guide and protect us from the carnage we see. Please forgive the Satanic worshippers for carrying out their dastardly ritual in this village. Please cleanse the soul of all who bear witness to this most heinous of bloodbaths. These people are good, kind, and honest men and should never be subject to such depravity and evil."

Forcing his head down, Malcolm muttered a few words in prayer before looking back up, astonished at what lay before them.

John barged past to see what was ahead and stopped, staring upwards. "How did that ceiling hold five cows? Surely the weight should have collapsed it."

"It is a well-constructed building," stated Jamie, coming in behind them. "The carpenter used oak and has built it with considerable skill."

"How do you ken that?" asked John, curiously.

"My father is a carpenter. I used to spend many a day learning how to cut wood and what timbers were best for what job."

"So, what made you give it up and become a soldier?"

"I am still a carpenter. I just choose to fight for my clan and country. Scotland needs every able-bodied man it can find. When all of this is over, I will go back to my wife and daughter in Calder and spend the rest of my life carving wood."

Father Patrick interrupted their conversation, "I dinna think we should spend too much time in here. I can feel the taint of evil everywhere."

"What makes you think it is the devil's work?" asked Jamie.

152

"If you look at the positioning of the bovine. They are in the shape of a pentagram. If you look below, where their bellies have been slit, you can see a pentagram marked out in cow's blood on the floor. This coupled with dozens of dead, naked bodies makes me think it is the work of Satan. I saw similar things in Inverness."

"What do you suggest we do?"

"If we had the time and didna want to attract the attention, then I would suggest burning the place down, but considering our situation, I reckon we should shut this mess behind us and get out of this forsaken place as soon as possible.

"The stench is disgusting," stated Jamie said, struggling to breathe, "You are right, we do need to be on our way. No more messing about, we need to find Hamish. John, can you grab the sack of food on the way out? We will make our way to the village square and see if there are any signs of the bloodthirsty Balliol."

"That sounds like a plan," replied Malcolm, the colour now starting to return to his face before closing the door and exiting the tavern, the others close behind.

The streets were empty apart from the random, distended corpse that was left decomposing outside a house or slumped atop a cart. Often there was a Heathen munching down on the plentiful food, a sight that still revolted. Unfortunately, there did not seem to be many survivors left in Carnwath as most of the population were either dead or had fled in fear.

Approaching the central square a few hundred yards away, they could see something odd, human shaped, attached to the column that indicated the start of the market. It was normally a popular event in the local area with farmers, blacksmiths, and local tradesmen all selling wares so that they could help feed their families and the rest of the village. Traders came from all over and his da used to set up a table there, selling off woollen clothes his ma had knitted.

Malcolm sighed, an exhale of sadness escaped, suspecting she turned into one of the monsters and lay on the bed thrashing away. He hoped they could find something that would cure her of the disease. Patrick wanted to send the soul back to the depths of Hell, to end the misery, but there was some life in that creature. Maybe it was more hope than anything, even blind faith, but he did cling on to it, knowing that acceptance of her passing would eventually lead to a break down and that was dangerous in the current environment. Shutting this to the back of his mind to block the pain, Malcolm trudged on, listening to the gentle banter of Wee Stevie talking about life in the various towns and villages of Scotland during his travels.

"Have you visited Edinburgh at all, Malcolm?" asked Wee Stevie, suddenly thrusting the conversation in Malcolm's direction.

Pensive, stroking his chin, Malcolm replied, "No, I have not. It is something I have always wanted to do. I often dream of exploring Scotland and seeing our beautiful country. Spending life on the road, sleeping in random inns or in fields whilst talking to different people. Since da left the village, I felt so trapped there. Especially with having to look after Donald."

"Sweet Jesus! What the actual fuck is that?" Jamie stopped unexpectedly, pointing ahead.

The others came to an abrupt halt beside him, colour evaporating from their faces. Patrick had dropped to his knees and was fervently praying whilst crossing himself, openly weeping on the ground. John stood hunched over, heaving the remains of his stomach over the stone surface. The thick, yellow vomit mingled with dirt, sludging down the slope towards the horror that unfolded before them.

Staring at the column, Malcolm could see a man attached to it, his eyes deep ruby, a deathly pallor replacing the normal vigour of life. His chest carved open with ribs hacked away, bent backwards underneath outstretched arms, a pair of ivory wings swaying in the breeze. The most disturbing part was the sight of spongy lungs draped over the shoulders and all the other organs hanging like a demented sculpture. It was one of the most harrowing things any of them had ever seen. Malcolm did not know how this abomination was able to move at all, never mind thrash about and snarl at their approach. On the ground below, marked in blood, was an arrowing pointing ahead and the initials *HB* under it.

"A blood eagle," whispered Wee Stevie in disgust. "Never in my lifetime did I ever think that I would see one of these. I thought that this practice stopped when the Vikings left Scotland."

"What the fuck? How do you even ken about this? It is fucking disgusting. How anyone could do this to their fellow man is beyond me!" Malcolm exclaimed.

"I learned of this from a friend that I met in Edinburgh," Wee Stevie replied despondently. "She is what Patrick here would call a Heathen, one of the few Scandinavians left who still believe in the old

Norse Gods and study their ways. Most of the Scandinavians have abandoned the old ways and have turned over to Christianity. Anja, who told me all this, said that the practice of the blood eagle was a ritual reserved for highest of nobles, it is an honour and used to punish them for their crimes. It is rarely used and one of the most heinous practices that the old Vikings performed. Ah, the memories, I wonder if Anja is still alive?"

"Stop reminiscing. What else did this Anna say?"

"Anja," corrected Wee Stevie. "Her name is Anja Jacobsen and she came over to Scotland from her homeland of Denmark with her father and sister. We used to spend many nights drinking and she told me many tales of the ways of the Vikings and the Norse gods. Seemingly this ritual is a sacrifice to the Norse god Odin. It was normally sent as a message to the other nobles that they too were subject to the laws as were the peasants. They are a strange people, the Vikings, but filled with honour. I miss my evenings with Anja, she was a nice lassie who had a good heart. I hope to God that she alive."

"I am assuming that Hamish has done this," replied Malcolm with worry etched over his face. "Where would he ken about this?"

"The initials HB indicate that this is the work of your nemesis," said Jamie, who was on one knee, using the sword to support his balance, head bowed to avoid seeing the horrific sight. "I can only assume that he must have met a Scandinavian who knew of the old ways that Wee Stevie has described. The message here is clear though, the arrow points to Lanark, Hamish is heading there for whatever reason. We had better hurry and hope that he has not caused too much chaos by the time we get there."

"I agree," replied Malcolm, still trying to avoid looking at the man on the column. "We need to get out of Carnwath as soon as possible, there have been sights here that will haunt my dreams for nights to come. I dinna want to see much more of this forsaken village."

"Right, everyone! Form up and dinna look at this disgusting slaughter. We need to get out of here immediately. Malcolm and Wee Stevie, if you take the front, you both have better vision than the rest of us and I dinna want any surprises. John, if you go behind them, myself and Patrick will protect the rear. Let us make haste and get as far away from this evil as we can," Jamie ordered with a renewed vehemence.

With that, the group got into their positions and walked towards the other end of town and onwards to Lanark.

CHAPTER TWENTY-TWO

THE LEGEND

A loud purring vibrated through the woods. What was seemingly the low growl of a bear permeated, waking Morag from a peaceful slumber. Having slept long enough for a crust to form over her eyes, Morag gave them a gentle rub, only further blurring her vision. The sharp glare of the midday sun forced Morag to throw an arm up as a shield. Taking a few more seconds to adjust and fully regain sight, stretching and moving joints stiff from the leisurely nap upon the downy grass, while casually surveying the surroundings, a deep yawn enveloped her.

Having never moved since being placed by the tree, Donald remained oblivious and trapped in his trance. Frustrated with the extra burden during an already tumultuous time, Morag was dismayed that Malcolm and his mother had concealed what was an obvious, serious problem with Donald. The full extent to which was only just revealed to she and Big Davie. It was hard not to be empathetic for the young lad, and now having first-hand experience, she did feel sorry for Malcolm's responsibility to find ways to snap his brother out of his own head. It was discouraging for all involved.

Trying to push aside the growing aggravation towards Malcolm for putting her and Davie into this situation by instructing Donald to journey with them, looking over at the slumbering giant, Morag could *feel* his throbbing snores. His massive chest heaved to the rhythm of the thunderous rumbles, harmonising with the incessant noise of the infected monstrosities. Curiously, it was almost hypnotic, tuneful in a strange way Davie and the surrounding Heathens grunting in unison. When they settled down for a snooze earlier, there was no sound of the creatures, only a pervasive, eerie silence. That could only mean one thing...

Snapping out of it, Morag shouted in panic, "Wake up, Big Davie! Those things are all around us!"

"Urrghhhh," mumbled Big Davie, slowly regaining consciousness, "yes, I would love to, lass but I dinna bend that way."

"*Davie!*" her voice high pitched with fright. "*Wake up!* Please!"

"Morag? Is that you? Where am I?"

Unable to wait any longer, Morag grabbed the water skin from her belt and threw the liquid over Big Davie's face.

"What the fuck! I am bloody soaking now, why the hell did you do that?"

"Listen," replied Morag, her fear abating. "Can you hear that?"

"I can hear those creatures. They have been groaning for a while; you should be used to them by now."

"No," insisted Morag, "when we stopped here for a break, there was nothing, it was quiet and there was not even the sound of an animal. When I woke up, all I could hear was you snoring and the moaning of the Heathens. Do you not get it? We are about to have company."

"Oh shit!" Big Davie jumped to his feet, brushing off the small seeds and leaves that had stuck to his breeches. "Arm yourself, lass, get ready to fight."

"What about Donald? Malcolm will kill us if we let anything happen to him."

"Donald is safe whilst I am alive. I willna let those monsters lay one finger on him. It does mean that we canna flee, we need to stand and fight. Get that poker of yours ready, lass, I have a feeling that you may need it."

"Big Davie, you are an amazing man. One thing that you have shown me during all of this, is that you dinna abandon your friends. Throughout this entire nightmare, you have protected everyone, whether they deserved it or not. A legend does not make a man, but the actions of that person defines the legend. You are famous because of who you are, Big Davie and everyone loves you for that."

"Morag, will you stop with this romantic nonsense and get ready. We are about to be attacked by God kens how many Heathens and you are standing here blubbering away. This willna save Donald and willna keep us alive. The only thing that *will* is us standing here and fighting for our lives. There is nothing more I would like to do than pick up Donald and run as fast as I can out of here, but we both ken that we would not get far before getting overwhelmed. This is a good place to defend ourselves, but if things do get bad, you need to run as fast as you can and head straight for Moderwell. You can get some help there and possibly an escort to Lanark."

Fiercely, Morag replied, "I willna leave you. We have been through too much."

"You may not have a choice."

Morag turned to give Big Davie a dry look, in doing so, out of the corner of her eye, she saw a shape emerge from the tree behind him, the familiar shuffling indicated that this was not friendly. Raising her poker, Morag called out, "Davie, watch out!"

Spinning, the large clansman turned to face the incoming aggressor. Sidestepping the lunging figure, Big Davie swung the axe, lopping off its head.

Morag watched as the crown rolled, teeth still grinding, before coming to a stop just a couple of yards beside Donald's slumped form. Gracefully striding over, Morag thrust the poker through the cranium, grimacing as grey-pink brains gushed out, matting the auburn hair.

"That is why I train every day." Big Davie laughed. "All the hours cursing my da as he rapped me on each part of my body that I left exposed. The welts, bruises, and pain that I suffered as he taught me how to fight. That is what kept me alive. Admittedly, your shout helped, but without the sparring, I would have been a goner there."

Another shambler emerged from behind the gloating clansman, inwardly Morag groaned in frustration. Big Davie was too busy self-congratulating and showing off to notice the threats. If this continued, she would be facing these creatures on her own. "Davie! There is another one. Stop boasting and concentrate or you are going to get us both killed!"

Big Davie looked to his right and dodged to narrowly avoid another Heathen who had decided to try and get a bite. Snarling with anger, he moved with the grace and speed of a cat, huge fist exploding into the face of his attacker, knocking it back against the unforgiving trunk of an elm. Davie followed through by stamping down and crushing the skull, twisting and grinding down to ensure that there was no chance of it getting back up.

"Will you stop shouting? You will bring more of these things down on us. I can handle one at a time, but if they attack in any sort of number, then we may be in trouble," Davie asked calmly.

Annoyance building, Morag replied, "Davie, you need to stop posing. One of those monsters is going to surprise you. I will stop shouting if you focus on what is going on around us."

"Understood." Big Davie nodded with concentration. Knowing that this would annoy Morag, he mockingly stood with one hand flat along his forehead and slowly spun round in circle, pretending to look out for threats.

"You are a total fool, you ken what I mean. Stop larking about." Morag giggled.

"Yes, ma'am," replied Big Davie, trying to keep a straight face. "Sorry, ma..... Morag, duck."

Instead of doing as instructed, Morag swivelled to face what had appeared. A blood-soaked pair of gnashers chattered at her from a few feet away. Taking a step back to gather momentum, Morag thrust forward with all her might to meet the creature head on. She skewered the solid iron rod through the left eye socket before using a leg to kick out, the force driving it into the mud, bodily fluids oozing and soaking through the soil.

Sweating profusely, Morag looked down worriedly at the remains of the body. A wave of relief washed over, the carelessness Big Davie lectured about was hypocritical as the same scenario almost unfolded in front of her. How could she be so tardy? The day-dreaming has almost resulted in death, the banter had distracted her to the point that they were both in danger. This needed to end before disaster struck. Putting the antics of the oversized fool to the back of her mind, Morag adopted a fighting stance, surveyed around the clearing, concentrating, trying to spot any movement, hoping that there would be no more incursions but the surrounding moaning told her otherwise.

"Morag, you need to concentrate more. If you dinna focus, you are going to get us both killed!" Big Davie said with amusement.

"That is not funny. They are getting here a bit too frequently. We both need to be more careful." Spotting movement, Morag pointed to the far end of the clearing to some rustling bushes. It could have been the wind but something in the pit of her stomach said otherwise. "I think we have more arriving. Davie, if you could check it out, I will stay near Donald." A worried look furrowed across her brow.

"I see them. Fuck, they are coming in their droves. Six of them, no seven…. eight…. Get ready, lass, this could get messy."

Infected appeared through all gaps in the forest, each one different. A large man dressed in overalls was the first to approach. It stood no chance as Davie swung his much-used axe towards the thing that had once been a farmer, the rough hands and tufts of wool caught on his leg confirmed this conclusion.

The aim was not quite true as the monster moved at the last minute, causing Big Davie to bury the blade deep into the top of its bicep, removing the limb clean, scarlet fluid spraying from the severed stub onto his chest. The force of the strike pushed it back into a nearby gorse bush.

Morag chuckled as she watched it struggle to escape its entanglement from the awkward shrub, the grey limbs flapping uncontrollably in the foliage. She was in awe at the speed of Big Davie. No sooner than he dealt with the farmer, a plump lady appeared. Wearing a blue and white checked apron, discoloured through age, a volume of gore stained the majority of it. Her once tousled, mousy hair was now a matted, tangled mess. Morag could imagine her standing over a cooking pot, similar to what Granny used to do on cold winter nights, mixing together a fat rabbit with vegetables. These monsters used to be people, men and women who had children, lived full lives, like her grandmother did. Now they were reduced to this. It was not fair on anyone, to finish your existence as a mindless bloodthirsty monster. The vision was soon disturbed as Big Davie decapitated it. The matron's head flew a few yards before becoming tangled up in the twigs of an overhanging branch above.

Pulling concentration away from her battle partner, Morag avoided the outstretched root of the oak that Donald was leaning against, placing herself in front of the stupored Douglas brother. Poker outstretched, she stood just ready in time for the next Heathen to attack. Stepping deftly to the side, avoiding a vulgar attempt to grab her, Morag drove the iron rod between the eyes of the strapping young lad. It was not much taller than her which made it easier to strike the killing blow. It looked strong, the sort of man that she might have fallen for if Malcolm was not in the picture. Thinking of these creatures as people had to stop. There was no chance of lasting long if she hesitated, even once. She chose to survive, deciding that it was more important to fight than become one of the infected. She was not certain if Patrick's theory was true, but not much else fit. These creatures seemed to have some sort of disease inside them that was passed on through biting others. Where this sickness originated, she was unsure, but Patrick's theory could also be correct. What if they were rejected souls sent back to their bodies due to their being no room in the afterlife? What if this was the battle between good and evil being fought out before them? What if this was the beginning of the end for them all?

Morag had little time to think as the next Heathen was a few yards away, but she sneaked a glance back towards Big Davie who was occupied with several of the creatures surrounding him. She was amazed at how he managed to fight multiple foes at once whilst avoiding being bit. She could see why he was the subject of all those rumours, today would just add to it. When they got to Lanark, she knew Malcolm would want to hear about the battle and then various versions of the story would make the rounds, each more ridiculous than the next. It was the just adding to the legend which would give the villagers hope in the days to come against the Heathen menace.

"Go, Big Davie!" shouted Morag in encouragement as another head went flying from the deadly axe blade of the Legend. "Try not to let them surround you."

"Aye! How about you fight all of these and see if you can avoid being surrounded instead of standing there watching?"

"I am guarding Donald," replied Morag, in earnest as she faced the next Heathen. "I have killed one already and am about to face another. I may not be the desire of every man in Scotland, but I am doing my best, Big Davie and you had better not forget it!"

"Sorry!" Big Davie loudly dodged another attempt to bite him, this time it was a small boy that was nipping at his heels. Big Davie's large boot extended out, sending the lad over the head of an incoming assailant as it landed several feet away, skidding along, narrowly avoiding the small beech to the left.

"I am in awe!" called out Morag as she blocked the lethargic lunge from an opponent with the metallic spike, leaving her neck open to the foul teeth of the Heathen as it bore down, hunger highlighted in the grey, bloodshot eyes. Shock almost rooted her to the spot, but the sight of the ugly beast forced her to leap back, before driving the poker through the side of its cheek. The mucous membrane leaked out of the Heathen's ear as it collapsed to the ground, spasming during the final throes of death.

"Nice move," encouraged Big Davie as three of the infected converged at once, a fist bursting through the skull of the first one as the curved wedge cleaved off the top of the second attacker's head. However, there was no avoiding the third Heathen as it sank its teeth into Big Davie's thick thigh, ripping a chunk of flesh out, feasting on the gigantic walking meal.

"*Aarrgghh*!" roared Big Davie in agony, as pain shot through the leg and up into his body. "One of those bastards bit me!"

"Oh no! I am so sorry, Davie, are you going to turn into one of those beasts?"

"I dinna bloody well ken that!" Big Davie screamed, hopping on one leg whilst blindly swinging his axe in all directions, hoping that some luck would come whilst the initial extremity of the pain subsided. "It just ripped a whack out of my leg. Now the bastard is munching on it like a raw chunk of beef."

"I hope not. You are scary enough alive, never mind as one of those creatures." Morag skewered another one of the Heathens, a teenage girl, a few inches smaller than her, its lack of height not diminishing any of the ferocity. "How bad is the pain?"

"It is like someone has booted me in the bollocks." Blood freely flowed from the wound, staining his kilt. "I am going to fucking kill the bloody lot of them!"

It was as if a blood lust had come over the burly Scotsman as numerous limbs suddenly went flying. Morag lost count of how many Heathens destroyed as the rage overcame him, twirling and thrusting with the metallic extension of his arm, with each strike swiftly ending the existence of the foes around. Big Davie's fury turned him into a monster, a beast created by the wrath anger as the desire for revenge and hurt took precedence with each fatal blow destroying anything in his path.

Morag dispatched the last of her enemies and turned to help the berserk warrior. Weakening from blood loss and exhaustion, Big Davie stumbled towards the tangled gorse bush where numerous infected had become trapped. Screaming, Morag was too late to get to him. Numerous hands shot out, grabbing his calves, pulling him to the ground like a lumberjack felling an oak in the forest.

Within seconds, the remaining Heathens swarmed atop Big Davie, ripping into his flesh, feasting on his body as the stunned Scotsman was unable to stop the remaining half-dozen from sinking their teeth into his arteries. A loch of blood formed alongside his dying body, the axe still swinging as he lay on the ground, screaming in both agony and defiance as he tried to kill as many as possible before his eventual demise.

Crying and stunned, Morag dispatched the remaining infected as Big Davie was now sprawled out, barely moving, pain etched across his face, trying to stop the inevitable tears from stinging his already gashed cheek. Rushing over, Morag held his hand, cries morphed to screams as Big Davie desperately tried to hold in his intestines, feebly attempting to halt them from spilling onto the filthy ground.

"You are not going to die!" Morag screamed defiantly. "I will bandage the wounds, they will heal."

"Get a grip, lass! I dinna have much time. My insides are leaking out and it willna be long before I go. I need you to do something for me," Big Davie replied weakly.

"What is it, Davie? Anything you want, I will do it." Morag sobbed, grip tightening on his fingers.

"I have a few things. Do them for me Morag, I need your promise," Big Davie answered, voice becoming hoarse.

"I swear on the life of my mother and my sister Mhairi."

Breathing laboured, Big Davie began, "First of all, when I die, dinna let me turn. I dinna want to become one of those things, stick that wee poker of yours through my head."

"I can do that."

"Secondly, dinna blame yourself or Donald for this. I chose to die this way, there was nothing that either of you could do about it. Try and wake that lummox up, you need him awake more than ever now."

"I dinna blame either of us."

"Good girl," he whispered, barely managing a weak grin. "Thirdly, you must get to Lanark as quickly as possible. I want to see you safe. You must move with haste."

"I will move with as much haste as we can."

"Fourthly," Big Davie was now spluttering blood as he spoke, "dinna let people forget me, but try to stop this stupid legend from getting out of control. I just hope that my death will finally quell this nonsense."

"I hate the legend as much as you do." Morag could not bear much more, she could feel his grip loosening.

"Finally," gasped Big Davie, his eyes starting to glaze over, "tell Mhairi that I love her."

With his last words ringing in her ears, Big Davie took a final breath and lay still. Morag atop, the grief inescapable. She cried for what seemed like hours, pounding his chest, hoping for a miracle, praying that he would breathe again, until she gave up and slumped over the corpse, feeling very much alone.

CHAPTER TWENTY-THREE

LANARK

The sloping, emerald hills levelled as they journeyed along the final part of the road to Lanark. Hamish was tiring slightly as a long and stressful day and the continual chatter from Andrew played on his already frayed temper. Sandy walked ahead with James, an amiable and relaxed conversation occurred between the two. It was almost as if they had known each other for years. What they were saying was beyond comprehension as every time their voices raised, he still was unable to make out what was being talked about due to Andrew's constant moaning. He wished that James would allow him to remove the head of the annoying man. Behind, Tam kept a vigilant watch, always on the lookout for trouble whether it be from the infected or one of the crazed Lowlanders, who did not seem to like the Balliols.

"I thay, old chap," said Andrew, trying to strike up yet another conversation with Hamish, "ith it going to be much longer? My feet are killing me."

"Not far now," replied Hamish, keeping an interested tone with the man, despite finding him tedious, "less than a mile."

"Oh goody! I look forward to a nice hot meal and a good nightth thleep. Do you have anywhere to thtay in Lanark?"

"I am not normally welcome in Lanark," Hamish said ruefully. "Lanark is under Bruce rule and our clans are not the best of friends these days after the recent conflicts."

"That is a shame," Andrew replied with genuine regret. "You must thtay at mine. We have plenty of roomth at the Baird Clanhouse. You would be a most welcome guest."

"That is a most generous offer, but I could not put you out of your way, what about my men? Where would they sleep?"

"They could thtay with the other tholdiers," replied Andrew, clapping his hands with glee. "It ith thettled then. You will thleep with me tonight."

Hamish forced a fake smile across his lips, hoping that Andrew would not spot the disdain. Hamish tried to bond with Andrew, but the little things irked an already fragile patience. His continual, pointless babble was frustrating. All this discussion about the weather was stupid, there was only so long one person could talk about the heatwave. Hamish's eyes glazed when Andrew tried to engage him about daisies or other flowers. He would have gotten on reasonably well with the chap if it was not for the fact that he was so pretentious.

After a few minutes, the small party could see the large barrier that surrounded the beautiful town of Lanark. Gothic architecture was plentiful. The long spire of St Kentigern's Church swept upwards, surrounded by the grey, flying buttress, decorated with intricate carvings of religious symbols. Stood to either side of the arched entranceway were two stone gargoyles, faces fierce and menacing, meant to ward off the evil spirits.

The wall was erected after the town was looted several times by invaders. Entry could only be gained via one of the four gates located at each compass point of the settlement. Two knights stood on guard in shiny metallic suits, ready for unwelcomed guests. Adorning their chest was a huge breastplate with the Bruce coat of arms, indicating loyalty to that clan. Two tall, spiked pikes were held in their right hands with small buckler shields being displayed in the other. As impressive as they looked, Hamish knew that is would not take much for him to breach their armour, at one of the numerous weak points, with his sword.

"Halt!" yelled guard one, his fiery hair peeking from under his helmet. "Who goes there? Friend or foe?"

"If we were your enemy, we would have killed you by now," Hamish whispered. "What a pair of idiots."

"Good day, thirth," Andrew answered, taking the lead. "I am Andrew Baird, nobleman of the Clan Baird. I am here on Clan business and the fine men are my escort during what are very troublesome timeth."

"Very good, sir," replied the guard, looking bored. "Can I see your papers please."

"Paperth!" spluttered Andrew in frustration. "One doeth not need to show any documentation to peathants like you. What ith your name? Who ith your thuperior? I will not be treated in thith manner. You are lucky that my man doeth not run you through. I am most offended."

"Sorry, sir. I am sure you understand that these are trying times. There is no need to get the commander involved, you may pass through. Please accept my humblest apologies."

"Before we do," began Hamish curiously, "please tell us what has been going on in the town. We have seen a lot of horrific acts over the last day. Carnwath has been overrun with the infected. How fairs Lanark?"

"Aye, well," answered the other guard, looking a bit embarrassed, "I think we have coped a bit better than most places. Most of that is due to Robert the Bruce making some sensible decisions. We managed to herd all the walking corpses out of the town and have trapped them in a sheep pen to the south of the city. We lost a few good men in doing so but it was better than losing the whole town. It was an ingenious plan, we put a couple of freshly killed bodies on the back of a cart drove it round Lanark, the monsters all followed it out of the gate and away from Lanark. The Bruce felt it was better to have them all in one space away from everyone than a slaughter inside the walls. Our garrison went around killing any of the stragglers and we have been very careful in policing the rest of the place. Our numbers are high and any resident is aware that they have to let us ken if anyone dies or looks to have this sickness. We then remove them from the town, making Lanark a safe place."

"That is brilliant," answered Hamish, his brain already devising possible ways to use this to his advantage. "So, Lanark is a safe town."

"From what I have seen, no place is safe, it was chaos here for a bit. It took the brains of The Bruce and the hard work of everyone here to get the place safe again. Admittedly, we still have a lot of work to do. The streets smell quite a bit, with the decaying bodies and puddles of urine from folk that were too scared to do anything else, but we are getting there. The people are removing the corpses, one at a time, and burning them outside to try and reduce the stench and get rid of the swarms of blood-thirsty flies, all whilst we contain the problem and stop the creation of more of these things."

"You have done brilliantly to make Lanark a haven," Hamish replied, trying to sound impressed, the scheming still going on in his head. "Where do you burn the bodies?"

"We keep the South Gate permanently open and guarded, which allows the residents to carry out the dead and burn them in the glens. The wind blows away from the town, so the stomach-churning odour does not blow back and make the streets unbearable to walk in. I am seeing more citizens walking about as life starts to get back to normal after the devastation."

"You have done a great service to the town," Hamish stated, thinking of the holes in their plan. "Each one of you should be proud of what you have achieved. Good day to you both, keep up the good work."

The group set off on their way along the cobbled streets of Lanark. The irregular stone made it hard going. Hamish found himself stumbling a few times, almost falling onto the unforgiving surface below. A few curses escaped his lips as they traipsed through the streets, passing sturdy, grey buildings. This, coupled with the slight incline in the road as they travelled north, caused the sweat to drip from their already reddening foreheads. Calves started to ache with the extra exertion used to climb towards their destination.

"My legs are killing me," complained Tam as they walked up another hill, the late afternoon sun beating down on him, eyes stinging from the salt in the sweat that had rolled into them. "How much longer to your Clan House?"

"Not long now, just round the next bend and it ith the large building at the end of the thtreet," Andrew replied, the chirpiness still evident in his tone.

"Thank fuck for that. I'm exhausted, I look forward to finding a good tavern and the company of a wench for the night."

"Tam," scolded James, his patience wearing thin with the continual complaining from the soldier, "you are in the company of nobles, please act that way and stop the cursing."

"Sorry, Mr. Douglas. I forget my station."

Despite the continual griping from Tam, they soon reached the building where the Baird Clan lived. It was a huge house that dwarfed the rest of the dwellings. The family crest emblazoned on an oversized banner, draped over dour grey masonry, covering the ugly walls. Beside it was a smaller residency, which again had the Baird colours adorned on it.

Hamish ordered, "Sandy, Tam, if you pair go to the barracks there, you can get a bed and some food from the quartermaster. Tell them that you are with Andrew and you will be fine. There is a tavern to the rear of the barracks, it is called The Freedom Arms, I will meet you there later, I have some business to take care of first in the clan house with Andrew and James."

"Yes, sir," said Sandy and Tam in harmony.

The door was answered by a burly lowlander, sword hanging deliberately by his side, showing the menace and unfriendliness that he meant to portray. This was not normal which worried Hamish, who was wondering what could have happened within.

"Halt!" demanded the Baird Guard, his flaming orange beard enhanced the ferocity. "Nobody is to enter by the order of Gordon Baird, leader of the Clan in Lanark."

"I am thure that I am an exception to thith rule," ordered Andrew, staring defiantly into the emerald eyes of the man. "Do you know who I am?"

"I dinna care who you are, there are no exceptions."

"I think you should go back inside and thpeak to Gordon and tell him that hith brother Andrew is thtood out here, hot and tired, whilst you treat me no better than the lowest peasant. I am thure that he will not be pleased that you hath disrespected me."

"Erm," stammered the Baird Guard, hesitantly. "He did say that in no uncertain terms, that I was to let anyone in."

"Well, do not dawdle, go and get my brother, I am thure that he will be delighted to thee me. What are you waiting for? Toddle on."

The man turned and disappeared back into the house, slamming the door behind him.

A scowl formed over Andrew's face as he turned beetroot with anger. "What a bastard. He ith not allowed to treat me like that. I will thee him flogged for thuch insubordination. I am fuming here. How dare he talk to me like that! I will not be treated thith poorly."

"Calm down, my friend," said James, trying to stop Andrew from exploding, "you are not achieving anything by ranting away in the street. I am sure that there must be a reasonable explanation to why Gordon has done this. Give him a chance to explain, there is more to all of this than meets the eye.

Inwardly, Hamish was chuckling, he loved to watch nobles being treated like dirt. It served him right, Hamish knew that Andrew had flogged his servants, much like most of the irresponsible upper class of Scottish society, it was something that he wanted eradicated. Hamish hated people being punished for doing their job. Hamish had seen first-hand the injuries that the upper-class administered on their poorer workers. Stripes down the back of a young woman's back for not polishing the silverware properly or bones broken in the beatings that cooks had endured for taking too long to make feasts for the over-indulged guests of the pompous idiots that swanned around looking for free feeds. Hamish got himself into trouble for dishing out the same punishment to the so-called lairds and ladies of Scotland, it earned him a few lashes, but it was worth it to see the agony on the faces of the spoiled rich folk.

Andrew's cheeks reduced to a deep scarlet colour, his previous anger had calmed considerably by the time the door had swung open and they were met instead by a smaller, blond-haired chap, well-groomed with no facial hair, which was normal for a nobleman. His features were similar to Andrew's, they had the same sharp nose and profound forehead. It was obvious that they were related.

"Andrew!" shouted the fellow in the hallway, striding over to give him a huge hug. "It has been far too long, brother. What brings you to Lanark?"

"Oh, you know, the usual," replied Andrew contritely. "Thex, drink, and betting on peasantth fighting."

"Seriously?" Gordon laughed as he removed his arms from around Andrew. "With all that is going on here, you are here to party?"

"No, you thilly dolt, we are here on a therious matter, one that I am not willing to discuss in public. Can we come in?"

171

"Of course. Come in, I will get rooms ready for you and cook to prepare some food. I am now intrigued."

CHAPTER TWENTY-FOUR

ALONE

A few seconds passed before Morag finally rose, looking over the sad sight of her fallen friend. Gripping the poker, she deliberated over whether to drive it through his head. It was the last wish of a dying man, but Morag found her arm refusing to respond. Big Davie looked so peaceful, it felt wrong thrusting the iron rod into his head and what if she did not have the strength to do it properly? *No.* Morag decided it was better to stand and watch. If there were any sign of movement, then action would be taken, but not before then. She felt so guilty for not fulfilling his wishes, but the serene look on his face was one which would be etched in her memory forever. A lot nicer than looking at brains oozing out his forehead.

It must have been five minutes of crouching before she decided that he was not coming back to life. A sense of relief washed over her and the iron rod dropped to the ground, clanging a few times like a church bell ringing on the Sabbath. Surveying the clearing, Morag saw carnage everywhere. Bodies were strewn in bushes and there was even one hanging over a tree branch. *This must be what a battlefield looked like*, Morag thought. Big Davie had done quite a thorough job dispatching the monstrosities.

Guilt plagued her soul. Davie's demise kept replaying, burning the horror into her brain. She should have done more, instead she stood there, taunting and teasing as he fought off dozens of the Heathens whilst she struggled to face the odd one or two. The bravery of the man was told in stories throughout the land, she vowed never to let these rumours die. Everyone had to know how courageous and humble a person he became. The tales never told of his kindness or generosity. Morag vowed to rectify this. Big Davie was meant to have a legacy that was deserving of the true hero of Scotland.

Thoughts of Mhairi came to mind. Morag knew that her sister was smitten with Big Davie. Now she had the unenviable task of having to break this devastating news to her. The hurt would be irreparable in the short term, but in time she would move on. The struggle was bad enough for Morag, but to put Mhairi through it as well was not going to be easy. Then there was Malcolm, poor sweet, kind Malcolm. *How do I tell the most important person in my life that his childhood playmate died whilst defending me as his brother sat, daydreaming, unaware of what was going on? How do I tell him that as I stood there, fending off a few foes, Big Davie was taking on a horde whilst Donald sat there, dreaming, unable to prevent the death of his dearest friend? How do I explain this to Malcolm without putting any blame or hatred onto his brother?* This was one hell of a fucked-up situation and she was not sure how to properly relay it.

Donald was still there but not there, breathing slightly laboured, for some reason. Severed heads were strewn about him, staring blankly back, oblivious to all that had unfolded. Anger boiled towards the man, no boy, who did nothing, who was unable to do anything. Morag knew Donald had issues but was not aware of how bad they were. Malcolm hid it all very well. Anytime she asked if Donald was alright, he avoided the subject, kept saying Donald was tired or ill. That did not wash, but upsetting Malcolm was the last thing Morag wanted to do, so there was no further probing on the matter. That was a decision she now regretted as Donald sat there, as useful as a lame horse. Fury welled up inside, at Malcolm who said nothing, and at herself for being so naive. She missed all the signs. It all made sense now. The times Malcolm could not see her due to an issue on the farm and the frequency their evening was cut short due to an emergency or Malcolm not wanting to stay out too late. Now she knew why. Beating herself up about it would do no good. Morag decided she was going to do something to wake him or it could be the last thing either of them would do.

Striding over, she could hear his low, babbling nonsense, head bobbing in intensity. Determined and at her wits end, Morag tentatively kicked his leg, then stood back waiting for a response.

When none came, it riled her a wee bit more and she lashed out again, this time with as much strength as possible. Again it was to no avail.

You utter bastard, thought Morag, blows now raining in as she continued her tirade of trying to wake the slumbering laddie. *How fucking dare you leave me to deal with this on my own? How fucking dare you sit there whilst I have to deal with all this shit? How fucking dare you sit there and do nothing, fucking nothing, when I am standing there trying to keep you alive? Big Davie died to keep us safe, do you get that, he fucking died for you and you are just sitting there. I hate you so much right now!*

With emotion getting the better of her, Morag struck out with the back of her hand connecting with the side of Donald's face. An almighty slap rang in the air, like the crack of a whip, but even that did not disturb him.

Frustrated, Morag kicked out at a small stone, sending it in the air and ricocheting off Donald's forehead, leaving a small red mark where it landed. Still nothing from Donald.

Storming off around the clearing, Morag almost missed the rustling of the leaves to the left and it was probably luck, more than anything, which made her swerve to one side to avoid a lone Heathen who wandered into thicket. *Fuck, it was probably all that noise I made that attracted it. Shit, where's that bloody poker I had? Och aye, I dropped it beside Big Davie, I am going to need it.*

Moving swiftly, trying to keep the creature away from Donald, she was not going to let all that effort keeping him alive go to waste. Morag snatched up the iron rod, nearly losing balance in the process. It took a few paces to regain composure as she turned to face the unwelcome intruder.

"I have had enough of you vile creatures killing my friends! I hate you all!"

With venom, Morag launched at the advancing shambler, eyes blazing as she brought the poker down with tremendous force, through the fleshy part of the cheek. Her momentum sent the Heathen to the ground with Morag atop it, stabbing furiously into the head until it finally stopped moving.

Morag removed herself from the corpse and brushed off the dust from her tunic before marching back over to Donald. With these attacks obviously the clearing was no longer safe. It would not be long before more dead arrived and the next time could be the last for them both. As much as Donald and his trances annoyed her, it would not be fair to leave him there. Morag loved Malcolm too much to abandon his brother. She felt guilty for leaving Big Davie's body like that, without a proper burial or memorial, but being selfless could cost them their lives, especially the way Donald was. Donald needed to move soon, this was ridiculous. Making the decision to try and wake Donald one last time, she pulled out her waterskin and threw it over the slumbering lad, hoping it would disturb him but unfortunately it failed to do so.

Accepting the inevitable, Morag wondered how Donald could be moved. There was certainly a height disparity by a good foot over her small frame, and a weight differential too. Morag suspected there was more than one bowl of porridge eaten by Donald in the morning. Taking a drink of the remaining water in her skin, Morag tried to heave Donald upwards to a standing position, using the tree trunk as leverage, until she finally managed to prop him against the large oak. Remembering how Big Davie supported him, Morag grabbed Donald's arm and thrust it over her shoulder until the weight was not too much of a burden and she could hold some semblance of balance.

"Bloody hell, Donald! You are one heavy bastard. I dinna ken how I am going to get you to Moderwell, but I will try. You better wake up soon. I really, really hate you just now and I may beat the hell out of you soon if you do come out of your slumber."

Taking a step tentatively forward, Morag moved Donald with her, concentrating on trying not to fall and taking things slowly. The poker now in her bag, she used a large branch as a makeshift walking stick. Luckily it was a sturdy piece of wood as she relied on it more as the journey progressed. The going was rough, and a couple of times they fell over, collapsing in a heap. It was a struggle to get back up, but sheer stubbornness pushed her onwards. An hour later they exited the woodland and were back onto the road to Moderwell. Morag was not sure what kept her going, probably a combination of anger, willpower, and determination. The random mumbling from Donald did not help as each time words were uttered, an urge to punch his teeth out was almost too tempting to resist. However, there was only so far that rage could take them. Exhaustion set in. Morag was not sure how much longer she could keep going and began to look for somewhere to recoup, cursing at Donald the whole way, occasionally aiming a sideways kick at him in frustration.

Spotting a small muddy path ahead, she made the decision to drag Donald up there, spotting a dense cluster of bushes within. A few minutes rest could not hurt. A chance to eat, grab some water, and possibly even relieve herself was too hard to resist. Thinking about water was not a great idea, soon Morag was crossing her legs which almost caused her to trip and fall.

"Donald Douglas!" screamed Morag in frustration, close to his face, "For fuck sake, wake up! I am sick of dragging your fat, hairy arse to Moderwell! End my suffering, you filthy piece of cow shit! Do something worthwhile and wake up!"

Despite her shouting at him, there was still no response. His face completely blank, like the morning sky with on a clear day. Morag was close to breaking point, tired, hungry and annoyed, more at Malcolm than anyone.

Fuck it, the need to urinate was more important than anything. Calming down, she took the time to roughly deposit Donald on the ground, propping him up against a bush before rushing behind a tree and peeing.

Quickly, she returned and flopped down beside Donald, wincing at the pain in her feet. It was a long day, a lot happened, and she had no idea what to do next. The thought was to head to Moderwell in the hope of finding her brother, but with no guarantee that Donald would come back, she honestly did not know how much further his dead weight could be dragged. A cart or a barrow would help, but there was no chance of finding one out here. Tired, the fight to keep her eyes open was a battle that even William Wallace could not win, an utterly exhausted Morag passed into a slumber.

CHAPTER TWENTY-FIVE

DISTURBANCES

The horrors of Carnwath spurred the group to leave the godforsaken town immediately. Jamie was keen to get them on the road again and arrive in Lanark as soon as possible. Nobody disagreed as the thought of spending a night there was not something any of them wanted.

Unfortunately, the sun had set and yet again, they were making a trip to a potentially dangerous place in the dark, a prospect that Malcolm was not looking forward to. The harrowing sights of Carnwath still played in his mind. The slew of bodies strewn across the tavern and the bloke who was 'Blood Eagled' as Wee Stevie had called it. He did not understand how anyone could do this to a fellow Scotsman and the sight of the dead man turned his stomach. Hamish Balliol was going to pay for each one of his indiscretions, he had made too many people suffer. It had to end. These mindless murders had to stop, no matter what the cost. If he did not kill the traitor, then there would a lot more devastation and Malcolm did not want that playing on his conscience.

"You seem distracted," said Father Patrick, walking beside him. "How is the leg?"

Snapping back to his senses, Malcolm turned to speak to the priest. "Ignore me, Father, I am just lamenting on what we just witnessed in Carnwath. I didna realise there were so many evil people in this world. The leg is fine, thank you. There are still twinges of pain, but the strapping Morag put on has really helped."

"I saw far too much evil in the world on my travels, but I never seen anything as bad as Carnwath. I wish there was more we could have done."

"Father, what more could we have done? In the pub, everyone was dead, there was nothing but death and blood. Apart from setting the place alight, what else could we have done? As for the town square, that was clearly Hamish and he is on his way to Lanark. The best thing we can do is get there and stop him."

"I never really knew Hamish, he rarely frequented the church. What is he like?"

"I think it was safe to say that we never really got on. Hamish used to tease myself and the other kids for being peasants and always turned his nose up at us. Big Davie hated him for that. A few times Hamish and his loathsome friends would get one of us on our own and start to beat up on us, but Big Davie would find out about it and we went and taught him a lesson or two. I feel ashamed, but I always used to deliver a couple of extra kicks to the snivelling toad, mainly to show him that not all peasants were weak. It was in vain as it never stopped him. He hated me more than Davie, but then again, there are very few people in the world who dinna like Davie, you canna help but love his antics and easy-going attitude."

"Dinna chastise yourself, lad," replied Father Patrick, pensively. "You were young and although I dinna condone violence, sometimes it is needed to teach the correct lesson."

The once sombre mood improved the more distance put between themselves and Carnwath. Patrick had stopped his fervent praying and Wee Stevie was bantering with John. Jamie remained quiet at the front of the group, he was busy concentrating on the route ahead. Malcolm brought up the rear, withdrawing himself from the rest of the party, missing Morag, regretting the decision to leave her. The gentle tone of her voice, the small giggle which escaped whenever she found something funny, and most of all, the soft touch from her warm, delicate hands entered his thoughts, causing the pace to slow. He did not notice the rest of the group had disappeared around a corner a few hundred yards ahead. Subconsciously, he kicked out at a loose stone lying in his path and continued to strike out at it as he rounded the bend. Each time contact was made, Malcolm winced with regret, cursing his stupidity at not using the other foot.

Ahead stood the large, metal entrance gate, surrounded by the imposing town wall of Lanark. Two guards were standing, deep in discussion, engrossed in whatever that they were talking about. Still lost in thought, Malcolm failed to notice the others a fair distance ahead.

"Malky," shouted Jamie, impatient at the tardiness, "will you hurry up, we have not got all day. I am exhausted and parched. Move your arse!"

Quickly, Malcolm snapped back to reality, shaking off his tiredness with a quick stretch of his limbs. A renewed spark appeared in his step, as for the first time, he saw the entrance to Lanark. He hurried to catch up with the others.

Joining the rest of the group, they approached the gate and were met by the guards who had finished their heated discussion. Dressed in the Bruce colours, their magnificent breastplate shone in the twinkle of the moonlit sky.

"Hark, who goes there? State your name and business!"

"Oh, for fuck sake, put that sword down before you stab yourself, Stewart. Have you not learned to use that bloody thing by now?" Jamie exclaimed in frustration.

"Jamie Fucking Douglas," mused Stewart in surprise, "is it not the Flagbearer of the Douglas Clan army? Have you lost your wee piece of cloth?"

"Piss off, you idiot. Are you going to just stand there or let us inside? There is a ale with my name on it and you are stopping us from getting acquainted."

"Lucky you," grumbled Alisdair. "We are on duty all night; Stewart here thinks that it going to be a cold one. Where is that big lump Davie? Usually, you pair are joined at the hip."

"Ach, has he not arrived yet? I was hoping that he would get here before us. If you see him, tell him to meet us at the Clan House. Ask him not to stop for any wenches on the way."

"Haha," said Alisdair, smirking. "That will be bloody right. I have more chance of finding a chest of gold pieces than Big Davie not stopping to shag a wench. Get yourself inside and if I see the big lump, then I will tell him where you are."

"Thank you, my friend. Keep an eye out for the Balliols, those miscreants are out to cause my cousin here a lot of trouble."

"I will keep extra watch for those slimy worms." Alisdair spat in disgust. "They have caused both of our clans enough problems, especially that traitor, King John."

"What is it like inside?" asked Malcolm, conscious of the threat that they had just escaped.

"We have cleared the streets," replied Alisdair. "There are none of those creatures in Lanark anymore. Robert the Bruce ordered everyone inside whilst the soldiers led those creatures out of the South Gate and into the glens. For all I ken, they are still wandering out there."

"You are an idiot. They are all holed up in a field, the gate is locked and there is no way through for them. We are quite safe in here." Stewart laughed.

"That is good to ken. I look forward to a good night's sleep for a change," Malcolm stated, relieved.

"Aye, lucky you. Stop rubbing it in. We're not getting relieved until dawn."

"Peace be with you," declared Father Patrick as they passed through the gate, "may the Lord look after you this night."

"Bless you, Father. May God be with you."

The streets were remarkably quiet, considering the normal hustle and bustle that accompanied a busy market town. Usually at this time of the evening the traders were packing up their stalls and heading home after a day of selling their wares in the main square of the settlement. However, all that the group could see was overturned carts and pools of blood splattered everywhere. There were no sign of any corpses littering and stinking up the road. Malcolm was impressed by the efficiency of the local guard and the great job that they had done removing the putrid carcasses.

The odd person was seen peeking out behind their shutters, but apart from that, there was not much sign of life. The taverns they passed were open for business, but there was not the usual noise inside. The eerie silence quickened their step which reduced the time to reach the Douglas Clanhouse at the southern end of town.

The entrance to the building was a large oak door with the clan crest displayed below the massive iron knocker. Answering the repeated banging, a guardsman, who upon recognizing Jamie, ushered them through a hallway and into a reception area where a small table was flanked by two benches. The walls were adorned with draping tapestries depicting famous Douglas Clan members over the ears. The centrepiece of the collection was William Wallace, his imposing features highlighted on the skilfully woven material.

"Do you think that Big Davie will be hanging there beside William Wallace?" asked Malcolm with curiosity. "His legend is growing and soon his feats will outstrip the achievements of our former leader."

"Probably," replied Jamie. "You do ken that it is his da that is in charge here?"

"Really?" asked Malcolm in shock. "I ken that father spent a lot of time in Lanark, but he never really spoke about the rest of the clan and Davie never said anything about his parents."

"They dinna get on well at all. I think that his da wanted Davie to be a nobleman, but the big fool was more interested in fighting and going to battle with the rest of the clan. His natural size and fighting prowess led him to the bed of many a pretty lady in town. Our large friend soon got bored in Lanark and William Wallace was only too eager to have him in his army, much to the annoyance of Brian. Your da spent a lot of time brokering the peace between Brian and the scourge of the English, who promised Brian that he would keep an eye on his son on the battlefield. In return, Brian promised that he would not summon you or Donald until you were ready. It turns out that Brian didna need to make that promise as Big Davie was more than capable than looking after himself. I believe that it was your da who started the Legend of Big Davie to annoy Brian, but he will never admit to that."

"Hopefully Brian will be able to tell us if he has any news of where my da is," Malcolm replied with worry.

"I am sure that he will be fine. He is a clever and strong man, he can more than take care of himself. You have nothing to be concerned about."

"Thanks, Jamie, you are a good friend."

"Brian Douglas will be here shortly," announced the guard, interrupting the discussion. "He has been made aware of your arrival."

"Thank you, we eagerly await his presence," Jamie said.

After a few minutes, a rotund man strode in, his auburn hair had mainly aged to a sparkling silver with patches of baldness adorning the crown of his head. Wearing a well-groomed suit, he looked every bit the noble that he was.

"Welcome, fellow clan members," declared the bloke, puffing out his chest. "My name is Brian Douglas and I am Laird of the Douglas Clan in Lanark. We have plenty of space here, my staff are preparing rooms for you. I hope that Joe, my personal guardsman, has been looking after you."

"Yes, he has," Malcolm piped up, watching Brian's left eyebrow raise with curiosity. "I apologise for our ungainly state, it is quite wild out there outside of Lanark."

"No need to apologise," Brian said warmly as he glided over to Malcolm. Extending a hand, he clasped Malcolm's and shook it. "I dinna believe that I have made your acquaintance."

"I am sorry. That is most rude of me. My name is Malcolm Douglas, son of Cameron Douglas from the village of Forth. I believe you have already met my cousin Jamie. The small, offensive looking man is Wee Stevie Galbraith from the city of Edinburgh. The balding chap beside him is John Wilson, also from Edinburgh, and the priest is Father Patrick Murphy who preaches at our local church in Forth," Malcolm said sheepishly.

"What a curiously odd group of people you have assembled, young Malcolm," Brian mused. "Pray tell, the last that I saw of young Jamie, he was on his way to Forth with my rascal of a son David. I was expecting to see David with you, but to my surprise, there is no sign of him. What tavern did you leave him in?"

A chorus of laughter erupted from the group, easing the tension that had formed after meeting the senior Douglas for the first time. Malcolm noticed their host guffawing at his own joke with the rest of them joining in.

"If Big Davie had his way, it would be every tavern." Malcolm laughed. "Your son is not with us. He left Forth with my brother Donald and our friend Morag to help find her brother Rabbie. They were on the road to Moderwell, we are expecting them to join us soon. In fact, we thought that they might have arrived before us."

"It is a shame, I would have liked to have seen my son in the flesh, to know that he is safe," Brian replied with a hint of regret.

"I ken that feeling," muttered Malcolm. "Have you heard any news of my da?"

"Ah yes, your father, Cameron Douglas. Now let me see. The last I heard, he was in England trying to take as much territory as they could. I have not heard any news since all this nonsense started. I have sent a couple of riders, but they have not returned as of yet. I am as eager to know where they are as that force contains a good portion of the Douglas army."

"I was hoping for better news," stated Malcolm despondently. "If you do hear anything whilst I am in Lanark, please let me ken. I am desperate to ken what has happened to him."

"I understand that, young man. If I do hear anything, I will tell you. Now on to more pressing matters, why are you here? I am eager to hear about your journey."

"This could take some time," Jamie interrupted, "we have been travelling for most of the day. Do you have any food prepared? I am not sure about the rest of my friends, but I am absolutely famished."

Murmurs of agreement came from the others. A small grin appeared on Brian's face before he summoned over Joe, the guard. After a brief conversation, Joe hurried out of the room.

"Of course." Brian smiled, keeping the warmth in his voice, "You must be thirsty too. If you follow me, we can go through to the main hall. Joe has just left to ask Cook to prepare a small feast in your honour, with wine and ale to wash down the fine food."

"That is too much. A plate of stew and a tankard of water would suffice, we dinna want to put you to any trouble," Malcolm said humbly.

"Nonsense!" boomed Brian defiantly. "Any son of Cameron Douglas is a welcome guest in our house and shall be treated with the same respect and hospitality that your mother and father would show to us. I willna take no for an answer. Come, let us get you lads fed. I am eager to hear your tales."

Soon the group were relaxing in the dining area, sitting around a giant table filled with chicken, beef, and all sorts of vegetables. Each of their tankards was filled with ale, the snowy froth spilling over the side, looking teasingly at Malcolm who was parched after a hard day in the sun. Flagons of wine were prevalent, and after a few minutes, the rest of the clan joined them. Malcolm was keen to keep his wits about him and stuck to drinking water after the first tankard. The feast and heavy drinking continued long into early hours of the morning, when most finally staggered off to their beds.

CHAPTER TWENTY-SIX

AWAKENING

The final strikes were made and the arduous battle finally ended. Donald surveyed the carnage. Bodies lay scattered on the field from one end to the other, with both sides having taken heavy casualties. Limbs and heads were separated from the carved-up corpses as Donald shook himself down, trying to get rid of the pain of the numerous wounds received by the blades of the English Army. A deep fatigue was starting to set in, and although there were not many survivors left in the Douglas Army, he could see Big Davie and few others looking bedraggled, hands on hips, trying to catch their breath.

"Davie!" yelled Donald, frantically. "Over here!" Donald jumped up and down for several minutes, but Big Davie did not respond. It was strange as Davie always had near perfect hearing. Concerned, he walked towards the large legend but for every step taken, Big Davie got further away. Frustrated, Donald broke into a run, but the faster he got, the more Big Davie faded until ultimately vanishing into thin air.

"That is weird," thought Donald aloud, as he came to a halt, "I could have sworn that Big Davie was there a minute ago."

"Me too," said a voice from behind. "He just seemed to disappear, almost as if he ceased to exist."

Spinning around, Donald turned to face whoever had just spoken but there was no-one there. There was nothing apart from lots of corpses lying strewn in front of him.

"Who said that?" Frantically Donald swung his head side to side, trying to catch a glimpse of the commenter, but once more, there was no sign of life.

"This is getting stranger and stranger," said Donald, scratching the top of his head. "First Big Davie disappearing and now I am hearing strange voices. I wonder if I am going mad?"

"You are not going mad," replied another person. This time, Donald could swear that it was the voice of a woman, one about the same age as he. There was a familiarity about it, almost recognisable. In fact, it sounded like someone that he knew very well.

"Mhairi, is that you?" Donald called out, expecting to see nobody. Yet there, in front of him, was the unmistakable sight of Mhairi Douglas, Morag's sister. Naked, without a stitch on, milky white skin shined in the midday sun, full breasts highlighting her fantastic figure. Donald could do nothing but stare at the perky pink nipples that stood at attention. His arousal becoming more obvious.

"Erm," Donald muttered with embarrassment, head dropping feet becoming the focal point after realizing that he stared at her bosom for too long. "Are you not cold standing there like that?"

"Cold?" queried Mhairi with a puzzle look upon her face. "I am standing here naked, ready for you, Donald Douglas, and you ask if I am cold. I have needs, I have wants. Ravage me now, Donald!"

Oh my, thought Donald, unsure of what to do next. *What if she doesna like me? What if I am not good enough?*

"I like you, Donald." Mhairi smiled, arms opened wide, inviting. "You will be good enough, now take off your clothes. I want to see your muscles."

Stripping quickly, Donald stood nude in front of her, penis proudly standing at attention in anticipation. With a reassuring grin, Mhairi strode towards him, stepping over the decaying corpses. Without hesitation, she grasped his member, causing a shudder to escape him.

"Do you like that?" Mhairi asked, gently moving her hand up and down with an exaggerated flair as she reached its base. Gasping, Donald leaned forward and held one of her full breasts, carefully caressing around the mound before pressing down and flicking each nipple which resulted in Mhairi gripping and tugging with her fingers more vigorously. Continuing to play with her tits, Donald arched forward, nibbling on her lips before embracing them into a full kiss, feeling a tongue enter his mouth, exploring, all the while rhythmically masturbating him. Passion grew with each passing moment, not knowing how much longer he could hold it in.

Closing his eyes, the anticipation built as he let out a small groan. Pleasure coursed through his heightened body, ready for the next stage, knowing that this was finally it. There were one or two girls he had canoodled, but none had engaged in the act of love making. Donald was ready to finally lose his virginity.

Fully awake now, the scene changed. Instead of lying on a battlefield, he was sprawled against a tree. The sun had just peeked over the horizon, the shadow of the oak providing some respite from the heat. Intertwined with his body was Morag, and surprisingly, her pair of small breasts were being fondled by his overeager hands. Massaging away, Donald was unable to stop them. A pair of lips moved up a bare shoulder, blocking the view of the naked form ahead and engulfed his, a tongue thrust inside, exploring within.

The shock of it all was too much. Why was it Morag kissing him and not Mhairi? *This was surely a nightmare, where did she go? Why was Morag lying there, her beautiful hair matted with a combination of dried blood and dirt? What am I doing here? Why am I kissing Morag? Morag is Malcolm's girlfriend, not mine!* Yet her point sat soft, tender between his forefinger and thumb, a moan escaped as more pressure was placed on it. *Why am I continuing to fondle her?* Donald could not understand why he did not stop. Her silky mouth moved around as she raked fingernails up and down his biceps. Donald gasped in pleasure.

Unexpectedly, her eyes shot open and lovely, deep irises gazed upon him. A look of horror flashed across her face. Before Donald knew it, his cheek was stinging after a loud crack reverberated from her outstretched palm.

"Remove your hand from my breast now, Donald Douglas!" Morag ordered with a dangerous tone, one that Donald had never heard before.

Quickly removing his other hand from her chest, Donald looked embarrassed as Morag's murderous glare cut like a butcher's knife carving through a shank of beef. Carefully, they disentangled themselves and Morag stood up, still looking disapprovingly at him.

"I am sorry, Morag," Donald stammered, backing off slowly, "I dinna ken what came over me there. I didna realise that it was you until it was too late."

"Donald, I am glad to see you back to normal," said Morag flatly, "but if I ever catch you groping me again, I will put my poker through your bollocks. Do you understand me?"

"Yes, Morag," muttered Donald, in shock at her ferocity. "It willna happen again. One minute I was with Mhairi and the next..."

"Hold on," Morag interrupted, her temper starting to spiral, "I am out here killing Heathens and protecting you from certain death whilst you are in dreamland, fantasising about having your wicked way with my sister?"

"Erm, well, I am truly sorry. I dinna ken why I go into these trances, but I am sorry that I have caused you distress. I didna mean to disrespect you or your sister. Oh dear, I feel so embarrassed, I hope that one day you will forgive me."

"Of course, I will forgive you," replied Morag, softening, "I was just taken aback by your actions. It was a traumatic time when you were away."

"What happened?" asked Donald, confused. "And where is Big Davie? I dinna see the big lug anywhere."

"It is my turn to be sorry. Big Davie is no longer with us."

"I can see that. What happened?"

"We got ambushed by a large group of the infected. There was just simply too many for him to fend off and they ripped him to pieces, killing him outright. He did kill most of his attackers before dying. He was a brave man, Donald, one of the best."

"Did you remove his head afterwards, to stop him coming back as a Heathen?"

"No, I never," replied Morag, thinking, "the funny thing is, he never came back as one of those creatures, he just died."

"Now that is strange, I wonder why that was?"

"I have no idea. I guess he was destined for Heaven."

"What a lot of shite!" shouted Donald, angrily. "That idiot Father Patrick thinks religion explains everything. His theory is stupid. My mother was one of the purest people in Scotland, she would not harm anyone and she came back as one of the infected. He is talking out of his arse."

"Donald Douglas!" scolded Morag in shock at his attack of the priest. "Show some respect to Father Patrick. He is a kind, honest person and a man of the cloth. He must be respected. His words are the words of our Lord. I am a good Catholic woman and I willna listen to your blasphemy."

"I am sorry, Morag, but my mother is not a Heathen. She was a good woman. I willna have anyone talk ill of her."

"Calm down, Donald. I do understand. I would be upset if I had lost my mother. We need to focus. We still have not found my brother yet and Malcolm will be waiting for us both in Lanark. We have to move. I spent too much time dragging your sorry carcass around yesterday and not getting far. I honestly dinna ken why you are ill like this, and to be frank, I dinna care."

"It is not my fault, it just happens. It all started a few years ago when me and Malcolm were mucking about by the river. I tried to jump onto a swing and missed. I ended up cracking my skull and if it was not for Malcolm, I would have died. It was after the accident that the day dreams began. Days and days of lying there doing nothing was boring and I started to fantasise about all sorts of things. It lasted for a few months before we got it under control."

"What happened?" asked Morag, "You have dreamt at least twice in the last couple of days, that one lasted an age."

"I think it was when da went to war with the clan. The dreams returned not long after that. Ma and Malcolm tried their best to help but nothing was working. I could see the frustration in their eyes and I kennt they were ashamed of me. I am useless, like a lame dog at times, but Malcolm has always been there for me, until now."

"He was wrong to abandon you for his revenge against Hamish. I will talk to Malcolm about this when we get to Lanark. Please try and stay awake this time, you are far too heavy for me to be carrying everywhere. Now move before I kick your sorry hide again."

Quickly, Donald gathered up his bag and they left, an uneasy silence hanging over as the long, arduous journey resumed.

CHAPTER TWENTY-SEVEN

STEALTH

It was the middle of the night when Hamish finally managed to convince Andrew and Gordon they had to leave. The survival of their two clans in Lanark depended on them vacating the town and heading back to Peebles immediately. This did not leave him with a lot of time to carry out his plan, and it also meant disturbing Sandy and Tam who were last seen in the local tavern sinking a few tankards of ale. Hamish felt a pang of guilt as the pair needed some downtime, but danger from the other clans meant that he needed to act fast or risk being recognised and hung.

Approaching the door of the drinking establishment, Hamish was met by a burly man who looked as if he was there to keep people out rather than encourage business. The Baird clan crest was prevalent on his shirt. Large scars adorned either side of his bald cranium, bushy eyebrows and thick beard adding to the menace.

"No entry for you, sir. This is Baird territory, try somewhere else," the doorman stated with a glare.

"Well, that is not very friendly, sir," Hamish answered with his own dangerous look. "I am sure that Gordon Baird would not be happy to hear that his honoured guest is not allowed inside, he may even have your head for this."

"The only head that will roll tonight is yours," growled the doorman, getting very annoyed at Hamish's arrogance. "Now piss off, you are not welcome here."

"Oh, but I think that you will find that I am," replied Hamish smugly, handing him a parchment. "Now be a good lad and open the door for me, it is getting a bit chilly out here and I have business inside."

It took several minutes for the man to examine the document before stepping aside and letting Hamish through, albeit begrudgingly. Hamish entered the tavern with a smug grin, scouted around for Sandy and Tam, hoping that they were still there as he did not fancy the trek back to the Baird Clan's barracks.

The watering hole was typical for Lanark, made of stone and hastily built, it usually housed the scum and villainy of the town. It was furnished with overturned tables and broken benches, where patrons either slumped over them drunk, or sat having deep and meaningful conversations with someone random they just met. Luckily for Hamish, Sandy and Tam were there, faces coated in the froth of the ale from their drink, telling stories with the locals and having fun with the wenches. Hamish hated these types of establishments, usually due to the smell of urine and vomit, often stale as a result of the lack of cleanliness.

Approaching the pair, Tam hailed over, slurring badly, "Hamish! What are you doing here?" Tam sloppily swigged down some ale from a half-empty tankard. "You are supposed to be tucked up in bed with the nobles, drinking their posh wine, and shagging their ugly servants."

"Aye, shagging their posh wine and drinking their ugly servants," piped up Sandy, looking a bit worse for wear than Tam. "Wench! Where is my drink? I seem to be dry here!"

Hamish laughed, shaking his head. "It is in your hand, you idiot! Come on drink up, we've got work to do, I will explain on the way."

"Oh, come on!" exclaimed Tam, looking annoyed. "We still have a few hours left of drinking. The wenches were just starting to get warmed up as well."

"Look, you pair of idiots," snapped Hamish in frustration, "things are about to kick off here and you can either be lying in your bed ready to be hanged in the morning, or you can move your drunken arses outside and help me. Your choice."

"I choose the ale! The ale chooses me too. The ale says that I have to order another full tankard and bring it with me. The ale believes in what you do but the ale has told me that it wants to see what you are doing. Long live the ale," Sandy replied.

"Long live the ale!" shouted Tam, encouraging him. "I want some ale too. If you want us to go, we need ale."

"Idiots." Bemused, Hamish laughed. Turning to the wench that was clearing up the table beside them, he smacked her bottom playfully. She squealed teasingly before turning around to face them.

"Wench, three ales for the road and hurry up, we have not got all night."

The buxom blonde flashed a smile, adjusting her bosom, and tottered off behind the bar, golden hair bouncing as she strode, glancing back and winking at the drunken Balliols.

"What is going on, sir?" asked Tam, downing the remainder of the ale that remained. "Why are you rushing us away from a fine evening?

"Ssshhhh!" hushed Hamish, hastily. "I will explain when we are out of here. We need to be leaving soon."

"It willna be long, sir. The ale has told me that it is being poured now and that it will be joining us shortly. It wants us to be merry. It wants us to sing and dance," Sandy slurred merrily.

"I was speaking to the ale before I left," said Hamish, slyly, "it told me that we need to be quiet and whisper or we will end up on the noose tomorrow."

Looking sombre, Sandy replied, "The ale is wise, I shall obey its instructions. Long live the ale!"

The barmaid returned with three full tankards. Hamish thanked her and tipped a couple of shiny silver coins as they made their excuses and left. The doorman sneered at him on the way out, Hamish evilly smiled back, knowing the man would be dead in the morning, along with the wench and the other tavern patrons.

The group hurried along the streets, having to stop every once in a while, as Tam took a swig from his ale or Sandy tripped over rubbish left lying. Each time this happened, Hamish made sure a swift kick in the ribs served as a message that he was not happy at their inebriated state. Both men stank of booze, the stench almost overwhelming despite being out in the cool air. After hauling Tam out of a couple of alleyways he had wandered down in error, bringing up the contents of his stomach each time, they finally reached the door to the Douglas Clan House. The words *Jamias Arraire* greeted them atop the crest that emblazoned the door. That phrase burned through Hamish's soul. Anger started to build at the arrogance of their motto which meant 'Never Behind'. After tonight, Hamish would make sure that they would never be in front again.

Signalling to the pair of drunks to cease the uncontrollable giggling, Hamish gingerly placed a hand on the handle and turned it, hoping their way in would be simple. To his surprise it was, as the oversized door eased open to reveal a pitch-black hallway beyond, the glow of the moon was the only source of dim light.

Motioning to the tipsy duo, Hamish waited for them to join before creeping up the stairs located to the right, just after the empty, silent great hall. The smell of chicken, veg, and various rumps of beef wafted past his nostrils on the way past. A small rumble reminded him of the lack of food consumed at the Baird Clan House and the temptation to nip in and grab a leg of lamb was almost overwhelming.

A smile crept across his face whilst ascending the first flight because he knew that most of the clan, if not all, would be lying passed out, sleeping off the evening's celebrations. This should make things easier. Rubbing hands together in glee, Hamish continued up, passing the second floor, hearing the rhythmic snoring that confirmed his suspicions. One more climb and they could start causing mischief. The thought of potentially wiping out most of the Douglas Clan in Lanark, along with his arch enemy Malcolm, whom he hoped had taken the bait and followed him to the town, nearly caused Hamish to miss the top step which flattened out to reveal a short foyer where the open door for the upper level was located.

"Right," whispered Hamish to Tam, "you ken what to do. When we go in, put the barrier in place and go down to the second floor and wait for me. When I pass you, you put the barrier in back in place and we'll go down to the first floor. When the barrier is in place there, you go downstairs and wait for us outside. Do you understand?"

Although Tam was still not fully concentrating, his head nodded in comprehension. Doubt filled Hamish. *What if they were too drunk to follow simple instructions? Fuck! What if they trapped me inside? If I'm caught, the hangman's noose would be waiting, or more likely, I would be killed on the spot by a filthy, vengeful Douglas, probably Malcolm or Big Davie.*

"Sandy," Hamish directed his next set of orders to the other man, "you follow me into the room, then you walk quietly to the other end of the dormitory and wait for me. Once I am through the door on the far side, put the barrier in place and then follow me down to the second floor. Then I'll give you more instructions. If I dinna come through, bar the door and get out of there quickly."

"Got it, sir," said Sandy, smiling. "The ale will keep us safe."

Shaking his head, Hamish muttered expletives under his breath and nodded to Tam who closed the door behind as they entered the first dormitory. It was a large room, filled with beds which spanned two rows ahead. There was a narrow walkway between the footboards. Sandy carefully staggered along, trying not to crash into any. A sigh of relief escaped as he saw Sandy reach the other side without disturbing or waking anyone. Seeing a thumbs-up signal, along with a goofy smile, Hamish withdrew a long dagger from his belt and grinned, knowing that this was where the chaos began.

Creeping over to the first bunk on the left, Hamish saw an auburn-haired chap, roughly thirty years old, lying under a stained brown cover, his chest moving up and down in time to thunderous snoring. Slashing with as much force as he dared muster, Hamish slid the knife across the throat of the slumbering soldier. He grinned as a trickle of blood soon became a fountain, copper permeating the thick air, the victim gargled before choking and becoming lifeless. Knowing that time was of the essence, he rushed to the unconscious Douglas member on the bunk opposite. With haste, Hamish repeated the killing strike. Not hanging around to watch, he moved quickly to navigate to the end of the aisle, glancing over to see the first corpse turning into one of the monsters.

This was just the start of the shenanigans, but Hamish felt elated seeing the creatures slowly starting to rise. Reaching the last two beds, he sped around to the right and again drew the blade over the neck of his third sacrifice. With a joyous bounce in his step, Hamish closed in on the final target, swiftly ended his life.

Rushing over to the door where Sandy stood guard, Hamish could see both of the newly created monstrosities shamble over to the next bed, lean over, and gouge teeth into the forms of their unsuspecting warrior brethren. Gleefully smiling, Hamish counted over thirty Douglas Clansmen, all lying there, unaware of their impending fate. Signalling to Sandy, Hamish started his way down the stairs to the level below as Sandy barred the exit. Muffled screams filled the room, morbid sounds of death dampened by the thickness of the huge barrier that entrapped them within.

Hamish bound down to the next landing. Again, alcohol induced snoring vibrated into the hallway like thunder rolling in on a stormy afternoon. Popping his head into the dormitory, Hamish checked to see if anyone was disturbed by the ruckus upstairs. All seemed serene. No-one was stirring, not even the scurrying of a mouse could be heard as it shot across the floor on the hunt for cheese, over the rumbling noises coming deep from the throats of the sleeping Douglas Clan.

Sandy quickly joined him. Hamish stood, head shaking at his bumbling friend who missed a couple of steps, nearly falling. If not for the sturdy oak bannister, Sandy would have landed in a heap, no doubt ruining all of their hard work.

Frustrated, Hamish snapped in a whisper, "Are you alright? You look a bit unsteady. I think you have had too much ale. If you want to leave after this floor, you can."

"I am fine, sir, I willna let you down. We can do this, for you and the Balliols." Sandy garbled slightly incoherently before raising his voice, "Long live the Balliols!"

Hamish snatched Sandy by the arm and hissed, "Ssshhhh! Are you trying to get us killed? Save the loyalty for when we are on our horses and on the way back to Peebles, not in the middle of a night time massacre. I swear, Sandy Balliol, if you fuck this up for me, I will slit your throat and leave you to the Douglas'. Now get ready to bar the door behind me and meet me on the level below."

"Yes, sir, sorry, sir. It was the ale who got me into trouble, I will be having words with it when you are inside."

Standing aghast, Hamish just looked disapprovingly at Sandy before turning and sneaking into the room, head shaking as he walked, eyes adjusting to the light, or lack thereof, within the dormitory. Again, he reconnoitred, checking for any movement within, a sign that someone was not really in dreamland. The layout was identical to the one above. However, the stench of stale alcohol and flatulence filled the air making Hamish gag slightly, the ale that he had consumed previously bubbled away in the pit of his stomach. Swallowing it down, Hamish pulled the dagger out once more and went to the first bunk. This time a smaller man, ginger haired and freckled, was lying tucked up, cosier than a swaddled baby.

Right, Hamish, he thought, *one more floor after this one and then we are on the road back home with your own bed waiting for you.*

Rearing back, the blade was thrust into the man's larynx, bubbles of blood formed, slowly suffocating him on his own fluids. Hamish rushed over to the opposite bed, copying the same maneuver, killing another unsuspecting victim. It was all good so far, similar to the previous floor. The dead rose, turning into one of the vile flesh-eating monsters.

Breaking into a short jog, Hamish knew that time was of the essence here if he wanted to carry out the remainder of his plan. Unfortunately, a pair of boots, kicked off by one of the drunken Douglas soldiers, lay strewn in his path, tripping him. Hamish fell, landing face first, almost bursting his nose.

"What the fuck was that?" exclaimed a voice to the left of him. "Will you pipe down. It is the middle of the fucking night."

"Shut up, William," replied someone else, "I am trying to sleep."

"I canna sleep, Matt's snoring is too loud," said William.

"This is all I need" muttered the second man, "my head is pounding."

"I can hear someone."

"You are dreaming, leave me alone."

"Who the fuck are you?" shouted William, spotting Hamish back on his feet trying to make a run for it. "Get back here, you bastard."

A combination of fear and excitement spurred Hamish on to the exit.

"Intruder!" yelled William, in a panic. "Intruder!"

"Fuck the intruder!" the other man shouted in response. "There are infected monsters in here. If we dinna get out, then we are all going to die!"

"Yes, you are," muttered Hamish as he helped Tam close the wooden door before securing the barricade. "Die, you Douglas bastards. Long live Clan Balliol!"

CHAPTER TWENTY-EIGHT

MODERWELL

The uneven roads, coupled with stiff legs, meant the going was cumbersome on the journey to Moderwell. Surrounding were overhanging trees, emerald leaves partially hiding acorns recently nibbled by hungry squirrels. Morag often stopped, not only to look at the beauty of the area, but to rest her stiff limbs, aching from all the recent trekking. To the side of the woodland were various bushes, each bursting with colour as tempting smells of tantalising fruit teased her taste buds.

There was obvious tension between the pair with the moroseness of Big Davie's death playing heavily on their minds. Morag regularly forced back tears, her anger still focused on Donald for not being there to save Big Davie, and towards Malcolm for not telling them about Donald's condition. On occasion, frustration overcame and she kicked out at a loose stick, sending it flying into the foliage. To further her aggravation, it narrowly missed Donald, though she deliberately aimed for her companion. Big Davie's good nature would have relieved the awkwardness between them as his natural wit would have kept the mood light.

"I keep thinking about him," said Morag, trying to break the silence which bubbled between them for most of the journey. "I keep wanting to make a comment or a joke like he would, but everything I think of is lame compared to what he would say."

"I ken how you feel. If he was here, Big Davie would be teasing me about the way that I walk or laugh at something daft that he had seen in the trees. It is not fair that they killed him, it should have been me."

"No, Donald," snapped Morag, annoyed, "it was who he was. Whether you were awake or not, Big Davie was the type of man who would have not done anything differently."

"I could have been there to do something. I am an embarrassment to my family and my clan. I train to be a warrior and when the first fight happens, I am lost to the world, kept alive by my brother's girlfriend. What an idiot I must look."

"Look," said Morag, sick of his self-deprecation, "you may have something wrong with your head but I will slap your bloody face if you dinna get over this and move on. You need to find a way to stop this dreaming or whatever it is. You seemed to snap out of it pretty quickly when you had your hands on my breasts. Perhaps that is the answer."

Donald's face turned the deepest shade of red. "Erm, I am sorry, I dinna ken what happened. One minute I was there with Mhairi and the next I am there with you. The light was poor, if I had kennt it was you, I would not have kissed you. Please accept my sincere apologies."

"Apology accepted. Although I am not sure I can forgive you for it."

"Each time that I dream, I end up on the battlefield," said Donald, trying to justify his actions. "This one took a bizarre turn, I saw a fading Big Davie and then your sister appeared, it was all very surreal. I have kissed Mhairi a couple of times when you and Malcolm were away, but it was never anything more than a kiss. I wish it was more, but she seemed to be fixated on Big Davie, so I never took it any further. Your relationship with my brother made it weird for a bit."

"What you and Mhairi do in private is none of my business, but if Rabbie was to ever catch you, he would flog you until you were black and blue."

Desperately trying to change the subject, Donald said, "Speaking of Rabbie, was there any sign of him during the attack?"

"Thankfully no. I checked every body that we killed and not one of them was my brother. I just hope that we find him in Moderwell, I am really worried about him."

"I am sure we will. If he is not in Moderwell, then he would have journeyed onto Lanark or Glasgow. Dinna give up hope on finding him."

"I am not. The plan is to go to Moderwell and if he is not there, then we will head south to Lanark and meet up with your brother and the others to plan our next move. I ken that you are anxious to hear news about your father, as am I. So, I want to kill two birds with one stone and see if there is news about our das or any sign of Rabbie. I am hoping that it willna come to that and Rabbie turns up safe and sound in Moderwell."

"I hope so too." Donald pointed to a sign ahead. "It willna be long until we found out, look, there is the two-mile sign. If we hurry, we can get there in no time."

"With all that has happened over the last couple of days, I am not keen to rush into any danger. I think that we need to have more caution from now on, else we could find ourselves suffering the same fate as Big Davie."

The conversation continued for a quarter of an hour until Donald's attention started to wander and he spotted the next sign indicating that Moderwell was a mile away. Putting his hand on the sword hilt, Donald warily surveyed the area, looking for buildings or any indication that there was some habitat nearby, but all around was nothing but bushes and fields which was frustrating.

Morag looked confused. "Rabbie always went on about Moderwell, I thought it was a big village or a town, but I dinna see anything. Have we missed it?"

"The sign says one mile to Moderwell, there would not be a sign there if there was no village. How strange."

"It is not far. We should just follow the road and see where it leads to, even if it is just a few houses, it is better than nothing. Hopefully, the people there have seen Rabbie or at least will put us up for the night."

"I think we should be ready for any possibility, keep that poker of yours handy, it may be needed."

Nodding, Morag pushed onwards, striding along the path, legs weary from the arduous walk. What she would not give for some hot water to soak her feet in. This, coupled with yesterday's exertions, meant that her pace had slowed somewhat, and she now trailed a few yards behind Donald. Morag felt a pang of jealousy at the elongated rest he got during all the chaos. It was only anger and determination that kept her going.

Quarter of an hour later, they rounded the final bend that revealed the straight road that led to the heart of Moderwell. The size of the village shocked the pair. Ahead was no more than a dozen houses and a tavern. The pungent waft of horse manure reached their nostrils, as welcoming as her parents were when Malcolm first came to dinner. It took a few weeks for them to warm to him, but his kind nature soon won them over. Malcolm would often take time to read a story to Mhairi or clean the shit out of the barn for father.

It was still, like walking through Forth during harvest time when all the villagers were out in the fields bringing in crops for winter. It reminded Morag of long afternoons she spent out with her mother. Many days were spent cutting wheat and corn, then storing it in the barns, but it was all worth it for the huge celebration to signal the end of the season. Morag enjoyed the dancing, singing, and general merriment when everyone got together. She loved to twirl her skirts in time to the piper, often jigging into the early hours of the morning. It was here where she first met Malcolm, a few years ago after he interrupted when she was gambolling with Rabbie, who scowled at the handsome lad. They partied and chatted well past the end and, without warning, their lips met. It was then she fell for him. The pair often snuck off in private to the woods or a hiding hole Malcolm made at the back of the barn.

Morag sighed at the pleasant memory, the late afternoon breeze rustled her brown locks, the strands partially blinding as they danced in front of her face. She juggled the poker and bag, making each attempt to sweep it back futile as it became more unkempt before she put them down and fixed the strands properly.

"This doesna look promising. I dinna think there are any people here, never mind Rabbie. This trip looks to be for nothing." Morag sighed.

"We will have a look around, find some food, and maybe somewhere to sleep tonight. If we dinna find Rabbie, then we head for Lanark at first light and meet back up with Malcolm. We have lost too much time as it is, Malcolm will be getting worried about us."

As the houses loomed closer, the splatter of blood on the walls and the stench of decay permeated the evening air. Morag assumed a violent battle had occurred, yet there were no bodies to be seen. A combination of the cool breeze, the lack of people, and the putrid smell had her hackles raised. The nervous tapping on the hilt of his sword indicated Donald was just as wary.

Immediately noticeable was that the door to each small house was blocked off. The first dwelling had a wooden cart in front of it, the sort that farmers used to transport their turnips from the field to a barn. Curiosity piqued, Donald moved to investigate further.

"Look at this, the spokes of the wheels have been damaged. This cart is not going anywhere fast. Whoever did this is not wanting anyone inside. I wonder why?"

"It is none of our business." Morag shifted uneasily, a small voice telling her to flee.

"What if your brother is inside? What if he is trapped in there with no food and is unable to get out? You kept saying that he was in Moderwell, now we are here, you are not willing to look in the houses to find him?"

"I guess that it willna hurt to have a look, but I am not expecting him to be there. Rabbie is probably dead. I should just accept it."

"Dinna give up on him. We have journeyed a long way looking for him, have some faith, we will find him."

"Will we though? Everywhere we look, the dead are walking, eager to kill and eat people. It is a horrible place that we live in. Why should I believe that Rabbie hasna been attacked by one of those creatures? If Big Davie could be beaten by them, then what chance would Rabbie stand? I ken that I am sounding down, but do you blame me? Look at all the people who are dead, your ma, the villagers in the pub, Big Davie. Rabbie has gone, Donald, and the sooner that I accept it, the quicker that I can get on with my life."

"That is not the Morag Douglas who I ken. It is not the Morag Douglas who stood up to Malcolm and came out here looking for her brother. It is not the Morag Douglas protected me whilst I was out of it, fighting off certain death for us both. It is not the Morag Douglas who has kept going despite everything that has happened. Now, stop this nonsense and help me move this bloody cart."

"I have been a fool, Donald. I am sorry but I feel like everything has fallen on me at once. I dinna ken how much more I can take. What was it you wanted me to do?"

"With all you have been through, it is no surprise you are struggling. We have been through too much together for you to quit on me now. If you go to the back of the cart with me, we will try and shove it out the way. We have a chance to move it with both of us pushing."

Hesitantly, Morag followed Donald to the rear of the obstacle. Placing both hands on the barrow and pushing with as much strength that she could muster. Muscles strained as pressure increased, sweat trickled down her back exertion and stifling heat.

"Push harder!" exclaimed Donald excitedly. "It is moving."

"*Stop!*" boomed a deep voice in the distance. "What the hell do you pair think you are doing?"

Startled, Morag spun around, brandishing her crude weapon, squinting in effort to spot where the shout originated from, her hand shaking in both fear and anger for not being more aware. There was no sign of anyone. No shadows against the abandoned buildings whose walls were smeared with dried blood. No obvious presence of life on the stone road that was choked with overgrown weeds.

"Over there," said Donald, pointing behind the tavern at the far end of the road, "there is a man coming towards us with an axe over his shoulder."

"Where?" asked Morag, squinting to where he indicated. "All I see is buildings and fields.... wait, I see him now, he doesna look like my brother."

"I never said it was Rabbie. Maybe he kens what happened to him."

"Maybe, maybe not. Whoever he is, I am glad to see him."

"Perhaps he willna be glad to see us. Whoever he is, that axe makes him dangerous. I think we should be careful, just in case he is not friendly."

Unconvincingly, Morag said, "I am sure that we have nothing to worry about, there are two of us and only one of him."

"That meant nothing to Big Davie, he took on thirty at once and won."

"You do ken that most of his legends are exaggerated? Each new telling of the tale got more outlandish. Big Davie himself said that some of the stories were bordering on the ridiculous," Morag replied smugly.

"I ken that, but there is some truth in them. He may not have taken out thirty, but he did take on more than one and they were certainly more skilled warriors than us. I just think that we should show some caution and be prepared for anything, our lives depend on it."

By the time the stranger was ten yards away, Donald's sword was drawn, ready to attack at the slightest aggressive movement. This was an older man, perhaps in his thirties, long amber hair matted with drying mud. A deep scar sat just above the top of his brow, giving additional menace to his natural snarl. Donald was taller but not by much. The stranger's muscular frame implied a strength Morag was certain would overwhelm Donald with ease.

"I wouldna go in there if I was you," said the man, with a wry smile. "Not if you want to live."

Curious, Donald asked, "Why? Are you going to kill us for whatever it is that you have hidden in there?"

The stranger laughed. "No, I have nothing of importance in there. I used the building to store all the corpses I killed. It was better than stinking out the streets. My name is Gregor Munro and I am the last surviving inhabitant of Moderwell. Now, can I ask who you are and what you are doing here?"

"I am Donald Douglas and this is my friend Morag. We come from the village of Forth and are on the hunt for Morag's brother Rabbie who was heading here looking for her. Do you ken of him at all?"

Stroking his chin absently, Gregor replied, "Aye, I ken Rabbie. We spent more than one night drinking what crudely passes for ale in the tavern ages ago, but I havena seen the rogue recently. Perhaps he took a different route."

"That may well be the case. Can I ask what happened to everyone here?" Donald asked.

"You can ask, but before you do, please tell me where you plan to go to next?"

"We are going to head for Lanark to meet my brother Malcolm and our friends. We are thinking that if we havena seen Rabbie, then perhaps he has seen sense and travelled there. We are going in the morning but were hoping to find somewhere to stay tonight."

"There is an empty house here that you can sleep in, but I am not sure that you will want to be in the same village as me after you hear what I did," Gregor said with hesitation.

"Look, friend," interjected Donald, trying to keep the peace, "it canna be any worse than what we have seen already. Scotland is fast becoming a truly frightening land with the dead rising and loved ones dying in droves around us. Whatever you have done, it is to survive, and we willna judge anyone for that."

"I think it may be best that I tell my tale, then you can decide after that. But first, let us find some shelter and some food, you two must be hungry."

"We are," stated Morag, feeling the pangs in her stomach, "please lead on."

Gregor went to the tavern at the far end of the village. Leading them through the entrance, they quickly sat on a bench inside, and without delay were tucking into bread and ham and a flagon of watered-down ale. The room was remarkably clean, there was not much dust on the surfaces. The floors looked recently scrubbed and no dead bodies were left in the room. In some ways it was spotless, which was unusual for a pub. Most were often dirt-ridden dives. If not for the alcohol, most folk would make their own entertainment at home.

"So," said Donald, munching on a piece of meat, "what happened to the all the people here?"

Absently stroking the hair on his chin, Gregor said, "Now that is a story to tell. It all began a few days ago when I was out hunting for rabbits. I was feeling hungry and wanted something different in the cookpot, so I got my knife and went out into the woods over yonder to bring home some game. I had been out for most of the day, eating whilst on the hunt, and was quite happy with the eight rabbits that I had snared. I knew that something was wrong when I approached the village. There were a number of people roaming the streets, walking as if they had shit themselves. As I got closer, I could see limbs missing and blood everywhere, I knew that something serious had happened and I was not going to get caught out unawares."

Intrigued, Morag asked, "What did you do? The village looks spotless."

"I used my brain. I knew that I had time so I picked them off. I used my speed and knowledge of the village to trap or kill them in ones and twos. If there was too many gathered, I ran out of the village to a safe place and regrouped, doubling back on myself. Once all the villagers were either killed or trapped, I spent my time cleaning the place up so that it would attract no others. Once clean, I took my time to rid each building of the creatures that I had trapped, the house that you were about to enter was the last one left to deal with."

"That is impressive. Did anyone else survive or have you seen anyone passing through?" Donald asked.

"I have not seen a soul. It has been quite lonely the last few days. Once this last house is clear, this will be a safe place for people to stay. I just wish that more people in the village had survived."

"You are more than welcome to join us on our journey to Lanark. We could do with another pair of hands," Morag said.

"It does get lonely here, let me think on it and I will let you ken in the morning. First, tell me what has happened to you pair and we can relax before getting some much-needed sleep."

"That sounds like a great idea," replied Morag before launching into the story of how she and Donald had journeyed to Moderwell.

It took about an hour for them to relay their tale with much prompting and many questions coming from Gregor before they climbed into bed for the night, exhausted.

CHAPTER TWENTY-NINE

CONFRONTATION

BANG!

Waking with a start, Malcolm rubbed his bleary eyes, trying to focus, his head pounding from the fright. Malcolm did not dream much, last night was disturbed in particular, due to the number of people in the room. A rhythmic vibration was felt as each exhale echoed through the room like a thousand purring cats after a good meal. Donald's issues meant that Malcolm was never fully out of it, continually worrying that the next morning would be the one where Donald would not wake. This turned Malcolm into a light sleeper, the smallest sound usually waking him.

Malcolm groggily looked around to try and see what had caused the disturbance. Inky darkness dominated the room with rasping snores still prevalent. Malcolm groaned in annoyance, the sound grating on his fraying nerves. A pungent smell of alcohol and stale farts tortured his delicate nostrils. Stretching stiff limbs, he pulled up to the edge of the bed, easing out of the cosy blanket as bare legs met the chill of the night air.

Bugger, thought Malcolm as he tried to adjust to the lack of light. *Which one of these drunken bastards is making all that noise?*

A lot of ale and wine was consumed at the feast and most of the residents had joined them in the dining room. The result was now the majority of the clan lying comatose in bed, oblivious to everything in the room. Malcolm decided not to drink a lot, a combination of wanting to be up early in the morning to resume the hunt for Hamish and needing to be sharp for when the confrontation happened. The aching ankle dampening enthusiasm, the injury was still giving him bother but the worst of it was healed which was a relief. The heavy strapping Morag put on kept it supported and although his movement was restricted, it meant that he was able to walk with minimal pain.

Another bang from above interrupted his train of thought. Pulling on his warm woollen coat, Malcolm hobbled to the door, ready to walk upstairs to check that everything was alright. Darkness hampered his progress as the uneven placement of the beds provided painful obstacles.

Shaking his leg to reduce the agony, Malcolm eased the dormitory door open. A blast of air titillated the end of his nose causing a strand of hair to dance like crickets playing in a field. Rubbing his hands together to generate a bit of warmth, Malcolm could hear more thumping and what sounded like groans intertwined with vibrating snores of the sleeping soldiers above. Oddly, the stairwell was blackened. Malcolm did not recall the torches being extinguished before he settled down for the night.

Easing over the summit, suspicion gripped his mind as shadows danced in the darkness above. Uncertain if his imagination was playing tricks, Malcolm took a step up to try and get a better look, not sure what was happening. Could it be his head fooling him, was someone there or was one of the others sleepwalking? He soldiered on, trying to put all that nonsense to the back of his mind. Keeping tight against the wall, he tried to blend in with the inkiness, avoiding detection as he ascended towards what could be waiting.

More movement, this time no shady image, it was real. Malcolm could make out a figure standing beside the open door, watching intently at whatever was happening inside. *Who could it be? Why was he not in bed like the rest of the clan?* Feeling his side, Malcolm discovered he was without weapon, exposed and vulnerable, especially if this person was an intruder.

Suddenly, the door slammed shut. The figure hoisted a large wooden beam and inserted it in the slots, trapping everyone within. Catching a glance of the face, Malcolm realised it was not one of the people that they had dined with earlier, leaving him concerned that this was an unwanted guest. Caught in the midst of indecision of whether to confront him or to go and get some help, Malcolm felt a light breeze as the stranger rushed past and down towards the bottom floor.

"Excuse me!" Malcolm called, but it was to no avail as the figure disappeared out of sight. Curious to what was happening upstairs, Malcolm continued on, rather than pursue the intruder.

Reaching the top landing, Malcolm examined the barrier, confused at why it was put in place to secure the exit. He lifted it, balancing it against the wall before thrusting the door open, eyes squinting to try and make out what was unfolding inside. Malcolm could see a few figures bent over sleeping soldiers but was unable to make out what they were doing. Suspecting foul play, Malcolm decided to sound the alarm.

"Wake up! Wake up! Intruder in the building! Wake up, you fools!"

Commotion ensued as slumbering bodies rose to see what the fuss was about. People were falling over each other in the dark as they stumbled out of bed to investigate.

"Infected in the room! We are under attack!"

Confused voices abound, shadowy shapes were now fighting soldiers who were on their feet and trying to work out what was going on. At the far exit, some men discovered it was barred and battered the wood futilely before realizing there was no way out. The noise attracted the newly created monsters and soon the men were desperately fending off attackers. One of the infected had sensed that Malcolm was fresh meat and was bearing down on his position, but good fortune held as a blade flashed before him and removed the head of the creature.

Realising that help was required, Malcolm took the opportunity to dash down the stairs to wake the everyone resting in his dormitory. A few were already disturbed and were rising, but he wanted to focus on rousing Jamie, who he knew would be able to organize the room quickly. The figure who rushed past worried him. Malcolm knew that Brian slept on the ground floor along with his personal bodyguards and if there was more than one intruder, then he could be in trouble. The urge to warn him and prevent any further unnecessary death was too great, but the delay was unavoidable as there were so many lives that needed to be saved.

Approaching the larger bed at the end of the row, which was often reserved for the most senior clansman, Malcolm shook the body lying atop the stale, sweat stained sheets, praying his cousin would wake.

"Wake up, Jamie!" Malcolm shouted in his ear, his arms moving vigorously, trying to interrupt Jamie's sleep. "We are under attack, there are intruders and Heathens in the building!"

Groggy, Jamie muttered, "What? Is that you Malcolm?"

"Yes! You have to get up, before we lose most of the men."

The shock of the statement brought Jamie back to reality. Sitting up abruptly whilst rubbing his eyes, a large yawn escaped his cracked lips, disturbing a few of the soldiers that were still sleeping nearby.

"What the hell is going on? How the fuck did Heathens get into the building? I thought the town was free of those creatures."

"I am not sure. I heard a noise and went upstairs to investigate. I saw someone put a bar on the dormitory door and rush past me back downstairs. I opened the door to see confusion and people turning into Heathens. I came back down here to get some support. If you can lead a group upstairs to help, I will go downstairs to find out where that fucker went."

"You are not going down there on your own," insisted Jamie, getting out of bed and putting his boots on. "What if there is more than one intruder?"

"We dinna have time to argue. Joe is downstairs so I willna be on my own and you need to get upstairs quickly."

Nodding agreement, Jamie stood and unsheathed his weapon, barking instructions at the rest of the men. Seeing that his orders were being obeyed, Malcolm hurried out of the room and down the stairs to the level below, taking care not to trip and fall on his descent.

There was no sign of the intruder when Malcolm stepped out into the expansive hallway. Squinting as far as his eyes could focus, neither door at the end of the corridor was lying ajar and did not look disturbed.

Malcolm's mind was still playing tricks on him, random movement kept catching his attention at the corner of his vision but there was no-one. Or was there? Nerves jangling now, butterflies danced in his stomach as he moved onwards, continually looking around, convinced that someone else was there.

Was there another person inside? Could it be the person upstairs earlier or was it just his imagination, Malcolm did not know but the feel of the sword he had grabbed was a comfort. *Who in the town had this grudge against the Douglas Clan? Was it even aimed at them? What if it was Hamish? If it was Hamish, surely then he would have killed me on the landing.* There was a lot for Malcolm to ponder. He let his mind run amok as Brian's room loomed closer.

When he reached the entrance, Malcolm found that it was slightly ajar, but no glare escaped from inside, it was darker than Big Davie's mood before lunch. Grip tightening on the weapon, Malcolm thumped heavily on the door a couple of times.

Shuffling was heard before a panicked, squeaky voice responded, "Who is there? Is that you, Joe?"

"No, Brian. It is me, Malcolm. There is an intruder in the building, I thought I saw him down here. I was just checking that you are alright."

"I am fine," replied Brian, still sounding groggy. "Give me a moment and I will come and check round the house with you, no-one knows this place better than me."

"Do you need some light? I can light a candle for you if you want?"

"Aye, that would be great. There should be one just outside the door. If you could light that one please."

"Will do."

Malcolm picked it up and went to the centre reception area to set the wick alight. Flame dancing like an elegant lady on a ballroom floor, he continued back to Brian's room. Above, the commotion could be faintly heard as the battle ensued. Jamie was a competent leader who could more than handle himself in a fight, but the rest of the group was fairly inexperienced. The majority of veteran fighters were with the clan and his father in Cumbria, warring with the English and hoping to gain land down south.

Carefully making way back to Brian, Malcolm noticed the larger man standing at the doorway, struggling to get into the hall. Brian seemed to be walking with his back arched, as if he was in pain. The contour of his face showed a combination of fear and discomfort, a sign that something was seriously wrong. The glint of a blade, held tight against his throat, confirmed Malcolm's suspicions.

"Malcolm, old chap," a familiar voice echoed down the hallway, "it has been far too long. How the devil are you?"

CHAPTER THIRTY

DECISIONS

Malcolm could not believe what he was seeing, Hamish bloody Balliol standing before him with a knife to Brian's throat, chatting away as if they were old friends. Anger and revulsion built up like a raging storm ready to unleash a barrage of thunder and lightning on the land. It took all of his willpower to swallow it down and not beat the daylights out of Hamish.

"I have had better weeks. I was not expecting to see you here," Malcolm replied through gritted teeth.

Mockingly, Hamish sneered. "Really? I left you enough clues."

"Clues! Those were barbaric acts. You are one sick bastard, Hamish. I will end your life for all that you have done."

"For all that I have done!" Hamish laughed in disbelief. "What about you, Mr. Fucking Perfect? Every day when I was younger, you and that ugly big bastard Davie would set upon me at school and beat me to a pulp. I hated going to school because of you. You made my childhood a misery and now I am going to make your life even worse."

"How much worse can you make it? You have butchered my ma, killed my dogs, and made life a living hell for the last few days. Do you not think that you have done enough?" Malcolm asked incredulously.

"I have only just started. There is so much more to come. In fact, as we speak, a large horde of infected people are on their way to Lanark. They are going to destroy you and your wretched clan and I will love every minute of it."

"You are an idiot, Hamish," taunted Malcolm, trying to goad the man into a mistake. "There are two things that you have forgotten. The gates are all down with guards protecting them and I will kill you tonight."

"It is not I that is the idiot. The gates are all up and sabotaged. Each of the guards have been taken unawares and murdered. You have too much to worry about tonight to kill me. There is the incoming threat from the glens and there is the threat within. As we speak, many of the Douglas Clan are being murdered in their sleep and instead of you helping them and saving their lives, you are down here blethering to me."

"How the hell did you manage that? You are on your own here and we would ken if there was a gathering of Balliols inside the wall. The Bruce hates you as much as we do."

"We had a little help inside the city. Not all the clans in Lanark are supporters of The Bruce, some of them are sympathisers with us and the English. You are too naïve to see that though and it will be your undoing. As for what is happening upstairs, I may have sneaked in with a couple of my men and started murdering your clan in their sleep, barred the doors, leaving them to turn into monsters and kill the rest of the room."

"You evil bastard," gasped Brian, struggling to talk with the blade digging into his neck. "That is my friends and family that you are killing. You will hang for this."

"Who is going to hang me? You? The Bruce? You will be too busy to think about me. It is going to be chaos in here and I have no plans to stay around and watch."

"What do you plan to do?" asked Malcolm, worried that more foul deeds would befall him.

Hamish laughed. "Now that would be telling. Let me just say that I plan to make a wee detour on the way home to Peebles, to a place that you are very familiar with."

Malcolm stepped forward. "I am going to destroy you! You willna do any more harm to my friends and family."

213

"Back off!" warned Hamish, pressing the knife further into Brian's throat. "Or I will kill your leader."

Stopping suddenly, Malcolm glared into the smug face of his childhood enemy, trying to evaluate what he was likely to do next. The slightly unhinged look displayed across his face said it all. This was a man who had killed before and was not afraid to do it again. The thought of his ma thrashing away on her bed flooded into Malcolm's vision, closely followed by the sight of the bloke in Carnwath nailed to the Town Centre, helpless and hungry, snarling at passers-by.

"I thought that would stop you," mocked Hamish. "Not so brave now without that big idiot beside you. Talking of Davie Douglas, where is the gigantic fool?"

"That is my son that you are talking about," Brian hissed through clenched teeth.

Surprised, Hamish retorted, "Really? You must have gone through a lot of food. That stupid lump eats like a bloody horse."

A muffled knock, followed by two more quiet raps on the door, sounded behind Hamish. A smile crept across the Balliol's face.

"I am afraid that I must bid you farewell." Hamish grinned as he pulled the knife across Brian's neck, severing the artery, blood spurting as the man collapsed. "Give my love to Big Davie, tell him that I absolutely meant to kill his father."

With that, Hamish disappeared out of the exit into the stillness of the night, leaving Malcolm with the choice to chase after or tend to the dying man. The decision was a no-brainer as he rushed over to the fallen leader, pushing a hand against the open wound, trying to halt the flow of blood as it coursed through his fingers.

They were soon joined by the rest of the clan. First on scene was the guardsman Joe, rushing to check on his charge, worry etched across his face. Close behind was Jamie and Father Patrick, both concerned at the sight.

"Is he dead?" asked Joe, frantically, seeing the pale face and still haunting eyes staring blankly back at him. "Who fucking did this?"

"He is alive for the moment," replied Malcolm, tears streaming down his cheeks. "It willna be long before he does pass away. He has lost too much blood. I came in to see Hamish fucking

Balliol with his knife across Brian's throat. There was nothing I could do."

"Friend, I ken that," said Joe morosely, putting his hand on Malcolm's shoulder. "I promise you that we will get the bastard who did this. We will hunt him down and beat him to within an inch of his life, then leave him for those creatures to feast on his worthless hide."

"And I will be there to make sure that the rat suffers," muttered Malcolm, growling, teeth gnawing in anger. "But we have more pressing problems."

"What can be more pressing that sending that worthless rat to Hell?"

"Hamish Balliol and his followers have released the town's infected from the field where you had put them. They have sabotaged the gates so that they can enter and cause havoc. We have a matter of hours if we are lucky."

"I will kill each person that is responsible for doing this," Joe said bluntly. "What do we do? We have to go after him."

"If it was up to me, then I would take every clansman and go after him," answered Malcolm venomously as Brian took his final breath and slumped to the ground. "He is gone. Quickly, Joe, you must remove his head, he wouldna want to come back as one of those creatures."

Stepping away from the corpse, Malcolm said a short prayer as Joe brought his blade down on the spinal cord of the dead clan chief, severing the head from the rest of the body. Joe wiped the sword clean with a cloth attached to his belt before bending down on one knee, head bowed before paying respect to the fallen leader.

Standing beside him, Malcolm put his hand on Joe's back, as a comforting gesture, the tears flowing down both of their cheeks. Anger coursed through Malcolm's veins, a fist smashed into the stone wall. The sheer venom of the strike bruised and scraped his knuckles. Malcolm cursed as it felt like someone had put a knife through his hand.

"We need to go after him," said Joe in a low voice, "he canna get away with this."

"I ken. What about the threat to the town?" Malcolm asked, holding his reddening fingers.

"Others can deal with that; they willna miss a small group of us going after him. Fraser will gather an army against the incoming infected. We need to hunt that bastard down."

"You do ken that he is not alone. I dinna ken how many, but he does have help."

"Aye, but they dinna have the skill or passion of the Douglas Clan? Did he tell you where he was headed?"

"Aye, Hamish told me that he was going back to Forth, he wanted to destroy my home village."

Joe punched a fist into his palm. "We have to stop him! There are good men and women in that village."

"Who do we take? Fraser willna like us stripping the clan of much needed fighters before an upcoming battle."

"You leave Fraser to me," replied Joe with a wry grin. "There are four of the best men that I ken are a part of Brian's personal bodyguards. The six of us will make a nice group to go after him."

"What about the lads that I brought? I trust each and every one of them in battle."

"Fraser will need Jamie in the command group, there are too few experienced men still in the town. He willna let Jamie go, that lad is too valuable. The priest has to stay, what we are about to do willna get God's approval."

"What about Wee Stevie and John? They ken the road well and both ken Carnwath backwards."

"Aye, they are both good suggestions. Now, let us find a cover for the body so that we can pay our last respects before leaving. Get the priest to do a eulogy or something. The men need to see that Brian was a man on God's mission, it will inspire them," Joe said.

"Aye, that they do, what is left of them."

"What happened up there? I heard the commotion from my sleeping quarters and the next thing I knew, you were standing there holding Brian's body."

"I am not quite sure. From what I could see, Hamish and his men sneaked in, blocked the dorm doors, and killed a few clansmen, turning them into those creatures whilst everyone slept. It was luck and skill that we never lost more than we did. As it was, we lost at least thirty men from what I can gather."

"This means war, the Balliols will pay for what they have done. They have not heard the last of the Douglas Clan."

The rest of the troops started to make their way into the hall, wondering what all the noise was. Soon, the place was bulging, confused over who lay dead under the blanket. Joe turned back around and faced the group, waving his hands to hush the crowd.

"Gentlemen, please. Under the cover is the leader of our clan in Lanark, Brian Douglas."

Gasps of shock and murmurs could be heard from the group causing a bit of a ruckus.

Hands raised to quiet them down further whilst Joe quickly summarised what Hamish told Malcolm earlier. Incensed chatter rose from the crowd at the news and Malcolm stepped forward to speak. "This is not good, whatever way that you look at it. For some reason, the Balliols, Hamish in particular, have an issue with our clan. They now have an alliance with another clan in Lanark and have left to go after my home village of Forth. I plan to chase them down and get revenge for what they have done to Brian and my ma, but I do need help. I would love to pursue him with a full army of Douglas behind me but there is a more pressing matter. Our enemy have unleashed a huge group of infected upon us. The town's own people who were turned into these creatures have been freed from their confinement in the glens to the north and are on their way towards us as we speak."

Rallying cries of support echoed throughout the room. One elderly clan member started to bang his cane rhythmically on the floor. Soon others joined in, chanting "Die, traitor, die!" This was followed by "Kill the creatures!" Passion and a thirst for revenge was evident on the faces of each man.

The battle cries continued for a few minutes, the crowd getting stirred up with rage before Joe stepped forward again. "I am going to go after Hamish with Malcolm and a few others to hunt him down and make him pay for his attack on our clan. Fraser will take command of the clan's forces and make preparations for the defence of the town. I ask that you give him your full support as he will need every one of you in order to make Lanark safe."

With that, Joe and Malcolm walked through the crowd, clasping hands and hugging people as they passed. Wine was thrust into their palms, weapons offered for the journey ahead. To a man, everyone wanted to join them to smash the Balliol menace. Joe thanked each one and promised he would decide soon on who would join them. The clan were like a pack of wolves, hungry to take down their prey, thinking only of blood and vengeance. Joe and Malcolm walked into the map room, pride in their hearts, ready to plan the death of Hamish Balliol.

CHAPTER THIRTY-ONE

PREPARATIONS

Before dawn, Gregor woke Donald and Morag and informed of his decision to journey with them. A hearty breakfast, courtesy of their new friend, was feasted upon before belongings were quickly gathered and they hit the road just after first light. Morag was still feeling a bit sluggish after the exertions of the previous day and soon settled in a few yards behind Donald and Gregor as they walked south towards Lanark.

In an attempt to break the silence, Donald tried to engage Gregor in conversation. "Erm, sorry to disturb your thoughts, but I was wondering how you ended up in Moderwell? You dinna seem the village type."

Laughing, Gregor looked at Donald, a quizzical look upon his face. "What makes you say that?"

"You are handy with a knife and are great at hunting. Your body shape is that of a traveller, rather than a man who gets heartily fed by his wife or mother, and the brogue on your tongue is not from around here."

"Very perceptive, young Donald. We may make a woodsman out of you. Aye, I am all of that. I grew up near Inverness, up in the Highlands but soon got sick of village life and when I was roughly the same age as you, I wanted to find my place in the world. I worked as I journeyed from village to village. On nights where I could not find work, I learned how to hunt, it was that or go hungry. It was difficult at first but after much practice, I like to think I became quite adept at it. Moderwell was one of the places I found work and the old couple who took me in were kind to me. I enjoyed life in Moderwell and became good friends with a few of the villagers, including Rabbie. I was ready to leave just before all this senseless slaughter happened."

"Does it get lonely?"

"That is the only downside to life on the road. You have yourself as company. When I get lonely, I find the bed of a tavern wench or a local lass looking for a thrill. I have to be careful when I do that as I have been chased out of many a village before for bedding the wrong farmer's daughter. It can be hard at times, but I find it invigorating."

Glancing back, Donald noticed Morag lagging behind before upping her pace and almost catching up again.

"If Morag keeps doing that, she will keel over with exhaustion and I dinna fancy carrying her the rest of the way to Lanark," said Gregor, concerned.

Sighing in frustration, Donald replied, "I would talk to her, but she is still annoyed at me."

"If you two want to survive, you need to settle your differences or one of those monsters will have you both for lunch."

"It would not be fair on her to die at my expense. I already have too much blood on my hands. I will settle it with her."

Donald summoned Morag over. After a quick lecture from Gregor, they called a temporary truce and she kept pace with the pair, though sometimes shooting murderous glances in Donald's direction which left him feeling very uncomfortable.

Any villages passed were deserted. It appeared as though the Heathens were either killed or had lost interest as survivors fled into the countryside. The trio travelled for most of the morning, finally approaching the large western gate that protruded from the long, stone wall that surrounded Lanark.

Donald wiped the sweat away from his forehead as they approached the entrance to Lanark. The guard post was unoccupied, immediately arousing suspicion. "That is not good," Donald said, breaking the uncomfortable silence that had descended. "Should there not be guards there?"

"Aye, laddie, Robert the Bruce does not like any of the gates to be unguarded, this is most unusual," Gregor pondered.

Their pace slowing as they neared, Donald asked, "How do you ken that, have you been here before?"

"Old man Graham had me running errands to and from Lanark, it was a good place to sell livestock and eggs. On a good day, we could pick up quite a few coins or some good quality wheat or barley in barter. I normally visited at least once a week."

"So, you ken the town well then?" queried Morag, interested in what the more experienced man had to say.

"Aye, that I do, lass. I got friendly with one of the other traders and we would look after each other's wares whilst one of us explored the town, sometimes getting a well-earned ale or a good wench to fuck. The taverns were good places to pick up news about the fighting down south or what was happening in Lanark."

"Does that mean that you ken where the Douglas clan house is?"

"Aye, that I do, lass. I have passed it a few times on the way to a wench's house for an hour's pleasure, although I have never been inside."

"You must take us there immediately them," Morag demanded, taking charge once again. "We need to find Malcolm and the others. I am worried that something may have happened to them."

"I think we need to show some caution," replied Gregor, sensibly. "We dinna ken what is happening in the streets. I ken you said that this was a safe town but what if that has been compromised? You are right, we do need to get to the clan house as soon as possible, but not recklessly. We should be on our guard, have weapons ready, and not take any risks on the way. I dinna like what I have seen, something is not right here."

Nervously surveying the area, Donald said, "I agree with Gregor, we have already lost Big Davie, I woulda like either of you to become one of those creatures."

"Sorry," groaned Morag, begrudgingly, "I just want to get to the clan house and see Malcolm. We have been too long apart and I miss him."

Gregor looked at the pair of them, before speaking. "I do understand, but I would rather get you there in one piece. Now have any of you got any berries? I am feeling peckish."

Reaching into her bag, Morag handed both Gregor and Donald some fruit which they greedily devoured, one of them keeping watch whilst the others ate. Once finished they hastily resumed their journey to the Douglas Clan Headquarters. The streets were surprising sparse of both people and Heathens, curtains were pulled at most houses. Either no-one was home or they did not want to be disturbed in fear of what was lurking. Taking advantage of the quietness, the group picked up the pace, ever wary of any surprises but always looking round, nervously, thinking they were being watched.

A mile later, they were standing outside the front door, ready to rap the knocker when a middle-aged man brushed past them, placing his hand on the handle, about to enter.

"Excuse me," said Donald, putting his palm on the person's shoulder, "is this the Douglas Clan house?"

"Yes, son, it is. If you dinna mind, I am busy, I have a lot to do."

"Sorry to disturb you, but my name is Donald Douglas, I am here looking for my brother Malcolm. Do you ken if he is inside?"

"Follow me," he replied, opening the door. "I am Fraser Douglas, I will get one of the others to talk to you."

Cautiously moving behind the clansman, the trio made way into the hallway. Donald's jaw dropped, never had he seen such luxury and class. From the heads of various wildlife, stuffed and mounted on the walls, to the velvet drapes brushing the floor that drifted to cover the wooden shutters that blocked the windows. There was a lot of bustle as various people were either talking or scrubbing the floors. Recognising his cousin Jamie at the other end of the corridor, Donald was about to call out when Fraser suddenly barked out an order.

"Jamie, come here! We have a lot to discuss, get one of the men to gather the rest of the commanders, we need to start planning. Can you also get someone to look after this lot behind me? They are looking for your cousin, Malcolm."

Spotting their arrival, a warm smile swept across Jamie's face, chipped, battle-worn teeth highlighted through the grin. Crossing the gap quickly, Jamie wrapped his arms around Donald and enveloped him in a long hug, reminding the younger man that there was a friendly face inside the building.

"It is good to see you, lad," said Jamie, releasing Donald from his embrace. "Where is Big Davie? Is he not with you?"

"I am so sorry," started Donald, hanging in head in a combination of respect and shame. "I am afraid that Davie was killed by those monsters. We were ambushed in a clearing on the way to Moderwell and the sheer number killed him. I ken he was your friend."

A gasp escaped Jamie's lips, followed by a sob as grief overtook. Taking a couple of steps back, Jamie slumped against the wall, pulling knees up to his chin. Donald settled down alongside, extending an arm and engulfing him, the warrior's tears dampening Donald's grass-stained shirt.

"I am sorry, Jamie. Big Davie was a hero to the end, we would not have made it here if it was not for his courage. He will be remembered, there is no greater man than the legend that was Davie Douglas."

"Get up!" yelled Fraser from afar. "We dinna have time for reunions, we have a battle to plan for and I need your help. Move it!"

"Sorry, Donald," muttered Jamie, wiping the tears from his reddening eyes, "I have to go. If you wait here, I will get Father Patrick to bring you up to speed. It is good to see you."

"Jamie," said Donald, hoping for news of his brother. His cousin stood up before looking back, a pained expression, making it clear that there was no time to waste.

"Patrick will talk to you, I will catch up later." There was no waiting about as Jamie disappeared into one of the side rooms, hastening after Fraser who seemed to be in charge.

The group sat in the padded velvet chairs in the reception area, waiting for Patrick as the hustle and bustle continued, clansmen rushing as if something serious was about to happen. Donald became increasingly concerned as the wait was longer than expected and not one person had bothered to check up on them. Worried that no mention was made of his sibling, Donald sat pondering about the meeting with Jamie. *What if something had happened to Malcolm? Where was my brother? Why was the place in such chaos?*

"I think they have forgotten about us, lad," spoke Gregor, eyes constantly following the action around them. "Something is wrong here and I would like to ken what it is."

"I think you are right, friend. It is very unusual for Jamie not to stop and chat to us. It is not like him at all."

"Perhaps the shock of Big Davie's death was too much for him," said Morag, unsure what to make of the proceedings. "We were both devastated when it happened."

"No, it is not that." Donald reached a hand up and scratched the beginning of a beard on the end of his chin. "Jamie seemed as preoccupied as the rest of them and he couldna have moved quicker when that man called him, what was his name again?"

"You mean Fraser? Aye, I noticed that. Fraser looked as if he was in charge and he expected Jamie to obey. Something happened here, whatever it is, it has everyone in a right mess. Not one person has taken any notice of us," Gregor answered.

"I saw that too," stated Donald, before spotting the figure of Father Patrick. "Here is one man that will surely give us some answers though." Raising his voice, Donald called over to the priest, "Father Patrick! Over here!"

The scrawny priest, hurried to join them, plopping his bottom onto one of the comfortable chairs beside Donald. Out of breath, Donald gave him a few seconds to gain composure before opening the conversation.

"Father Patrick, am I glad to see you. No-one will speak to us. I am frantic with worry. Have you seen Malcolm?"

"I am sorry, Donald, but your brother is not here. He left this morning to pursue that rogue Hamish Balliol," replied Father Patrick who then proceeded to tell the story of their travels to Lanark, the cruelty encountered at the hands of Hamish Balliol and the people picked up on the journey.

Turning around, he continued, "Morag, it is so good to see you. I am glad that you and Donald are safe. We do seem to be missing someone and have gained a stranger. What has happened to our giant?"

Donald and Morag spent the next few minutes summarising the tale of their journey, from Donald's descent into his dream world, to the death of Big Davie, and the meeting of Gregor in Moderwell, before explaining about the journey to Lanark and what they had seen. Once they finished, a look of concern spread over Father Patrick's face.

"That is quite some tale. I am sorry that Big Davie has passed away, despite his flaws, he was a good man at heart, perhaps as pure a man as I knew. I will always remember his kindness to others. He was a special man. I shall certainly shed a tear tonight." Changing the subject, Father Patrick continued, "Did you find your brother Rabbie? I have been praying for his safe return every day since we parted."

"Father, there was no sign of him. He was not in Moderwell or amongst any of the Heathens that we encountered. I fear that he became one of those vile creatures. I still hold some hope that Rabbie is alive, but my heart says otherwise."

"That is a shame," said the priest, making the sign of a cross in the air. "Let us bow our heads and take a moment to remember those lost to us."

As one, the group prayed and remembered the loss of Big Davie, who had given his life to save theirs. Rabbie, who had went off to look for them and was now missing, presumed deceased, and Jean, who was the unfortunate victim of a crazed madman. The death toll was rising and Donald knew that it would get worse before much longer.

"So, Jamie is in one of those rooms, planning for a war with Fraser," said Donald, trying to take it all in. "I take it that it will be all hands to the front line to defend the town?"

"Yes, that is correct. The Bruce has issued an order for the clans to provide armies to defend the town, to try and delay the Heathens whilst they get all the townsfolk inside the castle. Only the Wallace and the Douglas Clan have enough men to provide their own force, the rest of the town will combine under a third. Fraser is commanding our clan with Jamie as the runner between all three armies. We dinna have long until the Heathens are upon us, I suggest that you all come with me and I can make arrangements for your role in the upcoming battle."

"Thank you, Father. I have a feeling that today willna be a good day to die," Donald replied grimly.

CHAPTER THIRTY-TWO

THE CHASE

It was a few days since Malcolm rode a horse and the prolonged trip to Forth was proving to be a sore one for his backside, the large brown mare taking every bump and rough patch on the journey. Brian's bodyguard Joe was alongside, fury etched upon his face. Malcolm spoke a couple of times to him on the route and he showed nothing but compassion and love for Big Davie's father.

To the rear was the pair of lads they picked up in Carnwath, Wee Steve and John Wilson. Both were in a sombre mood as they kept pace behind them. Knowing that Carnwath was lost, the two men were invaluable in finding an alternative way around the hamlet, across the vast, lush meadow which proved to be a comfortable canter for the animals. The only obstacles were the boundary fences built by the farmers to keep their livestock enclosed. The final quartet was four of the clan who survived the attempted murder in the dormitory on the second floor. Each soldier hand-picked by Joe and were fiercely loyal to Brian. His demise not only shocked but also infuriated the men vowing to kill Hamish in the most gruesome method possible.

As they neared Forth, plumes of smoke danced above rooftops as a light breeze caught and played with it like a woman twirling her scarf. Panic set in as Malcolm realised that some of the buildings were on fire. It was coming from the area where Morag lived.

"We may be too late!" Malcolm called, digging his heels into the beast. "Come on, we need to get a move on!"

The group were soon at a gallop, Malcolm streaking ahead with Joe a few paces back. As they approached the hamlet, residents were outside passing water from the wells to stop the blaze spreading.

Hastily dismounting, Malcolm grabbed the nearest bucket and helped tackle the blaze. The fire raged on as the others joined in, flames dancing about, singeing the hair from their beards. A couple of villagers pulled back due to a severe burn on an arm or leg, but perseverance and a tremendous effort from the locals soon extinguished the threat.

"Good job, everyone," said Malcolm, smiling at the battered group behind, catching the eye of an aging woman, her long auburn hair greying with age but not detracting from the mature beauty she possessed.

"Thank you for helping, son. The whole village is on your debt. Tell me, where have you travelled from?"

"Erm, it is me, Malcolm Douglas, son of Cammy and Jean. I stay out in the outskirts of the village on the farm."

"I ken who you are, laddie. I am just wondering who you have come with and where have you been?

"Agnes, your curiosity will get you killed one of these days." Malcolm laughed. "This is Joe Douglas, personal bodyguard to Brian Douglas, clan leader in Lanark, and these are his men. Please, tell me what happened here?"

"What are you doing hanging out with senior clansmen? Are you looking for trouble, son?"

"I think trouble has found me, lass. I am just glad to have such skilled men supporting me. Once again, do you ken what happened here?"

"I really dinna ken a lot. I was sitting in my chair, having a nap, and the next thing that I kennt, there were flames and Murdo was shaking me awake. We got out as quickly as we could and the rest of the villagers helped us. That is all I ken."

"Does anyone else ken anything?" Malcolm shouted to the rest of the crowd. "We have been chasing a very bad man and we need to ken where he has gone to."

"I saw what happened," a young woman with jet black hair called out, hypnotic hazel eyes met his. Skye often went to church with her parents, sat at the back deep in prayer. An attractive lass, around about Morag's age, there was some interest from his side but the growing relationship with Morag nipped it in the bud. There were snippets of conversation overheard but he did not catch much. The family fled from the north-west coast of Scotland after escaping by boat from the Isle of Skye, her birthplace. Rumour spread through the village and one he heard was the family moved into Forth during the night, with the swaddling babe in hand. Whispers were rife amongst the locals for a few years, gossiping about the reasons for the hurried escape, but nothing was ever confirmed or denied. She was a couple of years older than him and spent a lot of time fending off potential male suitors. A lack of interest gave her the reputation of being a witch, something that was soon refuted by Father Patrick, who was quite protective of the Forth congregation.

"Speak up, lass, you have nothing to be afraid of. We are not going to do anything to you, Skye."

The audience parted to allow her to come closer to Malcolm and the others. As she approached, a warm smile enveloped the pale, pretty face and an enchanting smell caught his nostrils, one of a deep musk that exuded from her. If there was not love and a commitment to Morag, then this was one girl he would have definitely pursued.

"I was standing outside blethering to Mhairi, talking about Big Davie. You ken that she really likes him. Well, we were so both distracted fantasising about his big muscles that we didna notice a group of men riding into the village until it was too late. There must have been at least thirty of them. Well, they got off their horses and started killing some of the men here and setting fire to the houses. Mhairi got all upset and yelled, telling them that Big Davie would come back and take care of them. They seemed to take exception to that and slapped her hard and she fell to the ground clutching her face."

Fists tightening, face reddening, Malcolm felt rage build inside, threatening to blow. "Those bastards! What did you do?"

"There was not much that I could do. If I had stood up to them, then I would have been treated as badly as Mhairi. So, I tried to blend in with the walls as much as possible, but they spotted me. Their leader strode over, he was one scary man, let me tell you that. Well, he looked me straight in the eyes and told me that he was going to burn half the village to the ground. He said to pass a message to you, that this is your doing and if you want to see Mhairi again, then to come to Peebles and give yourself up where you will stand trial as a traitor to the Balliols. Do you ken this man, Malcolm?"

"I do, Skye, I have kennt him for many years and he hates my guts. It is Hamish Balliol and it sounds as if he has a lot of protection and men at his disposal now. Thank you for your help, I willna forget it."

"Just get the bastard who did this. I like Mhairi, she has been a good friend to me. I would hate to see something happen to her."

"I will try my best, lass. Does her ma ken that she is missing?"

"Not that I ken. The last I kennt, she was inside having a nap and I didna see their house on fire. She must still be in there."

"Ah shit. That means that I need to tell her."

"If it helps, I will come with you, it is not fair on you to do this alone," Skye said, concerned.

"Thank you, I will take you up on that offer. Now, tell me, what has happened to all the infected in the village? I dinna see any."

"It was Mhairi," answered Skye, with a tear in her eye, "after you all left, she went door to door and rounded up all the able people and we all worked together to rid the village of those creatures. Then she started patrols. We all walk in pairs when she told us to. We havena had any problems with Heathens since yesterday."

"If only everyone was like that. I need to get some men together so that we can go after Mhairi, she deserves to be rescued after what she has done. Joe, can you sort that out for me whilst I go and speak to Sheena Douglas about her daughter?"

"Aye, Malcolm, I will see who I can find," Joe replied.

Walking towards a gathering of locals that had formed a couple of hundred yards away, Joe was soon in deep conversation, trying to recruit them to join the small force. Malcolm took Skye by the hand, her touch soft like a nobleman's silk shirt, and led her to Morag's home before entering through the door and making the short climb up the stairs.

"Sheena! Are you there?" called Skye, hoping that a friendly voice would not frighten the poor woman. "I have brought Malcolm Douglas, he has news about your daughter."

"Give me a second! I am not decent! I will meet you in the kitchen!"

Trudging back down, Malcolm and Skye sat at the small table beside the cauldron, a sombre look on both their faces. It was only a couple of days ago that Malcolm had last been in the house with Morag, it was surprising how much had changed in a few days.

"You look as if you have the weight of the world on your shoulders," began Skye, disturbing the momentary silence, "I havena seen you in a few days, what have you been up to?"

"You ken, this and that, not a lot. Travelled to Carnwath, met some nice people, saw some horrible things. Went to Lanark, had a feast, watched a man die, you ken, the usual."

"Malcolm Douglas, you make light of what seems to be some adventure. What on earth have you been doing and where is Morag?"

"It may be best to explain it all when Sheena comes down, it is a long story, but she will want to ken about her daughter first."

"What about my daughter?" Sheena interrupted, entering the kitchen, auburn hair tied up in a shawl, wearing a worn brown dress. "I thought Morag was going to Moderwell with Big Davie? Have they found Rabbie yet?"

"Not Morag, I have not seen her since we parted ways a couple of days ago. I mean Mhairi."

"Where is Mhairi?" asked Sheena, suddenly curious. "I have not seen her in a while. Is she not with you, Skye?"

"I am so sorry, Mrs Douglas," said Skye, morosely, "Mhairi has been taken."

"Taken? Who would take my daughter and why? She is a gentle girl, she would not hurt anyone."

"I ken that but there was a raid on the village when you were asleep. It was the Balliols, they snatched Mhairi and have taken her to Peebles. There was nothing I could do. I tried to stop them." Distress was evident in Skye as her head sank down between her arms, sobbing and wailing. The guilt and grief escaping as she continued to torture herself whilst taking the full blame for Mhairi's abduction.

"It was not your fault, Skye," comforted Malcolm, moving to comfort the girl, "if you had done anything else, you would have been killed. Hamish Balliol is an evil bastard and will pay for his crimes, I will see to it. If it is anyone's fault, it is mine. It is me that he wants to kill, he is trying to destroy everything that I love. I am sorry, Sheena, I couldna get here in time to stop this."

"Will you two stop it! All my children are missing and all you can do is mope around feeling sorry for yourself. Now, tell me Malcolm, what has happened since you left us a couple of days ago?"

Sheena and Skye listened intently as Malcolm told his tale, Skye helped fill in the blanks and answer any questions that Sheena had. It was a relief to be able to let it all out and tell someone everything he endured. Sheena was a patient woman who at the end of the story was more worried than anything else.

"Well, Malcolm Douglas, that is all well and good, but what are you going to do to get my daughters back?"

"There is not much I can do about Morag. Donald and Davie are looking after her. As for Mhairi, I honestly am not sure, it will take a large force to try and take Peebles. Joe and the others that came with me are trying to recruit men from the village to mount a rescue, but I fear that it willna be enough. Every minute that she spends with that vile bastard is one too many for my liking."

"I am coming with you. She is my friend and I want to help," Skye stated.

"Dinna be daft, lass," snapped Sheena, indignantly. "What use will you be to the men trying to rescue her? You will just get in the way. It is best to leave the fighting to the menfolk, like I plan to do. I will wait here for their return."

"Excuse me, you of all people should not be talking like that, not after what Mhairi has done for this village. She has proved that women can make the difference and I want to help her, it sounds like Malcolm could do with all the help that he can get."

"My daughter was a fool, look where it got her, kidnapped by a bloody Balliol. Do you want the same fate?"

"Ladies," Malcolm interrupted, "calm down, it is my decision and I really could do with as many hands as possible. I am not happy for Skye to go with us, but I have no choice, I need her if I have any chance of getting your daughter back. Even with her help, I am not sure if we will have enough to mount a rescue straight away. I will have to see how many people Joe has managed to recruit before I make that decision."

CHAPTER THIRTY-THREE

GLENS OF THE DEAD

The mist rolled along the glen, obscuring anything that was a few hundred yards in the distance. It was typical weather in Scotland for this time of year, but considering everything that happened, it was not something that was going to help the ragtag Lanark army as they stood ready, awaiting the approaching horde.

"Douglas Clan!" Fraser Douglas yelled as he paced up and down the line. "We will stand firm. Our tactics are simple and if we stick to them, we will be victorious. Keep the monsters at length; they are unable to bite us if they are not close enough. Use your polearms to stab and your shields to fend them off. If they get through, that is when you drop your shields and use your hand to hand weapons with your bucklers. You have got archer support from atop the town walls, so keep them within range of our bowmen so that we can maximise their skills. We have no cavalry today, most of our horses got eaten by the infected and the bastards seem to have a taste for it."

"Is that why you are riding one then? Are you going to be the bait?" one of the clan shouted from the rear.

Arrogantly, Fraser replied, "Dinna be ridiculous, I am far too valuable for that. You need my leadership and military expertise to win this battle. Now, if things start to go awry, we fall back to the glen outside the castle, using the town as cover. Unfortunately, as you already ken, the mechanism to lower all the gates is stuck and we reckon that they have been sabotaged by our enemies. This means the town is exposed and we are the last line of defence between the monsters and the townsfolk. We are here to give as many people as possible a chance to get to safely inside the castle. We may not have huge numbers, but we can get this victory. We are the centre force in this battle. On our left are our close allies, the Bruce Clan, and on our right are the combined army of the rest of the clans within Lanark. We are outnumbered by the infected, but we willna be defeated by them. We are Douglas and we dinna yield, ever."

"*We are Douglas, we dinna yield*!" came the chanting from the troops.

Donald felt hackles rising as the words were repeated continuously by each man standing around him. Hands started beating chests, the rhythm was in time with the rousing phrase inspiring the soldiers, preparing them for the looming battle ahead. Nerves fluttered about in Donald's stomach, which was only natural before a skirmish which did not look winnable, but he was starting to feel a bit more at ease. It felt strange standing there in the middle of an army of people who he did not really know. Although Jamie was in the group, he took his normal position as standard bearer beside the second in command, ready to defend the flag and the fight the Heathens with everything that he had.

There were many similar fights in his daydreams which Donald replayed. However, on each occasion, either Big Davie, Malcolm, or his da was standing beside him and they were always up against the Balliols or the English. Never a foe that did not use combat tactics, an enemy so ferocious it did not care who it attacked, as long as it could gorge on human flesh. Donald shivered at the thought, goosebumps formed on his skin as the possibility of becoming dinner for the monsters was now becoming a reality.

Quickly, Donald checked his weaponry, ensuring each item was in prime condition for the upcoming melee. The wooden buckler was placed on the floor behind him, with a sword lying in its sheath at his waist, ready to be drawn if the creatures were able to get past the initial defences.

"Are you alright, son?" Donald's thoughts were interrupted by a query from a broad Irish accent. Taken by surprise, Donald turned to see a tall, slightly built, red-haired soldier who was leaning on a huge metallic shield.

"Yes, I think so. It is my first proper battle and there are an awful lot of those creatures coming for us," Donald replied with hesitation, nerves jangling.

"Ach, dinna worry so much. You will be fine, son. Just concentrate on what is in front of you and trust the lad either side to take care of what they are facing. I will be on your left, so you willna have anything to worry about from me. The name is Seamus, Seamus O'Neill." The gangly man outstretched a hand.

"Donald, Donald Douglas, son of Cammy Douglas, from the village of Forth. Sorry for being nosey, but are you not in the wrong army?"

"My mother is a Douglas, my father is an Irishman," said Seamus, grinning. "I was born in Ireland and grew up there, but we moved to Carluke to be with my mother's family. I found a good Irish lass, too good for the likes of me, and before we knew it, the local priest married us, and we set up house together. Would you do me a favour, Donald? If I die, can you go to Carluke and tell my wife Claire that I died a hero, if she is still alive?"

"I passed through Carluke on the way here, there was not a lot of infected in the streets and all the people were inside and keeping to themselves," Donald answered, grasping the jovial man's hand and squeezing it. "I promise to return and tell your Claire about your heroic death if you dinna make it. If I die, will you find my da Cammy and tell him that I died honourably? He is in Wallace's army down south, fighting in Lancashire."

"I will do, son. Just you stick close to me and we will both be fine. You look like a handy lad with a sword, have you ever fought any of the infected yet?"

"A couple of times," replied Donald cautiously. "I was lucky, I had Big Davie beside me. That man was like a small army on his own. I saw him take down thirty of the infected while, the rest of us were taking on one or two at a time, Davie was scything through them all. He was a great fighter and an amazing man."

"Big Davie is a legend. I met the guy a couple of times and he is every bit the fearsome warrior that he is portrayed in the stories. A giant of a man with a pure heart, there are not many like him," Seamus said with a hint of pride.

"There *were* not many like him," corrected Donald, regretfully. "He is dead now."

"No fucking way!" gasped Seamus in astonishment. "I refuse to believe that anything could kill the legend that is Davie Douglas, the man was an animal on the battlefield."

"There was no man like him," Donald whispered with a tear in his eye. "He was a true friend and like a brother to me, I just wish he was still here."

"Use that to spur you on in this battle. Do the big man proud, you two were obviously close. Show him that you are a true warrior and I am sure that he will be proud of you.

"I am not so sure about that. I blame myself for his death," Donald said ruefully.

"You are being too harsh on yourself. I am sure that it was not your fault. It must take something special to kill a legend, I am sure whatever you did would not have made a difference. Stop beating yourself up about it."

"It was my fault though. I was lying there in a trance whilst both Davie and Morag fought off those monsters. I could have helped but instead I was out of it on the ground. Some friend I am."

"Look," started Seamus, trying to reassure the lad, "Big Davie was a one-man army. What could you have done differently that he couldna have? Stop blaming yourself and get your head straight and ready for this fight. I need you focussed, this will be a bloody battle and I willna be left exposed because your mind is elsewhere. Now show some courage, young Donald, there is a lot of dirty, hungry beasts that are wanting to eat us and we canna allow that to happen."

A faint rhythmic beat, like a harras of horses thundering their hooves, vibrated through the ground below, interrupting the conversation. The whinnying of mares to the rear caused Donald to look up to see a long line of bodies in the distance, steadily moving up the incline. A stench of urine wafted by as a few of the less experience men soiled themselves. Donald barely held control of his own bladder, relieved the time was taken to empty it earlier. Hands shaking, Donald's knuckles turned white as he clung onto the fifteen-foot spear, hoping not to let go.

Struggling to reign in his mount, Fraser paced back and forth in front of the rows of troops. "Douglas Clan! Our enemy is now in sight, you ken what faces us. Raise your shields, prepare your pikes, we are about to fight, and I dinna intend us to lose!"

Yells of agreement came from within the ranks. Donald found himself unwittingly joining in with the camaraderie, it was not something that he was used to. The conversation with Seamus had put Donald more at ease, but the sudden realisation that he was about to fight for his life had brought the fear back, the thought of potentially dying and returning as one of the creatures horrified him. "Stand fast, Donald, you will survive. They willna kill you," said Donald to himself, trying to concentrate on what lay ahead.

"Archers!" shouted Fraser once again. "Get those damn bows ready and be prepared to fire at will. The more that you kill, the less we have to face. I want to see the battlefield littered with bodies!"

Donald checked the buckler and sword were easily accessible before raising the shield and picking up his pike. There was an unfamiliarity with the weapons, which were a new discovery in warfare, one the Douglas Clan had adopted only recently. Although he felt disadvantaged, they looked simple enough to use. He remembered what Big Davie used to say about using weapons. Keep a hold of the big stick and use the weight of his body to stand fast whilst poking the incoming foe with the pointy bit. It seemed easy when he thought of it like that. Donald just hoped that he was heavy enough to stop himself falling and being crushed.

The slow ascent of the incoming enemy soon turned into a thunderous rumble as the sight and smell of the Lanark army spurred them on towards the next meal. Donald heard multiple twangs as arrows loosed from the long bows of the archers who stood atop the town walls. He peeked out from the side to see what sort of damage they were doing and was shocked. The monstrosities were being littered with numerous shots that penetrated into their festering torsos, which they seemed to ignore while trudging on through the grass, leaving a foul ooze behind.

"Aim for the heads, you idiots," came a shout from the command group, the voice sounded like his cousin Jamie who seemed to be close by. "You are wasting arrows!"

The steady stream of fire stopped as the bowmen readjusted aim, but by the time their target was acquired, it was too late. The horde was upon the Douglas Army, teeth gnashing and snarling as the pikes thrust into midriffs, knocking out some of the projectiles embedded into chests. The elongated spears did not stop them as the creatures pushed onwards through the protruding poles, guts hanging from the spike at the other end. Donald's stomach started to retch at the sight of the gore and entrails adorning the weaponry. Much to his horror, the first infected was joined by another, then a third as the weight of more bodies pushed against straining arms. Donald knew that it would not be long until they reached the shield and he was not sure if the sheer volume would overwhelm him before the archers ran out of arrows.

"They are going to crush us! The pikes are not working. We have to go hand to hand," Seamus yelled.

"I agree," chorused several voices along the Douglas front line.

The number of beasts was close to overwhelming them. A feeling of dread came over Donald as the thought of being trapped under the thrust of the advancing horde was terrifying, giving him an extra boost of strength to keep defences steadfast. Looking to the right, one of the other clansmen was on his back, confined by the sheer weight of the enemy atop the long shield, ripping chunks out of the screaming man. Donald knew that whatever happened, he did not want to meet his maker that way.

"Drop your pikes," commanded Fraser. "We fight for our lives. Aim for their heads, show no mercy!"

A sense of relief washed over Donald as he let go of the wooden shaft, using a spare hand to wipe away the moisture to prevent his vision blurring. Jumping back, he dropped the cover and deftly picked up the buckler and sword, standing ready.

The first attacker came, a fat noble, guts hanging over his belly and a gaunt complexion intermittently stained with the spray of gore. Discoloured teeth were bared as the monster prepared to pounce and sink them into Donald. However, at the first sign of movement, Donald neatly dodged, bringing his arm up to smash the shield into the creature's face, blood spurting out of both nostrils as a vessel ruptured. Slashing with the blade, he cut through the eyes of the infected, hoping that if it could not see, then it could not eat him. Unfortunately, it seemed to make no difference as the attacker moved forward again for a follow-up strike, trying to knock the weapon from his grip. Surprised at the tactic, Donald stepped towards the creature, thrusting with the shield, moving it back whilst using his left foot to push it over to the ground. He followed through and stabbed through the orbit for the killing blow. An eyeball was left skewered on the sword as he rapidly withdrew the blade, trying to wipe it off on the grass. Donald stood panting, hands on knees as the reality of the situation hit him. He had put in such effort just to kill one of the monsters and there were hundreds more out there, all wanting a pound of flesh. Determined not to let Big Davie down, he stood straight, just in time to see a few more approach. The pike thrust into them earlier still protruded through the duo but the third one managed to break free from the others.

The ridiculousness of the pair was lost on Donald, as he did not see a comedic duo, knocking into everyone as they walked, but a double threat trying to break free from the spear and dine on Donald. There was nothing funny about the way they kept rebounding off the long shields of nearby clansmen. All he could see was two of the infected wanting his flesh and he was not going to let them chew his calf like a noble munching on the leg of a spit-roasted pig. Keeping a defensive stance, Donald waited until they were within striking distance before stepping to the side and using his huge boot to kick out at the side of the lead attacker, forcing it to fall, its partner tumbling in tandem. Deftly, he moved towards them, avoiding limbs that tried to entangle around his ankles and hands attempting to grab hold. With a leap, Donald vaulted in front of the pair, turning to slash across the larynx in a double motion, severing arteries as blood spurted from their throats, killing them on the spot.

Grimly, Donald scanned either side to see that the rest of the clan was not faring as well. Numerous men had fallen and were either being feasted upon by the creatures or had turned and become one of the undead themselves. It felt galling that the very people that he had just fought beside had now become the enemy he feared. Whilst the Douglas Clan numbers fell, the amount of foes stayed roughly the same as they pushed the army back towards the town wall. Donald knew that it would not be long until the retreat was called, and they were forced to flee inside the walls of Lanark.

Murmurs flowed across the ranks, a general buzz sounding from the far right and speculation was making its way towards him.

"Fraser has fallen, the infected have taken him and his horse. The command group are in turmoil, the only one now left is Jamie Douglas and even he is struggling against them!"

Rumours were always spread during battle, or so Donald was told by his da. Often these were not true, but one had to look for the signs just in case they were.

Donald found himself missing the quiet evenings with his parents, sitting, listening to tales and the banter with Malcolm. What he would give for da and Malcolm to be there just now. Loneliness crept up too quickly, engulfing his spirit. Although Seamus looked out for him and Cousin Jamie was nearby, the nerves were still there. *Did Big Davie piss his pants before battle?* Donald witnessed a lot of the men involuntarily soil themselves when the dead were close. He suspected this was the reason that a lot of them did not don underwear, not that he went out of his way to look.

Focusing back on the threat ahead, a group of four were making way towards him. Looking around for support, there was no-one nearby who was not already occupied with one or two of the creatures. Seamus was fighting three at once and had already taken a couple of bites to the arm. Donald could see mustard coloured puss ooze from Seamus's wounds integrate with the blood running from the cut. Donald knew that Seamus would die soon but vowed not to let his new friend turn.

Faced with a horrible decision, Donald quickly weighed the options. His choice was to deal with the immediate threat or to help out Seamus and face seven, potentially eight, of the monsters on his own if Seamus was to become one before he got there. Failing to reach him meant someone else in the Douglas Clan would have to face them and Donald had enough on his conscience without adding more to it.

The decision proved easy. Donald raced toward the ailing Seamus. The path clear, Donald's heart ached with the sight of so many clansmen being slaughtered. Stomach churning from the ghastly odours, he was not deterred. Spurred on by determination to keep his word to Seamus, Donald hoisted the sword, and with a mighty swing, cleaved cleanly through the neck of the muncher. Body flopping with a plop to the ground, surprisingly, the beast's jaws were still firmly clamped upon Seamus' limb. The Irishman's teeth were grit with agony, yet the warrior bravely fought to fend off the onslaught of bites and scratches reigning in.

Incoming from the right was a well-endowed, blonde, teenage girl. Normally such attention from a young lady would have Donald stuttering nervously, but her once creamy complexion was now withered and gaunt. Wrinkled skin streaked with shades of scarlet made Donald almost feel sorry for her, though not enough to stop him from decapitating her. This left the two that were still attacking Seamus, who promptly dispatched one, using a knife that he could barely grip due to the damage to his forearm. The precise slashing at its throat was nothing short of spectacular given his severe injuries.

"Watch out, son, there are more behind you!" called a voice from behind Seamus.

Worried, Donald spun around to see the trio of terror had caught up to him. A low growl met him as the small group he avoided earlier had followed through the battlefield. Readying a defensive stance, Donald stood his ground, awaiting the incoming attack from the slavering threat.

"Come on then," Donald taunted, swaying sideways, trying to weigh his next move. "How about you, Fatty? Or maybe you, Beardy? Or even you, Old Man? Which one should I kill first?"

"*Mwwoooaaaarrrrr!*" screamed Beardy. Worryingly it sounded like he was issuing a challenge. One that the hairy beast was not going to back down from.

Donald smiled wryly. "So, Beardy, you want me to shave your beard off? I dinna blame you. It is looking very tangled and you seem to have gotten some food and drink in it. You seem to be a very messy eater."

The ensemble howled in unison before quickly rushing in, their speed surprising. Jumping to the right, Donald stabbed the abdomen of the elder, rupturing its side, guts disgorging. Ignoring the trauma, Old Man moved towards him whilst the others tried to react to the speed of the teenager.

"I guess you found my jokes funny," Donald quipped as Old Man kept coming. "You are splitting your sides with laughter!"

The remark was met by an aggressive retort as Donald ducked the initial strike, bringing the buckler up to fend away the attack. A quick step towards the beast was followed by a thrust forward of his forehead, connecting squarely with the nose, blood and broken bone spraying everywhere. The ferocity of the blow forced it back, staggering slightly as it tried to regain its footing. Meanwhile the other pair joined it and began their attack on the young soldier.

"Fatty, were you missing your friend?" Donald once more taunted his opponents. "Or were you just looking for an excuse to eat him? I hear you like the blood of a Scotsman, well you willna drink mine."

Fending off, the incumbents, Donald could see Seamus struggling against the monsters he was facing. "Are you alright Seamus?"

"I am perfectly fine, I may die today but I am taking down as many of the infected as I can in the process," Seamus replied, a huge grin spread across his face as another beast stumbled towards him.

"What do you mean, may? Have you not seen that huge poisonous gash in your arm? You are going to end up one of them."

"Nonsense," stated Seamus, confidence seeping through him as he squared up against his aggressor, "it is but a flesh wound. I will live."

"That disgusting, seeping, yellow puss says otherwise," replied Donald, disbelievingly as he dodged another blow from an attacker. "Look, when you die, I will remove your head and stop you from turning into one of them."

"You should concentrate on what is in front of you and not worry about me. I will be fine and if I am not, I ken that you will remove my head."

With those words ringing in his ear, Donald focussed on the immediate threat as three more of the fiends closed in. It took a few minutes to dispatch them, removing each head whilst avoiding the slobbering mouths. Seeing a break in the action, Donald took a few seconds to catch his breath and compose himself, wiping away splattered blood from his forehead and taking a gulp from the water pouch.

Hearing that Seamus was still fighting, Donald turned with intent to render assistance but stopped in awe at what transpired in front of him. Barely recognisable from blood streaked clothes and skin, Seamus was on his knees, close to death as the remaining four monsters had attached themselves to his flesh, feasting on the warrior. Donald could see the fight had left Seamus and his time was close.

Rushing over, Donald shoved his buckler into the first enemy, pushing it off Seamus before releasing the rage and anger onto the others, kicking and punching at them until all that was left was squashed remains. Now unencumbered, the collapsed warrior struggled for breath though unstoppable, still attempting to use the buckler to get back onto his feet. Donald booted the ribs of the closest corpse in frustration at the sight of the dying man.

"*Retreat!*" bellowed a cry from behind, the voice sounding a lot like Jamie. "We will regroup in front of the castle! *Retreat!*"

Donald looked at Seamus. The soldier's eyes glazed over as he slumped face first into the ground, strength depleted, unable to support his own weight. Boundless monsters closed in, teeth bared, dinner lying helpless in front of them.

CHAPTER THIRTY-FOUR

EVACUATION

The word chaos would be an understatement, not sufficient enough to describe the scenes Morag witnessed. All decorum was lost as she was bumped, kicked, and knocked by passing townsfolk as they scrambled along the streets. It was amazing how much people could carry and run at the same time. One woman even had a huge iron cauldron strapped to her back. How she never fell, Morag did not know. The rats were even scurrying away from the thick leather boots pounding the stone surface, squeaking in fear of their lives.

All in all, Morag's head throbbed from the noise and her arm was covered in red marks from the constant carelessness of others. Never before had she witnessed so many people all in one place. This was busier than outside Old Ma Mary's place on baking day. All the kids in Forth and the surrounding villages queued outside in the hope of a taste of her delicious treats. It was rare when a child went home without a bun or a cake. A few times, the hubbub was too much for Morag so hands slapped over her ears to try and dull the commotion. She was close to the breaking point and Father Patrick was not helping. Every time she looked for the priest, he seemed to be helping someone in the crowd, whether it be picking up dropped clothing or helping a fallen woman. He was everywhere. It was quite a sight to behold, but frustrating as he kept getting in the way causing townsfolk to try and avoid him which was why she was continuously getting hurt.

"Will you watch where you are going!" Morag screamed, grasping her left foot in agony after a plump lady stood on it. "I may not be tall, but I do exist. I am not a ghost!"

"Sorry, miss," the woman mumbled in quick apology, hurrying up the road, bumping into other people before tripping and landing on her bottom.

Morag's smug grin was short-lived as Father Patrick hurried over, offered a hand, and pulled her back up, before she uttered thanks and continued up the street.

Making her way to the side, Morag stood against the wall of a small house and called out, "Father Patrick! Over here!"

It took a couple of attempts before he heard and glided over, daintily dodging the masses trying to thrust past. He rested, standing by her side, his breath shallow with the exertion.

"Morag, how can I help?"

Morag closed her eyes, thinking of sheep grazing in the field in an attempt to calm her mind. "I was thinking. We really are not doing much to help the people in the streets. They are all scared, more interested in fleeing the town than anything. There must be lots of folk still in their houses, afraid to move due to the crowds or simply not aware of what's going on. Would it not make more sense to find and try to help them?"

"Morag, you are a clever lass. Why did I not think of that?"

"I think you have been too busy trying to help people that you are not seeing how scared they are. It sickens me to watch all this panic whilst Donald and Jamie are out there putting their lives on the line, and for what? To save them." The disgust was evident in her voice as she gestured towards the townsfolk. "Do they really deserve the sacrifice that those brave men are making? Do we deserve the sacrifice they are making? No man should have to give up his life to save another. It is not right."

"Morag, lass," said Father Patrick, gently, "you are being a bit too harsh. Who are we to decide who is to be saved and who should live? It is God's will that good men like Donald and Jamie are able to allow the unworthy to have a chance in this world. They will get their judgement in the afterlife, the same as you or I. We need to keep being the best we can be, keep being decent people. If we can do that, then it is not our soul being plagued by the demons of our past."

"Thank you, Father. Your council is wise as usual. I do try to live a good life, but all these people infuriate me. I swear the next time I get bumped; I will punch them."

"You need to reign in your temper, lass. Come, let us see if we can find people who truly need our help."

The pair slipped away from the main road and went down the nearest side street, a long narrow, cobbled pathway. Father Patrick stumbled a couple of times, nearly going over his ankle.

"Whoever invented cobblestones belongs in Hell beside the man who invented swords and fishermen."

"What is wrong with fishermen?" asked Morag, curiously. "I thought Jesus was a fisherman."

"Do you not listen to my sermons, lass? Jesus was a carpenter. It was his disciples that were fishermen."

"I thought his disciples were good men. Why do you despise them?"

Laughing, Father Patrick responded, "It is not the disciples I despise; it is the modern-day fishermen. They drink, curse, and spend most of their days in sin and debauchery. If modern day fishermen were more like Peter and Andrew, then we would live in much better place."

"I have never met a fisherman."

Solemnly, Father Patrick spoke, "I pray, for your sake, that you never do."

"Shall we try the first door on the left?"

"After you, child."

Morag thumped on the small door. Pounding away, the sound echoing down the narrow alleyway. After about a minute, she gave up, shaking her hand in the air, trying to ease the dull throb.

"I think I may try the next one. Perhaps you should not hit the wood with such vigour. If you keep doing that, you will injure yourself. You are no good to me or God with a bleeding hand.

Sheepish, Morag replied, "I think that would be wise."

Rapping at the next premises, it was answered by a short, thin woman. The smell of stale sweat pouring out the door almost overwhelmed them.

"What do you want?" Without giving them time to answer, she continued, "Never mind. I can see you are a priest. Whatever you are selling, I am not interested. I dinna want any of your religious bile." Abruptly, the door slammed shut.

A stunned silence ensued before Morag spoke, "Erm, I dinna think she likes you. Do you ken her?"

"I have never seen her before in my life."

"Do you think we should try again. She really should be evacuating with the others."

"I think it is your turn," replied Father Patrick, tentatively. "I have a feeling you might have more luck than I."

Nervously, Morag raised her hand and pounded the wooden surface a couple of times, stepping back, not wanting to be within striking distance. This seemed fruitless but they needed to try. Big Davie would have burst into the house and emerged with the woman over his shoulder, marching up the street to the castle, not giving her any choice in the matter. The fool would probably tell jokes as her fists pummelled into his back.

"What is Heaven like?" asked Morag as she waited on an answer.

Father Patrick pondered for a few seconds before replying, "I honestly dinna ken. Why do you ask?"

"I have no doubts that is where Big Davie is. I just want to ken that he is at peace."

"I have faith he is. I can only guess at what Heaven is like. It is God's house. I am sure it will have everything Big Davie needs to be at peace with himself. I honestly believe he is probably watching us just now."

Waving up to the sky, Morag spoke quietly, "Hi, Davie. If you are watching, I am sorry that I never put my poker through your head. I couldna bring myself to do it. I miss you and I hope you are happy."

"I said I didna want anything religious here!" Morag jumped back at the voice as it echoed through the door.

"We are not being religious!" Morag yelled back. "The town is about to be under attack. You must evacuate to the castle!"

"Is this some trick to get me to church?"

"No, your life is in danger!"

"I really dinna want to go to church. The last time I went, they shouted at me for falling asleep!"

"I will shout at you if you dinna come out and head to the castle!"

"Is there some massive prayer session at the castle? I bet there is. You religious people are devious!"

"Look, the monsters are going to attack the village. You need to go to the castle for your own safety. There is no prayer session there and nothing religious. We just want to see you safe!"

"If you promise me there is nothing religious, then I will go to the castle!"

"For God's sake," Morag cursed in frustration.

Father Patrick hurriedly admonished her, "Morag, dinna use the Lord's name in vain."

"I knew it was religious!" shouted the woman triumphantly. "I will be staying here!"

"Come on, lass. There is nothing we can do here. This woman is impossible. There are others to try and save."

Feeling downhearted, Morag agreed and they continued banging on doors, trying to convince townsfolk to exit their homes and vacate to the castle. Before long, a few of the archers were seen running along the main street, sprinting for their lives up the steep cobbled slopes.

"Morag, we need to run. If we dinna hurry, we willna get back to the castle in time. That is some of the men who were fighting in the battle down there."

"Can you see Donald or Jamie?"

"No, but if we dinna move, then it willna be Donald or Jamie we see but the Heathens. Run, Morag, run for your life!"

With that, the pair sped to the gate, exiting the town, and into the castle to safety, just before the portcullis was lowered, trapping all the residents inside. Slumping down, Morag panted.

"We were very lucky."

"Were we?" replied Morag. "With all the people in here, it will take just one death before the whole place turns into a bloodbath."

"Let us pray that doesna happen."

CHAPTER THIRTY-FIVE

RETREAT

For a few moments Donald stood rigid, unsure of what to do next after watching Seamus fall. The despair of seeing a strong warrior drop hit hard, coupled with the fear of being infected. However, the command to retreat was clear. In order for the army to survive, they needed to regroup and take a final stand outside the castle. Torn, Donald did not want to leave Seamus to the clutches of the beasts to feast upon. The threat of being isolated was also at the forefront of his mind. It would not take much for the situation to worsen, and with no support, the chance of being surrounded by his worst nightmare was not a prospect that he relished.

Making a quick decision, Donald strode to Seamus. The stricken soldier managed to turn over, his face pleading to end it sooner, rather than later.

"You ken what to do," Seamus croaked with resignation. "Remember your promise, Donald Douglas. Thank you for not forgetting me."

Eyes heavy and falling shut, Seamus went to meet his maker. Donald uttered a small prayer before swinging his sword and thrusting it through the mouth, sending Seamus to the afterlife.

"God bless your soul, Seamus O'Neill," Donald whispered solemnly, tears streaming down his grimy, bloodied cheek. "May you now be at peace with yourself and the world. It was an honour to ken you. I vow to tell your widow Claire how brave a man you were. I vow to tell how valiantly you died. You were a hero."

Slathering beasts no more than a few yards away, Donald turned, wiping away the dampness on his cheek before running as fast as he could towards the open entrance to the walled town. With death hot on his trail, it looked like every surviving clansman had already retreated.

Donald was on his own. A horde of infected villagers and reanimated brethren were gaining fast behind.

Not daring to look back, Donald burst through the opening and into the town, following the same route as earlier, hoping to find a way through the maze of streets and not run into a dead end. The worn roads made the going tough as his leather boots scuffed a couple of times whilst running along the cobbled surface. A scattering of the enemy loomed ahead, but they were in groups of one or two and not the mass horde that had initially attacked on the glens. Several turned to face him, sensing the heavy breathing exerted from his overworked lungs and the sweat dripping from his boiling head. Donald could feel weariness from battle creeping into his aching body. Arms sore from continual use of the buckler and sword, Donald pushed on, forcing his legs to sprint while avoiding confrontation, knowing that stopping would mean the creatures would converge on him.

Bodies lay strewn, obstacles on the stone path as he pushed onwards up the sharp incline. Each corpse had several beasts feasting upon it, stripping skin and muscle, scooping out organs, stuffing mouths full. Donald wanted to do something to prevent further carnage, yet being heavily outnumbered and exhausted forced him to go on, distraught as the reality of war was unfolding in front of him.

One of the infected broke away from the fallen soldier it was feeding on and turned its attention to Donald. Its grey skin hung loose through a ripped tunic, stained by a combination of the putrid liquid of the victim devoured and mud from the glen. There were not many options for Donald, he could either avoid it by finding a side street to traverse, but in doing so, he risked being trapped, surrounded by buildings and the bloodthirsty. Or, he could stand and fight. Though not keen on this, Donald knew that it was the best chance for survival.

"Fuck! This is the last thing I need." Digging deep into his store of reserves, Donald burst forward, aggression pulsing through aching muscles, washing away the stiffness that had weighed down his thighs. Spinning, he avoided an attempted grab by his foe, and with one swift stroke, he removed the arm from its socket, blood spurting in a cherry coloured fountain, staining the ground below. Grinning, Donald turned and blocked a swinging fist aimed for his head with the buckler, stepped inside and beheaded the monster, crown bouncing a few times before gently rolling down the hill.

The brief skirmish did not disturb the other feasting infected. Deciding not to hang around, he continued up the slope towards where the rest of the defenders were waiting, ready for the incoming horde less than a few hundred yards behind Donald. The short delay had cost precious time and distance as the thunder of footsteps could be felt vibrating through the ground underneath.

One more delay could mean death. Face set with determination, Donald grunted. "This is not good! Hopefully the town square is close, this bloody hill is punishing."

Up ahead, a sharp bend came into view, an aging gothic building, windows long and colourfully decorated, sat on the corner beside it. Within the depths of his disturbed mind, Donald recalled that this was the townhouse of Robert the Bruce, the sheriff and infamous clan leader. It was a place his da had always talked about, describing the beautiful velvet curtains and luxurious furnishing within. If there had not been a group of festering foes behind him, then he would have sneaked a look behind the door to see what da had always raving about.

Paranoia ensued. Donald took hasty glances over the shoulder, willing himself up the final few yards. Ahead, just over the breast of the hill, the menacing silhouette of a sole figure stood. Donald gulped, hoping it was not a creature, praying it was one of the other warriors waiting to help with stragglers.

The undead were gaining, they did not seem to be affected by pain, tiredness, or injury. They kept the same pace, lolloping steadily, driven by the smell of sweat and excrement that emanated from the fleeing living. Monster lips dripped slobber, infused with the blood of their unfortunate victims. Donald was now convinced that the horde would catch him before he reached the summit. The sleeve of his arm wiped at his sweat sodden face, the hilt of the sword narrowly missing the top of his brow. The fear of death breathed heavily down his neck, overwhelming as the snarls of the hungry got steadily louder until Donald finally crested the hill and the ground levelled out.

Daring to sneak another look behind, the ravenous rabble was less than two hundred yards away, further than expected. Relief coursed through him as the going was easier over the flat stone surface, giving Donald the chance to finally round the corner where Robert the Bruce's house was.

Coming into focus, Donald recognised the man waiting as Gregor, the surly hunter they met in Moderwell. Looking fresh as a daisy, Gregor smiled warmly, clapping him on the back as he panted in exhaustion, hands on knees trying to recover breath after the punishing ascent.

"It..is..good..to..see..you.."

"Save, your breath, lad," said Gregor, stroking his beard, "we need to move soon, those things dinna seem to be slowing. I was worried about you, lad. I told Jamie I would wait behind and look for you. He told me not to wait too long."

Donald raised his head slightly ready to respond.

"Dinna talk, lad. Recover as much as you can before we set off. He was concerned for your welfare. I told him you were still alive and I would wait for you. I ken he will be glad to see you when we get to the castle."

Nodding, Donald took a couple more gulps of air before standing up. The chasing cadavers were closer now by a good fifty yards.

"Pull up your britches, young sheepherder, it is time to move. They have our scent and I am keen to put as many yards as possible before we meet up with Jamie."

Running for his life seemed to be the norm rather than the exception. Donald scampered back into a jog; his legs stiff after the brief rest. Gregor was beside him, bloodied axe in hand as he kept pace with the younger man. The top end of the town was the affluent area with extravagant houses adorning the streets, the lavish gold and brass fittings glinting, causing them to wince a few times as temporary blindness hit.

Donald was astonished to still have the energy left to sprint. It was amazing what people could do when their lives were in danger. Stretching his arms whilst running, he could feel the soreness all over from the travel and extended battle over the last day. It was painful to see that Gregor was not showing signs of exertion while Donald struggled to find any sort of rhythm in his step.

"Try and relax when you run. You are going to injure yourself," Gregor said, trying to help.

"How can I relax with over a hundred of the hungry chasing us?"

The duo cut down a side street, trying to shake off their pursuers. "Fair point, laddie. I ken it is tough but try and get a rhythm to your stride rather than being tense all the time. Your legs willna ache as much. Move your arms as well, it will help your balance. You run as if you have shit yourself and that canna be good for you."

Gregor did not even appear winded.

"Like this?" Donald started to flap his arms about, looking more like a constipated chicken than anything.

"Maybe not that relaxed." Gregor laughed. As they got a full view ahead, his voice changed to a more concerned tone, "Fuck, that is a dead end, those bastards are not that far behind us. What a fucking idiot."

"Oh God! What do we do?" Donald frantically looked round the alleyway for another exit.

"From what I can see, we have three choices. We could try and scale the wall ahead, we could try and go through one of the houses and hope that there is a back door, or we could go back the way that we came."

"Going back is not an option. We will walk straight into a shitload of the creatures."

"I meant to ask earlier, why do you call them creatures and not Heathens, like Father Patrick does?"

"We have no time for that! We either go over or through the houses. Give me a lift up, I want to see what is over that wall."

"Ha, I dinna fancy heaving your bulky frame up. It may be quicker to try the door and go through the house."

"What if things are worse on the other side? Or there is no way through?"

"It is a chance that we have to take. They are getting too close now, I think we will need to kick the door in."

Turning back round, they positioned themselves in front of the entrance to the nearest house. Gregor lifted his boot and slammed it hard. It would not budge. Swearing under his breath before motioning over Donald to assist, he lined up for a second strike. This time Donald stood alongside to add to the force. Both men lashed out at the same time, again to no avail. Numerous attempts ensued but each time the door remained steadfast.

Suddenly, from above, the shutters flew open. A woman, raven-haired with a touch of grey streaking the sides, appeared, face rouged with anger. If looks could kill, then Donald and Gregor would be six feet under.

"What the hell are you pair of idiots doing? The noise that you are making is going to bring those creatures down on me! Go away and leave me alone!" At this, the lady disappeared back into her house, the tension and anger could still be felt in the air around them.

A moan interrupted as the first of the Heathens had found its way down the alleyway. A naked girl, who had once been attractive, stood in front of him, entrails dragging behind her. As disgusting as this looked, it did not seem to hinder her, which momentarily surprised Donald. On the top of her left thigh, there appeared to be a pentagram etched into it, but he was not keen on hanging around to investigate further.

"The wall!" yelled Gregor, reluctantly. "We have no choice but to scale the wall, otherwise we will be trapped against it, in a fight for our lives. Quick, whilst we still have some time."

Running, Gregor leapt, trying to grasp the top of the wall but fell short by a few inches, sliding back down to the ground below. Seeing this, Donald pulled out of his attempt and stood at the base, looking up at the structure that loomed over.

"I could give you a boost up," said Donald, after a brief pause, "it should be enough to get you up there."

"What about you? I am not leaving you here."

"I will be fine," replied Donald, with false confidence, "I will find a way to survive."

"Dinna be daft, I wouldna let you die alone. I can reach down and use my shirt to pull you up. That way we will both be safe."

"Great idea, you had better hurry up though, they are getting close."

Putting his arms down to form a cup, Donald interlinked his fingers before Gregor stood on them. Testing the weight of the older man, he heaved mightily, thrusting Gregor upwards until fingers grasped the top of the wall. Gregor pulled himself up atop, a grin forming on his face at the success. Quickly stripping off his shirt to expose his toned muscles, scars crisscrossing from various hunting accidents of the past. The scratches varied from wolf to a rabid wildcat. Gregor spoke about these on the journey from Moderwell, how he fought off the angry beasts. Reaching down, Gregor extended the garment towards Donald, just as the nude infected girl reached them. Donald grabbed the sleeve and began to climb, leg just missing the swinging limb of the monster who had made an attempt to haul him back to the ground. Sweat poured from the ascension, Donald flopped over the cap and joined Gregor atop. The entire town lay before them.

"It really is a lovely place to live," Donald stated, admiring Lanark's landscape. "If I was to live in a town, I think I would like to live here."

"Ach, wait until you see Linlithgow or Stirling, they are both amazing places to visit, although Edinburgh is as pretty a city that I have seen."

"When all of this fighting calms down, I think that I would like to visit these places. I really havena seen much outside of the village. I lead a very sheltered life."

"If you dinna mind a grumpy loner tagging along, then I would like to experience this with you. Although standing here and blethering is not going to get us anywhere." Gregor saw the infected beginning to gather below. "I am getting a bit nervous here. Come on, let us get moving, we have an army to catch up with."

Taking care with each step, the pair made steady progress as they moved south towards where the exit to the castle was. A couple of times progress was hindered by a break in the wall, but a hop over the gap only delayed a short time. The makeshift path went past ten rows of houses before emerging from the last pair of buildings. The two warriors jumped down onto a large road running east to west. The street was empty, there was no sign of the dead townsfolk or any of the fighters that had fled from the battle. Worried that they had went in the wrong direction, Donald stopped, squinting, looking for the way out or something that would tell them the way to go.

"I think we are lost," Donald exclaimed, shrugging his shoulders, trying to get a better look at the surroundings. "Do you have any idea which way we should go?"

"We came from the right. I think that I can see the road that we were on before we took the shortcut. Look, we could either head back that way and risk running into trouble or go the other way and risk hitting a dead end or getting lost."

"The road best travelled is the one that we ken the destination of," said Donald, sagely. "I reckon that we head right and risk that they havena caught up with us. We should start running now, before it is too late."

"Agreed, now move your hide and do try to keep up." With that, Gregor broke into a light jog, gradually building the pace. His relaxed running style made it look effortless as Donald struggled to keep up whilst going at the same tempo.

The houses at outer part of town were all single level buildings, built on a budget to accommodate the poorest of residents. Flimsy doors either hung by a thread or lay shattered in pieces on the ground. Like the rest of Lanark, this area was filled with carcasses of the residents who perished when the initial outbreak occurred, but everyone had pitched in and cleaned the streets, removing the rancid smell of decaying meat.

Finally arriving at the junction, Donald looked down the hill trying to see how far away the approaching horde was. The buildings on either side looked familiar, although he could not be sure as this was the first time in Lanark. The dark shadows, formed from the houses, made it difficult to see the shuffling figures.

"Fuck, this is not good." Donald groaned with frustration. "There must be a good fifty of them there. They are a stone's throw away. We need to move now."

"Right," replied Gregor looking up the other route, "it seems to be clear up ahead. Are you up to another run?"

"I am fine, old man. I still have some puff left. Come on, we are spending too much time gabbing, we need to move."

"They give me the creeps too," Gregor stated casually, "try and put them out of your head."

"I wish I could, but I have seen too much carnage for it not to affect me."

"We both have, laddie. But we have to move on, or we willna survive the day. If we stop and feel sorry for ourselves, then we give those creatures a chance to catch up and eventually we will die or become one of them. Our only option is to run just now because they heavily outnumber us. Now, stop worrying and run faster."

The motivational speech from Gregor seemed to have an effect on Donald as extra determination flowed through the weary bones of the young clansman. It reminded him of the encouragement that father used to give when he struggled to shear the sheep or milk a cow.

After a couple of minutes Donald excitedly exclaimed, "I see it! I see the gate. We are almost at the castle."

Weary, Gregor replied, "Finally. I hope that we get enough of a rest before having to face the infected again. How far behind are they now?"

"They are double the distance away from when we joined the road. I reckon that they are a good few minutes behind. I just hope that we have the numbers to fight them."

"Come on, son, let us make that final push and get to the castle, then we can assess it from there."

As he passed through the open exit from the deserted town of Lanark, a light breeze wafting through the air cooled the sweat that dripped off Gregor's beard, soaking the shirt, making it cling to his torso. The large stone castle appeared at the south east of the town. Sat upon a small hill, adorning the corners of the wall, massive stone turrets rose into the sky, flags flapping in the wind. The building was the centrepiece of the area, where the Lord of Lanark normally resided. Big Davie often told them stories of sweeping velvet drapes hanging from the main hall. The gaps in the wall served as lookout points for the small garrison which used to be stationed there, most were now dead after the carnage on the glen on the other side of town.

A gathering of about a hundred men stood drinking water from their skins and munching on dry bread. The drawbridge was up, iron trellis lowered, preventing entry into the fortress leaving Donald in no doubt that they were going to have to face this fight without any possibility of sanctuary.

The castle sat about a mile away from the town proper. Stone walls helped make it easy to defend against marauding English forces. This was a castle used for residence, unlike most of the castles in Lowland Scotland, which were hastily erected to defend against the English army. It was a large structure and could easily hold the town's remaining population, but with the little time they had to evacuate from the raiding horde, Donald hoped that the people left behind were few and far between. It was used by the Sheriff of Lanark, Robert the

Bruce, who was popular amongst the residents, mainly due to his earlier support of William Wallace in the fight against the English. A few sessions of parliament were held there, due to the central location in comparison to other venues in Scotland. Lanark was easily accessible to both the loyal Scottish clansmen and the English sympathisers.

A large meadow, highlighted by deep emerald grass well-tended by the locals, stood in front of the mound where the rest of the settlement had retreated. Just off to the side of the main body of troops, a small group of men sat talking to each other. Within, Donald could just make out the thin figure of Jamie, who seemed to be in quite an animated discussion with a couple of clansmen. Seeing that his cousin was there, Donald pointed to Gregor and they adjusted their route to aim for where he was located.

A few minutes later and they were stood in front of Jamie, bent over, hands on top of thighs, panting, trying to regulate breathing again after the punishing run for their lives. Jamie was bemused at the pair, both of whom looked very rough and exhausted.

"What the hell happened to you two?" asked Jamie, not quite sure what to make of them. "I had given you both up for dead."

"Donald thought that it was a good idea to take a short cut down a dead end," began Gregor, deliberately trying to bait the younger man, "I tried to talk him out of it but you ken what young men are like these days, headstrong and stubborn."

"Aye, he gets that from his father. Cammy liked things done his way or not at all. Usually his judgement was good, but when it was not, he always found a way to get us to safety," Jamie replied.

Indignant, Donald argued, "I didna lead us down that dead end. I followed Gregor down it, I resent that slight on my…." Stopping mid-conversation, Donald stood shaking his head as Gregor guffawed with laughter, a huge hand placed over his face to try and hide it. "You bastard! I will get you back for this, if we survive the day," he finally chuckled.

"We will survive, lad," stated Gregor, seriously. "I am sure that Jamie here has a plan. Whatever it is, I hope it is good because they will be here in a few minutes, they were not far behind us when we left Lanark."

"Fuck, that is not good," said Jamie, worry etched upon his face, "are you sure?"

"Aye," they both affirmed simultaneously. That was enough for Jamie who turned to the rest of the army.

"*Get ready! The enemy is approaching. They will be here soon!*"

CHAPTER THIRTY-SIX

THE BATTLE OF LANARK CASTLE

Every soldier on the field was bedraggled after the gruelling effort that it took to fight in previous skirmish and panicked retreat thereafter. The incoming horde was at the other end of the meadow, after just exiting the town. This time there was no running away from the bloodthirsty threat. Opposite, a huge line of clansmen waited to stop the monsters advance and assault on the medieval castle.

In the middle was Donald Douglas, who stood tall, despite all the adversity over the last couple of days, wiping the last of the gore from his blade. To his left was Gregor Munro, the tall hunter was receiving final instructions from the battle commander and Donald's cousin Jamie. Morag was in the fortress above, along with the local priest, Father Patrick Murphy, who helped evacuate the town before the Heathen horde was near. Cousin Jamie led the tattered army after the majority of the leadership were slain and eaten. Now they faced down the same enemy, whose numbers had remained constant whilst the Lanarkians had reduced.

"This is it," said Gregor, looking ahead at the festering fiends, "we live or perish, there is no retreat. Are you nervous, son? I ken I am."

"I am struggling to control myself," replied Donald, bouncing up and down on the spot, "the shaking willna stop."

"That is only natural, son. Just keep focused and stay mobile, your life may depend on it. Stick close to me, we have a better chance if we help each other. I willna lie, I dinna expect to live, but I do want to give myself the best chance of survival. Your cousin Jamie is a clever lad, if anyone can keep us alive today, it is him."

"I ken that it is going to be tough, but I also ken that I have to fight with my brains as well as my heart if I am going to stand a chance of surviving. Thank you for choosing to fight beside me. If I die, will you remove my head? I dinna want to come back as one of those creatures," Donald said, weariness overtaking his tone.

"I will, son, if you would have the honour of doing the same for me. But that is defeatist talk, we willna be vanquished on the battlefield, for we are Scots and we wear our hearts on our sleeves. We willna lose."

Emboldened, Donald started the chant, "We willna lose! We willna lose!"

"*We willna lose!*" shouted the rest of the Lanark army as the Heathens edged closer.

Each man stood ready, weapon in one hand and shield in the other, waiting to begin the fight for their lives, knowing that with overwhelming numbers against them, this was likely to be their last day alive. Above, Donald could hear the residents of the town, leaning over the castle walls, taking up the war cry, cheering on the brave heroes, awaiting their doom. Trying to lift spirits, they kept yelling the phrase repeatedly in the hope that this would revitalise the exhausted troops and give them the energy needed to win this skirmish.

A wave of Heathens launched at the defensive line, rotting teeth bared, trying to grab a hold of an arm, a thigh, or any other part of the body that they could latch onto. A gurgled moan emanated as the taste of the next meal was within grasp. Seeing the threat, Donald side stepped, heaving up his wooden buckler, smashing into the jaw of the infected attacking him, a raven-haired, bearded chap, dressed in silk finery, with a stomach that overhung his belt through years of overeating and drinking. The remaining teeth of the monstrosity exploded into the air, scattering as he drove the sword in a sweeping motion, clipping the ankles of his aggressor, knocking it to the ground before removing the head. The last moments of life escaped, a slight twitching of the festering torso before it lay still, no longer tormenting

Donald or his friends. A couple of the creatures that were behind it dove atop the corpse, ripping into the grey flesh of the fallen fiend. They paid no attention to Donald as he deftly removed each of their heads, reducing the number by another two.

Affording a glance to the left, Donald could see Gregor holding his own in battle, with a few fallen figures strewn around. Grinning, a determined face looked back, nodding, letting Donald know that there was no problem so far in facing the monsters.

Turning, he found himself engaged with another couple of beasts. Their relentless drive pushed him back. Donald used every bit of speed that he possessed to fend them off as jaws and claws tried to sink in. The sheer numbers forced him into a prolonged battle with the pair before another found a way through to join the attack. Donald was exhausted, continually feeling down as wave after wave of attacks came. *How much longer can I last out here?* Each time one died, another took its place and they never seemed to thin in numbers. *Was this how battles really were? Did da have to face the same overwhelming odds?* Despite this, his father survived, albeit with injuries. That's what Jamie told Malcolm. If he could do it, then surely Donald would.

Removing the doubts from his mind, a new resolve came over Donald as his attitude changed. Taking a few seconds to reason things out, Donald knew that this pace was too brutal to sustain for any length of time. Instead of continuing to dodge and block, he decided to take a couple of risks. Charging the one on the right, using the shield to prevent the others from latching on, Donald leapt high into the air bringing a knee up before driving it into the chest of the fiend, knocking it over to the dried mud below. Landing beside with a thunderous thump and battle cry, the hideous creature was decapitated with a single blow.

Donald roared. "Take that!" Fist pumping in the air, weapon still clutched, he spun to face the remaining savages, their gruesome grins snarling. "Come on then, I will destroy you both now!" shouted Donald feeling refreshed, using this to push forward, trying to gain the advantage by striking first at the opponent. However, this time they were more prepared with the second infected converging on him as the powerful blade rung true, slicing through the jaw of his victim. Blood and bone gushed like a waterfall into a river, bleaching the battlefield with a grim reminder of the fallen brave. Feeling another one behind, Donald thrust an elbow backwards, connecting with the chin, causing it to stumble back a couple of steps, allowing Donald to regain balance before driving the sword through the cranium, brain matter oozing out through the wound. The creature slumped to the ground, perished.

The battle raged on. Donald and Gregor fought, working together against the murderous menace, back to back at times, the body count soaring as more creatures fell to their demise. The numbers were proving to be overwhelming for the whole army. Clansmen fell to their deaths before rising again and joining the undead. Jamie's tactics proved effective and the opposition lost more numbers than before, but the advantage of soldiers reanimating meant that the Lanarkmen were facing a losing battle.

Donald had never been so scared. Fear was helping push him past the pain pulsing through his muscles, making it difficult to move. Each time that things looked bad, he was able to run, just far enough to escape the impending doom. Terror filled his mind, forcing thoughts about his family, the loved ones that were no longer. What happened to them? Would he ever be reunited with anyone? Tears threatened to spill as the thought his ma lying on that bed, thrashing as one of the hideous beings invaded his brain. A fate that he did not wish on anyone. Where was Malcolm? Why had he decided to go after Hamish rather than defend the town with his clan? He was usually a man of honour, not someone who abandoned it to seek out vengeance. That was exactly what happened. Donald prayed that when he died, Malcolm was able to find Morag and spend the rest of his days with her. Finally, Donald thought about his da, Cammy, raging war with the English down in Cumbria or Lancashire. He was a brave, fearsome warrior, but facing battle against these monsters was a fight that even Big Davie failed to win. There was the chance that either his da or Malcolm were still alive, but Donald had that feeling that he would be meeting them in Heaven with Big Davie.

Shaking off the forlornness, Donald rallied and moved to block a strike coming into Gregor's blind flank. Using his left arm to push it away, the animated corpse flew back, knocking over another couple that were incoming. It was like the games of skittles he used to play in the barn with Malcolm and Big Davie when they were younger. Stopping for a moment to regain some composure and scratch his arse which had itched for the last couple of minutes,

Donald once again looked to the meadow, trying to catch a glimpse of his cousin Jamie, hoping he had avoided being gorged upon or turned during the battle.

The united clan army was now less than fifty and facing a horde that tripled in number. Each soldier was engaged in melee against at least two of the infected while other savages feasted on the remains of the Lanark force who bravely perished. The strength of the attack had pushed the heroes back against the hill behind, the steep slope stopping them from retreating further. It was literally an uphill battle. Donald knew it would not be much longer before they all were destroyed, eaten by the monsters, left to become one or rot alone in the meadow.

A brief respite came as arrows rained down from above, embedding themselves in the forehead of the second line of enemy that were pressing in.

"Push them back!" yelled Jamie, a distance away to the right. "Show them what we are made of! We willna be defeated! Push those damn bastards back!"

Jamie's words brought mixed emotions to Donald. They spurred him on, giving an extra push as the latest of the foul cadavers was trying to latch itself onto his wrist. There was also a sense of relief which washed over him, knowing that Jamie was still alive and in charge, leading the fight. It was his tactical expertise and keen awareness which encouraged the men to aim for the heads and necks of their enemy. Leaping over a stray head caused Donald to trip, lying beside it, balking at the lifeless eyes staring back.

Immediately, two infected rushed in and jumped on top of him, the foul stench of their rotting breath overwhelming. Instinctively, he fought to keep their faces from biting away at his limbs, using every bit of strength to hold them off, weakening with each passing second. Humid air, coupled with the weight of his enemies, made it difficult to breathe, expending more energy as he prepared for the lonely ascent up to Heaven.

"Come on, you stupid bastard," taunted Donald, trying to use willpower to bring forth extra fortitude. Vision dimming, Donald slipped closer to losing consciousness, the darkness reaching, but sheer stubbornness prevented it from enveloping him.

Suddenly, the pressure eased. One of the infected rolled off, quickly followed by the other. Gasping for air, a sense of relief washed over Donald, knowing that this was a lucky escape. Once more death was cheated. A hairy arm stretched down and grabbed his shoulder, hauling him back to a standing position.

"You will live, son," the familiar voice of Gregor sounded as Donald tried to find his bearings, taking a few seconds to allow his vision to clear. "But for how much longer, I am not sure. It willna be long before we are overrun and scrambling for our lives. You have fought well. If I die, I couldna think of a better person to die beside on the battlefield."

"Aye, but we are going to live," said Donald defiantly, "I have no plans to die today. It is them or us and I want to see the sunrise tomorrow morning. So, stick your chest out, dunderheid, we have monsters to kill."

Just as Donald finished the speech, another small group of beasts launched a strike at the pair. The game of cat and mouse continued, each side probing, trying to find the advantage and deliver the killing blow. The heroes were severely hampered by the exertions of the previous battle and the long run fleeing from the horde. It showed as swings of the blades either did not find their mark or glanced off the opponents. The rest of the Lanark army were in just as bad shape with the remaining soldiers almost dead on their feet, exhausted, struggling to fend off the relentless onslaught. The festering fiends outnumbering them now five to one. This was the final stand, the living could not hold out much longer.

"Form a circle! We can only win if we fight together and move as one. We can do this, rally to me and form a circle!" Jamie yelled, now standing not far from Donald's right side.

Shattered cries of "Lanark" came from the remaining clansmen as they maneuvered over strewn corpses to where Jamie was stationed. Donald and Gregor took position in the circle beside Jamie in one last desperate effort to repel the infected. This formation was normally used against cavalry, but Jamie had adapted it for use against the dead by keeping the men tight together and mobile along the battlefield, preventing them from being isolated against multiple threats.

Despite the initial success of the circle, the infected kept eating away at the soldier's numbers, with more of the defenders turning when they died. The circle was a tactic Jamie saw used on the battlefield by William Wallace, but not one that would provide a victory in the long term against the horde. Quickly Jamie realised this and ordered the army to turn into mobile strike units, using squads of four to rush in at a couple of beasts, kill them, then move away, keeping the enemy from focusing on one point. However, this was exhausting for the already beleaguered army. Soon, due to tiredness, the Heathens got the upper hand.

A deafening noise emanated. Donald looked up. Expecting dark storm clouds, he only saw blue skies. Confused by the sound, his concentration wandered.

Behind the cadavers, a score of horses thundered in, riders flashing a sea of blades, removing the heads of copious infected. Numbers quickly dwindled due to the newcomer's mobility and onslaught. Cheers erupted from the weary Lanark troops as salvation arrived on steeds, handing the savages a severe beating. Pushing forward in their circle, the infantry which numbered around twenty, picked off smaller groups until the meadow was clear. Finally, the skirmish was over and the townsfolk collapsed to the ground, utterly exhausted from prolonged fighting. A couple of men dismounted, one Donald did not recognize, but the other was his brother Malcolm. Disbelieving, Donald rubbed his eyes before rushing over to embrace him in a massive hug, almost knocking Malcolm to the ground.

"I am so glad to see you," said Donald, relieved, tears streaming down his cheek, "I thought you went after Hamish?"

"I did," replied Malcolm, his face sombre, horrified with the amount of life lost, "the bastard was not there. He took Mhairi and tried to burn the place down. We managed to get most of the fires out. I gathered the lads that were left in the village and we rode here as quickly as we could. It was that or go after Hamish and we didna have the numbers. The other villagers told me that there were dozens of men with him."

"I honestly thought that we were done for there, things were bleak for a while."

"I can see that. What about Morag and Big Davie? Are they alive?"

"Morag is," answered Donald, watching the relief wash over his brother. "Big Davie was killed though. We were attacked in a clearing on the way to Moderwell, we were quickly overwhelmed and Big Davie lost his life. It was a sad day."

"That man will be a huge loss," said Malcolm, bowing his head, "I am just happy that you are alive, brother. You look a mess though. Let us get you all up to the castle and get some food and water, you have earned it."

With that, the Douglas brothers walked off towards Lanark castle, along with the rest of the army. Celebratory pats on the back and hugs continuing as they approached the fortress. Donald allowed himself a moment to look back upon the battlefield and say a small prayer in memory to the glens filled with the dead.

EPIL⊕GUE

Nervous, Morag paced the ramparts, watching Malcolm, Donald, and the rest of the Lanark army as they strode towards the castle, jubilation exuding as cheers erupted from within. As happy as she was for the victory, Morag will still furious at Malcolm for abandoning her and she did not look forward to telling him about Big Davie's death.

The battle was a hard for all, especially Morag who felt so helpless at not being able assist. When Donald appeared, she tried to exit the portcullis, but guards prevented her from opening it, explaining with a long pike that it was not in the interests of the inhabitants for it to be opened. Morag tried a couple more times before being chased off by the sharp end of the weapon.

On the wall was not much better. She could see the fighting but was too far away to make any difference. She felt embarrassed to be shouted at by Jamie when her usual accuracy with the bow went awry. Instead of hitting the monsters, the arrows embedded in the chests of a couple of Lanarkian soldiers. The other so-called archers never fared any better, with more shots missing the Heathens than hitting them. All in all, it was a very frustrating time. Robert the Bruce himself ordered the cannons not to be used for fear of growing the horde and hindering the cause of the brave men fighting on the glen.

When Malcolm arrived, Morag cheered with the others, but jubilation soon turned to trepidation as the very meeting she knew was inevitable loomed large. To begin with, Morag wondered who accompanied him, but she soon recognised the men and women of

Forth who rode beside Malcolm, or in the case of Skye, rode *with* him. Now the battle was over, and it was time to get this over and done with.

Hurrying down the steps and into the courtyard, Morag tried to keep a low profile from the rest of the townsfolk who were gathered trying to set up a temporary camp in the castle. Babes clung to mothers and children scampered about, playing tag to try and occupy their time whilst keeping out the way of the adults. It was a short walk to the main entrance, the portcullis now raised to allow the heroes into the keep.

Two lines of sentries flanked the army as they entered, saluting Jamie at the head of the party. Robert the Bruce stood at the other end of the honour guard, dressed in a red velvet robes, waiting for the battered and bloodied soldiers as they trudged onwards. A spontaneous round of applause exploded as every person in the area put their hands together in appreciation of sacrifices made. Robert the Bruce hugged each man and woman as they passed, before ushering them through huge mahogany doors into the main hall where a feast awaited the heroes. The finest wine and meats flowed as Morag barged in, trying to get to her beloved. Malcolm was in the corner, chatting away to a nobleman dressed in white tights and a short yellow jacket, looking ridiculous on the diminutive chap.

"Morag! Am I glad to see you."

Morag sighed and dragged him off out the hall, into a quiet corner in the courtyard.

"Well, did you manage to find that brother of yours?" Malcolm asked as he enveloped her in a tight hug.

Morag's faced sagged before straightening up and looking him in the eyes. "I couldna find him. I suspect he turned into one of those creatures."

"Fuck," replied Malcolm, annoyed, "I promised your ma I would bring all her children home."

"We got as far as Moderwell, at least Donald and I did, but the only person there was Gregor who had not seen my brother. I fear he is lost. What do you mean bring all her children home?"

"Erm, I have bad news, my love."

Morag stomped her left foot before replying, "Dinna 'my love' me. What is the news? I have suffered much hardship over the last few days, you dinna need to sugar-coat anything."

"It is your sister Mhairi…"

"What about Mhairi? Look, stop beating about the bush and tell me straight, Malcolm Douglas or God help me, I will kick you hard on your sore ankle."

"It was Hamish. He set the town on fire and kidnapped Mhairi. I fear he has taken her to Peebles."

"Well what are you doing here, why are you not in Peebles trying to get her back?"

"We did not have the numbers to chase after them. I came back here to try and get more men so we could go back out after her. Thank the Lord I got here when I did, Jamie and Donald would not have lived much longer."

"You are so vain, Malcolm. Jamie and Donald were doing fine without you. In fact, everyone seems to be doing fine without you."

Malcolm stood there aghast. "What do you mean?"

Unable to help herself, Morag launched into a tirade. "Big Davie, Donald, and I did fine without you, so fine that Big Davie died and Donald was asleep whilst I dragged his sorry backside halfway across the country. Why did you not tell me he was sick? You bastard, I told you everything about my family."

"Well, I…"

Morag cut him off before he could finish. "I am not interested. It was your fault he died, Malcolm. *Your fault.* You left me and Big Davie to care for your sick brother whilst you went off gallivanting after bloody Hamish Balliol, and for what? To satisfy some twisted revenge notion in your head. What about me? What about Donald? You abandoned us."

"That was not my fault…"

Again, Morag interjected, not giving Malcolm a chance to explain. "It bloody well was and you ken it. What about Lanark, Malcolm? Hamish Bloody Balliol set loose a shitload of Heathens because you angered him and what did you do? Did you stay to help the good people of Lanark? No, you disappear and go after Hamish, still trying to satisfy your hunger for revenge."

"That is not fair…"

"I dinna care what you think. I have had enough of being treated like dirt. It is not good enough. You need to put my needs and Donald's needs first. You need to stop being so bloody selfish and take responsibility for your life."

"I am sorry, Morag."

"Sorry does not cut it this time, Malcolm. Man up and stop being a coward. We are leaving tomorrow to get Mhairi."

With that, Morag stormed off, leaving Malcolm on his own to lick his wounds. She would let him stew on that and pick up the pieces in the morning, hoping he would feel guilty enough not to enjoy the fine wine and food laid out for them.

✿✿✿✿✿

The sun set over the western horizon, plunging the courtyard into darkness. The gothic stone structure was magnificent in stature. Father Patrick Murphy sat inside in the private dining room of Father John Comryn, priest of St Kentigerns Church and the senior religious figure of Lanark. Only Robert Wishart, Bishop of Glasgow, was recognised as having a higher stature within the Clydeside area. Father John invited him for dinner the night after the mass battle by Lanark Castle. The church was located within the town, which was now secure, the gates fixed and emptied of the Heathen menace.

Father John came shambling back into the room, holding a large flask filled to the brim with wine, which was sloshing about as he carried it. Miraculously, not a drop spilled before he placed two deep silver goblets onto the table and poured a generous amount into each. Grabbing one of the cups, Father John brought it to his mouth and ingested a sizeable amount before refilling the chalice and exiting to the rear. Once Father John left, Patrick held his drink in his hand before tasting a small bit. The flavour burst onto his tongue like an explosion of gunpowder from a cannon. He never tasted anything so good and savoured each mouthful as he sampled it.

A couple of minutes later, Father John returned with two huge bowls, again filled to the brim. A brown stew, mixed with carrots and turnips, the gamey smell wafting towards his taste buds. Patrick's stomach was now complaining that none of this had entered into it. The food had barely touched the stone surface of the table when his spoon thrust into the meaty goodness as he devoured each tasty morsel. Amused, Father John watched as Patrick finished the meal within minutes. Patting his lips with a cloth napkin, Patrick satisfied his thirst with another gulp of the fruity alcohol.

"I am guessing that you were hungry." Father John laughed, taking a sip from his goblet. "If you want another helping, the pot is in the other room, there is still plenty left."

"I did not realise how famished I was until I smelled the stew. That was delicious, if you dinna mind, I will go and get some more. Do you want another portion as well?"

"No, thank you. I have been taking too many second portions recently. I need to reduce some of this extra belly I am carrying."

Looking at the portly priest, Patrick could see his point. Although he had aged well, Father John had quite a sizeable stomach that had grown considerably over the last few years which he was sure worried the Bishop. The Bishop of Glasgow was known for not wanting his priests to be fat, hours of chatting to the parishioners had taught him that people engage more with someone if they look as if they have endured hardship, rather than an old man with a fat midriff.

Picking up his bowl, Patrick strode to the kitchen where a large cauldron, surrounded by an array of knives, sat bubbling away. On a small bench sat a fresh loaf which was baked in the kiln that morning. Hunger still not satiated, Patrick refilled the dish before hunting about for a wooden tray, placing the bread and a sharp blade onto it. The doughy waft caught the edge of his nasal passage and more drool escaped his lips before dripping onto the tunic.

Balancing the food in one hand, he used the other to push open the door, using his bottom to keep it from rebounding. It did not take long to negotiate through the entranceway and back into the cosy dining area where Father John waited.

"I see you have found the bread," remarked Father John, about halfway through his meal, "I baked that early this morning, it is very nice. I had a couple of slices earlier."

"Do you want me to cut you a slice now?" Patrick asked as he placed the tray on the table. Putting his food by his place setting, he eased the knife into the thick crust, rasping through it into the soft, pillowy loaf.

"Would you? That would be awfully kind. This stew needs mopped up afterwards, otherwise the bowl can get very greasy. Tell me, what was your theory on the infected, I believe you called them Heathens?"

"I did. I have observed these creatures and the people that they once were, and it is my belief that they are Heathens and as such they must be sent to Hell.

"Oh my!" exclaimed Father John, slurping some of the gravy into his mouth. "What has brought you to that conclusion? It is quite a wild assumption."

"Sorry," said Patrick, absently moving the utensil back and forth over the tray. "I have seen the creatures and not one of them could be called godly. The people of the village have fornicated or killed in one way or another. Poor Malcolm believed that his mother was pure, but the rumour was that whilst Old Man Douglas was away, Jean did play. I heard that she was having illicit meetings with Henry Douglas, the local tanner. The parishioners often told me that the two fornicate in the barn whilst the sons were out tending the sheep. It is a sad state of affairs, a village of debauchery in my opinion, I will be glad when I get my next assignment."

"That seems a very awkward place to be in," replied Father John with skepticism. "A lot of the townsfolk in Lanark got infected, most of them seemed decent folk. I am not sure of this, Patrick. Have you got any evidence?"

"I have seen them change myself," Patrick continued, sensing that Father John was not believing his tale, "one of the villagers I witnessed dying in front of me, his eyes glowed a deep crimson before he came back to life. I swear that I saw the devil in him! That was just before Big Davie removed his head."

"Big Davie? *The* Big Davie, the man who killed a thousand strong English Army with nothing but a fork?"

"That is the chap. I spoke to Morag Douglas who was with him when he died. According to her, Big Davie never came back to life. It looks like his soul was pure and accepted into Heaven by God."

"I can see your logic, Patrick," said Father John dubiously, "but I am not convinced by it. Do you have anything else to back it?"

Agitated, Patrick queried, "What about the battle? You must have seen what happened this evening?"

"What did you see, Patrick?" quizzed Father John, becoming a bit more interested.

"The demon, you must have spotted it out there. It had a large black muscular body, huge bull horns, and grey smoke bellowing out of the huge nostrils on his face. It was frightening, it drove the

Heathens on, making them more powerful and stronger, we were lucky to win the fight with that thing spurring them on."

"I think you must have been having visions, Patrick. I am afraid that I saw nothing. Are you sure that it was not your imagination?"

"No, I thought you would miss it," Patrick murmured, an evil smirk forming across his face. "You are too pure to see it. I suspect that you will find your place in Heaven, shall we find out?"

Just as he was finishing the sentence, Father Patrick thrust the blade out, slicing the throat of the priest, watching blood gurgle out as he slumped forward over the cold, hard table, spraying all over the remains of his dinner.

"I bet your God will be happy to see you," Patrick taunted the lifeless body. "I reckon he will sit there and say, well done, John, you served us well, sorry you got killed. Guess what? It does not matter now. My lord has prevailed here. Satan is in control and his minions are roaming the Earth causing havoc. There is nothing that you or your Christian freaks can do about it, is there?"

A loud cackle escaped the lips of the mad Satanist at the demise of the former head of St Kentigerns Church. Grabbing Father John's eyebrows, Patrick pulled his face up and looked at it in disgust before slamming it back down against the stone.

"I was rather hoping that you would turn!" Patrick snarled with derision. "I was looking forward to slaying you again. After all the effort I took to start this on the glen. I sacrificed virgins to the Dark Lord to turn everyone into blood-thirsty creatures. Do you ken the effort it took me and my fellow disciples to get to this point? And you are too bloody pure to turn into one. I am disappointed. Oh well, there is nothing that we can do about it now."

Grabbing the loose cloth at the top of his tunic, Patrick hauled the massive minister from the seat and dragged him along the unforgiving floor before letting him sag at the exit to the foyer.

Pausing to catch his breath, Patrick kicked the body several times, then started a new rant. "May the Dark Lord burn your family, you fat bastard! If you had eaten less in life, I would not be burdened with dragging your holy highness to your final resting place."

Patrick's foot continued to pummel the side of the corpse. The frustration of having to hide his true beliefs from the others and the growing hatred of them all could finally be vented. There was no better man to take it out on than Father John. Father John, who thought himself the most holy of men in Lanark. Father John who preached to his congregation about making sacrifice in God's name, whilst he ate and drank like a nobleman. The hatred and loathing of all that Father John had stood for drove Patrick to Satanism. It was when he visited the Highlands recently that he was finally fully inducted into the ranks of the Chosen. Patrick felt power surge through him from the Dark Lord, using it to enhance his strength as he dragged the body through the door and onto the stone altar in the main hall.

"Do you not see the irony of this?" Patrick began to preach at the lifeless figure. "Here you are, as dead as half the world, but instead of you coming back alive, you sit in your pious throne in Heaven. Well, guess what? I am going to impeach your soul, ruin your body. I am going to sacrifice you to Satan at your own God's altar. Is that not funny?"

The crazed laughter continued as Patrick positioned the deceased within the stone precipice, until it was trapped, no part of it leaning out.

"Now, let us finish your evening, Father John. I hope you enjoyed your last meal and supper, pity about the bread."

Carefully walking to the side of the room, Patrick deftly removed six candles that were secured onto the side before positioning each one in the shape of a pentagram to the left of Father John, watching as the scalding liquid wax melted onto his skin. Keeping the last one, Patrick lifted it above his head and started chanting in Latin before bringing it down and setting John's cloak alight.

The rest of the cloth soon caught fire as each of the points added to the flames dancing around the burning Father John.

Satisfied his job was done, Patrick exited into the stillness of the night whilst the church blazed behind, black smoke spiralling into the inky sky. Laughing, he disappeared into the shadows, leaving no trace of the dastardly deeds behind.

THE END

ACKNOWLEDGEMENTS

First, I want to thank my editor Christina Hargis Smith. I could not have done this without her. Her encouragement, belief, attention to detail, feedback, and advice has turned this into a novel I can be truly proud of. I'm so very proud to be part of the Optimus Maximus Publishing Family and I look forward to working with her on future projects.

I want to thank my beta readers for picking up the errors that I missed, so a huge shout out to Craig Deegan, Angela Smith, Emma Thompson, Joan McLeod, Heather Kennedy, and Ricky Fleet. You guys have all been amazing and it's through you, I've ironed out the rough.

I want to give a huge shout out to the excellent Jeffrey Kosh for creating the cover that Christina and I envisioned. Jeff, you are a talented man.

I would like everyone to sympathise with my wife and kids for putting up with me during this whole writing process. You guys are the best.

I want to thank Gillian Downing, David Dougal, and especially Claire O'Neill for believing in me and helping run my Facebook Group called Matt's Cats.

Aaron O'Neill, you are a genius for designing my website. It looks fantastic.

I can't leave out the wonderful Freedom Matthews for being the best writing partner a man could have. Her wisdom, encouragement and positivity have helped me get this book finished.

A couple of years ago, a young lady did something special when we were raising money for Little Princess Trust. Her name is Ellie Hyde and she worked tirelessly doing chores around the house to raise some money to support my daughter and I wanted to show my appreciation by thanking her here in this book.

Most of all I want to thank YOU, the reader. This book has been a two and a half year labour of love, a book that I've thoroughly enjoyed writing and one I hope you have enjoyed reading and I hope you choose to pick up Book Two when it's released.

ABOUT THE AUTHOR

Based in West Lothian, Scotland, Matt Hay first found his love of horror, hiding behind the sofa whilst watching Diana devour a mouse in the excellent V. Nowadays, much older and allegedly wiser; he devours as many books as possible. A project co-ordinator by day, Matt escapes the daily grind by immersing himself in the horror worlds he creates. When he's not spending quality time with his wife and kids, Matt can be found relaxing at the Mull of Kintyre, savouring the gorgeous view of the beach or at his local football ground watching his beloved Livingston FC.

If you want to connect with Matt, you can find him on Facebook as Author Matt Hay – https://www.facebook.com/mannequinglangon

On Twitter – https://twitter.com/Glangon

On Instagram – https://www.instagram.com/mannequinglangon/

On his website – http://authormatthay.com/

Feel free to join Matt's fan group, Matt's Cats – https://www.facebook.com/groups/145631362745616/

Glens of the Dead is Matt's debut novel, but he has written a few short stories that are available for your pleasure.

From Optimus Maximus Publishing

Maximus Shock Anthology https://www.amazon.com/Maximus-Shock-Collected-Madness-Terror-ebook/dp/B01N9W6Q6J

(Matt has the short stories called Mannequin and A Wolf In Sheep's Clothing in this anthology.)

Sporm https://www.amazon.co.uk/Sporm-Matt-Hay-ebook/dp/B07CNWCYBQ

(A standalone erotic horror short story, also available on audiobook)

From Wolfgang Anthologies

Night of the Living Cure

(Matt has The Postman in this charity anthology)

From ZPR Productions

Splintered Dreams – A Guide to the Apocalypse – Volume II

(Matt has The Mertians in this Anthology)

In a dungeon nobody cares about your scream.

SPORM

MATT HAY

Graphic content! Ages 18+ Horror and erotica mixed in a short story…Sporm, the half-spider/half-worm, is rejected and humiliated by his friends and strikes out on his own in search of the fabled Pink Pleasure Cavern. He soon experiences erotic and horrific adventures as he explores some of the seediest places in Amsterdam, hoping for the ultimate thrill whilst trying to survive one of the most dangerous areas of The Netherlands

CHECK OUT THE OMP WEBSITE FOR
A COMPLETE LIST OF OUR TITLES

WWW.OPTIMUSMAXIMUSPUBLISHING.COM

BOOKS ARE AVAILABLE IN BOTH PRINT
AND ELECTRONIC FORMATS

RICKY FLEET

HELLSPAWN

SERIES

10.35 AM, September 14th 2015. Portsmouth, England.

A global particle physics experiment releases a pulse of unknown energy with catastrophic results. The sanctity of the grave has been sundered and a million graveyards expel their tenants from eternal slumber.

The world is unaware of the impending apocalypse. Governments crumble and armies are scattered to the wind under the onslaught of the dead.

Kurt Taylor, a self-employed plumber, witnesses the start of the horrifying outbreak. Desperate to reach his family before they fall victim to the ever growing horde of shambling corruption, he flees the scene.

In a society with few guns, how can people hope to survive the endless waves of zombies that seek to consume every living thing? With ingenuity, planning and everyday materials, the group forge their way and strike back at the Hellspawn legions.

Rescues are mounted, but not all survivors are benevolent, the evil that is in all men has been given free rein in this new, dead world. With both the living and dead to contend with, the Taylor family's battle for survival is just beginning.

Book 1 in the Hellspawn series.

Kurt Taylor and his family have battled the living and the dead and now find themselves on the run, their home reduced to ashes. With unimaginable horror lying in wait around every corner, the onset of winter and the plunging temperatures only add more danger to their precarious existence. They decide to forge ahead and try to reach the protection of others who have hopefully survived the zombie apocalypse. If this fails, their only choice would be to try and reach an impregnable fortress, a sanctuary that has stood for a thousand years.

Standing between them and salvation are the villages and cities of the damned, a path that will test their spirit and resilience unlike anything they have faced before. More companions are rescued from the jaws of death and join them in their perilous journey. Mysterious attacks befall the group and it becomes clear the dead aren't the only things that lurk in the darkness.

Tempers fray and personalities clash. The group starts to fracture and Kurt is forced to commit acts that cause him to question his own morality. Can they survive the horror of their new existence? Will they want to?

The Hellspawn saga continues.

BALLYMOOR, IRELAND, 1891

Patrick Conroy, a young American student of medicine in Dublin, decides to take a break from the hustle and bustle of the big city and spend a month in the quietude of the wild and beautiful Glencree valley, County Wicklow. However, surrounded by local legends and myths, he is soon dragged into an ancient mystery that has haunted the village of Ballymoor for centuries. Set on the background of the tumultuous years preceding the War of Independence, and colored by Irish folklore, the Haunter of the Moor is a ghost story written in the style of Victorian Gothic novels.

A modern dark urban fantasy, telling of two powerful families who uphold a secret duty to protect humanity from a threat it doesn't know exists.

Though sharing a common enemy, the two families form a long-standing rivalry due to their methods and ultimate goals.

Forces are coalescing in a prominent Central European city criminal sex-trafficking, a serial murderer with a savage bent, and other, less tangible influences.

Within a prestigious, private university, Lilja, a young librarian charged with protecting a very special book, finds herself suddenly ensconced in this dark, strange world. Originally from Finland, she has her own reason for why she left her home, but she finds the city to be anything but a haven from dangers and secrets.

Book One in a planned series.

Meet Mason Ezekiel Barnes, former NFL tackle turned successful author of the naughty ninja adventure series Mia Killjoy. Mason is obsessed with winning a Pulitzer and is thwarted by his fellow author and nemesis, the twerpy little gnome Conrad Bancroft.

Perk Noir is full of comedic relief, pop culture, NFL, jazz, a little touch of romance, and flashbacks of Lightning and his family during both the first half of the 20th century and later during the Civil Rights movement. Mason and Shelly and their adventures is a fun filled thrill ride that will appeal to all readers, there is something for everyone at the Perk.

Two hunters pursue the same prey.

Fate has forged the slayer, Trey Thomas and the Sandrian vampire, Adalius, two natural enemies, into an uneasy alliance against an evil more powerful than either have ever faced. Only together do they stand a chance of defeating Anna; if they don't destroy each other first.

As they pursue Anna, the apprehensive Lycan watch as a confrontation looms on the horizon between vampires, the New Bloods and the Old Guard, which threatens to plunge the vampire world into civil war and trigger an all-out supernatural conflict which in the end could destroy them all.

Killing is the sole province of the religious fanatics, an axiom as true today as it was some five hundred years ago; and no nation, region or person is immune.

Europe had clawed its way out of the Middle Ages with the dawning of the renaissance, only to be plunged once more into darkness, as the dogs of war circled to destroy its resurgence during the 16th century. The Islamic successor to the Roman Byzantines, the Ottoman Caliphate, flexed its muscles to conquer much of Western Asia, North Africa and South-Eastern Europe. Christian Europe shuddered when the once invincible bastion of the Knight's at Rhodes were defeated; and now trembled as the Ottoman army rattled the very gates of Vienna. No Christian army, it seemed, could withstand the ferocity of the Azabs, the Akıncı, the Sipahis, the Janissaries, and ruthless layalar's of the all-conquering Islamic hordes.

This then is the cauldron into which Gideon de Boyne is unwittingly thrust with his small army of dedicated Christian warriors. On the hostile island of Crete, at the doorstep of the Ottoman Empire, Gideon must face not only the overwhelming force of Muslim warriors but his own inner conflicts of the futility of war and his very Christian beliefs.

Will he succeed and come out of it unscathed?

Collected tales of Madness and Terror

Maximus
SHOCK

An OMP Magazine

Complete
Collection

MAXIMUS
SHOCK
0

16 Mind-Shocking Tales!

RICKY FLEET   JEFFREY KOSH   EMIR SKALONJA

KEITH MONTGOMERY   SCOTT CARRUBA   CHRIS GARSON

LORRAINE VERSINI   MAURA ATKINSON BUTLER   MATT HAY

LEON BROWN   WK POMEROY

EDITED BY
CHRISTINA HARGIS SMITH

www.ingramcontent.com/pod-product-compliance
Lightning Source LLC
Chambersburg PA
CBHW050712180626
46814CB00002B/393